THE
SECRETS
WE
KEEP

THE
SECRETS
WE
KEEP

A Homefront Mystery

Liz Milliron

Author Photo Credit: Holly Tonini

First edition

ISBN: 978-1-68512-555-4

Cover art by Level Best Designs

This book was professionally typeset on Reedsy.
Find out more at reedsy.com

For all the Rosies who blazed the trail for generations of women to come.

Praise for The Secrets We Keep

"Tough, big-hearted sleuth Betty Ahern will have you cheering her courage and smarts as she searches for a soldier's mother in WWII-era Buffalo. With Betty's growing confidence and the hint of a troubling new romance on the horizon, this may just be the best entry yet in Liz Milliron's fantastic WWII Homefront mystery series. A great read, fast-paced, dialogue-driven, and a moving exploration of the price paid by those who hide family secrets."—Mally Becker, Agatha Award-nominated author of the *The Turncoat's Widow*.

Chapter One

June, 1943

E veryone has secrets. They can be small things, like hidin' what your best friend bought her beau for his birthday. Or knowin' that your brothers broke your mom's favorite lamp, but not tellin' her. These might make you uncomfortable for a while, but if they come out in the open, the damage isn't bad. If it's a *good* secret, like the present, it can even be fun.

Then there are the whoppers. They might be about who you are, or where you come from, or things that will ruin you. They fester, like an infected cut, and make you miserable from the inside out. Secrets that big turn your world upside down, spin it like a top, and leave you wonderin' which way is up.

They can even get you killed.

It was the Monday before the Fourth of July. I sat in the corner booth at Teddy's Diner and sipped my coffee, savoring the taste. Much better than the chicory I had to drink at home. Next to me, my empty plate showed traces of a demolished breakfast, bits of scrambled egg, and the drippings of maple syrup from my pancakes. The diner had become my office until I made enough dough as a private detective to rent a real one. I'd met so many clients there, Judy, one of the waitresses, informally reserved the booth for me every morning.

She stopped by and held up a half-full pot of java. "Want a warm-up? Say, is that what I think it is?"

Two papers occupied the table. One was the morning's *Courier Express*. I'd read it cover to cover and now tried to put it outta my mind. The headlines were all about the bombing campaigns in Europe and speculation about where the Allies would go now that they'd defeated the Germans in North Africa. All I knew was that wherever it was, my fiancé, Tom Flannery, would prob'ly be there. He was serving with the 1st Armored Division. I didn't know much about warfare, but it was a safe bet any big action would involve tanks. It wouldn't be any more dangerous than Africa. Then again, it wouldn't be safer, either.

I also didn't need to read about operations in the Pacific, where my older brother, Sean, was no doubt involved in the invasion of the Solomon Islands. All I could do was light my candles at church every week and say a couple Hail Marys for 'em.

The other sheet cheered me up. There on thick cream-colored paper, in heavy black words inside a gold foil frame, was the result of a lot of studyin' and six weeks of waiting. "Yes, it is. I'm a professional now." The certificate, accompanied by my detective's license issued by the great State of New York, had arrived the previous Friday. I hadn't let them out of my sight since.

Judy whistled. "Congratulations! Breakfast is on me."

"Oh, no. I couldn't."

She poured the coffee. "Are you kidding? I'm tickled for you, Betty. I really am. A real private dick. Think of it. Some day, you'll be as famous as the movie guys, and I'll be able to tell my customers, 'Yessir, she sat right in that booth and conducted business.' This'll be the most popular diner in the First Ward, if not all of Buffalo."

I laughed. "Judy, you're a peach. I'm not sure I'll ever be as well-known as Sam Spade, but I'm sure gonna try."

"You told Tom?"

The question sobered me. I'd written him a letter immediately upon opening the envelope, but I'd waited until this morning to mail it. "I haven't heard from him in weeks. I don't even know where he is. Ten'll get you twenty, he'll be part of whatever is comin' next, but I haven't the foggiest idea if he's still in Africa or not. One thing's for certain, he doesn't have time to write."

"You didn't answer the question, and besides, that's not what I asked." She gave me a shrewd stare. "You haven't."

"Actually, I posted the letter this morning." I covered my uncertainty by taking a sip of my coffee, even though it was way too hot. "But I don't know when he'll get it. The mail will have to catch up with him, and who knows when that'll be. Once these boys get rollin', you know how it is."

She sat across from me. "He'll be proud of you."

"You think so?"

"I *know* it. Heck, he oughta brag to every one of his buddies about you. If he doesn't, well, never mind that."

A figure came up beside the table and coughed politely. "Excuse me, are you Betty Ahern?"

I looked up. A young man in sharp Army greens stood ramrod straight, his soda-jerk style hat tucked under his arm. The single stripe told me he was a Private First Class. He was prob'ly about six foot tall, his dark brown hair cut close at the sides, but the top showed hints of a curl. He filled out the uniform well. A thin scar, newly healed by the look of it, cut his forehead above dark eyes, and the line of his jaw was strong, almost too much. He wasn't drop-dead gorgeous, but there was a wholesome air about him that would appeal to any single young woman. Maybe even a married one.

Judy stood. "I'll leave you to business." She faced the private. "Can I get you anything?"

He looked at her, suddenly a bit awkward. "Thanks. A cup of coffee, please."

"Comin' right up." She hastened away.

I gestured to the vacated seat. "Take a load off. You've prob'ly figured it out, but I'm Betty. How can I help you, Private?"

He blinked. "How do you know my rank?"

I grinned. "My fiancé is in the Army. Now, have a seat. Judy'll be right back with your joe."

"You must think me a real dope." He slid into the booth and laid his hat on the table. His voice sounded pleasant, mild. It reminded me of Sean's.

I watched him. He fidgeted like an embarrassed schoolboy. "Nope, I'm observant. I have to be. You came to see me, Private. You must want something."

Judy came back with an empty mug, which she filled lickety-split. "You want anything else, you holler." She moved away.

He stalled and slowly rotated the thick white ceramic mug. Then, he appeared to make a decision. "I want you to find my mother."

"Is she missing?"

"I don't know. See, I don't know who she is."

I took my notepad and a pencil out of my bag. "You'd better start at the beginning."

He took a cautious sip. He must've decided the java was okay, 'cause he followed it with a bigger one. "I'm an orphan. I grew up at Father Baker's Home for Boys. The nuns found me in the back pew of the church when I was a baby. No note, no explanation. Only this." He fished a chain out of his shirt and held it out for me to see. It was a St. Christopher medal. "They baptized me Christopher because of this and gave me the surname Lake."

"The patron saint of travelers. Someone thought you'd go far."

"Also of soldiers." He grinned. "Appropriate, huh? Anyway, I never asked any questions. The nuns didn't encourage it. I won't claim to have had a great childhood, but I guess it was better than growing up in the street."

"What makes you think your folks were poor?"

He shrugged. "Why else would they leave me in a church?"

"I can think of several reasons, but let's leave that for a moment." I didn't want to say out loud that a baby coulda been an embarrassment under the right circumstances. "Why do you want to find her now?"

"I was injured in early May, in action against the Germans in Africa."

"Africa? What unit?" I shouldn't have interrupted, but I had to know. Maybe Private Lake knew Tom and could tell me if he was all right.

"34th Infantry. Why?"

My heart fell. "My fiancé is with the 1st Armored. I thought you might know him."

For a young man, his gaze was awfully understanding. "Sorry. Anyway,

I took a pretty bad hit. Shrapnel. They sent me back to England for a bit, and I got the chance to come back to Buffalo for a spell. I go back to the front in two weeks, the ninth." He leaned forward. "Miss Ahern, I've seen things. Things a person shouldn't have to see. I want to know my mother before I go back. I want this," he tapped his chest, "to go to her if I get killed. I've spent twenty years not knowing where I came from and not being very curious, to be honest. But something about living with the Grim Reaper at your shoulder makes you want to see certain people, like your mom. Can you help me?"

I thought a moment. An orphan, and his only lead was an old religious charm? "May I see that medal again?"

He pulled it out, slipped it off, and handed it to me.

I could tell at once it was quality goods, silver at least, maybe white gold. The carving of the saint was crisp. There were a couple of scratches on it, but the metal was remarkably smooth. I flipped it over. "What's this engraving on the back?"

"It's French, I asked the nuns." He closed his eyes. *"Avec tout mon amour.* With all my love."

"Your mother was French?"

"I don't know." He slapped the table, the first sign of frustration he'd shown. "Maybe. Or my dad was. Or they liked French. Who knows?" He pushed aside his coffee. "Please, I need to find her. Don't you understand? Can you help me or not? If not, tell me and I'll find some other detective. Although, the guy who vouched for you said you were pretty good."

The guy... I closed off the thought. Instead, I brought to mind my own parents. How would I feel if I'd grown up without them? If I had to go into harm's way without knowing who I was or where I came from. "No guarantees, but I'll try. May I keep this for now? I promise I'll give it back before you ship out again."

Private Lake leaned back. "Yes, yes, of course. Thank you. I, um, don't have a lot of money. I've saved some from my pay. It's not like I've got a family to send it home to, and there aren't corner soda joints in Africa. What do you charge?"

"My standard rate is fifteen dollars for the first week, plus expenses. After that, it's five dollars a day. Is that too much?"

"No, that's fine." He took a wallet from his pocket and laid down three fivers. "What else do you need?"

"The name of at least one nun from the orphanage would be handy."

"The nun in charge is Sister Mary Agnes."

"Swell." I jotted down the name. "If I gotta talk to you, where can I find you?"

"I got a room up near Our Lady of Victory." He recited a phone number. "That's for the house phone."

"I'll be in touch."

He stood. "Thank you. This means a lot."

"Like I said, I'll do my best."

He turned to walk away.

"Oh, Private Lake? One other thing."

He faced me. "What is it?"

"You said someone vouched for me? Who?" It didn't really matter, but I was curious. The only person I could think of was my friend, Lee Tillotson, and it didn't seem likely he and the private had met.

"Oh, he's a volunteer at the hospital. He's a Quaker, nice guy for a conscientious objector."

I immediately knew who he was talking about. Frank Hicks.

Chapter Two

Judy insisted on payin' for my breakfast. I left her a fat tip and skedaddled before she could argue with me about it. I did have Private Lake's fifteen bucks in my purse, after all.

Out on the sidewalk, I stopped to light up a Lucky Strike Green. The sun shone down, a few clouds in the otherwise clear sky. Pigeons and seagulls fought for scraps in the gutter. After a week of scorchers, the temperature had settled to a nice warmth. A perfect midsummer day.

What I wanted to do was march on over to Buffalo State Hospital and give Frank Hicks a piece of my mind. Assuming he still worked there. Since jobs were limited for a conscientious objector, I had no reason to think otherwise. I'd said goodbye to him at the end of Edward Kettle's case back in May, and he had no business butting back into my life. No, sir. He could keep his dark eyes, dimpled cheek, and Jimmy Stewart smile to himself, thank you very much.

If only my heart didn't do a little pitter-pat at the thought of him. It had no business doing so, either. I was engaged to Tom, the man I loved. End of story.

Common sense won over hot emotion. I caught a bus to Ridge Road in Lackawanna and got off near Our Lady of Victory Hospital. From there, it was a short walk to the church. The orphanage loomed across the street. I mounted the steps and went into the office. A lay person, a young woman maybe a couple years older than me, sat at the desk typing, her black skirt, stockings, and neat short-sleeve white blouse a perfect outfit for working at a house of the Lord. I coughed. "Excuse me."

She ignored me.

I tried a second time, a bit louder. "Excuse me."

She held up one finger and kept working.

Now, I was irritated. I wasn't dressed all prim and proper, but that didn't mean she could ignore me. I rapped on her desk. "Hey, I'm standin' here."

She looked up a cool light in her dove-gray eyes. She looked me over, then reached for a form. "How many months along are you? It can't be much. You're not showing."

I didn't have a response. *She thinks I'm pregnant.* 'Cause I was there or 'cause I wore pants and must be a knocked-up, khaki-wacky, unwed mother? "I'm sorry, you've got the wrong idea."

"Oh?"

"Yeah, you do. I don't need your help. Not in that way, at least. I'm here to see Sister Mary Agnes." I handed the secretary one of my brand-new business cards.

Her forehead crinkled as she frowned. "A private detective? Really?"

"Yes. I'm here on business. Is the sister around?"

She didn't seem to know what to do with me or my card. "It's highly unusual for someone to walk in off the street to see her."

"That's me, unusual." I was determined to get past the gatekeeper. I would have expected this kind of attitude from an old lady. Not someone with pin curls in her hair.

A woman in a black habit with a white wimple came out of the back office. Her face was lined, and her blue eyes a bit faded, indicating she was old. But the religious clothing made it hard to tell her age otherwise. "What is it, Jane? This noise is disturbing my morning prayer."

Jane ducked her head. "I'm sorry, Sister. But this young woman says she has to talk to you."

I held out another business card to Sister Mary Agnes. "I'm sorry to intrude, but I'm here on behalf of my client, Private Christopher Lake. Is there somewhere quiet we can talk?"

Sister Mary Agnes read my card. "Young lady, shouldn't you be at home instead of playing games? Watching your children? Or helping your mother?"

I held up my left hand. "I'm not married yet, Sister. My guy is overseas. I'm not pregnant, and I don't have kids. I have three younger siblings to help Mom plenty. My visit is strictly business. No games."

"I see." She tapped the card against her hand. "Well, since you're here and I almost certainly won't be able to get rid of you, come this way." She led me to a small office and closed the door. The furniture was plain wood, a desk and three chairs. The bookcases were prob'ly full of religious titles. A shrine to the Blessed Mother, fronted by a kneeler, was against one wall. A lit candle and open prayer book showed Sister really had been at prayer.

The sight made me feel guilty. "On second thought, I'm sorry, Sister. Maybe I *should* come back later. I didn't mean to interrupt your prayer."

"Please, sit down, Miss Ahern." Sister Mary Agnes pointed at a chair and sat behind her desk. "The Lord and his Mother are patient. They'll still be there when I'm finished. As I said, I don't think you're the type to be gotten rid of easily."

I sat and crossed my legs at the ankle. I wasn't sure how to take her words. "What makes you say that?"

"You have a determined look about you." Sister's eyes twinkled. "It reminds me of someone."

"Oh?"

"Myself at your age." She clasped her hands. "Now, my child, what can I do for you?"

I took out my notebook. "I told you in the outer office. I'm here on behalf of my client. Do you remember him?"

"Christopher? Oh yes. I remember most of our boys, but he was especially memorable. Such a kind child. And very responsible. I wasn't at all surprised when I heard he'd enlisted ahead of the draft."

"He told me you're in charge of the orphanage."

She inclined her head. "I don't have the title of Mother Superior, but yes, I do manage the daily affairs."

I held my pencil over the page. "What does that mean?"

"Oh, all the little things that make the place run. Handling the paperwork, overseeing the orphans' ration books, taking in donations of money and clothing from the laity, the list goes on."

"Would that include taking care of things when boys come to the orphanage?"

Her expression didn't change. "Such as?"

I wasn't sure, so I guessed. "Recording dates, either birth or the day they were admitted, what names the boys had, or were given, anything known about family or parents. That kind of thing."

"Yes."

She sure was big on short answers. I wrote some notes. "How does that work? Are they always babies, or do you get older kids, too?"

She eyed me. "Children come to us in all sorts of ways and at all ages. Some have lost their parents and have no other family. Some are left for us. Sadly, some have been given up by parents unable to care for them." She paused. "You haven't told me exactly what this is about, Miss Ahern. Is something wrong with Christopher? Is he in trouble?"

"No, Sister." She was sharp, whatever her age might be. She wouldn't be taken in by a fib, even if I could bring my Catholic self to lie to a nun. "He's home on medical furlough and hired me to find his birth mother. He told me he was left in a pew in the church. Do you keep records when boys come into the orphanage?"

She studied me over the tips of her clasped hands. "We do."

"May I see the ones for Christopher?"

"You may not."

I blinked. There was no anger in her voice, no maliciousness, no emotion at all. It was a matter-of-fact statement. "Why not?"

"Because they are none of your business."

"I disagree, Sister. They're my client's business, and that makes them mine. Doesn't he have a right to them?"

Sister Mary Agnes continued to stare at me, voice mild. "Have you, or he, thought of the fact that perhaps his mother doesn't want to *be* found? That perhaps the reason she left him is because she could not, or did not want to, keep him and therefore wished him to grow up ignorant of her?"

I couldn't read anything in her blue eyes. The fact is that I hadn't thought of it, and I'd never asked Private Lake. Maybe he knew and decided to search anyway. "Do you think that's fair, Sister? He's a young man who faced death. In two weeks, he's going back to the front to do it again. Can't you understand why he wants to know?"

She nodded, rather solemnly. "Of course. I think it's perfectly natural. When man faces his end, he wants closure, peace. Part of coming to a sense of peace could be reconciliation with family."

"Then why won't you help me?"

"Because while you only have an obligation to your client, I must respect both child and parent. I'm sorry."

I couldn't believe this. "You're not gonna tell me anything?"

"Beyond what Christopher himself has said? No." She stood. "I can see the decision upsets you, but it is final. I have no doubt you have the best of intentions, but you will find no help here. Good day, Miss Ahern. God's peace be with you."

I bit my tongue against a sharp reply. It wasn't the appropriate place, and I didn't have any business saying what I wanted to say to anyone, and definitely not a nun. It wouldn't have changed her mind.

But doggone it. At least she coulda given me a hint of what to do next.

Chapter Three

My thoughts about Sister Mary Agnes were not at all charitable after I left the orphanage. In my opinion, Private Lake's mother had lost all rights when she gave him up. If she didn't want to meet with him, that was her choice. But a young man, 'specially one going back to risk his life for his country, oughta know his mother.

However, my long experience with nuns had taught me I had as much chance of changing her mind as of stopping the water over Niagara Falls. Which put me in a pickle. If she wasn't willing to help, what else could I do?

I put my hand in my pocket, and my fingers brushed the chain of the Saint Christopher medal. I took it out and watched the metal gleam in the sunlight. The carving looked even crisper in the sunshine. I turned it over in my fingers. It was in such good shape after twenty years, or more, of wear. It had to be high quality. I knew of a jeweler down on Main Street in Buffalo. He'd know for sure.

A bell jingled as I walked into Henck's Jewelry, but no one was in the joint. I scanned the glass cases of sparkly stones, pausing over the diamond engagement rings. Mine was much smaller than anything in the case. Tom had never told me where he bought it, but it wasn't this place. I twisted it on my finger. Not that it mattered. The love behind it was the important thing.

A man with a chrome dome and a face like a winter apple came out of the back. He wore round glasses and a white shirt with black pants and black suspenders. "May I help you? Perhaps you're looking for a ring?"

I tore my attention away and went over to him. "No, I already have one of those. I'm hoping you can help me with this." I handed over the medal. "I take it you're Mr. Henck?"

"I am. Let me see." He carried the medal over to a bright lamp. "Hmm. Good quality. Silver, I'd think."

"Not white gold?"

"No, I don't think so. Gold is softer, even when mixed with other metals. How old is this?"

I leaned on the glass, then straightened. I wasn't afraid of the glass breaking, but I didn't want to leave marks either. "At least twenty years. The person who owns it has had it since he was a baby."

Mr. Henck turned it over in his long, slim fingers. "It's older than that. There's a date here."

"I thought that might be a deep scratch or dent."

"No, it's a date. I don't have my loupe and I can't quite make it out. Old eyes, you see." He rubbed it between his fingers. "Yes, silver. There are a few scratches, but not many. I think gold would have more marks on it. I assume he knows what the inscription means?"

"All my love. He doesn't speak French, but he had it translated."

Mr. Henck ran the chain through his hands. "This is particularly fine as well. Something I'd expect on a woman's necklace, not a man's. The young man can't ask his mother about the piece?"

"He's an orphan. The nuns at Father Baker's found him in the church, wrapped in a blanket and wearing that." I pointed. "No note, no other explanation."

"Ah." He handed it back. "What exactly do you want me to say?"

I pooled the chain in my palm. "Well, one thing you've already done. You said it's quality goods."

"Oh yes, no doubt. The metal plus the detail in the carving tells me that."

"Do you sell things like this?"

"Religious medals? No, that's not part of my normal inventory." He took off his specs and polished them with a cloth he took from his pocket.

So much for getting a tip. "Then you can't tell me anything else?"

"That depends." He put his glasses back on. "If you want to know who bought it, that I can't help you with. I don't know where it was made. Do you know if it was purchased from an American jeweler?"

I hadn't even thought of that. "Come to think of it, I don't. I assumed that 'cause the owner is American, his parents were. At least one of 'em. I s'pose an engraving in French doesn't necessarily mean a French parent."

"It does not." Mr. Henck pulled a book from under the counter. "It could be his parents were Francophiles." He saw my expression. "They loved French culture. Or if it is a family piece, it could have been passed down through generations and originated in France."

Why couldn't anything be simple? "Then it's a dead end."

"Not necessarily." He ran his fingers down a page. "Ah, here's what I'm looking for." He reached over and wrote on a pad, then ripped off the sheet and handed it to me.

It was a name and address. A French-sounding name. "Who's this?"

"Another jeweler in the city, one who immigrated from France and who might know more. That is the address of his store. I suggest you take the medal to him and ask your questions."

* * *

As soon as I got off the bus, I could tell the jeweler Mr. Henck sent me to was gonna be in a fancier place than his. It was on Main Street, not far from Best Street. The front door was under a deep red awning that managed to look both demure and moneyed at the same time. Trays of glittery rings and necklaces beckoned shoppers from behind the plate glass windows.

I pushed on a heavy glass door that had the name Dumonde lettered in gold and went in. A bell tinkled above my head. Even the inside smelled like dough. I smoothed my cotton blouse, and the thought crossed my mind that maybe I shoulda dressed up. *Nonsense. I'm a gumshoe, not a shopper.* The lights were just bright enough to create a sea of sparkle under the glass cases.

Before I'd even reached the register, a man emerged from the back. He was tall, taller than my client, but thin. His black hair was shiny and smoothed in wings away from a broad forehead that showed the deep creases of age. He had gold glasses on his beaked nose, the kind without arms, and one of those things jewelers used to look at gems perched on his head. The creases in his black trousers and the stiff collar of his white shirt told me he used a lot of starch.

He looked me up and down. "How may I help you?"

I was impressed. I thought he had been about to tell me to scram. I handed over one of my cards. "Are you Mr. Dumonde?"

He took it, his fingers long and slim. Was that a requirement to be a jeweler? "I am Monsieur Dumonde, yes." He spoke in an accent that reminded me of Maurice Chevalier. "What is it you want?"

Straight to the point. I briefly wondered if he faked that accent to impress his customers or if he practiced it to make sure he didn't lose touch with his homeland. "Mr. Henck, he runs a jewelry store downtown, he sent me. I'm looking for any information you can give me about this." I took the St. Christopher medal out of my pocket and handed it over.

Mr. Dumonde ran the chain through his fingers. "Ah, very fine work. Not one of mine, but it is like something I would sell."

"You have religious medals?"

"A few." He took a few steps to another case. "The French, we are mostly Catholic, yes? Medals to the Blessed Virgin and other saints are very popular. See?"

I followed. In the case was a small selection of medals in both silver and gold. The Virgin Mary was prominent, but there were a couple of others, including a young woman with a sword. *Joan of Arc was French, wasn't she?* "What makes you say mine is quality?"

He pulled the glass from his head. "Silver. It is old, but does not have many scratches. The detail in the engraving is exquisite, very sharp and detailed."

"How can you tell it's age?"

"Here." He pointed to the small indentation on the back. "This is small enough to look like a scratch, but with my loupe I can see it is a year. 1872. I think, perhaps, the year it was made, yes? And the inscription, you know what it means?"

"With all my love."

He nodded approvingly. "This is yours?"

"No, my client's." I briefly told Private Lake's story. "Do you think this was his mother's? Or his father's?"

Mr. Dumonde turned the medal over again, still looking through his loupe. "Mother's, I would say. The chain is too fine for a man. See these here? These are for men."

I followed his finger, which pointed at a selection of chains that were clearly thicker than the one on the medal. "I see your point. You said it wasn't something you sold. Do you know who did?"

"Not personally. I think whoever it was, you will not find the shop in Buffalo." He grinned. "One moment, please." He went into the back and returned a couple of minutes later. "My eyes, they are older but not too old. I was right. This mark right here, I recognize this as a well-known jeweler in Belgium. His family, they have been jewelers for generations. In the Great War, the Germans invaded, but his shop survived. I can only hope he does as well this time." Mr. Dumonde removed his loupe and handed back the medal. "You said your client is an orphan?"

"Yes."

"St. Christophe, he is not the patron saint of orphans."

"No, but he does look over travelers and soldiers. And you said this isn't a man's chain."

Mr. Dumonde inclined his head. "True. Then perhaps the young man's mother believed he would journey much in his life and need the saint's protection."

"Seeing as it was prob'ly hers to start with, someone thought the same of her." I took the medal from him and put it back in my pocket. "Can you tell me anything else?"

"I think I would not be telling you anything you do not already know, or believe, Miss Ahern. This woman you seek, she is French, perhaps Belgian. Or had French parents who gifted her with this when she went out into the world."

I thought of Canada. "French Canadian?"

16

"The Quebecois, they are French and, at the same time, not. They have their own culture. No, because the medal is from a Belgian jeweler, I think you seek someone with European roots." He stood and bowed. "You are wise for your years. Go with God, mademoiselle. And be careful."

The admonition startled me. "How so?"

His gaze was solemn. "A baby left in a church with no message other than this medal? That tells me this woman intended her identity to be a secret. Some secrets, they should not be trifled with, yes?"

Chapter Four

Outside Dumonde's, I leaned on a lamp post and lit up. What had I learned? Bupkis, that's what. I'd already known the medal was high quality and about the French connection. No, I decided, that wasn't quite true. Mr. Dumonde told me it came direct from Belgium around the turn of the century. That was somethin'.

But how did it help?

I watched the well-dressed shoppers stroll down the street while I exhaled a cloud of smoke. This would have been much easier if Sister Mary Agnes had been willing to spill what she knew. 'Course, if she had been, Private Lake coulda asked her himself, and he wouldn't need me. In fact, it was likely he did.

It wasn't that I expected the solution to every case to fall in my lap. Heck, I needed to do quite a bit of legwork to solve my past cases. But this was locating someone's *mother*. Why was it this hard?

Mr. Dumonde said he thought it likely she was Belgian or from a Belgian family. I still believed it was possible the father had been as well. Well, Buffalo didn't have many Belgian families. Germans, Irish, Poles, those we had in spades. Then, a thought hit me. What if Private Lake's parents weren't Belgian, but one of 'em had been *to* Belgium? Thanks to the Great War, we had plenty of men who fell into that category. Any one of 'em coulda bought a token for a sweetheart back home. Yes, the medal was expensive, and maybe that ruled out the average Joe in the trenches. Then again, perhaps not. If the jeweler was scared after the Germans reached Belgium, and he'd been trying to get out before he lost everything, he may have let it go for a song.

In fact, Private Lake's father coulda been a Doughboy on leave who met and wooed a local girl. Or he coulda been treated by a French or Belgian nurse. Maybe Private Lake's father had been an American officer who brought back a French girl as a wife. After all, just 'cause the medal was Belgian didn't mean the owner was. Both countries spoke the same language. It wasn't a reach to think a piece of Belgian jewelry would wind up in France.

The number of possibilities made me a little giddy, but I liked the ideas. Considering who St. Christopher gave his protection to, who better to bring a religious icon like that back from the war than a soldier?

But it sure didn't help narrow down my options.

I ashed my cigarette. I needed to approach this from a different angle. A mother had given up her child. What would make her do that? I couldn't imagine Mom giving up any of us under any condition. Didn't mothers and children usually have a strong bond? Why break it?

Private Lake's assumption was his mother couldn't afford to keep him. That might be true. Maybe she was a war widow. Maybe she was married, but her husband was unemployed, perhaps unable to work because of a wound or deformity. If she'd been a young woman, alone in the U.S. with a baby, she might have decided the child would have a better chance, being raised by the Church.

But if that was true, why didn't she hock the medal for some dough? Did it mean so much she couldn't give it away?

"No way." I shook my head. My family didn't have much money. With six kids, the younger ones wore a lot of hand-me-downs. But there was no way Pop or Mom would think of giving one of us up.

'Course it could be they'd never been that desperate.

A young woman in a stylish summer dress and high heels sauntered by. Her hair was perfectly waved, her makeup flawless. She had the soft skin of someone who never worked a day in her life. I watched her go down the sidewalk and noted the seams of her stockings. Stockings! I had one pair of nylons I only brought out when I was getting dolled up. Who could afford to wear them walking down the street?

A woman with money, that's who. The thought brought me back to another reason a woman would give up her baby.

Scandal.

What if Private Lake's mother had not been poor, but rich? If she'd gotten pregnant, the family would have gone to great lengths to hide that fact, 'specially if she was a debutante. A baby out of wedlock would ruin her chances for an acceptable match. Even if the father was well-to-do himself she mighta been forced to have the child in secret and give him away. Sure, if the father was willing to be pressured into marriage it mighta worked, but if he wasn't? Even worse, what if the father had been someone considered undesirable by her family? Or maybe he'd been a married man.

If that were the case, it was easy to think she coulda had nice jewelry. Maybe the medal had been a gift from her lover. It could even have come from a father, maybe one who served overseas or went to Belgium on business trips. If it was from the mid-nineteenth century, it might even have been passed down to her from *her* mother. And her last act had been to give it to her child.

"I like it." I looked around. The woman next to me, holding the hand of her small son, sidled away. "Sorry, talking to myself."

She gave me a once over and inched away some more.

I wanted to lecture her on her snooty behavior, but I didn't have time. I needed to find out if any socialites disappeared, then reappeared, about twenty years ago. Fortunately, I had a good contact who could help me out.

* * *

I pushed through the main door of the *Courier Express*. The joint was hoppin' with reporters bustling in and out of offices, men wearing visors and pencils behind their ears holding sheaves of paper crossing the polished floor, and even a few regular people mixed in. The news never sleeps, and it was logical that a newspaper office didn't either.

I went to an older woman seated at a desk with a small switchboard. "I'm lookin' for Melvin Schlingmann. Is he in?"

She looked up at me. "Your name?"

"Betty Ahern."

"Is Mr. Schlingmann expecting you?"

Mr. Schlingmann. It was beyond strange to hear my friend referred to as "mister," considering when we'd met, he worked for a grubby tabloid. I guess breaking a story about a murder, with an inside scoop courtesy of yours truly, brought him up in the world. "No, but if he's here, he'll see me. We're friends."

The woman's expression was doubtful, but she pushed a button on the switchboard. "Mr. Schlingmann, sorry to interrupt, but you have a visitor. A woman, Betty Ahern. Yes. Yes, I'll tell her." She replaced her phone. "You can wait over there. He'll be out in a minute."

I took my seat. Melvin had to love this job. It was exactly his cup of tea, his finger on the pulse of what was happenin' in the city, if not the world. I wondered if he'd paid his long-suffering landlady or maybe upgraded his digs.

When he appeared, I could see he'd improved his wardrobe. His clothes weren't flash, but they fit much better, and he didn't look so much like a weasel with his skinny neck poking out of his overlarge collar. He looked like he was eatin' better, too, or at least on a more regular basis. This was a Joe his girl, Irene, would be proud to be seen with. I stood.

"Betty! What's buzzin', cousin?" He gave me a brief hug. "Haven't seen you in a dog's age. I still owe you a lunch for helpin' me get this gig."

I waved my hand. "You wrote the story, Melvin. Not me."

He chucked me on my shoulder. "Maybe, Toots, but you gave me the scoop. But I'm sure you didn't stop to flap your gums. What's up?"

"I need your help."

Melvin rubbed his narrow chin. "With what?"

"Knowledge. Maybe research? Is there somewhere quieter we can talk?"

"Sure, there's a soda shop down the street." He glanced over at the receptionist. "Let me tell Myrtle I'm stepping out for an early lunch. Stay put." He hustled over to the woman, spoke, and came back. "Okay, let's go."

The soda shop was about a block and a half away from the *Courier's* offices.

We'd beaten the midday crowd, and we had our choice of seats at the counter. A pimply youngster too young to enlist came up to us. "What can I get ya?"

Melvin turned to me. "Coffee or a milkshake?"

I studied the menu. "Chocolate milkshake and a grilled cheese."

"Vanilla and the same for me." Melvin pulled out his wallet. "It's on me."

The boy jotted down our orders and left.

I leaned on the counter. "I can pay for my own lunch."

"I know, but like I said. I owe you. I'm getting off cheap." Melvin rubbed his hands together. "Okay, spill. What kind of assistance can I provide the city's most successful private investigator?"

"That's sayin' a bit much. I'm not sure how successful I am when I still can't afford my own office."

"You'll get there. Time is money, Toots. Talk."

I reached for a napkin, turning my back so he couldn't see my grin. Melvin hadn't changed much after all. I set the paper rectangle beside me. "I'm lookin' for a missing mother."

"Missing person?"

"Kind of." I told a shortened version of Private Lake's story. "I got the bum's rush at the orphanage when I tried to get them to give me the details."

"I'm not surprised. Those nuns are tough." Melvin paused as the soda jerk set down our shakes. "What's this woman's name?"

"That's part of the point. I don't have one. I've been calling her Mrs. Lake to myself, but that's all made up."

"It will complicate the search." Melvin rubbed his nose. "He doesn't have anything to go on besides the medal, huh? Can I see it?"

I handed over the St. Christopher. I stuck a straw in my milkshake and sucked. "I've been to two jewelers who both assure me that's a high-quality piece."

"I can see that." He turned it over. "French inscription."

"With all my love." The ice cream was deliciously cold as it slithered down my throat.

Our sandwiches arrived, perfectly toasted squares of bread leaking melted cheese from the sides. Melvin picked his up and immediately put it back down. "Wow, hot. What are you thinking?"

"I s'pose Private Lake could be right, and his folks were too poor to keep him. But that's gonna be hard to follow without more information. I can think of one other reason to put a kid in an orphanage that'd be an easier story to follow."

"A wealthy mother looking to avoid the embarrassment of a child out of wedlock. Makes sense." He tested his sandwich again, decided it was cool enough, and took a careful bite. Since he grabbed his shake immediately, it must still have been hot.

It didn't surprise me that his thoughts mirrored mine. Melvin may have worked for a seedy paper when we met, but I'd never doubted his smarts.

I decided not to scorch my mouth. "Bingo. Which is where you come in. I need to know if any debutantes mysteriously disappeared about twenty years ago. You know, went off for a cure or something instead of making her entrance to society."

"Or already *was* in society, fell out of sight, and came back about six months later. Gotcha." He threw caution to the wind and took a big bite of his sandwich. "But you can do all that yourself. You don't need me. All you gotta do is search the newspaper archive. That's simple stuff compared to things I know you've done in the past."

"Actually, I do." I told him about my deadline. "I have to follow up on other things. I don't have time."

"Okay. I'll bite and give you a hand. What's in it for me?"

"What do you mean? You're a *real* newshound now, aren't you? This is a fluff piece." I took a much more lady-like piece out of my own sandwich and savored the crunch of the bread with the melty goodness of the cheese.

"I'm flexible." He grinned. "I can build goodwill by giving a lead to the Lifestyles gang. Or who knows? Maybe there's a story here. You don't know until you know, right?"

"You're impossible. All right, if there turns out to be something, and that's a pretty big *if* in my opinion, I'll give you an exclusive again. Deal?"

In the blink of an eye, three-quarters of Melvin's lunch had disappeared. He still gobbled his food, but at least he wasn't as disgusting about it. And he stayed thin as a rail. We'd started lunch together, but I was willing to bet I'd finish it on my own.

"Deal. I'd shake on it, but our hands are all greasy." He slurped down more milkshake. "How do I find you with the results?"

"Call my house. If I'm not there, my mom or my sister will take a message. They know you now." I eyed the crumbs on his plate. "Tell me something. Do you always eat so fast? I mean, do you even taste your food?"

He threw some money on the counter and took another drink. "I told you. Time is money, Toots. After all, I have a disgraced society girl to find."

Chapter Five

I left the soda shop and paused on the sidewalk to consider my next stop. It would take Melvin time to run down the lead I'd given him. He might have his own deadline to meet first. There was no guarantee he'd find anything, either. Maybe it was buried too deep. Nah, I didn't need to worry. I could tell he'd been interested. Melvin was the kinda guy who would find the dirt, if it was there, even if he did have another assignment in the works.

Now that I'd set Melvin on the trail, I could go to Buffalo State Hospital to confront Frank Hicks. I couldn't decide if I was mad or grateful, or something completely different. My feelings were complicated, and I didn't like that one bit. Sure, he'd saved my bacon in Front Park on my last case. In the emotionally charged aftermath of the moment, things had gotten a bit heated. He'd admitted he liked me. Even admired me, somethin' that wasn't to be tossed aside lightly. Yes, he had turned my head a bit. I was engaged, not dead.

But I was committed to Tom and I was smart enough to recognize temptation when it leaned in for a kiss. I'd made it plain I didn't want Frank in my life. Not like that. I hadn't ever thought he'd start referring business once I'd shut the door on anything personal. Did he know I was a fully licensed private investigator now?

It didn't matter. It was better for both of us to let time and space cool whatever spark had been between us.

But I sure wouldn't mind seeing that dimple again.

I mentally scolded myself. I had more important things to think about.

There was one more reason a baby might end up in an orphanage. It hadn't occurred to me until Melvin left. What if Private Lake's mom had died and there'd been no one else willing to raise him? I could find a death certificate easy as pie by stoppin' at the county records office downtown. *At least Sister Mary Agnes coulda told me that.*

Unless it was the *way* she'd died the sister didn't want to talk about. It was bad enough knowing your mother was dead from illness or perhaps childbirth. But what if she'd been the victim of a crime, like murder? I laughed at myself. "Stop bein' dramatic, Betty." My history had me seein' murders everywhere, including where they prob'ly didn't exist.

But it was a possibility, one I couldn't ignore. Finding out if Mrs. Lake, as I'd taken to calling her in my head, had been murdered would require help from another old friend.

I hightailed it over to police headquarters and double-timed it to the desk sergeant, a man I knew well from previous trips to the building. "Good afternoon, Sarge."

His broad, weathered face under the close-cut cap of salt-and-pepper hair creased in a smile. "Hi there, missy. You looking for Detective MacKinnon?"

"I am. Is he in?"

"Should be. Hold on a sec." He picked up the phone and spoke to the person on the other end. Then he hung up. "He said go on up. But before you do, rumor has it you're the real thing. Passed your exam, did you?"

"I did." Since Sam MacKinnon had paid for the correspondence course, I felt obliged to tell him right off when I got my license. I wasn't surprised he spread the news around HQ, especially the officers I talked to regularly. Sam had never said it, but I suspected he thought of me as a daughter, or at least a younger sister. I took the envelope out of the bag I now carried and showed the sergeant the license. "Heard it from Detective MacKinnon, did you?"

He whistled. "You bet. He made sure everyone who mans this desk knew you were a professional and should be treated with courtesy. No more waiting in the lobby." He jerked his thumb toward the elevator. "You'd better go. Don't want to keep him twiddling his thumbs."

I thanked him and rode up to the detective's floor.

Sam was waitin' for me when the doors opened. "I thought you'd gotten lost." His shirtsleeves were rolled up over his elbows, and his tie loosened at the collar. He wasn't wearing a jacket, and his brown pants had crumbs on them, maybe from a lunch eaten at his desk. There was a glint of humor in his brown eyes.

"I've been here before, remember?" I followed him down the hall. "Sarge wanted to see my license. I hear you told everybody."

"Naturally." He held the door to a conference room. "To what do I owe the pleasure?" He sat at the table and leaned back.

I took the chair across from him. "I have a new client." I told him about Private Lake and everything I'd done that morning.

"Sounds like you covered all the bases. What could you need from me?"

"I got to thinkin'. Maybe Mrs. Lake is dead. 'Course, she wouldn't have been called Mrs. Lake, but to make things simple, that's how I'm thinkin' of her until I know her name."

He narrowed his peepers. "Good thought. Have you looked for a death certificate? Although without a name, that's a hard row to hoe."

"Not yet. I'm gonna do that after I leave here. I'm gonna have to look and see how many women of the right age died around that time. If she died of natural causes, well, that'd be a simple situation. But what if she was murdered? The case file might have more information that could help me locate her or any remaining family."

"Hmm." He hooked his thumbs in his suspenders. "I can't pull the file on every murdered woman on a whim."

I ripped a page out of my notebook and wrote Private Lake's birth date. I handed it to Sam. "Sure, but I was hopin' you could go back and see if any murders occurred near this date. You'd be looking for young women—I'd say no older than twenty—who were killed anywhere from a few days to a week after this date."

Sam took the page. "When was your private left at the orphanage?"

"The fifteenth of May in 1923."

"And his birthday is May 4?"

"He told me that was the date assigned by the nuns. They made a guess based on what the doctor said when he examined the baby."

Sam tucked the paper into his shirt pocket. "Do you know how old the mother was?"

"Nope. Like I said, I'm thinking no older than twenty, maybe as young as fourteen, if she had been raped or something. But heck, I s'pose she coulda been older." I spread my hands.

"I'm sorry, but I'm too busy for a fishing expedition at the moment. My captain will bust my chops but good if I ignore my current cases for something that might not even be a crime."

Rats. "I shoulda thought of that."

"Tell you what. Here's what I can offer for assistance. Go find your death certificates. If any of them indicate the woman was murdered, I'll do what I can to get you the details of the case. Deal?" He stood.

I did the same and held out my hand. "Thanks, Sam. You're a pal."

He grasped it. "Anything for a fellow investigator."

* * *

As soon as I left Sam, I headed to the county building. It was only a few blocks away, and the walk didn't take long at all. I barely had enough time to smoke half a Lucky before I arrived. I carefully ground it out and stuck it back in the pack before enterin' the building. I figured they wouldn't want fire around paper records and no way was I wastin' a smoke.

I used the building directory to find the records department. I handed over my business card to the gray-haired woman behind the counter. She had glasses, and her hair was pulled in a bun so tight it stretched the skin at her forehead. She fixed me with a piercing blue-eyed gaze. "What is this for?"

"I'm working a case, and I need to see death certificates for women in May of 1923."

"You can't barge in here and look for an unspecified record."

"My client is tryin' to find his mother."

"What does that have to do with me?"

Why did I always run into old women who didn't feel like helpin'? What I wanted was public information. Then again, I might be interruptin' a project she was workin' on and made her grumpy. After all, somebody had to fetch those certificates for me.

I glanced at her left hand. A thin band was on her ring finger. I didn't know if she had children, but I took a gamble and tried to appeal to her maternal instincts. "Private Lake, that's my client, is an orphan. He was left in a church pew when he was a baby and grew up at Father Baker's. Now he's in the Army. He was injured on the front, and he's home on furlough. He'd like to try and find his mom before he goes back. He's had one brush with death. He wants to know where he came from, and who can blame him?"

Her sharp eyes softened a smidge.

I leaned on the counter and used my best wheedling voice. "Those boys, they're fightin' a war and seein' all sorts of horrible things. Don't you think you could give me a hand here? Bring some comfort to a Joe who's going back in harm's way?"

She took a handkerchief from her pocket and dabbed at her eyes. "Well, when you put it that way. I guess I can spare the time and pull the records you want. What month did you say you are looking for?"

I thought. "Can I have April and May of 1923?"

"That could be quite a lot of certificates."

"I'm only interested in women of childbearing age. Say fourteen to thirty. Can you give me only those?"

She cocked her head. "I'm very busy, young lady. My sympathy only goes so far."

Of course. "Give me everything. I'll figure it out."

She walked away and returned a few minutes later with two piles. "Here's April and May. You can sit over at that table. They are filed in date order, so please keep them that way."

"You got it." I took the certificates and went to the desk. I had a hunch that what I was lookin' for would not be in April. I tackled that pile first. I paged through every one of 'em, passing over any men. I knew the name was meaningless, so I focused on age. But no women under the age of fifty had died in April 1923.

I moved on to May. I went through these a bit slower, as I figured I was more likely to find possibilities. I was right. Three women, all between the ages of eighteen and twenty-nine, had died that month. I wrote down the names and causes of death. Two had died of illness, one from a fall. I made darn sure the certificates were back in date order before I returned them to the desk. "Thanks."

The clerk thumbed through the paper and nodded with approval. "Did you find what you are looking for?"

"Kind of. I have three names."

"You don't have any idea which of them is the right person?"

"Unfortunately, no." The certificates did not list next of kin. It would be quite the research project to find the families.

She must've read my mind. "Start with the obituaries."

I looked at her. "Excuse me?"

"My advice is to look at the obituaries published in the paper. Those typically include who the person is survived by, things like that. I know it's twenty years ago, but parents and siblings should still be alive." She hitched her sweater around her shoulders.

Hopefully, they'd also still be livin' in Buffalo and be listed in the phone book. If any of 'em where relatives of the woman I was lookin' for, how would they feel about a surprise grandson or nephew? "Thanks for the advice. And for lettin' me poke around."

"I hope the young man finds his mother." Her voice softened. But then the hardness came back. "You'd better not spread the word I'm a soft touch. We can't be inundated with people looking for historical records. There might be a war on, but that doesn't mean this office isn't busy with other things. I do not have time to do research for every person in the city with a missing relative."

I stifled a sigh. "Wouldn't dream of it, ma'am."

Chapter Six

I coulda gone back to Melvin for help with the obituaries, but I'd already asked him for one favor. I headed for the next-best source of past newspapers, the library. It had been a helpful resource in past cases. I hoped I'd find what I was lookin' for this time.

Inside, I went directly to the desk where they kept magazines and newspapers, what they called "the stacks."

A young woman, maybe a few years older than me, sat behind the desk. She had pretty brown hair with gold highlights that shone under the overhead lights and a smattering of freckles across her pert nose. She was reading a book when I walked up, but immediately set it aside. "May I help you?"

I glanced at the title. *Moby Dick* by Herman Melville. It looked like something a teacher would make you read in class, not something a person picked up for enjoyment. "I'm looking for obituaries for these people." I handed over the paper with the names and dates.

She read it and looked up with a gleam in her intelligent gray eyes. "Do you know what paper they were in?"

I hadn't thought of that. My family members were *Courier Express* readers. But Buffalo did have another paper. "I don't. I s'pose I need both of 'em."

"Oh, if you're looking in 1923, there's more than two."

"Really?"

"Yes." She straightened on her stool. "Back then, the *Buffalo Daily Courier* and the *Buffalo Morning Express* were separate papers. Then there's the *Evening News*. There were others as well. I recommend checking in *The Bee*."

31

My mind reeled. "This isn't New York City. Why are there so many papers?"

Her answering laugh was merry. "The Buffalo newspaper scene is, and was, quite robust. Why don't I start with the *News,* the *Courier,* and the *Express*? If you don't find what you're looking for, I'll help you branch out from there. What dates?"

All I wanted were the stinkin' articles. "I don't know those either. How soon does an obituary run after the person dies?"

She tapped a finger on her chin. "Could be anywhere from a day to a week. It really depends on the family. I'll get you a week after the death." She hopped off her stool and disappeared into the back.

Seven papers times three publications. I had to comb through twenty-one newspapers? I knew I wasn't gonna get lucky and find it on the first try. I was in for a long afternoon.

The young woman returned a few minutes later. "Here you are." She thumped a stack of newspapers on the desk. "You can use one of the carrels over there to work. If you find what you want, please don't rip it out of the paper. By the way, did you know that Samuel Langhorn Clemens was an editor and part owner of the *Buffalo Express*?" She waited, obviously expecting a response.

I didn't have one.

"You know, Mark Twain! He lived in Buffalo for a while." Judging from her expression, she was extremely proud of this fact.

'Course, I knew the author. But Lee, who had done well in school and was somethin' of a history nut, would find this fact a lot more interesting than I did. But the clerk was bein' helpful, and that counted for a lot. Not everyone was as difficult to work with as the lady at the records office. "Wow, I didn't know. That's fascinating. You said I can work over there?" I pointed toward the small desks.

She nodded, and I hurried off before I got stuck in a long conversation about books. I didn't want to hurt her feelings, but I wanted to get to work.

I was right. The task took hours. Oddly enough, I found the old papers truly interesting and much of my time was spent browsing their contents.

The stock market had been booming back then, and Buffalo's economy was in high gear, with companies such as Bethlehem Steel leading the way. The Great War was over, but that didn't mean no war. The headlines talked about conflict in Turkey, Saudi Arabia, and even Italy.

I saw ads for Ford cars, patent medicines, and new appliances that ran on electricity. I remembered Pop telling me the utility was beginning to spread to households on a large scale when I'd been born. Same with the telephone. Pictures in the Society pages showed women in shorter skirts than the previous decade and even the old flapper dresses my mother considered somewhat scandalous. The men looked sharp in flash suits. "They sure did know how to party, didn't they?" I said to myself as I flipped the newsprint.

Eventually, I stopped my lollygagging and got to work. I decided to work through one day at a time and check each paper. Tedious, but a lot better than going through a week's worth of papers three times over.

It took a couple of hours, but I found what I was looking for. The woman at the records office was right. I got names of parents and siblings for all three women.

Now, to find the people, and hope they were still alive and living in the area.

I returned the newspapers to the desk. "If I was looking for a person, I don't s'pose there's a better method than checking the telephone book, is there?"

She took the stack. "No, sorry. At least, not that I know of. There might be more information in city records, but I don't think they open their doors to regular people."

I wasn't a girl off the streets, but I didn't have to go into that with her. Besides, it would be easy-peasy to look them up. I could always ask Sam for help if I failed with the telephone book. I looked at the clock. It was almost three in the afternoon. I had one more stop I wanted to make before five.

* * *

I got off the bus and walked to Buffalo State Hospital, planning my speech.

33

I had things to say and I couldn't allow myself to be distracted by Frank's movie-star looks and brown eyes that were so deep I could easily fall in and get lost.

Or that stinkin' dimple.

Once again, the park-like grounds of the hospital amazed me. I'd never seen the rooms, but if they were anything like the outside, they were pretty plush for a place meant to house crazy people. I remembered my run-in with the woman at the administration building the last time I'd come here looking for Frank. I wasn't in the mood to deal with any more gatekeepers. I decided to take a stroll and see if I could spot him on the grounds.

There were plenty of patients out tending the gardens and walking the paths. They were usually supervised by a nearby orderly, but I deliberately avoided eye contact with any of the solitary people strolling around. I'd had one encounter with a mental patient who'd insisted trees had a higher intelligence. I didn't want another.

I kept my eyes open for Frank. When I'd first seen him on the hospital grounds, he'd been with a group of patients tending the vegetable garden. Not today. The rows of plants were leafy and full. I could see tomatoes on the vine, and rows of feathery greens I assumed were carrots. But no people. They must've done their work earlier in the day, when it was cooler.

I wiped sweat from my forehead and kept walking. If I had to, I'd go talk to the secretary at the main office. I crossed my fingers. It was too nice of a day for a fight. It had gotten a little hot, but the sky was a brilliant blue, and the clouds had disappeared from the sky. I could imagine I was walking the grounds of the Albright Knox Art Gallery, also designed by Frederick Olmstead, instead of the grounds of a hospital.

Eventually, I passed another orderly, this one an older man who must be beyond draft age. "Hi there." I handed over a business card. "I'm looking for Frank Hicks. Is he at work today?"

He narrowed his peepers. "What does a private detective want with Frank? Is he in trouble?"

Yes, but it wasn't anything like what this guy thought. "No trouble. I know him. We're not friends, exactly. More like acquaintances. But on good terms. I have a question for him, that's all."

He continued to eyeball me, his distrust plain on his square face. Finally, he answered. "Frank is off today."

Darn it. "Is he at home?" I knew where Frank lived from my last case. I didn't want to bother the building supervisor, though. Not unless Frank was there. I didn't need rumors of female visitors spreading through the building, giving people the wrong ideas.

The orderly shrugged. "Beats me. I don't talk to Frank much outside of work. He's got funny ideas."

I knew exactly what he meant. "You mean how he objects to the war? Yeah, I understand. But it's 'cause he's a Quaker, I guess."

"I don't care why. I don't hold with conchies. Me, I'm too old. I did my time in the Great War. It's people like me who give Frank the right to hold all those fancy morals. Least he could do is his part, you know?"

"He thinks he is. He's helping here. Besides, it's not like he believes the Nazis are right or anything. He doesn't hold with fighting." *Why am I defending him?* I'd had this exact argument with Frank. I'd played the part of the person who didn't get it. I'm sure Frank could defend his beliefs to anyone. He prob'ly had done that many times, including to this man. Frank Hicks didn't need me coming to his rescue.

Except I couldn't help myself, and I didn't want to dig too deep for the reason why.

The man curled his lip. "I suppose you agree with him, huh, missy? I bet you don't even got the least clue what's going on over there. Do you even read the news?"

I stiffened. "For your information, my fiancé and my older brother are overseas. I follow the headlines. Not that it's any of your beeswax. Now, can you help me find Frank or not?"

He had the decency to flush. "Sorry. I guess he might be at home. Sometimes he visits his folks. He might also be volunteering down at Our Lady of Victory. He does that occasionally on his day off."

"I thought you didn't talk to him much."

The red on his face deepened. "I hear him talking to others."

Which meant he was a snoop. Oh well, so was I. But at least I was a *professional* snoop. "Did any of this eavesdropping tell you if he hangs out anywhere else?"

The orderly frowned. "I've overheard him talk about playing chess with some of the old geezers who spend their day at the Moose Lodge up on Tonawanda Street."

"Thanks." I turned away, but stopped. "You don't know the phone number at his apartment, do you?"

"What do I look like, a telephone directory? I told you plenty, now buzz off. I got work to do." He walked away.

I stared at his retreating back and squashed down the unreasonable urge to run after him and defend Frank. After all, Frank Hicks was nothing to me.

But if that was true, why was I chasing him down?

Chapter Seven

I was in the area, so it didn't take long to walk to Frank's apartment. He wasn't there. The building super smirked at me in a way I didn't quite like, but I also wasn't gonna waste time insisting I was there on business. It was easy to see it wasn't an argument I would win.

But it wasn't a wasted trip. According to the super, Frank was a regular up at the Moose Lodge on Tuesdays. I headed to Tonawanda Street. The parking lot was mostly empty, but the bar was full of old men, like the orderly had said. All of these guys coulda been my grandpa, never mind my father. They clustered around tables and at the bar, swapping stories of the Great War and talkin' about how if they were young enough to enlist, this current conflict would be over.

"I'd kick the Hun right back where he belongs," one elderly man boasted. "And send the Japs packing, too."

"You were in the Army, Ernie," his buddy said. "In the motor pool."

"Don't matter none. Ain't they fighting on land, too?" Ernie slurped his beer and dashed a hand across his mouth. He caught sight of me. "Well, hey there, missy. Can I buy you a drink?"

The bartender flicked a towel in Ernie's direction. "I told you earlier. You're cut off, Ern."

Ernie tapped the side of his nose. "You forget, men are scarce."

"Not that much." The bartender leaned on his folded arms. "Something I can do for you, miss? You don't look all that thirsty."

"I'm not." I passed him a business card. "I'm looking for someone."

An outbreak of shouting and a stream of cussing interrupted me and drew my attention to a group in the back corner. In the gaggle of bald heads and gray hair, Frank's mane of thick, dark waves stood out like a sore thumb. "Don't worry. I think I found him." I walked to the back.

Frank shook hands with the man who faced him across the chessboard. "Would you like to try for best three out of five, Mr. McNally?"

The old coot grumbled. "And lose what little sense of self-respect I have left? Not a chance, youngster." He caught sight of me over Frank's shoulder. "Well, now. There's a sight for sore eyes. Fellas, we caught ourselves a pretty lady. Fancy a drink, miss? Or maybe you're here to show up this whippersnapper on the chessboard."

Frank half-turned in his seat. When he saw me, he scrambled out of his chair so fast it nearly fell over. "Betty!" He caught the furniture before it crashed to the floor. "What do you want?"

One of the geezers gave a wheezy laugh. "You're not very smooth with the women, young man. You ain't gonna impress her that way."

Frank ran a hand through his hair. "I mean, it's nice to see you, but I didn't expect…is there something…what I mean to say is…"

It was cute, seein' him all off kilter at my appearance, but I didn't much care for the grins blossoming on the wrinkled faces gathered around the table. "Mr. Hicks, I'm glad I found you. I have a business matter I'd like to discuss. About the client you recently referred to me. Is there somewhere we can talk?" My gaze swept around the crowd. "Privately?"

"Sure. Let's go to the back tables." Frank looked over at the bartender. "Two waters, please, Mr. Sykes."

The bartender held up a hand in acknowledgment as Frank led me to a small table in the back corner. "Were you telling the truth? Just now?"

"I sure was. Did you think I suddenly had a hankering for your company?" I wiped a hankie over a chair and sat, hands folded in front of me.

Mr. Sykes came over with our drinks. "I'll try and keep the old fools busy for you, Frank."

"Thank you." Frank set his glass in front of him. Once Mr. Sykes left, he looked at me. "To be honest, I don't know what to think. After what happened in the park—"

I was swift to correct him. "What *almost* happened."

He dipped his head. "I'm rather surprised to see you."

In the low light, his eyes were dark and gentle, like a doe's. Had he always had such thick eyelashes? I forced myself to focus. "Private Lake found me."

"You took his case? Swell." The dimple made its appearance. It was as attractive as I remembered.

"I did."

"Tell me, did you pass your exam? Or have you not taken it yet?"

"I passed. I've got a license and everything."

"Good for you." He hesitated. "Betty, I mean it. It *is* good to see you. I thought about looking you up, but I figured, after the park, well…I didn't think you'd want to see me."

"I didn't." I realized that sounded rather harsh. I hurried on. "It's like I told you. I'm grateful and all. But I'm engaged, Frank. It's better we keep things professional. Quite honestly, when Private Lake mentioned your name, it was kinda shocking."

"Why?" He ignored his glass, which had beads of water on it.

I bought myself some time by taking a drink. "There was no reason for you to do somethin' like that. In fact, I came here intending to yell at you, but I guess that would be kinda rude, now that I think of it."

He twitched an eyebrow.

"I mean, it's not like I'm rolling in dough. I still conduct business out of a booth at a local diner. Thanks for mentioning me." This was not at all what I'd planned to say. I'd forgotten the impact of his face, the curve of his jaw, and the impossibility of resisting that Jimmy Stewart-like grin.

"You are quite welcome. I met Chris when I was volunteering at Our Lady of Victory. When he mentioned his desire to find his birth mother, I immediately thought of you."

Again, I stalled by taking a sip of water.

"See, he also mentioned that he didn't have a lot of time or money. I thought of all the private detectives in the city, you'd be most sympathetic." His hand moved, as though he wanted to reach out. "After all, you do have a big heart. I told you that before."

He had. "Private Lake didn't mention that bit. What can you tell me about him? I know about him bein' an orphan, growin' up at Father Baker's, and how he was left in the church."

"I assume he told you about the medal?"

"He did."

Frank looked over my shoulder. "There's a diner not far from here. Let me buy you a cup of coffee, if not dinner."

"Frank, I told you I want things professional between us."

"I understand. They don't."

I craned my neck. The geezers had gathered together, all eyeballs on us. Some of the wrinkled faces were creased in knowing grins, and a couple of 'em elbowed their companions. I got the message. Frank and I might understand the situation, but these guys were more than capable of making up their own version of events.

I gestured toward the door. "After you, Mr. Hicks." I spoke loudly and hoped they'd all get the message.

Frank stood. "Of course, Miss Ahern."

We left. Judging from the smirks, we hadn't changed a single mind.

* * *

At the diner, the elderly waitress seated us in a booth at the back. She laid down two greasy menus and took our order for coffee before shuffling off. Unlike the old men at the Moose Lodge, she didn't make any assumptions. At least, her face didn't change its long-suffering expression.

Frank pointed at me. "Are you sure you don't want to eat?"

I pulled out my pen and notepad. "Professional, remember? A meal makes this too close to a date."

His dimple flashed and was gone. "Businessmen have lunches all the time."

"Not dinners, though." I hoped my tone was tart enough to put him in his place.

"If you insist." The dimple didn't make a reappearance, but the light in his eyes twinkled.

Is he makin' fun of me? I decided to ignore it and press on. "How did you meet Private Lake?"

Frank folded his hands on the table. "I told you already. I volunteer on Monday afternoons at Our Lady of Victory Hospital. He was there for a check-up. He'd been injured on the front and treated in England, but they furloughed him home for a bit. He said he'd been told to check with a doctor when he arrived in Buffalo to make sure his wound was healing properly."

"Who struck up the conversation?"

"He did. I was crossing the waiting room, and he asked if I was a patient. We got to talking. After his appointment, we went to the cafeteria for coffee."

The waitress returned with two cups of java, which she set down without a word and moved away.

"At least the cream and sugar are on the table." I waved at them. "Did you tell him about yourself?"

"That I was a conscientious objector? Yes." Frank took his java black, like me, it seemed.

"What did he say to that?"

"Nothing." He lifted an eyebrow. "He didn't start lecturing me or storm out or anything like that. It seems the nuns taught him well because we had a good discussion about the similarities between Quakerism and the teachings of St. Francis of Assisi."

Not what I would have expected. "Who brought up his story?"

"I asked about his family, what they thought about him being overseas and had he had a chance to see them while he was home. That's when he told me the whole thing and showed me the St. Christopher." Frank took a sip. "He said he'd never wondered much about his mother when he was a child, but being injured had changed his mind. Unfortunately, he didn't think he'd have time to search. That's when I brought up your name."

"I guess I oughta thank you. But don't make a habit of it." I jabbed my pencil at him. "I'll think you're lookin' for excuses to see me."

He stared at the black liquid. "I wouldn't dream of it."

Was he bein' funny or sarcastic? I couldn't tell. It didn't matter. *Professional.* "Did he tell you anything else? Maybe things he'd heard from the nuns growin' up or something? I find it hard to believe they never talked about it." Private Lake hadn't told me, but our discussion this morning had been pretty brief.

"According to him, no. But he did start to have suspicions when he became a teenager."

Now, this was news. "Why? Did something happen?"

Frank slowly rotated his mug. "I'm sure your experience with nuns is more extensive than mine. But Chris said while most of them were very tight-lipped, one seemed to take a fancy to him. At least, she'd slip him sweets every now and then and spend more time with him."

I waited.

"One day, she said how even though he had nothing, he should never think of hocking or selling his medal. 'Some day, it will be the key to knowing who you are. By it, your mother can claim you as her own.' But when he asked her to elaborate, she refused to say anything more."

Huh. There was a certainty in those words. Had the old nun known who left him? Did that mean there'd been more with him in that pew? Or had he not been left, but someone had given him to Sister Mary Agnes directly. Someone whose name she'd pledged to keep secret?

It certainly sounded like at least one other person knew things about Private Lake's history beyond what he'd been told. "Does this nun have a name?" My coffee had cooled, and I took a gulp.

"According to Chris, her name was Sister Francis Claire. She retired several years ago." Frank shrugged. "Or at least she left the orphanage. He hasn't seen her since he was sixteen."

I wrote down the name. "Where would a retired nun go?"

Frank drained his cup, stood, and tossed a bill on the table. "How would I know? I'm a Quaker, remember? Isn't that a question for a good Catholic?" As quick as a wink, he leaned in and kissed my cheek. "It was good seeing you, Betty. Don't be a stranger."

He left before I could catch my breath and say anythin'. But the spot burned as though he'd touched me with a lit cigarette.

Chapter Eight

All the way home, I obsessed about Frank's kiss and the meaning. Was he bein' friendly? Did he mean more than that? Did he *want* more? Of course, he did. The more I thought, the angrier I got. *How dare he?* I'd told him there was nothin' between us but business. He had no right kissing me, 'specially in public. All those old men, leering at me as we left the Moose Lodge, as though there was somethin' between Frank and me.

Okay, fine, there was, but not what they thought.

Except a little part of me liked it. *Admit it, it's been a long time since a guy looked at you like that, and you don't mind one bit.* I focused on my engagement ring. Think of Tom.

Think of how betrayed he'd feel if he knew his girl was steppin' out on him.

Inside my house, the smell of food greeted me. Mom came out of the kitchen, still wearing her apron. "Betty, you're in time for dinner." She dried her hands and stared at me. "What's wrong?"

"Nothing."

"Your face is as red as a tomato."

My whole face or one spot on my cheek? "I'm fine, Mom. I'll be in my room." I grabbed the telephone book.

"Don't you want to eat?"

"I'm not hungry, thanks. I'll make somethin' later if I change my mind." I tried to push past her to the bedroom I shared with my sister.

Fat chance. She stood in front of me and put her hands on my shoulders. "I can tell you're upset about something. Talk to me."

43

Mom was not the person to unload my heart to, not right then. "It's okay. I...it's this case. It's got me a little wound up." I gave her a quick hug. "Go eat before it gets cold." I sidled past her, went to my room, and closed the door.

Inside, I sat at my desk and covered my face with my hands. 'Course, Mom spotted my trouble. I had to get my emotions under control. Mary Kate wouldn't bother me for a while, but she'd be in to do her homework after dinner. I planned to be somewhere else so my nosy sister wouldn't pester me with questions.

It took effort, but I pushed all thoughts of Frank to the back of my mind and got to work. The obituaries had given me half a dozen names to track down. I started with the brothers, figurin' they were more likely to be listed in the directory. Of the four, I found two names that matched. I wrote down the addresses and numbers.

One of my women was survived by her parents. I found that listing next. Finally, I looked for the names of the sisters, at least those that had different surnames and were prob'ly married. The trick was I didn't know the husband's first name. I found four matches. I'd have to call them all to see if any of them were the relatives I wanted to talk to.

Right on cue, Mary Kate threw open the door and flopped on her bed. "Betty, what's shakin'? Mom said you weren't hungry. Why? Haven't you been workin' all day? You should be starving." She stretched her neck and tried to read my notes. "Who are those people? Suspects?"

"Folks I have to talk to. Don't ask questions." I folded up the sheet of paper and tucked it in my pocket. I glanced at the clock on my dresser. Six thirty. Good. I grabbed my purse, made sure my smokes were there and headed for the front door.

I opened it and hollered, "I'm goin' out. Be back before long." I didn't wait for a response.

Outside, I lit a cigarette. Cat, the stray that had adopted me last fall, appeared and wound himself around my ankles. Then he stopped, sat, and fixed me with an accusatory feline glare. *Meow.*

I reached down and rubbed his ears. "Don't look at me like that. I'm sure

Mary Kate fed you."

Meow. He didn't blink.

I often thought Cat had better instincts than my mother, and I couldn't shake the feeling he knew exactly what had happened between Frank and me earlier that afternoon. "It's not my fault. I told him I was engaged." Cat tilted his head.

"Oh, go away. I'm going to see Dot. She'll know what to do." I headed off, my chaperone trotting behind me. I guess Cat wanted to make sure I made a full and honest confession to my best friend.

* * *

Dot Kilbride and I had been friends almost as long as Lee and I, which is to say, since early childhood. We'd been through a lot together, including working at Bell Aircraft and solving four murders. She and Lee had been goin' steady since spring, but they were tactful enough that I never felt like a third wheel. If anybody knew what I was s'posed to do about Frank, Dot would.

I rapped on the door, and Mr. Kilbride answered. "Evening, sir. Is Dot home?"

He invited me inside. "We haven't seen you in a while, Betty. How are your parents?" He went to the stairs. "Dorothy, you have a visitor."

"They're hunky-dory. Thanks for asking. How are you and Mrs. Kilbride?"

"We're fine. Mrs. Kilbride wishes Dorothy and Liam would get married so she can stop working and produce some grandchildren, but I suspect neither of them are in a hurry." He cupped his hands around his mouth. "Dorothy! Did you hear me?"

She appeared and ran down the stairs. "Geez Louise, I heard you. I was on the toilet." She took one look at me. "Dad, can I go out for a walk with Betty?" Dot was an only child, and her parents were way stricter than mine were. They were the only people I knew who called Dot and Lee by their Christian names on a regular basis. Heck, I was surprised they didn't call me Elizabeth.

Mr. Kilbride shook a finger at his daughter. "Be home before dark."

She grabbed my arm and pulled me to the door. "Thanks, Dad."

Outside, she pushed her curls off her forehead. "What's wrong?"

"Who said anything was wrong? Maybe I want to talk to my best friend and see how her day was."

Dot put her hands on her hips. Unlike me, she was short and curvy with a pinup girl's figure and bow-like lips when she smiled. "The look on your face tells me all I need to know. Somethin's wrong." She bent down, scooped up Cat, and nuzzled his head. "She thinks I don't notice anything. But we know her better, don't we?"

I threw up my hands. "Great. That's what I need. My friend and my cat conspiring against me." I took off down the sidewalk toward Conway Park, puffing my Lucky and ashing it in the gutter.

"Betty, don't be sore." Dot, who was several inches shorter than me, hurried to catch up. "I'll start over. How was your day?"

"I have a new case." I told her all about Private Lake and the story of his missing mother.

"Wow. He has no idea other than the medal? And the nuns won't tell you anything?"

"Nothing. If I'd been standing on the sidewalk, I think Sister Mary Agnes woulda slammed the door in my face." I kicked at a scrap of trash on the concrete.

"I can't imagine a nun doin' that. Have you called any of the names from the obituaries?"

"Not yet. I haven't told you the whole story." I filled her in on my meeting with Frank at the Moose Lodge, including our trip to the diner.

"He did not!"

"He did."

She stroked Cat, but her plump features were indignant. "Well, how do you like those apples." She stopped. "Oh, Betty. No. Don't tell me you liked it."

I couldn't look at her.

She trotted again to catch up. "What about Tom?"

"What about him?" I spun around. "I haven't heard from him in months. Yeah, I got a letter in May, but it was dated March. It's almost July, Dot."

"Come on. They don't have mailboxes on every street corner where he is. And he *is* kinda busy."

"One letter in four months?" I snorted and resumed walking. Stalking, was more like it. "I don't expect one every week. But a quick note, even 'hi, thinking of you,' would be nice. Instead, it's like I've fallen off the face of the earth."

"Betty—"

"What if he's met some local girl, huh? What if he doesn't want to get married anymore? Yeah, I know his last letter said he was lookin' forward to comin' home, but like I said, that was March. A lot can happen to a Joe overseas, away from his fiancée, in five months." What if he'd changed his mind? Despite my conflicted feelings about Frank, my heart sank.

"Elizabeth Anne Ahern, you stop right there."

Dot's stern voice made me face her. "Listen. You have no reason to doubt Tom, none at all. What on earth can make you even *think* those things?" Cat squirmed, and she let him jump down. He didn't go far, though. He sat and washed his paws, listening to the lecture. "Don't get me wrong, I understand. Frank Hicks is a handsome devil. He's nice. He thinks you're swell. But he has no right to kiss you, and you shouldn't let him."

Cat looked up. *Meow.*

"Seems my cat agrees with you." We'd reached the entrance to the park. I threw away my spent cigarette and headed to a bench, where I plopped down. "I didn't *let* him, Dot. He did it and left."

"And what bothers you isn't that he kissed you." She sat next to me and took my hand. "Is it?"

I felt hot tears building, ones I'd been keepin' at bay. "No. Don't get me wrong. I *am* mad. But a part of me, well, a teeny part, is happy to be noticed." I sniffed. "It's been a long time, Dot. I keep readin' Tom's last letter, and every time I do, it sounds worse. Distant. Like he's writin' what he thinks I want to hear and not what he means. Long distance is hard on a relationship.

War's gotta be harder. He's gonna meet all sorts of foreign girls who are gonna be happy to see American soldiers forcing out the Germans. They'll be showerin' those boys with hugs, and kisses, and, and, who knows what else. It's a lot, and I wouldn't blame Tom for lettin' it turn his head. A lot of 'em gotta be a lot prettier than I am."

Dot smoothed my hair.

"And here I am, at home, alone, and there's a guy, and he likes me, and, yes, I like him. What happens if I stay true, and Tom decides he doesn't wanna get married anymore, and Frank moves on? I don't wanna be a spinster like my Aunt May." I broke down and cried.

Dot, Lord love her, said nothing. She kept stroking my head and let me sob my heart out on her shoulder. Eventually, my tears slowed down. "Betty, listen to me. Remember my cousin, Annie?"

"I think I do. Isn't she the one engaged to a sailor?"

"She was."

It took me a second. I lifted my head. "Did he get killed?"

"No." Dot's gaze was solemn. "She became a Navy nurse and is stationed in Philadelphia. She met another sailor who got injured at Midway. I think that was it. Anyway, he'd been discharged 'cause of his injury. They got to talkin' and, well, one thing led to another."

"She left her fiancé?"

Dot nodded. "Annie and Gus, that's the new sailor's name, got hitched last month. She wrote Henry, her old fiancé, a Dear John letter and everything."

I wiped my nose on my sleeve. "What does this have to do with me?"

"This." She took my hands. "I know you love Tom. And I'm pretty sure he loves you. But this war, it does crazy things. The distance and time apart. Will he meet a girl in Europe or wherever he is? Maybe. You've met Frank, and clearly, you don't hate him. You might even have feelings. What you need to think about and decide is this. Is what you're goin' through genuine? Or is it your loneliness talkin'? If it's the first, well, you need to be honest with both guys and let your heart decide."

I picked up Cat, who snuggled close, like he knew I needed some comfort.

"But if it's bein' lonely? Betty." Dot lifted my chin. "Don't give in. 'Cause lettin' go of love 'cause you're scared will definitely set you on the path to spinsterhood. And you'll have no one to blame but yourself."

Chapter Nine

The next morning, I was sittin' in my usual booth at Teddy's, munching away on my toast, when a realization hit me. I muttered an oath and hoped no one was close enough to hear.

No such luck. Judy stopped at my table, coffee pot in hand. "Betty Ahern! I know your mother would wash your mouth out with soap if she heard you saying those words. Where on earth did you learn them?"

My cheeks warmed. "I did work at Bell Airplane for over a year, Judy. Plenty of the girls cussed. Some as bad as any man working at Bethlehem Steel."

"Well, I certainly didn't expect you to be one of them. What's got you swearing like a sailor?"

"This." I pushed my notes from yesterday toward her and explained my research project. "I wasted half a day on a worthless search."

"I don't understand." A small frown line appeared between her eyebrows. "It sounds perfectly logical to me. Why would you call it a waste?"

"'Cause if Private Lake's mother had family, she wouldn't have dropped him at Father Baker's now, would she?"

"Maybe they didn't know she was pregnant."

"I think it'd be pretty hard to hide. Besides, if they don't know, I still wasted my time 'cause if I call them now and ask, 'Say, did your sister have a baby twenty years ago,' they aren't gonna be able to tell me anything." I gathered my papers into a pile and heaved a breath.

"Okay, I get that. But you still know more than you did yesterday, right?"

"Sure, but I only have fourteen—make that thirteen—days to find this

50

woman. I don't have time to spend on useless tasks."

Judy hefted her pot. "I can't help you there. But I can offer you a refill."

I pushed my mug in her direction. "Might as well. Thanks."

Melvin appeared as though out of thin air. "Hiya, Toots. Why so glum?" He seated himself. "Coffee, two eggs over easy, toast, and a stack of pancakes, please. And as quickly as possible. I'm in a hurry."

I arched my eyebrow. "That's an awful lot to eat if you're short on time."

He snapped his fingers. "You're right. Skip the pancakes." He shot me a grin. "You don't have to add it to her bill. Although after I fork over my news, she might want to thank me."

Judy shook her head, jotted down the order, and went off for a clean mug.

I crossed my arms. "What are you so chipper about?"

"Good morning to you, too." He pulled a couple of napkins out of the dispenser. "You first. What's got your knickers in a twist?"

I told him about my wasted effort as Judy returned with his joe.

"Sorry, Toots. That happens. Going down the rabbit hole, I mean, and finding nothing at the bottom." He doused his coffee with some milk.

"I'm on a deadline, Melvin. I told you that."

"You did. Which is why you're going to thank me in about thirty seconds." He pulled a folded piece of paper from his pocket as he took a drink. He handed it to me with a self-satisfied smile on his face.

I opened it up. "What's this?"

"At your request, I went and schmoozed the Society writer. She's been with the *Courier* for ages, even before it merged with the *Express*."

"You better be careful who you're dallying with. Irene won't be happy." I knew Irene from the first time I met Melvin. She was a sweetie, but I was positive her tolerance didn't extend to her man cozyin' up to other women.

He waved his hand. "Don't worry. Irene knows that sometimes I'm required to pay compliments in pursuit of my goals. She made the line pretty clear. I have no intention of crossing it."

"If you say so." I looked at the name written on the paper. "Who is Marian Carstairs?"

"The lead of your dreams." His breakfast arrived, and he rubbed his hands together. He grabbed his fork and started eating.

"How's that?"

He swallowed. "The Carstairs family is big in Buffalo. The old man was involved in the steel industry for a while. He wasn't an owner at Bethlehem, but he played a big role in transporting the coke needed to make steel to the factory. You know, kinda like Frick did in Pittsburgh."

I was familiar with Henry Clay Frick in name, if not in detail. "And?"

Melvin pointed. "Marian is his daughter and oldest child. According to my source at the paper, she disappeared from society in the early 20s. Right around the time your private turned up at Father Baker's. She was gone for about six months. The family story was that she went to some sanatorium in the Adirondacks for 'health reasons.' But they were pretty mum about it. One day, she was the belle of the local ball, and poof! Next day, she was gone and only this vague story to cover. Once she returned, no one ever talked about it, although Gladys, she's my source, says plenty of people asked. Old Man Carstairs stonewalled everyone, and his darling daughter wasn't much more communicative. She got sick, she left, she returned. End of story." He winked. "Quite a tale, eh? And she never married."

"Definitely dodgy." It was a better lead than anything I'd spent time on yesterday. "You get the name of the sanatorium?"

"Nope. The family wouldn't even say that much. Gladys said people called places out in the Adirondacks fishing for dirt, but everyone clammed up tight." He pointed his fork at me. "Dollars to doughnuts Carstairs made a fat donation to whatever place it was to keep their lips zipped."

"But Marian wouldn't have been in a sanatorium if she went out there to have a baby, right? Maybe they don't have anything to say. Did anyone try the hospitals?"

"Come on, give us a little credit." He wiped up some egg yolk with his toast. "Granted, the Adirondacks cover a lot of ground. But there are only a few places the rich would have gone for a cure. Or to have an illegitimate child. At the time, folks at the *Courier* called all of them. No one had anything to say. Not even denying she'd been a patient. If that isn't suspicious, well, I don't know what is."

He was right. I could understand a hospital not admitting to treating Marian Carstairs. But if she hadn't been a patient, why not say that? "This is swell, Melvin. Really. You learn anything else?"

He slugged back some java. "C'mon, Toots. You don't expect me to do your whole investigation, do you? I gave you a name and a solid lead. The rest is up to you." He gave me a stern look. "Don't forget your promise."

"Yeah, yeah. Any story is yours, although I don't think there's gonna be one." I slipped the paper in my purse. "You're right, it's a good tip."

He said nothing, but held my gaze over the rim of his mug.

I sighed. "Breakfast is on me."

"You're a doll, Toots." He held up his hand to signal for a refill. "I mean that from the bottom of my heart."

* * *

I left Teddy's in a much better mood than when I'd arrived. I coulda continued contacting the people I'd found last night, but I didn't have much faith it would help me. On the other hand, Melvin's hot tip was promising. It would be easy as pie to find the Carstairs family. I knew they were one of Buffalo's big cheese families and almost certainly lived in the swanky Delaware Park neighborhood with all the trimmings that went with that address. But I didn't want to confront them without more information.

I headed back to the library for a dive into more newspaper archives.

The same young woman was on duty at the desk for the stacks. "Hello. You're back." Her bright eyes shone. "Did your search yesterday find anything?"

"It did, but I'm lookin' for something else today."

"What is it?"

I pushed forward the paper. "I'm interested in the history of the Carstairs family. Specifically, their daughter, Marian."

"I assume you're talking about *the* Carstairs family? The ones who helped build up the Buffalo steel industry?"

"That's the one."

She studied the paper. "What about Marian is important?"

I leaned on the desk. "She supposedly went to the Adirondacks for a cure in the early 1920s. I want to see if there was anything reported about it. After all, she woulda been a society girl at the time. I'm hopin' there would be news in the papers covering her absence."

The girl stared at me. "Why would you care? I mean, you're probably right because the Society pages are all about what is really gossip. The daughter of a wealthy family leaving the social scene would be exactly that. But how is that interesting to you now? Marian Carstairs is still alive."

I hadn't counted on her askin' questions. "I'm a private detective." I slid one of my cards across the desk. "It's for my current case."

Her face took on an animated expression. "Ooo, a real detective? That is the bee's knees. I've seen a few films with detectives, and it's always a man. I wondered why. And here you are. Can I, well, never mind."

Did she want my autograph? "Can you what?"

Her cheeks turned a pretty pink. "It's stupid."

"Tell me."

"Can I work with you?" Her words came in a breathless rush. "I've read some mystery novels. I don't think I want to be the detective because that's too much limelight for me. But a lot of times, the main character has a sidekick. I could, I don't know, be your research assistant or something. I love research. It would be a lot more exciting than working as a clerk at a library."

Aww, she was too cute. "What's your name?"

"Emmeline. Emmeline Schechter."

"Well, Emmeline, I'm not makin' enough dough to hire you. Although I gotta admit, having someone to help out would be swell. I'm not much on digging through piles of old newspapers."

She cast her gaze downward. "I understand. Being a junior librarian is kind of dull. A lot of times, I spend all day without talking to anyone. I guess I got carried away. What time period are you looking for again?"

She was disappointed. I could hear it in her voice and how the light in her eyes dimmed. "Tell you what. I can't pay you cash. At least not right now.

54

But if everything works out, I'll have an office someday and everything. If you're willing to do the work and wait for the payoff, I'd love to have a research assistant. Heck, I bet it would save me a ton of time. I could be talkin' to people while you look for information." I held out my hand.

She grabbed it. "Deal. Oh, this is nifty! Wait'll I tell my parents."

"You might want to hold off on that. At least until I get that office."

Chapter Ten

I left Emmeline with two tasks. The first was to find out what she could about the Carstairs family, including what might have happened to Marian in 1922. The second was to see if she could find a registry of girls who'd served as nurses overseas during the Great War.

"I'm on it," she said, snapping a salute. "Come back after lunch, and I'll let you know what I found."

"Are you sure that's enough time?" I glanced at the clock. "That's only about three hours."

"Oh, it'll be plenty. Unless half of Buffalo decides to come ask for back newspaper issues, this'll be a piece of cake."

I took her at her word. Outside, I lit up and dropped a nickel to call Private Lake. "Can you meet me?"

"Do you have news already?"

"Not really, but Sister Mary Agnes wasn't much help. I'm workin' on an angle. Meanwhile, do you remember Sister Francis Clare?"

"Sure do. She was my favorite."

"Swell. I want to talk about her. Meet me at Jimmy Mack's diner in half an hour."

I took a bus to Lackawanna. I'd chosen the place 'cause it wasn't far from Our Lady of Victory, the orphanage, and Private Lake's digs. He should be able to hoof it without an issue.

I was right. He was already seated in a booth when I arrived. "I ordered you a coffee. I hope that was okay."

"I take every opportunity to get real joe when I can. You boys in uniform prob'ly get the good stuff all the time, but here at home, it's almost always chicory." The mug in front of me steamed, and I inhaled. He must've arrived moments ago 'cause it was still too hot.

"What do you need to know?"

I sipped and took out my notebook. "I talked to Frank Hicks yesterday."

"He's a great guy, isn't he? Despite being a Quaker and a conchie." A shadow flitted across the private's face. "To be honest, now that I've been to war, I can't say as I blame him for staying home."

I wondered what he'd seen, but no way was I gonna press for details. Pop didn't talk much about his service in the Great War. Enough to let me know it'd been awful. This conflict didn't seem to be headed for years of trench warfare and mustard gas, but it had to be awful in its own way. "Yeah, he's a real peach."

Private Lake gave me a quizzical look. "It doesn't sound like he's one of your favorite people. I don't know why. He couldn't say enough good things about you."

I waved my hand. "It's complicated. It's also not why I'm here. He mentioned Sister Francis Clare. You shoulda said somethin' when we met the first time."

"I didn't think it was important."

"Everything's important. Tell me about her."

Confusion morphed into delight. "Aw, Sister Francis. I loved her. She was easily the oldest nun there and had the youngest heart."

"What do you mean?"

He leaned back. "Sister Francis mostly took care of the young kids. But not babies. She liked the kids who could talk but weren't so old they had developed a smart mouth."

"Before they got to school age?"

"Exactly. I remember her kilting up her habit to play hide and seek, or tag, anything on the playground. She loved pushing kids on the swings, and she'd even put the real young ones on her lap to go down the slide." He looked at the ceiling, clearly lost in happy memories. "She brought candy, too. Even though she wasn't supposed to. I swear, that habit held an entire store in its folds."

"She sounds swell."

"She was." He looked at me. "What was amazing is no matter what your favorite treat was, she had it. You wouldn't think a nun would have access to every sweet imaginable, but she did."

I thought of all the nuns I'd known. I wished I'd had a Sister Francis in my life. "What was your favorite?"

"Abba Zaba." He laughed. "Oh man, I'd get that taffy stuck on my teeth. Sister Mary Agnes busted me more than once because she asked a question, and my jaws were stuck together. But I never ratted out Sister Francis. I think Sister Mary Agnes knew, but she never heard it from me. When I was young, I'd get sent to bed without dinner, but when I got older, I got caned for lying."

"I've known a few nuns. They have a reputation."

"But they care. Most of them." He took a gulp of coffee. "Sister Francis retired when I was fifteen. Gosh, I missed those Abba Zabas."

I took a sip. My java had cooled considerably, but that didn't mean I wouldn't drink it. "Sounds like she kept sneaking you stuff long past childhood."

"It's funny. I hadn't thought about it, but you're right." A slight wrinkle appeared on his forehead as he thought. "Sister Francis had a kind word for any boy, no matter his age, but most of the time, once you'd gotten too old for her care, she stopped being such a presence. Not me, though. She would bring me to the nuns' house for tea to ask how I was doing."

Sister Francis Claire could be a gold mine. "Why do you think that was?"

"I don't know." He frowned into his cup. "I never asked. I was too happy for the attention. I mean, no teenage boy loves tea, but hey. It came with cookies or cake, and I wasn't gonna pass those up, that's for sure. Dessert was a treat, not a staple. Oh, not that they didn't feed us." He held up a hand. "But it was plain food. Nothing special."

"Do you think she might have known about your mother? Maybe had a little extra sympathy for you?"

He drained his coffee. "I can't imagine that was it. Some of those boys, they had stories at least as sad as mine. She didn't invite them over."

"She ever hint that she knew about your mom?"

"Never. I don't know why I was special to her."

Private Lake might not, but I couldn't shake the feeling that Sister Francis Claire was hiding a secret. "Is she dead?"

"No, would you believe it? She's gotta be almost a hundred years old, but last I heard she was living up at St. Ann's on Broadway." He chuckled. "I wonder if she still carries candy around with her."

I knew St. Ann's. Lots of old nuns went to live there after they were done with active service. "I'll ask."

He gave me a wide-eyed stare. "You're going to go talk to her?"

"I got a feeling she can help me with your case." I finished my coffee. "Thanks for the java. If I talk to her, anything you want me to say?"

He thought a moment and grinned. "Ask her if she still carries around Abba Zabas, will you?"

Chapter Eleven

My first instinct was to hop a bus to St. Ann's immediately. Two things held me up. Before I wasted my fare, I should make sure the elderly nun was still alive and kickin'. And up to havin' visitors. That, and instinct, told me I should have a little more information on hand. If I didn't have more background, Sister Francis Claire could tell me anything, and I wouldn't know whether to believe her or not. A nun might not be allowed to lie, not without goin' to confession. But I didn't want a replay of the conversation with Sister Mary Agnes. Not if I could help it.

Finding out if Sister Francis Claire was still in residence was easy. I dialed the number at St. Ann's and asked for her.

The woman on the phone didn't exactly sound suspicious, but she didn't answer my question right off, either. "Who are you, and what do you want with Sister Francis?"

I wondered if she was another nun or a lay worker. "My name is Betty Ahern, and I'm a private detective. I've been hired to find the mother of a boy Sister Francis took care of at Father Baker's, and I want to ask her some questions. If she's willing and able to speak to me, that is."

"A private detective? Is this a joke?"

Maybe I shoulda gone in person. "No, ma'am. I'm a real private dick, and if I was there, I'd show you proof. All I want to know is if Sister Francis is able to see me and if she can give me a little of her time."

"Sister is over ninety. She doesn't get many visitors. Then again, she loves talking about her time at the orphanage." She paused. "She's finishing lunch across the hall. If you can wait a moment, I'll ask if she's willing to speak with you."

"I'll hold on." While I did, I jotted a few more notes in my book. I couldn't explain it, but I felt hopeful about both Melvin's tip and what I could learn from Sister Francis. After my talk with Private Lake earlier, I really wanted to send him off knowing who his family was.

The woman came back on the phone. "Hello, Miss Ahern? Are you still there?"

"I am."

"You're in luck. Sister Francis is feeling quite well today. She would love to talk to you. How soon can you be here?"

I looked at my watch. It was nearly one. "Is three o'clock too late?" That should leave me plenty of time to chat with Emmeline and make it up to Broadway to see the nun.

"That will be perfect. Sister Francis can take her early afternoon nap, and she'll be waiting for you. But please be prompt. Disruptions to the life here can be very trying for our residents."

I assured her I wouldn't be late and hung up.

***

I got to the library a little after one. I thought about stopping at the front desk but decided to go straight to the stacks. I didn't need permission to speak to Emmeline. If she wasn't there, I had time to kill. Maybe I'd even learn something on my own.

She was at the desk when I walked up. "Perfect timing, Miss Ahern. I finished my report."

Report? "You don't have to call me miss. Heck, you can't be much older than me."

"I turned twenty this spring."

"That's barely a year older. You may be workin' for me, but no reason we can't use our Christian names."

"Oh, good." She put a piece of paper filled with handwriting on the desk.

"I hoped we'd become friends. Anyway. This is the abbreviated version of my research. I can give you the full report, including all the information, if you want."

Wow. She took this job seriously. "No, the summary is fine. Hang on to everything, just in case, but for now, I want the bare facts." I looked around. "Should we go sit somewhere else?"

"No. If we get a table, we'll get shushed, and I spent my entire lunch hour writing this up. I can't leave the desk."

"Emmeline, you didn't have to do that. When are you gonna eat?"

She waved a hand. "It's not a problem. I got into my work, and I'm not very hungry." She handed over the paper. "You read while I talk."

"Don't you need your notes?"

"I have a very good memory." She gave me a mischievous grin. "First, I checked for a record of women who served overseas during the Great War. That was not easy, let me tell you. Turns out the government does not like to give up service records to anyone. I said I was a local reporter, and I was researching women in the area who served as nurses, specifically in France, for a local color story about women in war."

"Was it a long list?"

"Long enough. After that, I did my best to locate them. Some have left the city. Page two is a list of the women who are still in the area. You'd have to call each one of them and hope you could get them to confess they had a child in 1923, a baby they left at Father Baker's orphanage. Honestly, I'm not sure that's where you should focus your efforts."

"Why not?"

"It's the same problem you had with deceased mothers. Many of those girls were working class. A baby out of wedlock would not have been scandalous. At least not as much as their upper-class peers. She might even have been able to pass the child off as legitimate if she had a sweetheart or got married when she returned home. It would not be the first time in history the baby's birthday happened a little on the early side, if you know what I mean."

She was right. I thought of my own situation. My parents wouldn't be thrilled if I got pregnant before Tom and I tied the knot. But all it would really do is hurry up the wedding. They wouldn't turn me out, and they wouldn't make me give up the baby. "Then what's your angle?"

"The lead from your reporter friend. I find it far more likely a society belle who got with child ahead of the altar would raise an eyebrow or two. It is very likely the family would demand the baby go to an orphanage. Especially if the father was undesirable in any way, either the wrong social class or, heaven forbid, a married man."

Which is what I'd thought. "A society girl would almost certainly know French. She might even have gone to a finishing school or something."

"Exactly. For that reason, I spent most of my time researching the Carstairs family. That sheet has my full findings, but I can give you the highlights."

"Okay, shoot."

She straightened her shoulders. "The first member of the Carstairs family arrived in Buffalo in the mid-1800s. He immediately got involved with the burgeoning industrial scene and started a small shipping company. Once the steel industry really started surging, Anthony Carstairs switched to almost exclusively shipping materials up and down the Erie Canal for the mills. He passed the daily running of the business to his son, whose name was also Anthony."

Emmeline's notes were top-notch. I wouldn't even have to write. "He was transporting coke and ore?"

"Yes. However, around 1890, he made investments in the coke industry that brought in a lot more money than simply shipping it. Anthony Senior wasn't a majority stockholder in Bethlehem Steel, but he made a good amount of money."

I knew a little of how steel was made from Pop. I wasn't surprised the elder Carstairs had made a bundle. "Is that still the main source of dough for the family?"

"No." She tapped the page. "While it continued to be a big deal, Anthony Carstairs, Junior, Marian's father, broadened the business considerably and moved into shipping by rail."

"Looks like the Carstairs family weathered the stock market crash pretty well. What about Marian?"

Emmeline continued her lecture. "There are two living children. Marian has a younger brother, Theodore. Both were very active in society, attended a lot of parties. Then, in the winter of 1922, Marian abruptly left Buffalo. The family story was that she went for a cure in a private hospital in the Adirondacks."

That tallied with what Melvin had found. "When exactly?"

"Early December."

I counted back months.

A faint grin appeared on her face. "Let me do the math for you. Yes, if Christopher Lake was born in late April or early May, that's six months, give or take, before his birth. Right about the time she would have started to show from a pregnancy."

"Hot diggity dog."

"I confirmed that no hospital or sanatorium in the area treated Marian Carstairs. My question is, where did she go?"

I put down the report. "You confirmed? How? My source at the newspaper couldn't get a word about anything from anyone."

Emmeline spread her hands. "I lied."

"You what?" It was one thing to pretend to be a reporter lookin' for public records. I'd done that. But this was access to personal information. For some reason, the thought of getting those under false pretenses gave me the willies.

"Oh, come now." She tossed her head. "Don't tell me you haven't been a little creative with the truth on occasion. I didn't break any laws. At least, I don't think I did. I called each hospital and said I was Mr. Carstairs's secretary. Marian had another breakdown, and I needed a copy of her patient file for her new physician."

Emmeline had moxie. I liked that. People had said the same thing about me, and I preferred to think it was a positive trait. But there was a difference between pretending to be a wife lookin' for a cheating husband and outright lying to gain access to private information. Wasn't there? Maybe not, 'specially in my line of work. It was something to ask Sam. There had to be a line and I didn't want to cross it.

For now, what was done was done. I could get the scoop and figure out the right and wrong later. "Please don't make a habit of that. At least not without checkin' with me first. What did you find out?"

"I told you. Nothing." She brushed her skirt. "Not from a sanatorium or the one hospital I considered a good location for an unwed mother to have a child in secret. If you're wondering how I got out of the jam, I simply said I must have gotten the wrong hospital and thanked them for their time. I took pains to sound a little flighty, too. I'm sure none of them suspect a thing."

I didn't know whether to be impressed by her initiative or dismayed at her casual regard for the truth. Perhaps a little of both. "Good job. I'm goin' to meet with the nun who took care of Private Lake as a child. Maybe she'll give up more details."

"If she knows them. I doubt she is aware of what hospital Marian Carstairs was treated at, but she may know who dropped him off. If you can get her to talk."

"I'm gonna try. But if she won't, that's not the end of the line. I got one more person to interview." I folded the paper. "When do you get off work?"

"Four-thirty. Why?"

"Want to come help me interview Marian Carstairs?"

Chapter Twelve

Emmeline agreed to meet me at four thirty at Lafayette Square. We could catch the bus to the Carstairs home in Delaware Park. I left the library and headed over to St. Ann's.

I arrived about half an hour before I said I'd be there. The building and grounds on Broadway were quiet, as befitted a place of worship and home for elderly religious. The somber stone and soaring spires gave it a dignified air. The mid-afternoon sun glinted off the giant rose window above the main entrance to the church. I'd never been inside, but it looked like the type of building that would have a lot of marble and Gothic touches. It stood right at the intersection of Broadway and Emslie, and the stairs came right to the sidewalk. Tall stained-glass windows marched around the sides. But I could see green space around back. That must be where residents could enjoy some fresh air. I imagined benches under the trees that peeped around the church. It was prob'ly a very peaceful space.

I walked to the front door of the rectory and pushed the heavy wood. It opened to a small front office. An elderly woman sat at the desk, a small leather-bound prayer book in her hand. "Hello."

She set it down and looked up. "May I help you?"

"I'm here to talk to Sister Francis Claire. I called earlier."

"Are you Betty Ahern?"

"Yes, ma'am. Is Sister still willin' to talk?"

"You're early."

"Sorry. My previous appointment finished faster than I thought. I can leave and come back." I had no clue where I'd go, but I'd rather spin my wheels waiting than be turned away.

She pointed at a chair. "Sit there while I see if Sister is able to see you now." She bustled from the room.

I took the time to study the space. A crucifix hung on one wall. The bookcases were filled with religious volumes. Several potted plants were on the windowsills, and deep blue curtains softened the stark white of the walls. The two metal filing cabinets looked out of place for a church and more like something I'd find in a government office. Maybe they'd been a donation. Churches didn't go buy fancy office furniture if a parishioner was willing to give stuff away.

The secretary returned. "Sister is in the back garden. You can see her, but don't be surprised if she falls asleep on you. She is quite old, and her thoughts often wander. Follow me."

She led me out a side door. I'd been right. Behind the church was a smallish park-like space. There were benches under the leafy maples and oaks. Squirrels darted here and there, bushy tails streaming behind them. They didn't seem very scared of people. 'Course, they might be used to humans by now. Heck, some of the residents might even feed the wildlife.

The secretary walked over to a frail woman who looked lost in her black habit. She held a rosary in her limp hand, and her head was down so far her chin almost touched her neck. The secretary laid a hand on the nun's shoulder. "Sister Francis? You have a visitor."

The nun's head came up, and she blinked. "A visitor?" Her thin voice matched her small body.

"Yes, you remember. The young woman who wanted to ask about Father Baker's."

"I loved every one of those boys. Such a joy."

The secretary stood aside. "I'll leave you to talk. You can sit here on the bench, Miss Ahern. If you need anything, please find me immediately." She bustled off.

I perched on the edge of the seat and studied Sister Francis. To say her face looked like a wrinkled winter apple was bein' unkind to the fruit. So many lines crossed her face it was hard to imagine her as a young woman. I couldn't see a wisp of hair under her wimple. She must have a small body, because the fabric of her habit swallowed her. But her eyes, set deep in her face, were sharp.

"Is she gone?" Sister whispered.

"I think so. Do you need something?"

She straightened. "Heavens no. Mrs. Fletcher is a busybody. I don't get many visitors. I don't need a chaperone when I do. I'm old, not incapable." The thin voice was brisk, not a trace of the faltering tone from earlier.

I revised my opinion of Sister Francis. At first, I'd wondered if she'd even remember anything useful. But the change in her voice and no-nonsense light in her clear blue eyes made me think she was as sharp as a tack.

She patted my knee. "She told you I was dotty, didn't she? That I might fall asleep on you or not remember much?"

"Sort of. Mostly 'cause you're ninety, and your mind might be slippin'."

Sister clucked her tongue. "I'm ninety-four, young lady. And there's not a second of the last seventy years since I took my vows that I don't remember. How old are you?"

"I turned nineteen this spring."

"By the time I was nineteen, I'd been in a convent for two years." She grabbed my left hand. "Engaged, but not married I see."

"We're gonna be as soon as Tom gets home. He's in the Army."

She cocked her head. "But you're not sure you want to."

It was clear I'd have to tread carefully around Sister Francis. I'd been with her less than five minutes, and she'd already put her finger on an uncomfortable subject. I withdrew my hand. "I've known Tom for ages. I love him."

"It is possible to love someone very much and still not want to marry him."

Time to change the subject. I cleared my throat. "Sister Francis, I'm not here to talk about me. I want to know about your time at Father Baker's orphanage."

Her steely-eyed gaze didn't change, but she followed my lead. "Those were the best years of my service. I took a vow of celibacy, but I had more children than any mother alive. I loved every one of those boys. Even the troublemakers."

"Then you must remember Christopher Lake."

She folded her hands in her lap. "Christopher was one of the special ones. Even when he was being a rascal, he could charm you into letting him off with nothing but a warning. And he was a rapscallion, make no mistake."

"How do you mean?"

"Mischievous. Too curious for his own good. Oh, not about his parents. But he loved cars and trains. If there was something mechanical around, he wanted to take it apart and see how it worked." She stared into space, lost in her memories. "We'd find him in the coal cellar, trying to figure out a better way of loading the furnace than shoveling. He followed our handyman around like a puppy. He loved climbing the trees. He tried to tame a fox kitten. If there was a way to get dirty, Christopher would find it."

"He never asked about his mother and father?"

She turned her gaze back to me. "I didn't say that. Back then, our Mother Superior told him he'd been left for God, and that seemed to satisfy him."

"Seemed?"

Sister nodded. "Sharp, aren't you? Yes, once he'd been put in his place, he never asked Mother about it again." She leaned in. "But he talked to me."

My heart sped up. "What did you tell him?"

"Oh, I'm sure he's told you his story and shown you his St. Christopher."

She's dodging me. "Yes, but with all due respect, Sister, that doesn't answer my question. What did you talk about?"

She smoothed the folds of her habit. "He fantasized about his mother, of course. The French inscription on the medal. Maybe she was a lost member of the French nobility. Or her family had taken her on a tour of the continent, where she learned the language. She'd show up someday to claim him, and he'd have a fabulous life." Her thin shoulders rose and fell. "Fairy tales, of course. Christopher had a very active imagination."

"And what did you tell him?"

"That romantic stories aren't always about princes and princesses."

Maybe the princess had fallen in love with the pageboy. "He told me you were especially fond of him. You gave all the young children candy, but even when Christopher got older, you had a soft spot for him."

She paused. "He was a special child. I always did wonder."

I waited, but she didn't continue. "You wondered what?"

"Whether he'd live out his childhood in the orphanage."

"Did you think he'd be adopted?"

She looked away. "Not precisely."

Her meaning hit me like a ton of bricks. "You thought his mother would come back for him someday."

"Not his mother."

But who else would take him back? "Wait, you thought his *father* would claim him?"

Sister Francis didn't answer me.

I'd never considered that Christopher's father was in the picture. Two jewelers had assured me the religious medal was a woman's piece. The inscription was a woman's sentiment.

Unless it had been from a man to his sweetheart. But an expensive piece like that meant *he* had dough, too. A pageboy couldn't afford that kind of gift. Had the princess fallen for another local lord?

My heart raced in my chest. "Sister, what do you know of Christopher's arrival at the orphanage? I mean beyond findin' him in a pew in the church."

She turned back to me. "Before I answer, why are you asking? Has something happened to Christopher?"

"No. Well, he was wounded in the war. But he's better now." How much should I say? "The whole thing has made him look at life a bit differently."

"I suppose it would. But why did he come to you?"

"He wants to find his mother. I'm a private detective. I'm not fibbing, I can show you my license." I opened my bag.

Sister reached out and stopped me. "You don't have to do that. I believe you. Any fool could see you're not like other girls your age. You remind me a bit of myself, to be honest. You have a passion for the truth, don't you? As well as a deep sense of compassion." She fixed that bright-eyed gaze on me. "Yes, I think you're very dedicated to finding answers for people who you think deserve them."

I shifted on the bench. I felt like a butterfly pinned to a collector's board, being examined with a magnifying glass. Wasn't I s'posed to be askin' the questions?

She kept me in place with her eyes. "Yes, I think you're different. I wouldn't tell this to most people, but I trust you'll do the right thing by Christopher." She leaned toward me. "The story he told you was only partly true." She held up a hand. "He didn't lie to you. It's what he's been told since he was old enough to ask questions. But it isn't exactly what happened."

"You know what did."

She nodded. "Christopher was not left on a church pew. He was brought to us, swaddled in a fine blanket. The medal was left for him to have when he got old enough. A protection. And a clue."

"To his mother?" I'd been right. There had to be something about the St. Christopher that set it apart from other items. "Did you see her when she dropped him at the orphanage?"

"Christopher wasn't brought to us by a woman."

I caught my breath. It could only have been his father. I stopped myself. No, it could also have been his *grandfather*. Either way, if I could get this man's name, I'd be well on my way to finding the mother. "No one ever came for him?"

"No. I saw a man once, hanging around the grounds. But he never came to the door, and he disappeared after a while."

Before I could ask my next question, the secretary reappeared. "Sister, it's time for your afternoon tea. After that, you have afternoon devotions."

Sister Francis transformed back to the fuzzy-brained elderly nun. "That would be lovely, Mrs. Fletcher," she said in her breathy voice.

Mrs. Fletcher looked to me. "I'll show you out, Miss Ahern. I'm sure you wouldn't want to overtax Sister."

I only had one more, you old cow. Why couldn't she have waited two more minutes? "Of course not." I stood. "Thank you very much, Sister Francis. You've been very helpful."

Sister's bony hand shot out and grabbed me. Given the way she'd been talkin' I shouldn't have been surprised at the strength in her grasp, but I

71

was. "May St. Christopher watch over your travels, my dear. And may the Father's love lead you to what you seek." She let go and closed her eyes, apparently exhausted.

"That's very nice, Sister." Mrs. Fletcher patted the nun's frail shoulder. "Let me take Miss Ahern to the door, and I'll be right back."

I shook myself back to the present. "No need. I can find my own way. Again, thank you very much, Sister. God bless."

I left with Sister Francis's words ringing in my ears. What was that about?

Chapter Thirteen

Emmeline was waiting for me when I arrived at Lafayette Square. I looked at my watch. "It's not even four thirty. What'd you do, leave work early?"

Her cheeks turned pink. "I may have pleaded a sick headache. It doesn't matter. I haven't had a visitor since you left me earlier this afternoon." She brushed hair from her face. "Did you speak to the nun?"

I went over what I'd learned from Sister Francis. "A man. It's gotta be either the mom's father or Private Lake's. Who else?"

"May the Father's love lead you to what you seek." Emmeline frowned. "It *could* be a blessing, you know. God the father. I mean, she is a nun."

"True, but somehow I don't think that's what she meant. Why tell Private Lake he was a foundling?"

"Simple. The father didn't want to be known either."

"But he left the medal in case Christopher wanted to find his family when he got older. And he does. That blessing is a clue. Find the father, and I'm one step closer to locating the mother." I looked around. "We'll take the next bus to Delaware Park."

Emmeline dusted off the bench and sat. "What about St. Christopher is so important?"

"What do you mean?" I sat next to her.

"Why a medal of him? I don't know anything about the saint."

I stared. "Do you mean it? How can that be?"

She laughed. "Because I'm Jewish. Couldn't you tell from my last name?"

It hadn't even occurred to me. "St. Christopher is real popular with

73

Catholics. He's the patron saint of travelers."

"Why?"

I rarely met a non-Catholic who was interested in the saints. Most people shrugged 'em off. "The story is that St. Christopher served God by helping folks cross a dangerous river. One day, he carried an unknown child safely across. Afterward, the child said he was Jesus. Because of that, Catholics pray to him before taking a trip. Lots of people carry a medal when they are traveling."

She tapped her lips. "Then someone must have thought the private would go places."

"Or was askin' for the saint's blessing as the child traveled through life. But it's why the nuns at Father Baker's named him Christopher. Least that's what Private Lake told me. St. Christopher is also the patron saint of soldiers."

"Why? Was he a soldier?"

"Not like we think of them. After he carried Jesus across the river, he went around converting people. Eventually, they killed him for it. He's considered a soldier for the faith. But anyway, Private Lake said that's why he decided to enlist, not wait to be drafted."

"Sister Francis invoked his name for your search. I guess he doesn't only protect physical traveling."

"No, s'pose not." Mr. Dumonde said the medal was old. Maybe it had been given to a son or daughter traveling from home?

"Well, we need all the help we can get." She stood. "Here's our ride. How do you plan to handle the talk with Marian Carstairs?"

The bus hissed to a stop, and the doors clunked open. I stood back to let Emmeline go first. "I'll figure it out when we get there."

* * *

I'd been to Delaware Park before, and I thought I knew what to expect. But the Carstairs mansion put the Witkop house to shame. It was huge, with wings off the back. The trees in front were so big they were obviously ancient. The brickwork was red and the white pillars and trim shone like they'd been painted recently. Dark green bushes lined the front of the house. A stone walkway led to the front, and a winding driveway led around back, prob'ly to a garage. Money didn't buy an extra gasoline ration, but I bet the Carstairs children found a reason to take their fancy automobile out at least once a week. I hadn't seen it, but with a house like this, it had to be top-notch.

For the first time, Emmeline shrunk back and seemed intimidated. "Gosh. Will you look at the size of this place? I bet you could fit three families in here."

"At least two big Catholic ones." I wasn't gonna let her see my own nervousness. I walked up to the door and banged the brass knocker.

A man answered the door. "May I help you?"

I assumed it was the butler. Ordinary people didn't wear black suits with bow ties that weren't tuxedos. I held out my card. "I'm looking for Miss Marian Carstairs. Is she home?"

He took my card between two fingers. "Is she expecting you?"

"No, sir."

"Then I'm afraid you'll have to make arrangements to come back. Miss Carstairs doesn't entertain unexpected visitors, especially this late in the afternoon." He started to close the door.

I put out a hand to stop him. "I think she'll see me and my associate."

"Why is that?" His expression didn't change, and his voice stayed polite, but there was a hint of disdain under the polished response.

"'Cause I might have information about a family member. Would you please give her my card? Tell her I want to talk about late 1922."

He looked me up and down, but never glanced at Emmeline. "Wait here." He closed the door.

Emmeline fingered her purse strap. "Shouldn't you have mentioned the sanatorium or Private Lake?"

"No. That might have gotten me turned away without a word." I wanted to light a cigarette to calm my nerves, but I didn't. "By mentioning the year, she might be curious and want to hear what we have to say."

Emmeline thought about that a bit and nodded.

My ploy paid off. The door reopened, and the butler waved us in. "Miss Carstairs will see you in the sitting room. This way."

I was immediately struck by the swanky interior. Much fancier than the Witkop home. Every piece of furniture was dark wood that gleamed within an inch of its life, betraying the liberal use of polish and lots of elbow grease. Every lamp, including the overhead chandelier, dripped with crystals. Plush carpets lined the floors.

Based on the entryway, I expected the sitting room to be dark. But the butler led us to an airy space with big windows. The satin draperies were pulled back to let the late afternoon sunshine pour in. The fireplace was unlit, but clean of stray ash or any wood left from the last blaze. The marble mantel was covered with photographs, some of 'em quite old. The walls held rich-looking paintings, including a man with giant moustaches. Maybe the original Anthony Carstairs. On the table was an old shot of three young people, two boys in their teens and a girl dressed to the nines in clothes I'd seen in pictures from the 1910s. It had to be the Carstairs siblings. The chairs were chintz, and there was something my grandma would have called a day bed, with two raised sides and a small pillow, boasting plush velvet. Another thick carpet protected the floor.

Our hostess lay on the day bed, a book on the mahogany table by her side. It was the middle of the week, but she was dressed in fancy duds. Maybe the Carstairses wore clothes like that to dinner all the time. Her brown hair was pulled up on top of her head. Her porcelain-pale face was unremarkable except for her eyes, which were almost violet in color. Their gaze bored into me with the power of the drills I'd used when I worked at Bell Airplane. Her jawline was almost like a man's, and her nose was sharp, like a hawk's beak.

Like Private Lake's.

"Please have a seat." The butler pointed at two wingback chairs. He turned to his boss. "Should I bring refreshment, miss?"

"That won't be necessary, Evans. I don't think they'll be here long." Marian Carstairs waved her hand, a lazy gesture. "You're dismissed."

Evans gave a short bow and backed out of the room. He closed the door behind him.

Marian picked up my card from the table. "A private detective. I have to admit, curiosity is the only reason I let you in. Strange profession for a young woman."

"I'm all about breaking tradition. I used to make airplanes."

She raised an eyebrow. "Who is your companion? Another detective?"

"This is Emmeline Schechter, my research assistant."

Emmeline bobbed her head. "It's a pleasure to meet you."

"Hmm." Marian didn't turn her attention from me. "Evans said you wanted to talk about 1922. Why on earth would that particular year interest you?"

"Because that was when you left for the sanatorium. That's the story, anyway." I tried to match her statue-like expression. If she wanted to act like this conversation didn't matter, two could play that game.

I was rewarded by a tightening of the skin around her mouth. Slight, but I noticed it.

"How did you, oh, of course. The paper reported it." She sneered slightly. "Gossip columnists were as bad then as they are now. Maybe even worse. I still don't understand why that insignificant tale would interest you nearly twenty-one years later."

"I've been hired by a young man, Private Christopher Lake."

Not even a flinch followed the words. "What does that have to do with me?"

"My associate made some phone calls." I nodded at Emmeline. "Why can't she find any record of you bein' in a hospital upstate that winter and the following spring?"

Some color came into Miss Carstairs's face. "How dare you meddle in my private business?"

Emmeline bowed her head and mumbled a response.

"Because of my client," I said swiftly. "I'm investigating any leads to find his mother. You mysteriously left society in the early winter of 1922. Private Lake was born in the late spring of 1923. That's about six months later."

Marian was sharp enough to understand the implication. "You think I left to hide a pregnancy?"

"You gotta admit, it's a possibility. 'Specially, as I said, we can't find any record of you bein' in a sanatorium, like the papers reported." I paused. "You woulda left Buffalo right about when you couldn't hide it any longer and returned after it was all over." A thought drifted across my mind. *Why did she bring the child back home?* Unless she hadn't gone upstate and that was why we couldn't find any records. Maybe she'd stayed closer to home. I pushed the thought aside for the moment.

"You impudent chit." Marian lifted her chin. "This conversation is over." She reached for a small handbell next to her book.

"Wait a moment, please."

Marian's hand froze over the bell.

"I'm here on an honest errand, Miss Carstairs. I will not tell the press about this. My only intention is to bring comfort to a young man who's serving his country. He's been through a lot. He grew up without family." I looked around me. "In a place a lot less flash than this. Looks to me like you've had it pretty nice, even with the Depression and all. Can't you find it in your heart to give him some peace?"

She lowered her hand but didn't say anything.

I glanced at Emmeline, who gave a tiny twitch of her shoulders. *Hurry up,* the gesture seemed to say. I did. "When Private Lake was left at Father Baker's, the only thing he had with him was a St. Christopher medal."

Marian studied her fingernails. "I'm not interested in some orphan brat's tawdry keepsake."

The words burst from Emmeline. "How do you know it's cheap? You haven't even seen it."

I laid my hand on her shoulder. "Miss Carstairs, I apologize for my associate's outburst. But she has a point. Your words make it sound like you know more than you're tellin' me. Naturally, that leads me to wonder."

Marian narrowed those glorious eyes. Then she snapped her fingers. "Give it here."

I pulled the medal from my pocket and put it in her hand.

She ran the chain through her fingers. Once again, her face tightened at the corner of her mouth, and a spark flashed in her peepers. She gripped the medal, then handed it back. "As I thought, this piece is not familiar."

She's lying. Why? I'd lay money the sight of the medal made her angry, not nostalgic. Because she'd had to give up her baby? Or something else?

"I was in a sanatorium for my health. I find it quite natural that any hospital would deny I was ever a patient, especially as we asked, and paid, for discretion." She stood. "I'll send Evans in to show you out. Don't come back. That's not a request." She swept from the room, leaving Emmeline and me behind her.

Chapter Fourteen

I looked at Emmeline, who appeared as baffled as I felt, although I hoped it didn't show on my face.

"Should we wait for the butler?" Her whisper was loud in the silence.

"I don't think so. We know the way out." I got to my feet.

Before I could take a step, a man came in, but not Evans. This guy was a shade taller than the manservant. Like Marian, he wore nicer clothes, but ones that stopped short of being a traditional suit and tie. His long jaw was covered by a neatly trimmed beard, and his nose was similar to Marian's, but on him it looked aristocratic, not intimidating. His brown eyes shone with warm light, and his dark hair was wavy. A lock fell over his forehead. "Well, hello. I expected to find my sister, not strangers. Who are you lovely ladies?" His voice was a pleasant baritone.

It hit me. *Private Lake has the same jaw.* His features weren't quite as strong as the Carstairs siblings, but there was no denying the similarity. I'd found one-half of his family, no doubt about it.

I stepped forward and held out my hand. "Betty Ahern, pleased to meet you. This is my associate, Emmeline Schechter."

She bobbed an almost curtsey, clearly tongue-tied by the man in front of her.

He gave us a dazzling smile in return. "Your associate? You sound like you're some kind of professional, Miss Ahern."

"I am." I held out a card.

He took it and turned it over. His fingers were long and graceful. "A private detective? What can you possibly be looking for here?"

"We came to talk to your sister. I assume you are Mr. Carstairs the younger?"

He pocketed the card. "I am. Theodore J. Carstairs, at your service. Marian's younger, ne'er-do-well brother, as she's constantly reminding me. My friends call me Theo."

"Are we friends?" I asked.

"We might be." He glanced at Emmeline. "You haven't told me the purpose of your visit."

I wondered how much to say. *Why not go for it?* "We came to talk to Miss Carstairs about her supposed visit to a sanatorium in late 1922."

"Why on earth would you want to do that?"

I told him briefly about Private Lake.

Theo's face blanched. He reached out toward a chair, missed, and staggered a bit. "A sad story and the young man has my sympathy, but I don't see what it has to do with my sister."

"I don't believe she went to get mental treatment." I watched him. "I think she went away to avoid the scandal of having a baby out of wedlock."

Theo's voice became solemn. "She admitted that?"

"No. But the timeline fits. If you could see Private Lake, he looks like her. And you, now that I see you. Plus, there's this." I held out the St. Christopher.

Theo took it tenderly. He ran his thumb over the engraving, and a faraway look came into his eyes. "Ah."

It was an odd reaction to jewelry that belonged to a sibling. "You've seen this before."

He cleared his throat. "You must excuse my sister, Miss Ahern. She doesn't like remembering that period or speaking of it. I'm sure you can understand. It was a tumultuous time. For both of us. Our lives could have been much different. Or should have been. Had things gone differently, you understand."

I could. I thought I understood her anger now. Marian Carstairs had not only given up her child, but her future. She'd never married and was doomed to be a spinster. Did she pine for her lost love? "I was told a man brought my client to the orphanage. I assume that was your father?"

His gaze had been fixed on the medal, but now it rested on me. "My father. Yes, the old man was quite devoted to maintaining the Carstairs family name. A hard man. In many ways, Marian is like him."

"Private Lake is home from the war but is returning to the front soon. Would it be possible for him to meet with your sister?"

Theo's hand clenched around the medal. "No, I...I think that would be unwise."

"You don't want to meet your nephew? He's a good person. I think he would do your family proud."

"That may be, but no. There's too many painful memories there. For all of us." He took my hand and put the medal in it, letting the chain puddle in my palm. He closed my fingers over it before turning my hand over and kissing it. "I wish your client well, Miss Ahern. I truly do. I'm sure he grew up with fantasies of a father and mother who loved him. I'd wager most orphans do. Let him keep that. Don't let it be spoiled by a bitter woman's anger." He patted my hand. "It's better to let some secrets stay buried, Miss Ahern. For all our sakes."

* * *

Theo Carstairs escorted us outside, where he once again wished us well before firmly closing the front door.

I stared at it. "That's a man who aged ten years in ten minutes."

Emmeline adjusted the strap of her handbag. "What do you mean?"

"When he walked in the room, he was a good-looking guy near forty, if that. Although he's gotta be at least thirty-eight, otherwise he'd have been drafted." I pulled a Lucky out and lit it. I struck out toward the bus stop.

Emmeline trotted behind me. "The scandal would have touched him as well. Imagine being the brother of the woman who had a child on the wrong side of the blanket back in those days. He was younger, too. What girl's family would have attached themselves to the Carstairs family under such a cloud?" She *tsked*.

"And yet neither of them married." Marian, I could understand. She'd been parted from a man she loved enough that she bore his child. But why hadn't her brother moved on with his life?

"True." She looked back to the house. "He's still a handsome fellow. I'd take him in a second." She snapped her fingers. "You know, if he was Jewish. I bet he was a real looker in his twenties."

We reached the stop in the nick of time to catch the departing bus. After paying our fares, I moved to the back and took a seat. A handsome guy indeed. Like Private Lake. The Carstairs family had given him a lot, even if he didn't get their name or dough.

Emmeline settled in next to me. "What are you going to do now?"

I exhaled a cloud of smoke. "I'm gonna tell Private Lake I might have found his mother." It was the fastest I'd ever solved a case.

Why didn't I feel more excited?

* * *

Emmeline and I parted ways. I promised I'd let her know how it went with Private Lake. Then, I rode back home to the First Ward.

I didn't go straight home. Instead, I walked down to the Tillotson house, where Mrs. T answered the door. "Lee and Dot are in the back. Would you like anything to drink?"

"No, thanks anyway, Mrs. T."

She reached out to brush some hair off my face. "Are you okay, Betty? You look worried."

"Yeah, I'm swell. I've got a lot on my mind. The backyard you said?" I hurried around the house.

My two best friends sat side by side, holding hands. They looked nothing alike, but somehow went together like peas and carrots. Lee was tall and lanky, yet strong from his work at General Motors. Sitting down, you didn't notice the bum leg, the result of a childhood dare gone wrong that made him limp and kept him outta the army. Dot was the exact opposite. I'd been the one who kept Lee outta prison, but Dot was the girl who'd won his heart. I wasn't jealous. I had my guy.

And don't forget Frank.

I pushed that thought right outta my head. I knew Lee wouldn't approve of me abandoning his best friend. Dot had already given her lecture. "Well, look at you two lovebirds. Aren't you too cute for words."

Dot turned a pretty shade of pink, but she didn't let go of her beau's hand. "Aww, cut it out."

Lee squeezed her hand and grinned, a lit cigarette in his other paw. "You're wishing you and Tom were here to keep us company."

"Heck, if Tom were here, we'd be married and off tryin' to start a family, not double-dating with you two." I leaned on the house. Another thought that didn't make me as giddy as it used to. Between my work at Bell and my new gig as a private dick, I wasn't eager to give it all up for a house with a picket fence and kids. "How's tricks?"

"Good." Dot gave me a once over, like she knew what I was thinkin'. She prob'ly did. "What about your case?"

"I think I solved it." I told them about finding Marian Carstairs and the trip to Delaware Park.

Dot's face became outraged. "You've replaced us already?" 'Course she'd pick up on Emmeline, not the details of my discovery.

"Don't snap your cap. Nobody'll ever take the place of you two." I went to sit by her and gave her a squeeze. "But if you're workin' all day and hanging out with your guy at night, when are you gonna have time to come sleuthing with me?"

"How do you know I couldn't make time if you didn't ask?" She grumbled, but it was fake. Mostly.

Least I hoped that was the case. "Anyway, I think I set a record with this one. One day. And all I spent was bus fare to Delaware Park."

Lee let go of Dot and stretched out his hand. "Can I see the St. Christopher?"

"Sure." I handed it over.

He clamped his cigarette between his lips and studied the medal. "Nice work. You had someone look at this?"

"Yeah." I told them what Mr. Dumonde had said.

Lee ran his finger over the inscription. "Is this original?"

"What do you mean?" I asked.

"I'm no jeweler, but I've done enough metal work to know that it looks newer. Like someone added the inscription later."

Dot leaned over it. "Maybe it was added before Miss Carstairs gave it to her son? You know, so he'd know she loved him even if she couldn't keep him."

"Maybe." The idea tugged at my mind. "You're sure, Lee? About the engraving."

He gave it back. "It's an idea. Maybe your jeweler can tell you."

The glance Dot gave him was quizzical. "You think it matters?"

"Don't know." He threw away his smoke. "The jeweler said the piece was old. If the engraving was added later, Betty might be able to find out who did it. That might help positively identify Private Lake's mother. Or his father, if the engraving was meant for her. It's more knowledge, right?"

I put the medal back in my pocket. Lee was right. If I could figure out who added the words, I might be able to tell Private Lake about his father as well.

All for fifteen bucks.

Chapter Fifteen

I wasn't s'posed to meet Private Lake until I called him with any news. But when I walked into Teddy's Tuesday morning at eight thirty, he was sittin' in my booth.

I snagged Judy's sleeve. "When did he get here?"

She glanced over her shoulder. "Twenty minutes ago. I told him you weren't in yet, but he wouldn't leave. I gave him a cup of coffee and a seat. Should I have gotten Bob to haul him out?" Bob was the cook, a beefy man who'd served in the Great War and brooked no nonsense.

"No, it's jake. I didn't expect to see him this morning, that's all." I hated winging it.

"You want your usual?"

"Please. Did Private Lake eat anything?"

She jotted down my order on her pad. "Nope. Only the joe."

I gave him the once over. He looked jittery, like a kid who had ants in his pants and was barely keeping himself together. Had he eaten anything at his boarding house? "Bring him some scrambled eggs and toast. Unless I miss my guess, that isn't his first cup of java this morning. If he doesn't put some food in his stomach, he'll either explode or be sick."

Judy nodded and headed for the kitchen.

I rolled my shoulders to relax them and went to my booth. "Morning, Private. What are you doin' here?" I slid into my seat.

"I couldn't help it. What have you found out?" He gulped from his mug.

"It's only been twenty-four hours."

"But you must have learned something since we talked yesterday. Haven't

86

you?"

Instinct told me not to tell him anything yet. "A little bit, yes."

He leaned forward, peepers wide. "What? Tell me."

"I don't think that's such a good idea. It's early goin', and in my experience, giving you information now, before I'm absolutely sure of my findings, could mean trouble. For me and you."

He reached forward and grabbed my hand. "Come on. You have to tell me something. Please. I paid you. Doesn't that make me your employer or whatever?"

I pulled my hand, but he held it tight. "Private, let go of me, or I'm gonna make a scene and have you tossed out."

He let go as if his hand grasped a hot pan. "I'm sorry, it's just this whole thing has me on edge. Please. A crumb is all I need. I've wanted this for so long, and to think it's in my grasp is torture."

I sighed. "That your first cup?"

"Third." He gave me a sheepish grin. "I had two with breakfast this morning. Frankly, I don't remember eating."

I held up my hand. "First things first. You're gonna eat the food I ordered for you. I don't need you gettin' sick. I'll get kicked out, and I don't have anywhere else to conduct business. Do that, and we'll talk."

I bought time by laying out my notes while we waited. This was not how I wanted to do it, but Private Lake wasn't gonna take "no" for an answer. I could tell he wanted to jump right in, but I wasn't gonna do that. I was hungry. More important, I wasn't gonna be led around by my client. He might have thought it took forever, but Judy appeared with our food in minutes.

She set the plates down and filled my mug. "You need anything else, holler."

Private Lake pushed his eggs around on his plate. "The food is here. Are you going to tell me anything?"

I pointed at his plate. "I told you. Eat first. Talk after." I buttered my toast and used it to break one of my eggs.

Judging by the look on his face, he wasn't happy with me. But he ate. It seemed to calm him down. At least he stopped shaking in his seat.

I wiped my hands on my napkin and handed him Emmeline's report. "I have a good lead on your mother."

He practically ripped the paper out of my hand. "Who is she?"

"I think her name is Marian Carstairs. Here's the story." I ran down what I'd learned from Melvin, what Emmeline had discovered, and my conversations with Marian and Theo from yesterday. "I've got a few more things to check out."

"But this is her?"

I took in his appearance before I answered. His face was flushed, his hands shaky. There was a bright gleam in his eye like the one people had when they had a fever. "I *think* it is. As I said, it's a good lead. The best I have right now. But there are a few details to confirm." Boy, I hoped he wouldn't make me regret this.

His head came up. "Like what? Her brother practically admitted it. What more do you need?"

"I'd want to place Marian in a hospital around the time of your birth. Or in a home for unwed mothers. Maybe even find someone who saw her back then. For extra proof. I want to make this clear. This is only what I've found out after a day. Things could change in a split second." I ate the last piece of my toast. "You're acting like my little brothers when they're full of sweets. Why?"

"I need to get this done."

"You've still got twelve days until you leave. That's plenty of time."

"Not if I want to get to know her. I don't want to find out her name and have to get on a train the next day." His gaze ran over the paper. "Is this her address? The house on Nottingham Terrace?"

I hesitated. He was too anxious. I remembered what Sister Francis had told me about him as a boy. He'd been impetuous and headstrong, and how it had gotten him into trouble more than once. I'd already given him more dope than I wanted to. But if I didn't tell him, he might show up at the Carstairs house anyway. "Yes. Private, you aren't thinking of going there, are you?"

He clutched the paper. "Why shouldn't I? You said this was her."

"No, I said it was a good lead, and it *might* be her. Be smart and take my advice. Give me a couple more days. At least the rest of this week. I'll tell you Monday morning whether it's a good idea to visit." I picked up my coffee and looked at him over the rim of the mug.

"I don't think that'll work for me."

I set down the java. "You don't charge a German line without a plan, right? I'm askin' you for time to come up with one. When I do, we'll go together."

He stared at the paper, and I could almost see the wheels turning in his head. "I can't wait. More importantly, I don't want to."

"Try real hard. Don't do anything that'll mess this up. You might not get another shot."

He laid down the paper and tried to smooth the crinkles out from where he'd clutched at it. "Can I keep this?"

"No, that's my only copy. I'll give you a full report when I'm done."

"Fine." He stood up, tossed a couple bills on the table, and bolted for the door.

* * *

I planned to spend all day at home making telephone calls. I wasn't gonna use all my nickels and take up the day on a pay phone. That didn't mean there wasn't a cost.

Mom shook a spoon at me. "Elizabeth Anne! I shudder to think what the bill will be next month."

"I promise. I'll pay for it. I got the dough. Please don't make me go find a public phone." I put my arms around her and kissed her cheek. I tried to keep my detecting out of the house out of respect for my family, but sometimes I didn't have much of a choice. "I'll be quiet, too. You'll barely know I'm here."

Mom sniffed, but it was clear to me she wasn't as angry as her words made her out to be. "You stay in the hallway. You can take a chair from the kitchen."

"Yes, ma'am." I pecked her cheek again, grabbed a chair, and went to the telephone to make my calls.

Like Emmeline, I found a fat lot of nothing. None of the sanatoriums I called were willing to admit they treated a patient named Marian Carstairs in the early 20s. The thought came back. Could be I was lookin' in the wrong hospitals.

I'd spent all day makin' calls. I stood and stretched muscles stiff from hours of sittin' in a wooden chair. As I did, there was a knock on the front door. "I'll get it."

On the doorstep was my friend, Detective Sam MacKinnon of the Buffalo police. "Good afternoon, Miss Ahern."

"Sam. This is a surprise. What's shakin'?" I held open the door.

He entered and took off his fedora. "Is there somewhere we can talk?" My younger sister, Mary Kate, stuck her head out of the front room. "Privately?" he added.

"The kitchen is as private as we're gonna get around here." I went to pick up the chair.

"Allow me." He lifted it and followed.

Mom turned from the sink, where she was peelin' potatoes for dinner. "Hello, Detective. We don't see you much around here these days. Is something wrong?"

He set the chair down in its place. "I need to speak to your daughter."

His words put me on edge. Not Betty. *Your daughter.* He'd greeted me at the door with *Miss Ahern.* "Is something the matter, Sam?"

He glanced at Mom. "We really should speak alone."

Mom put down her knife, wiped her hands on her apron, and crossed her arms. "I don't like your tone, Detective. If Betty is in trouble, I'm staying right here."

He held up a hand. "I assure you, Mrs. Ahern. Betty is not the subject of my visit. But she may have some information. Please, would you leave us alone for a few minutes?"

I laid a hand on her arm. "It's okay, Mom. I'll even finish the spuds."

"If you're sure." She untied her apron and hung it over a chair. "I'll be

90

right in the front if you need me."

After she left, I invited Sam to sit. "Don't mess with an Irish mother. Can I get you somethin' to drink? There's no coffee on, but maybe you'd like a glass of water?"

"That would be very kind." He sat. "I've heard the same about Jewish mothers. Any mother, really. Especially if she thinks you're after her children."

I set the water glass in front of him. "You didn't come by to chit-chat about family, Sam. What's the story?"

He took out his notepad and a pencil. "Do you know a man named Christopher Lake?"

The question was so outta left field, it took me a second to respond. "I do. He's a client. Why?"

"What do you know about him?"

Not for the first time, I noted Sam's tone. It was carefully professional. Not rude, but he wasn't here for fun. "He's a private in the Army back in Buffalo on medical leave. Why are you here?"

"What do you know about his family?"

Two can play this game, Sam. If he was gonna be all uptight, I wasn't giving up any more dope than necessary. "He doesn't have one."

"Why did he hire you?"

"That's my business. And his."

Sam's answering gaze was sharp. "When did you last see him?"

I crossed my arms. I didn't like the tone of this conversation. We'd always had an easy way of talkin' to each other. The man in front of me wasn't my friend, Sam. He was Detective MacKinnon.

"Miss Ahern, you need to answer the question. Out of courtesy, I came to your home. We can just as easily talk downtown."

He didn't raise his voice, but he didn't have to. Something was very wrong. I'd have to tread carefully. "This morning. We had breakfast at Teddy's at eight. He left around nine."

"What did you talk about?"

"Sorry, Detective. That's between him and me."

Sam wiggled his pencil. "Did he say where he was going? When he left the diner?"

"Nope. I didn't ask him. I haven't heard from him all day." I leaned forward. "Sam, what's this about? Be square with me. Is Private Lake okay? Is he in some kind of trouble?"

"Physically, he's fine. But he is in a rather tight spot."

"Why?"

Sam tilted his head. "You really don't know where he went after he left you?"

I'd had my suspicions, but I hadn't known for sure. Instinct told me not to admit anything, not yet. "I already told you, no. I'm not gonna say anything else until you tell me what this is about." I slapped the table. "Spill! What's happened to my client?"

Sam closed his notebook and laid his pencil on it. Then he folded his hands. "Private Lake has been arrested. For the murder of Marian Carstairs."

Doggone it. I *knew* I shouldn't have told Private Lake anything.

Chapter Sixteen

"When can I see my client?"

"Not until tomorrow at the earliest." Sam tugged his fedora on. "You aren't going to tell me what he hired you for? Why would he be interested in Marian Carstairs? How would he even know her?"

I liked Sam a lot. He'd put me on the path to bein' a private detective. Even paid for the correspondence course I'd taken to get my license. But I couldn't talk to him. Not yet. "I'm sorry, Sam. I gotta talk to Private Lake first."

"Fair enough."

"Can you tell me how you found him? I mean, you've never spoken to him."

Sam laughed. "It wasn't hard. I backtracked from the Carstairs house and looked at likely bus routes. I asked if anyone had seen a solitary soldier. He wasn't hard to remember." He eyed me. "We could be on different sides this time."

"I know." I rubbed the door. Unlike last time, when we'd thought we'd be opponents and wound up workin' side by side. "Do you think he's guilty?"

"Eyewitnesses put him at the house earlier today. He was quite angry when he left. They heard him shouting at the victim."

"No one visited her after that?"

Sam looked like he was fightin' with himself. "We haven't found anyone yet. Shortly after the private left, the staff left on daily errands and didn't return until early afternoon. The downstairs maid took tea to her mistress around four, as usual. That's when she found Miss Carstairs. Dead."

"Dead, how?"

"Shot." Sam's look was grim. "Allegedly with a German pistol. The maid said Miss Carstairs's father brought them back from the Great War as souvenirs. He kept them in his desk."

"Did you ask Private Lake what happened?"

"I did, but he refused to say anything. He's at least smart enough to realize talking to me is not necessarily the best decision."

I made a note to ask Private Lake about the gun. As a soldier, he would be very familiar with handguns. It didn't even have to be his. I didn't remember ever seein' him with a pistol. I was certain he hadn't been carryin' one this morning. 'Course he was enlisted. Pop said only officers got handguns. "Did anybody hear the shot?"

"Not that they remember."

"I guess they didn't see him, either. Are his fingerprints on the gun?"

"The gun was clean. No prints at all."

I paused. It didn't make sense. "How can that be?"

"It's very likely he wiped them off."

I pictured Private Lake as I'd seen him at the diner. "C'mon, Sam. If this had been thought out, maybe. But I don't buy it. You won't convince me Private Lake went to see Marian, argued with her, shot her on a whim, then suddenly thought about wiping his prints off the murder weapon."

Sam raised an eyebrow. "How do you know he didn't plan it? Nobody witnessed the shooting."

I gave him my best mother's stare. "The guy was jumpin' outta his skin when he left me. He wanted to talk to her, Sam. Not kill her. I don't buy him as the shooter, but even if he did, it woulda been somethin' he did in the heat of the moment."

Sam gave me a slight grin. "I have my doubts as well. I don't think the gun we found had been fired. We didn't find a weapon on your private. Would he have had the foresight to throw it away? He came off as a scared kid when we picked him up. I'm not sure he's our man. But he's the only suspect we have, and he very well *could* have done it."

Poor Private Lake. "What did they talk about? Him and Marian?"

"The staff only heard raised voices, not words." Sam stepped outside and stopped. "Are you certain you won't tell me why Private Lake hired you?"

"Sorry, Sam. You've been swell." He'd loosened up in the last five minutes, and it felt more like our normal relationship. But I had a duty to my client. "I know you didn't have to give me all that dope. After I talk to him, I'll tell you." I paused. "You didn't say what you thought. About him bein' guilty, I mean."

He chuckled. "Haven't I told you before? It doesn't matter what I think. Only what I can prove. But it looks bad, Betty. I hope you understand."

"I do." Heck, if I was a cop, I would have arrested him, too.

"Will I see you tomorrow?"

"I'll try. 'Bye, Sam." I shut the door.

I should have followed my instincts that morning and kept my yap shut. I suspected where Private Lake was goin' the minute he split from Teddy's, although I'd hoped I was wrong. Despite my urgings, Private Lake had taken the news I'd delivered and rushed off to Marian Carstairs. She must have denied him. But I couldn't see the private shooting her over a simple rejection. What else had she said?

I thought of my client. An orphan boy who grew up to serve his country. Who carried a saint's medal in his pocket. I thought of his innocent-looking face and open expression. Murderers came in all shapes and sizes. I knew that first-hand. But I couldn't believe Private Lake was one of 'em.

I grabbed my purse. "I'm going out."

Mom came out of the front room. "Where are you off to in such a hurry? What about the potatoes?"

I yanked open the door. "Sorry, Mom. I gotta go to Delaware Park."

It was close to five thirty by the time I reached the Carstairs mansion. The police were long gone, and the neighborhood was its normal, quiet self. I knocked on the front door. Evans answered. "You again. I have nothing to say to you." He tried to close the door.

I stopped him. "Did a young man visit earlier today? Wearing an Army uniform?"

Evans's voice was coldly correct. "If you are referring to Private Lake, yes,

95

he did. A most unseemly gentleman. He insisted on seeing Miss Marian. Pushed his way into the house, as a matter of fact. If she hadn't come out of her sitting room and told me to admit him, I would have thrown him out. Forcibly. Soldier or not."

I didn't believe Evans would have been able to do that. The private was younger, stronger, and bigger. "Did you hear what they talked about? Maybe Miss Marian told you?"

"I did not. Private Lake was in an extreme state of agitation. I had errands to run, but I told Miss Marian I'd stay. She said it wouldn't be necessary. I left. When I came home later that afternoon, Madeline, that's our downstairs maid, was in hysterics. Miss Marian was dead, and the police were here."

"Did she get any other visitors?"

Evans drew himself up. "I find your questions impertinent. I already spoke to the authorities, who, I might say, have far more business here than you do. As far as I'm concerned, this is your fault."

"Mine?"

"I don't think it's a coincidence that you showed up yesterday morning and an aggressive man came today. Now the lady of the house is dead. In fact, I think I'll be calling the police to add that to my statement." He slammed the door.

I never shoulda told Private Lake anything, not until I was sure. Now, he was in a pickle. And it would be tomorrow morning before I could do anything about it.

Chapter Seventeen

I woke up early the next morning, full of determination. My first stop was the city jail. I knew they'd be holding Private Lake there from his arrest through the trial, unless he could make bail, which I thought was a long shot. I doubted the Army would do that and he didn't have any other relatives. The guard gave me a hard time, but eventually told me to take a seat while someone fetched the prisoner.

I met Private Lake in the same room where I'd talked to Lee, when he'd been in jail last spring. I picked a seat between two other visitors. Maybe their talk would muffle us.

The young man who came out didn't look much like the handsome soldier in his dress uniform. His clothes were rumpled, and his naturally rosy complexion was washed out. A night in a cell added lines to his face. Jail time must do that to a person. "Hey, Private. I'd ask how you're doin', but I think I can tell for myself."

He tried to smile and didn't quite make it. "Got myself into quite a jam, didn't I?"

I wanted to give him a hug, but it wasn't the right time or place for that. "I told you not to go see Marian Carstairs. Why didn't you listen?"

"Honestly? I don't know. It seemed like a good idea when I had it. I wish I had taken your advice. This isn't the first time I acted before I thought." He lowered his head. "Guess this time maybe the lesson will sink in."

I knew from visitin' Lee not to expect any privacy. But for some reason, maybe out of respect for a soldier, the prison guard kept his distance. "Do you have a lawyer?"

"The local JAG office sent one over in time for my arraignment last night. It's standard procedure, I guess." Private Lake rubbed his chin, which showed a bit of stubble. I must have looked baffled, 'cause he added, "Judge Advocate General. The Army's lawyer boys. I'm gonna plead not guilty, for all the good it's going to do me."

"Hey. Listen to me." I rapped on the desk. "You knock it off, right now. I know the lead detective. He's not gonna pin this on you so he can close a case. If you're innocent, you'll get out in no time. Second, you've got me."

"Do I?"

"Of course, you do." I paused. "You didn't shoot Miss Carstairs, did you?"

"No!" He sounded desperate, not indignant. "I went there, but she, well, it didn't go as I'd planned."

This would be the tricky part. Gettin' his story without the guard overhearing. "Tell me about it. Quiet like." I lifted my chin toward the guard, who stood twenty paces away. "I don't think he's tryin' to eavesdrop, but if he hears anything, it's not a secret, you understand? Not like talking to the JAG lawyer."

Private Lake glanced at the guard and inched his chair closer to me. "After I left you, I hopped a bus north. I've got a good memory. I didn't have to see that address for more than thirty seconds to remember it."

As I feared. "Go on."

"The butler answered the door. I guess that's who it was. He didn't want to let me in. But then she came out of a front room, Miss Carstairs. I told her who I was, that I needed to speak to her. She seemed, I don't know, amused, I guess. She dismissed the butler, and I followed her into some kind of room a lady would have. Lots of fancy furniture and knick-knacks."

To this point, his story matched Evans's, which was good. "Go on."

He rushed on. "I told her my tale in a hurry and asked if she was my mother. The look on her face was not what I expected. First, she looked stunned. Then, it was more outraged. Then, it's hard to describe. She was angry, I could tell. But not with me, at least not only with me. She stared at the door, and I swear I heard her mutter something like 'what an idiot.' But I don't think she was talking to me. Anyway, I expected her to order me out."

"She didn't, though, did she?"

He swallowed again. "She *laughed*. Called me a poor, deluded bastard child. Then she said I was better off as I was, that no one was going to claim me. Because I wasn't good enough. My parents had given me up. It was obvious they didn't want or need me around. She told me to go back to the war and forget about ever being more than a lowly private. 'Unless you win a medal or something, and what are the chances of a throw-away bastard child doing that?' Her voice. It was hateful."

I couldn't even imagine how he'd felt. To be sure you'd found your mother after years of dreaming about that moment and to be confronted by spite. I hated Marian Carstairs in that moment. She coulda let him down nicely. Instead, it seemed she'd gone out of her way to hurt him even more. I no longer thought of her violet eyes as commanding. They were hard, unfeeling. "What did you do?"

"I tried to argue with her. But she pulled a gun out of her desk and threatened me with it. She told me to get out. I grabbed it and yanked it out of her hand."

"You touched it?" Then there shoulda been fingerprints.

"Yeah, but I didn't point it at her or nothing. I didn't! I took it away and tossed it aside." His eyes were wild. "You gotta believe me."

The guard glanced over at us.

"Shhh, keep it down." I waited, but the man went back to surveying the room. "What then?"

"She stopped laughing. She told me to get out before she called the police. That a bit of trash like me had no place in her world." His eyes gleamed, and he dashed his hand across them. "I stammered something, I don't even remember what, and ran out of the house."

"You didn't pick up the gun again?"

"No."

"You didn't fire it, wipe it off, and drop it again?"

"For the last time, no!"

"You didn't get angry?"

"Well, yeah, I yelled. A lot, I think. After she laughed at me, it all gets kinda fuzzy." He composed himself. "Her words hurt, I admit it. Even if she wasn't my mother, she didn't have to laugh. I'm an orphan. But I'm not trash. I go to church. I go to see the chaplain when I can. I enlisted instead of waiting to be drafted. And if I make it to the end of this war, I'm going to find a way to help out at Father Baker's." He took a deep breath. "She had no business being mean. I wanted to slap her. Or send her to see Sister Mary Agnes. But I didn't kill her."

I studied him. I'd seen a picture of Theo as a young man, beardless, in Marian's sitting room. It was easy to spot the similarities. The jawline. Private Lake's ears were exactly like Theo's. His eyes were almost the same color. Sure, the hair was darker, and Private Lake's nose was not as straight. His cheekbones were a little higher, more freckled.

And it hit me. I hadn't been wrong. At least not about Private Lake being a Carstairs. I'd fingered the wrong sibling. The differences, those would be from his mother, whoever she'd been. But I had no doubt I was lookin' at Theo Carstairs's son.

Theo did recognize that medal. Why didn't he say something? It wasn't great, fathering a child when you weren't married. But society didn't look at men with the same scorn. They'd say boys like Theo were "sowing their wild oats" or some such before settlin' down. Heck, an older man might even approve of his son's behavior. But something about Theo's case was different. I had to find out what. 'Cause that's what would tell me what I really wanted to know. Who the woman was who stole a young man's heart and had given birth to the Joe in front of me.

Private Lake cocked his head. "What are you thinking?"

"I made a mistake. Of course, I did tell you to wait. If you had, maybe we'd be havin' this talk at the diner instead of at the jail, but no matter." I took a deep breath. "You aren't gonna like this, but you gotta give me time to keep investigating. I need all the facts before I say anything else. I already goofed. I'm not gonna make the same mistake again."

He mulled that over for a good thirty seconds. "Fair enough. You're right, I don't like it. But I shot myself in the foot once. It might be harder to do from a jail cell, but knowing me, I'd do it."

"I do have a question. Did you see Marian's younger brother while you were at the house? His name is Theodore. Maybe you spoke to him?"

"No. I didn't see anyone except Marian. And the butler." He clutched the edge of the table in a white-knuckled grip. "Betty, am I gonna hang for this? I didn't kill her, I swear."

"I believe you. I'm gonna get to the bottom of this, and I'm gonna find your mom, too." I put my hand on his. "And I won't let you meet her in the pokey."

Chapter Eighteen

I left the jail and hurried to the nearest payphone. Private Lake was innocent. He had to be. That meant I had two cases: the one I'd been hired for—to find a lost mother—and the one I volunteered for. To prove a young man was not a murderer.

I called the library and asked for the stacks. "Emmeline, I need you to do something."

"What?"

"Look through the papers over the last, I dunno, two or three years. Start with the *Courier-Express* and the *Evening News*. Pull any issue that mentions anything about the Carstairs family."

"Got it." She repeated the instructions. "The whole family or just Marian? I read about her when I came into work this morning."

"Any Carstairs. I wanna know what they mighta been doing to be worthy of murder."

She paused. "The story said the police arrested Private Lake."

"I don't believe he did it." I had no doubt he'd been angry and maybe even had done something reckless. But that was way short of killing. "I want to know if Marian, or her dad, double-crossed anyone in business. Or made them angry any other way."

"Got it." The sound of paper ripping came over the line. "I'll get started reading."

"Get the papers. You don't have to do the research. I want to be there to do it."

Her voice turned defensive. "Don't you trust me?"

"'Course, I do. But two sets of eyes will be better than one. Besides, I'm not entirely sure what I'm lookin' for. That makes it hard to tell you what to do."

"I suppose. When will you get here?"

I glanced at my watch. "I have one stop before I go to the library. Let's shoot for noon, but I'll call you again if I'm gonna be late."

"Here." She rattled off a phone number. "That's a direct line to the desk here. That way, you don't have to go through the switchboard. I'll talk to you later."

One task started. The next step was to talk to Melvin's source at the *Courier*, the one who wrote for the Society pages. What was her name? Gladys. I didn't have a last name, but hopefully, there was only one Gladys in that department.

* * *

Once I arrived at the newspaper building, I was directed to the office for the Society pages. It was up on the third floor. It wasn't tiny, but you coulda dropped three rooms that size in the News department. Overflowing file cabinets lined the wall. No one was at the desk. Darn it.

I snagged the arm of a young woman who passed me in the hall, her arms full of newsprint. "Excuse me. I'm looking for Gladys. She writes for the Society section."

"Gladys Tutwiler?"

"If she writes social news, I guess that's her. There's no one in the office. Is she not working today?"

The young woman shifted the paper in her arms. "She's here. Maybe she went to the ladies'. Have a seat, and she'll be back." She hurried off without another word.

I followed directions and plopped myself down on the plain wooden chair in the office. Would someone tell Gladys I was there? I didn't want to catch her off guard. Scaring a potential source wasn't the best start.

After about ten minutes, as I was thinkin' Gladys had taken a powder or gone off for a story, a woman in her late forties or early fifties entered the room. Her makeup was thick, and her hair set in rigid curls. Her fingernails boasted a perfect manicure. She had the broad figure of a woman who'd never been called "slender," but her clothes set it off perfectly. She looked sophisticated, not dumpy. She was reading a page and talking to herself. "I'm going to strangle that man. He told me he'd never again change my copy without consulting me. This whole first paragraph is absolutely not my style. So much for keeping his word." She proceeded directly to her desk and didn't once look in my direction.

I cleared my throat. "Miss Tutwiler? Or is it missus?"

She jerked her head up. "What the devil? Oh, right. Arlene mentioned a visitor. Seeing this hatchet job drove it right out of my mind." She pulled out a pack of smokes and lit one. "Call me Gladys. Who are you?"

"Betty Ahern. I'm Melvin's friend."

"The detective." She held out the pack. "Smoke?"

I waved it off. "No, thank you. I'm sorry to bust in on you like this. But the matter is urgent."

"Honey, nothing in this department is urgent. You're thinking of those boys in the newsroom." She leaned back in her chair.

"Trust me. I'm about to make you as important as they are. To me, at least."

"That is a tantalizing statement." She blew out a cloud of smoke. "How on earth are you going to do that?"

"I need information regarding a recent murder victim."

Gladys drew on her cigarette, leaving a ring of deep red lipstick on it. "Marian Carstairs."

I nodded. "Good guess."

"It wasn't a guess. You asked Melvin about Marian's mysterious disappearance back in the 20s. I read about her death this morning. I can connect the dots. Not only that, she's the only murdered woman who could bring you up here. Otherwise, you'd be squeezing the News writers and good luck with that. They take the phrase 'tight-lipped' to a new level. Except Melvin, on occasion. I may get my copy altered, but I can always tell exactly what the deal is. My boss makes that mistake all the time. He underestimates me."

I liked this woman. She had a hard edge, but I could tell she was whip-smart. I pegged her as the type who'd rather be writing about the headlines of the day, but she'd been shunted into this dingy space, doomed to writing what men considered "fluff" stories about who married who, or who brought who to the latest gala. Instead of giving up, she made the best of it. "How long have you been writing for the *Courier?*"

She pulled over a heavy glass ashtray filled with butts and tapped her cigarette on it. "Officially? Twelve years. I was a *secretary* to the man who held the job before that."

I heard the slight emphasis. "What do you mean by that?"

"I wrote the stories, and he put his name on them."

"That's horrible! You didn't get your own byline?"

"No, but I got experience. When he left, I convinced the editor to give me a week's trial. I turned that into a career. But enough about me." She ground out her smoke. "You want to know the dirt on Marian."

"I think the cops got the wrong guy. But until I know more about her, I'm in the dark as to who has motive. Tell me about her disappearance. It happened before you worked at the paper, how much do you know?"

She rose and went to a filing cabinet. "It was before my time, but a newspaper keeps everything. That's in addition to what I read back then. I have followed that family for years. I was in my twenties, and I read every story about the Carstairs family. Buffalo isn't New York City or Los Angeles, but that doesn't mean we don't have our local celebrities. When I was younger, I wanted to be like Marian. Thin, gorgeous, rich, always wearing the best clothes. Any man she wanted, like that." Gladys snapped her fingers. She removed a thick folder and returned to the desk. "Here."

It held stories on yellowing newsprint. All of them were about the Carstairs family. Marian and Theo were prominent in all the photos. She was usually by herself, but Theo seemed to have a different girl on his arm in every one. "Doesn't look like she did, though."

"Have you met her?"

"I've talked to both of 'em."

"Then you know Marian has, shall we say, an edge to her."

Once again, I thought of those violet eyes, hard as amethysts. "Yeah, I got that impression."

"Of course, to be fair, she had to be like that. It wasn't only men after her money." Gladys lit up again. "When her older brother died, Marian was thrust into the role of heir apparent."

"Not Theo?"

She clucked her tongue. "Theo was the life of any party and a womanizer to boot. He could afford to be when his older brother was alive. Second son and all that. All the ladies loved Theo, and he loved all of them. Or so it seemed to the press."

The sly note in her voice made me look up. "You think there was more to it."

"He wouldn't settle down, and it struck me one day that it was because he really *was* in love. But he couldn't have the girl. Here." She reached for the folder and paged through the stories. "Take a gander at that." She handed me one.

In the picture, Marian and Theo were leaving Central Terminal. He was looking at his sister until I took a second look. "He's focused on this girl, here." I tapped the paper. "Who is she?"

"Very sharp, Miss Ahern."

"Betty."

Gladys dipped her head. "That is Noemi Gerard, Marian's maid. Pretty little thing, isn't she? French, as I understand. Or Belgian. I can't remember. Her parents left their homeland ahead of the Germans in the Great War."

I thought of the inscription on the St. Christopher medal. "You think this was the girl he loved? Were they caught?"

"Oh, there was never a public scandal. They were never seen alone together, and no one ever heard a whisper. But any sharp observer could see them making doe-eyes at each other on the few occasions they were in the same place. Me? I think he was head-over-heels. Of course, it would have been completely unacceptable, even for a second son. Well, maybe had Anthony III lived, Theo would have been left alone."

"Tell me about Anthony, the older son."

"Not that much to tell." Gladys exhaled a cloud of smoke. "He was your typical eldest child. Right from the start, it was clear old Carstairs was grooming him to take over. Unlike his younger brother, Anthony never put a toe out of line. He served briefly in the Great War. Got a degree in business from Canisius College. There was a girl before he went to Europe, but nothing came of that. Seeing the two boys out and about reminded me of a royal family."

"The heir and the spare?"

"You got it." She ashed her cigarette. "But then Anthony III died." She took the file and paged through its contents. She handed me a clip. "Here. He contracted Spanish flu, right at the end of it all. Old Man Carstairs must've taken one look at his remaining son and put his daughter at the front."

"Then Marian went away. What happened to Noemi?"

"She was dismissed. No cause given, at least not publicly."

I took out my notebook and pencil. "When was that?"

"Right after Marian went to the sanatorium. Now, it could be her services weren't required with her mistress gone. Could be she and her employer had a falling out." Gladys exhaled a cloud. "I always thought it strange, though. Even back then. Marian wasn't going away forever. It made more sense to give Noemi a vacation or put her to work elsewhere in the house. If she'd been dismissed for legitimate reasons, why be secretive?"

"What happened to Noemi?"

"She disappeared from Buffalo, never heard from again." Gladys leaned in, a wicked gleam in her eye. "Question is, why? Why didn't she get hired somewhere else? Where'd she go?"

"You have an idea."

"In the spring of '23, a midwife tried to sell a story that she'd been summoned to a house on the West Side, where she'd delivered a baby boy to a single mother. According to her, that woman was Noemi Gerard. But when my predecessor tried to run down the story, the house was empty. Woman and baby had split. No one in the neighborhood copped to knowing where they'd gone or even if the midwife was telling the truth." Gladys dropped her voice to a conspiratorial whisper. "If I understand Melvin right, you've found Theo and Noemi's son? Do you think he'd be willing to give me an interview?"

I doubted that, but I didn't want to offend my new source. "Maybe later."

Gladys nodded, as if I'd agreed Private Lake would talk to her. I hoped I hadn't. "Back to Marian Carstairs. Out of curiosity, did you ever find out where she went? And why didn't Noemi keep her baby?"

"To answer your first question, no. The Carstairs family was able to keep a lid on that. As for the second, my guess is they didn't want even a hint of a scandal. Remember, Old Man Carstairs had a lot of moolah back then. The stock market was booming. Five'll get you ten he paid Noemi off, took the kid, dumped him somewhere, and boom. Problem solved. Heck, he probably paid off the neighborhood to keep mum."

I wrote the name Noemi Gerard on my pad. Dead or alive, I had to find her. I couldn't see any resemblance to Private Lake in the grainy photos, but that didn't matter. "All this is interesting, but how does it relate to Marian?"

"It doesn't really, except whatever her father preached, Marian sang the same tune. Theo wouldn't have had any support from his sister. She's kept him on a tight leash since then. Imagine being a man tied to a woman's purse strings. After twenty years, it'd be enough to drive him bonkers. Maybe he finally snapped. He's not the only suspect, though. There are plenty of people who hated Marian and the family." Gladys pulled open the bottom drawer of her desk. She took out two glasses and a bottle of scotch. "Want a drink?"

"I don't think—"

"Honey, if you're going to be a gumshoe, you're going to have to loosen up a little." She held out a glass with a small amount of amber liquid in it. "Bottoms up."

I took the glass and sipped. The scotch burned my throat and set me coughing.

Gladys grinned. "First taste of hard liquor?"

I couldn't speak. Eyes watering, and gasping for breath, I nodded.

She laughed. "You'll get used to it." She took back the story about Anthony

III and paged through the folder, scanning the contents. "Take a gander at this. Old Man Carstairs made quite a stir in the city, putting his daughter in place after the heir apparent died. It changed her. That and the trip upstate. Before, she'd been a bit aloof. After, she became ruthless."

I studied an earlier picture of Marian at a party. She looked young, softer. Not as easy-going as her brother, but definitely not the hard-edged woman I'd met. "What do you mean?"

"Marian didn't have quite the reputation that her brother did. That didn't mean there weren't stories with her at the center." Gladys leaned back and tapped her fingers on the arm of her chair.

I tried another small sip of the scotch. It burned, but not as bad. "Like what?"

Gladys shrugged and took a much bigger drink than I had. "There were rumors that fall she was going to get married to Robert Newcombe. He worked for Marian's father. I don't remember what he did. But nothing came of it. Newcombe married another girl in the spring of '23."

"Before or after Marian returned from her cure?"

"Before." She finished her drink and smacked her lips. "I kinda feel sorry for her. Marian. She lost her chance at marriage. And it has to be hard, being a woman managing a business surrounded by men. No wonder she was a terror."

There was still a good bit of scotch in my glass, but I couldn't bring myself to finish it. I handed it back to Gladys. "Thanks for your time. And the drink."

"Any friend of Melvin's is a friend of mine. You sure you aren't gonna finish that?" She pointed at the glass.

I eyed the amber liquid. "I think I'll stick to Coke. Sam Spade and I don't have to have *everything* in common."

Chapter Nineteen

I left the *Courier* offices and hotfooted it over to the library. Gladys sure had given me a lot of social background on Marian and Theo. The problem was, I couldn't see how any of it was important twenty years later. Would Marian's former beau hold a grudge that long? Unlikely, but it wasn't the first time the past had come back to bite a person. I'd have to dig further into Robert Newcombe to be sure.

Once at the library, I made my way to the stacks. Emmeline was at a table, two small piles of newspapers in front of her. "Hi there."

I pulled out a chair and sat. "What's this?"

She waved at the papers. "I pulled some issues of both the *Courier* and the *Evening News* to get us started. I focused on ones from the last two years and looked for stories that mentioned anything about the Carstairs family, either socially or from the News sections. These are the ones that had information that could be useful. Some only mentioned the name, and I figured you wouldn't be interested in those."

"I thought I told you I wanted to look at everything myself." I'll admit it took some effort to keep the annoyance out of my voice.

"I know, but be reasonable. Did you really want to go through years of stories? All I did was look for mention of the name and the context. All of this might be worthless." She raised her eyebrows. "Don't you keep telling me we have a deadline? Now that Private Lake has been arrested, isn't time even more important?"

Doggone it, she was right. "How'd you do this so fast?"

"I've been at it for three hours, and I read quickly. I told you before. I love research."

Perhaps I'd been too harsh on her. "Well, good job partner. Let's get crackin', shall we?"

We divided the papers. She took the *Evening News* while I examined the *Courier.* "Theo really was a ladies' man, wasn't he?" I held up a paper. "This is at least the sixth time his picture appeared in a write-up about a party, and he's always got a different girl on his arm." Just like Gladys had told me.

"He was quite handsome. Still is. But I think there are two reasons a man doesn't settle down." Emmeline peered at a photo. "One, of course, is that he doesn't want to stop sowing his wild oats. Either because it's fun or because he wants to annoy his family."

I smoothed the paper. Theo posed with a beautiful woman in what had to be a shiny flapper dress. Even in the black-and-white photo, it seemed to gleam. But his smile looked false. As though he didn't really care about the girl. All he was doing was mugging for the camera. The look reminded me of a similar forced smile I'd once seen on Sean's face when the girl he'd asked to a dance turned him down and he went with someone else. "Or he wants a girl, he can't have her, and he's tryin' to make the best of it and not succeeding."

Emmeline nodded.

I flipped to the Local section of the paper. Below the fold was an article about Carstairs and his operations in Lackawanna. I tapped my pencil against my chin. "There's somethin' else we need to check."

Emmeline frowned, and lines creased her forehead. "What?"

"Who gets control of the Carstairs business now that Marian is dead." I stacked the papers. "I think Theo gets the family dough. Let's clean this up."

"We still have papers to read."

"I've got enough for now. If you have time while you work, keep goin'. I'm gonna hit the streets."

She collected the scattered papers from the table. "Why would Theo get the company?"

"Marian doesn't have kids. Theo's her next of kin." I paused. "I need to confirm that. I s'pose it's possible she left everything to someone else.

But that doesn't feel right. She was a proud woman. She might not have approved of her brother, but she wouldn't let the family fortune go to a stranger."

We carried the newspapers back to the stacks. Emmeline waved at a desk. "Put them there, and I'll reshelve them later. How much money do you think we're talking about?"

"That was a flash house. The company is still successful. My guess? A lot." I pushed hair off my face. "How much you want to bet Theo had an allowance?"

"Maybe he wanted more, and his sister wouldn't give it to him."

"Or she cut him off." I told Emmeline about my idea, that Private Lake was Theo's son. "What if they argued after Private Lake left, Marian said she was gonna toss her brother out for embarrassing the family, and he got mad?"

"But your police friend isn't sure the German gun is the weapon. He did say *allegedly*. I think he has doubts."

"It doesn't matter. Theo could easily have his own gun. He's in the best position to shoot his sister, drop his dad's pistol as a distraction, and hide the real one. So far, he's the only person we know was at the house aside from Private Lake. According to the cops, the staff all claim to have been out."

Emmeline drummed her fingers on the desk. "You're right. It doesn't seem likely a person would wait twenty years before killing in revenge. Why wait?"

"Exactly."

Her expression turned doubtful. "What do we do now?"

I hoisted myself up. "Seems like I have to talk to Theo again."

Chapter Twenty

When I arrived in Delaware Park, I didn't allow myself to be distracted by my surroundings. As the sun beat down on me, I hustled up the sidewalk and felt sweat dribble between my shoulder blades, even though it wasn't the warmest day ever for summer in Buffalo. Evans would prob'ly be horrified by my appearance.

I didn't care. The butler wasn't gonna shut me out again.

I knocked on the door to the Carstairs mansion. It wasn't long before Evans opened the door. "Can I help—good Lord. You again. I told you yesterday to go away. Your appearance today doesn't inspire me to do otherwise."

I ignored the gibe. "I need to talk to Mr. Carstairs."

"Mr. Theodore is busy. And you are in no fit state to enter the house."

"Look, I don't much care about proper appearances. I need to talk to him."

Evans opened his mouth, prob'ly to retort, when Theo appeared. "What's the trouble?" He gave me the once over. "You're the girl who was here yesterday talking to Marian. Miss Ahern, wasn't it? The detective?"

"That's me. I need to speak with you again."

"Whatever for?"

"It's about your sister." I shot a look at the butler. "I think we should do this without an audience."

"I told you yesterday, Marian doesn't…didn't like to talk about that time in her life."

"She's dead. It doesn't matter what she likes, does it?" I knew my words were blunt, but I had to convince this man to talk to me. "I think I can help find out why and who's responsible. You want that, right?"

Theo's gaze was thoughtful. Then he nodded. "Let her in, Evans. We'll go to my study."

Evans's outrage was plain. "But sir—"

Theo gently pushed him aside. "This way, Miss Ahern."

I followed him back to the room we'd talked in earlier. The only difference was a short glass with a small amount of amber liquid over ice took up space on the table next to the chair. Otherwise, the room looked untouched. I wondered how much time Theo spent in here and what he did. There were no papers on the desk. None of the books appeared to have ever been read. The leather on the spines was perfect and uncreased.

"Please, have a seat." He settled in the chair and picked up the glass. "They arrested a young man already. The police informed me of that last night. What's the issue?"

"I don't think they have the right man." I took out my notebook and flipped to the page I'd written on earlier. "I've been doin' some digging into your family."

"Whatever for?"

"I told you yesterday I thought your sister might be Private Lake's mother. He came here to meet her."

"I said you were mistaken. You shouldn't have let him."

"I know that, but the private wouldn't listen to me. It doesn't matter, 'cause I've changed my mind. I need you to be honest with me so I can clear his name. Tell me about Noemi Gerard."

A strange, closed expression came over Theo's face. "I believe she was my sister's maid. Way back in the twenties."

"You know she was." I focused on him. "She was fired right after your sister went away. Why?"

He tried for a laugh. "I...really, Miss Ahern. Why would I be at all concerned with such matters?" He got up and went to the bar.

"Maybe 'cause you loved her."

"That's pure gossip." He kept his face averted as he poured another drink.

"That doesn't make it untrue." I watched as his hand shook and scotch splashed onto the gleaming wood. "I saw a photo of her, with your sister. She was a pretty little thing. French?"

He closed his eyes. "Belgian."

"You said you barely paid attention to her. But you know where she's from."

"I did." The stopper rattled as he put it back in the bottle. "She was always reminding people about it. It stuck in my memory, that's all."

"The story I was told was that your family let her go." I paused for effect. "She had the most beautiful blue eyes."

His response was swift. "Brown. She had brown eyes."

Ah ha! I pounced. "You know where she's from and the color of her eyes, but you didn't pay attention to her? C'mon, Theo. I've seen pictures of you from back then. I've seen how people look at each other when they're in love. I see it in my best friends. I'll give you credit. You tried hard. You fooled a lot of people. But not me, not once I really looked."

"Please don't do this. Don't bring it up again."

"Everybody says what a ladies' man you were, but I think it was a sham. You recognized that St. Christopher. It was hers, wasn't it? Did you give it to her? Or have it engraved? All my love, it says. In French. Clever, doing it that way. She could pass it off as a gift from her parents or a family heirloom."

He clenched his hand.

"I bet your father was furious. His boy, younger son or not, in love with a servant? Scandalous." I leaned forward to see his face. "Marian must've flipped her wig."

Theo's shoulders sagged. "She was lovely. Noemi. Even her name. I used to tease her about, oh, everything. Her accent, the tiny gap in her front teeth, her nose, her freckles. She hated those freckles. She gave it all right back. Oh, in a respectful manner and never when my sister was around. But if we were alone? She was funny and smart and a joy to be around. There wasn't much of that in my life."

"When did you realize you loved her?"

"It all simply happened. One evening, I dressed to go to yet another party.

She helped me with my bow tie and told me how lucky a woman was to be with me. I joked I'd rather take her than some vapid society heiress. I realized what I said was true." He took another drink.

"You started an affair."

Theo returned to his chair. "At first, it was flirting, a couple stolen kisses, that's all." He stared off into the distance. "One night, my father and Marian were gone. We made love in the gazebo on a pile of blankets. It was summer. The mourning doves serenaded us." He brought his gaze back to me. "I wanted to marry her, truly. She said it was impossible. I said why not? This is America. Who gives a damn? That's what this country is about, right? Equality?"

It was s'posed to be. "What went wrong?"

"We were very careful, or we thought we were. My father threatened to pack me off to oversee a new office he was building in New York City. The same day, Noemi told me she thought she might be pregnant. I was overjoyed. I would marry her no matter what, even if I got disinherited."

"But you didn't. Why?"

"It's such a jumble, even years later. Marian had her breakdown. That part is true, by the way. It had something to do with a man, very uncharacteristic of my sister. I didn't pay attention. I was too caught up in my own troubles. Noemi was supposed to be here when she got back. But my father fired her. I was furious. I spent months looking for her. I swore when I found her, we'd get married. No luck."

I stayed quiet, letting him relive the memories.

"One day, Father pulled me into his office. Marian was there. They said Noemi and the baby were dead, and that was the last time she would be spoken of. Father told me I could live at home and be given an allowance, or he'd arrange a suitable marriage. I couldn't bear the thought of living with another woman. After he died, Marian doubled down on Father's arrangement."

"How did she do that?"

"She said all my expenses had to be personally approved by her. I couldn't appear in public with any woman she deemed unsuitable. It wouldn't be appropriate for her to arrange a match, but privately, she let me know if I ever wanted to get married, I needed her permission. She said Father had been soft and she would not give me another opportunity to embarrass her, not when her success at the company demanded everything be perfect." He swirled the liquid in his glass and downed it. "I've been a kept man all these years, Miss Ahern. Living on my sister's whim. I have no skills, no job, no place in the company. I've been dependent on her. And she never let me forget it. Never."

"I don't understand. Why didn't you leave?"

He shook his head. "Easier said than done, Miss Ahern. I was weak back then. When I was young, I spent a lot of money in gin joints and at the craps table. I got in trouble more than once. Father bailed me out, of course. Quietly. Well, as quietly as possible. I had a reputation. One night, I lost more money than I should have to a man who, shall we say, it wasn't a good idea to be indebted to. It was about when Noemi told me about the baby. Father paid off the mobster, but the price handcuffed me to this house. I had to let her go and not tell a soul." He tossed back the last of his drink. "In fact, you're the first person I've said anything to since the night it happened."

I couldn't even imagine his anguish, even though I could see the grief written on his face. No wonder he hated his sister. "Now that she's gone, who inherits?"

"There's the irony." He set down the glass and spread his hands. "Yours truly gets it all in the end. The house, the money, the company, all of it. Marian's inability to get hitched and have kids has left me in charge. Funny how life works out, isn't it? And I don't care. Without Noemi and my child, it's all meaningless."

"Why not leave everything to a business partner or someone else?"

"For all my faults, I'm still a Carstairs. Marian was proud, like Father. She'd never let the money and company go to anyone outside the family."

His story gave him a swell motive for murder. He seemed to realize it, because he laughed, a bitter sound. "Now you're thinking I shot her. Sorry to disappoint you, Miss Ahern. I didn't. You'll have to take my word for it. I hated Marian, yes. But if I was going to shoot her, I would have done it back then, when I could have kept Noemi with me. I have nothing to live for now, no reason to break free of my gilded cage. Impulsive actions like that belong to the young, like that poor soldier from that morning."

I stashed my notebook. "Mr. Carstairs."

He got up and went back to refill his glass. "I told you, please call me Theo. Mr. Carstairs makes me think of my father, and I can't stand it."

I debated how much to tell him. "I can't give you Noemi back. At least not now. But I can reunite you with your son."

He didn't move. "My son is dead."

"No, he's not. Private Lake is your child, yours, and Noemi's. If you'd see him, talk to him, you'd know."

Theo's laughter was loud and held genuine mirth. "Cruelty, Miss Ahern? Did my sister pay you? One last parting shot?"

"I'm tellin' the truth."

"Enough." He slapped the bar with his hand, then faced me. "All I have left are my memories. Did your private think my sister would pay him? That he'd be welcomed into the family, a rags-to-riches story? Maybe he believed the Carstairs name could get him out of his service overseas."

I marveled at the depth of Theo's pain. I was handing him the family he'd mourned all these years. All he could believe were the lies he'd been told. I hoped he hadn't killed because of them.

"I think it's time you leave." His face was pale, and his hand shook.

"Theo, please. I'm not tryin' to hurt you, and Private Lake isn't lookin' for money or favors. I really do think he's your child. Are you gonna let him take the fall for a crime he didn't commit?"

"Get out."

I heard the warning in his voice but pressed on. "Maybe Noemi is still alive, too. You can find her together. Be reunited as a family. I'll help. It's what I do. I don't think Private Lake is guilty. You gotta go talk to him, meet him."

"Get out!" Theo whipped his hand sideways, and the glass flew across the room. It hit the wall like a small grenade and shattered. Glass flew everywhere, and scotch puddled on the hardwood floor. He glared at me and breathed heavily through his nose.

I grabbed my purse and scurried to the door. Theo's face made me think of a picture I'd seen of a bullfight in Spain, the wounded animal angry and dangerous. Why? He'd truly loved Noemi. I could hear that in his words. Finding a son he thought was dead should have made him happier than a pig in mud.

Unless he'd framed that son for murder.

Chapter Twenty-One

I escaped the Carstairs house without runnin' into Evans, thank goodness. Outside, I took a deep breath. *You're lucky Theo didn't throw that glass at your head.* He'd been angry enough to do it. I said a quick prayer of thanks and debated my next move.

An urgent voice caught my attention. "Miss, miss. Wait up, please."

I looked around. An older woman beckoned to me from near the house, about ten feet away. Her gray hair was cut short, and she wasn't very tall. From a distance, I could tell she had to be fifty, if not sixty. But her thin frame stood ramrod straight, and her bearing gave off an air of energy. I walked closer. "Are you talkin' to me?"

"Yes. Were you visiting with Mr. Theodore?" Her deep blue eyes had a worried gleam.

"I was."

"I heard the shouting and came to see if you are okay. I hope he didn't hurt you. He's a nice boy, but he has an awful temper." She wrung her hands in her apron.

"I'm fine. He threw his scotch glass at the wall. I didn't even get cut by the shards."

"May I ask what you spoke of?"

I wanted to trust her, but not yet. "Who are you?"

"Mrs. Vance. I've worked for the Carstairs family for forty years. I started as the downstairs maid, and now I'm the housekeeper."

She must have known Noemi. She'd sought me out. I could use an inside source. "We were talkin' about Noemi Gerard. Miss Carstairs's maid back in the twenties."

"Oh dear. No wonder Mr. Theodore was upset. He doesn't like being reminded of Noemi." She glanced back at the house. "As long as you're not injured, I should go."

"Wait." I reached out my hand. "Did you see the young man who visited this morning?"

"No. My understanding from Evans is that he spoke with Miss Marian. He shot her, didn't he? I believe the police arrested him."

"Yes, they did, but I don't think they got the right person." I fumbled for my notebook. "Did you see anyone else?"

She waved me off. "Put that away. If he sees me talking to you..." She threw a look back at the house. "Tell me, why did the man from this morning want to see Miss Marian?"

I needed an ally, and I sensed this woman might be one. "He thought she might be his mother. But I think he's Noemi and Theo's boy."

Mrs. Vance's hands flew to her mouth. "We were told they were dead."

I thanked my lucky stars for Mrs. Vance and her concern for a stranger. "I can't say about Noemi, but her son sure isn't. Are you sure you can't talk to me?"

"Not here. Not now. But Noemi...oh dear. If I can help find out what happened to that dear girl..." She twisted the apron so hard it should have ripped. "I leave for the night at six. I can meet you."

"Can you come to the First Ward?"

She nodded.

"Teddy's Diner. Say six thirty?" I handed her one of my cards. "If you can't make it, call this number and leave a message."

She snatched the card and scurried back to the house.

* * *

I lit a Lucky and strolled down the street, tryin' to put my thoughts in order. Theo's life under his father and sister sounded awful. Had he inadvertently framed his kid for murder? That would sure make me mad.

I could also see where the police would think Private Lake was guilty. He confronted the woman he thought was his long-lost mother and, stung by her rejection, grabbed the gun from her and shot her. Maybe. If Sam was right in his guess, and the German pistol wasn't the murder weapon, where was it? Where would a private get a handgun?

Dummy. He'd come back from the front. He could easily have a gun.

Mrs. Vance puzzled me, too. What was she gonna spill? Would it clear either of the two men or convict them?

I flicked ash from my gasper. "No use worryin' about that yet. Focus on Newcombe. Where is he?"

I went to a nearby soda shop and started where I always did, with the Buffalo phone book. I found four listings for Newcombe. Of course. I took stock of my change purse. I needed more nickels. "I need to change this for nickels, please." I handed a dollar bill to the boy at the cash register.

He took it. "Are you gonna buy something? You can't sit here and use the telephone."

Good grief. "Uh, I'll take a vanilla malt." It wasn't as if there was a line for the phone. The joint was empty. Hopefully, it would stay that way until I'd finished my business.

The soda jerk came back with my malt. "Two bits."

I handed him a quarter to go with the dollar. "I still need the nickels."

"You got it." He opened the register and counted out the coins. "Say, doll. I get off work at four. Wanna go to the pictures?"

If this kid was older than fifteen, I'd eat the glass with the malt. "Sorry, kid. I'm workin'. And I'm engaged." I showed him my left hand.

"So? Not like he's gonna know, right? C'mon." He leaned over and waggled his eyebrows in what he probably thought was a suggestive, flirty way.

Yuck. It was like bein' propositioned by my younger brother. "No way. I'm not that desperate. I'm too old for you anyway. Try someone else. I've got a piece of free advice, too."

"Yeah?"

"Don't do the eyebrow thing. It's creepy." I took my malt and went to the phone booth. I dialed all of the Newcombe numbers. No one answered at the first two numbers. The third denied knowing the Carstairs family. At the fourth number, a woman with a listless-sounding voice answered. "He's dead," she said in response to the question.

"Oh. I'm very sorry for your loss." This was awkward. "How were you related to Mr. Newcombe?"

"He was my husband."

"Gotcha." I'd not seen this coming at all, and it made my questions sound crass. But I had to know. "By any chance, did your husband know Marian Carstairs?"

Mrs. Newcombe's voice turned sour. "Can't she leave him alone, even from beyond the grave? He chose *me*. Me! And she ruined him for it. All I want is what Robert was due."

I pulled the phone away from my ear. What? "Um, Mrs. Newcombe, it sounds like you had a beef with Miss Carstairs. Or maybe her father? Anyway, I'd like to talk to you about it. Could you meet me?"

"I'm a grieving widow. I can't bear to drag it all up again. Talk to Marian."

She must not have read the paper. "I can't. She's dead. Anything you can tell me would help."

"I have nothing to say. Goodbye." Mrs. Newcombe hung up.

Whatever had happened between Mrs. Newcombe, her late husband, and Marian Carstairs, it hadn't ended well. It sounded like Marian had been a jilted lover. But after twenty years, what could have happened that would lead to murder?

Chapter Twenty-Two

I needed to know about the crime scene. Since Evans wouldn't let me in, that meant I had to go to my best source.

I greeted the desk sergeant at police headquarters, who got on the horn for Sam. Minutes later, he appeared. "Let's go across the street to Moe's." He slipped on his suit coat.

I glanced at the sergeant and back. "Are you still in the doghouse?" Sam had gotten in hot water in the department not that long ago. I felt kinda responsible, since it had been my case that caused the problems.

"No." He held the door open. "I missed lunch, and I'm hungry."

The midday crowd was long gone at the diner, and we were able to grab a booth easily. We both tried to sit in the seat facing the door. "Sorry." I slid into the opposite bench. "Habit. When I go to Teddy's, I always sit so I can't be surprised from behind."

"It's a wise move." Sam loosened his tie. "But I'm pulling rank on you here."

The waitress came by with menus. Sam ordered the meatloaf with mashed potatoes and gravy. "I'm guessing you want to know about the Carstairs scene."

"A Coke for me, thanks." I handed the menu back. "Could be I wanna say hi to a pal."

He reached for the napkins and gave me a look. "Don't play me for a sap, Betty. I'm always glad to see you, but this isn't a social call."

"You got me." I took out my notepad. "I went to the Carstairs house today. Evans shut me out. I need to know about the scene."

124

"I shouldn't talk to you."

The waitress set down our drinks and left.

I took a sip. "That doesn't mean you won't."

"Are you going to return the favor?"

What could I tell him? Nothing he didn't already know. Anything I did give up might incriminate Private Lake. "I can't, Sam. I don't have anything." I saw him start to speak and put up my hands. "I promise. As soon as I have something solid that doesn't point back to my client, I'll come straight to you."

He sighed and put sugar and milk into his coffee. "Fine. One more time, and that's it. As always—"

"I didn't hear it from you. Got it."

"According to the butler, this Evans, everybody was out of the house at the time of the murder. I told you that when I came to your house. Everybody except Theodore Carstairs, who had been in his study all morning, which was very typical. Private Christopher Lake was the only visitor. Evans said he showed the private to Marian's sitting room, then left to run some errands."

I stirred the pop with my finger. "Then how did Evans know Private Lake and Marian argued?"

"Evans said they went at it pretty quickly. He could hear a heated exchange as he left."

I licked the Coke from my finger. "Let me get this straight. He took a stranger in to see his employer, then left the house. Oh, and there was shouting coming from the room? I don't buy it."

Sam's food arrived, and he grabbed the salt and pepper. "You have fine instincts. I asked Evans the same question. He offered the explanation that Theo was in the house if something truly went wrong."

"The guy who was holed up in his study?"

He took a forkful and chewed. "We couldn't shake Evans from his story. He seems very devoted to Marian. He's known her since she was a girl."

"I guess if you work for someone for twenty or more years, you build up some loyalty." But the story was very odd. "You told me Marian's body was found mid-afternoon."

"By the downstairs maid. She said the house was quiet when she returned."

"From where?"

Sam washed down another mouthful with a gulp of coffee. "She went out after her morning tasks to pick up a dress Marian had sent out for alteration. She says she often took care of such matters."

"She leaves to get the dress, comes home, and finds Marian when she brings in the tea. Any sign of a struggle?"

"The room was as neat as a pin. Except for Marian's body lying across her day bed and the pistol on the floor." Sam drank some joe. "Either there wasn't a fight, or the suspect put the room back together before he left."

"Or she."

Sam raised an eyebrow. "No one mentioned seeing a woman."

My retort was swift. "They weren't at home."

Sam raised his mug a little.

"What about the housekeeper? Where was she?"

"Mrs. Vance was out doing her weekly shopping. She left early and didn't even see the visitor arrive. She told us she arrived home around one but didn't look in on Marian. She told the cook to make the afternoon tea as usual and gave it to the maid. Then she checked with the cook to see how dinner was coming along."

I drummed my fingers on the table. "Then the only people in the house at the time of the murder were Marian, Private Lake, and Theo."

"That we know of, yes." Sam's words indicated he was leaving the option open for other suspects.

"What about Theo? What did he say?"

"He went into his study late morning, had lunch there, took a nap, and never left. He didn't hear anyone arrive and claims not to have heard a gunshot."

I stared at Sam. "You gotta be kidding me." One look at my friend's face told me he didn't buy it either.

"That's his statement, and again, he's not budging. Of course, I detected a whiff of bourbon on his breath when we spoke. My assumption is he'd been drinking for some time."

Had Theo passed out drunk and didn't want to cop to it? Why not? He didn't have much use for his sister, and the feeling was mutual from what I heard. His story didn't wash, though. "What about the gun?"

"No prints at all."

I sat upright. "That's impossible. It belonged to the elder Mr. Carstairs. Private Lake said Marian threatened him with it, and he took it away. How can there not be fingerprints?"

Sam chuckled. "Atta girl. Not only that, it's not the murder weapon. I was right. Ballistics don't match. It's the same *type* as the gun that killed Marian, but not the exact one."

None of that helped. I could hear the argument. Private Lake was home from the war. He coulda gotten a German pistol there. He could have used a different gun, wiped down the one left by the body as a red herring, and thrown away the real weapon after shooting Marian. I didn't have any trouble accepting that he'd fly off the handle and overreact. It was his actions after that bothered me. They were too cool and calculating to be from my impetuous and childishly innocent client. "Anything else?"

"That's all I have. Or rather, that's all I'm going to give you. I've stuck my neck out enough. But except for the information about the gun, you could have gotten that out of any of the employees at the Carstairs mansion. I don't feel guilty about sharing."

"You're a rock, Sam."

His expression turned sober. "Anthony Carstairs, Junior was a successful man. And a hard one, from what I've learned of his reputation. His daughter followed in his footsteps. As always, watch your back."

I stood. "Success can breed enemies. Thanks again, Sam." I opened my purse and took out a bill. "Lunch is on me. Don't argue."

"I'm a public servant, Betty. You can't buy my lunch." He pushed the money back.

"I bought a Coke for myself, and I left a very generous tip." I walked out of Moe's, my friend's laughter ringing in my ears.

* * *

I glanced at my watch. It was three thirty. I wasn't gonna meet with Mrs. Vance for another couple of hours. I had time on my hands.

I could visit Mrs. Newcombe in person. But I didn't know anything more than what I'd did this morning. Who cared if she fought with Marian over something that happened years ago? I needed a motive from now. Finding someone who'd seen her in Delaware Park wouldn't be bad, either.

The whole thing had happened in the middle of the day. The area was full of rich people. The folks who lived there wouldn't be at jobs, they'd be lounging at home doing whatever those who had dough did with their day. Plus there'd be servants. Somebody musta seen something.

I went back to the neighborhood to knock on doors. I started with the houses closest to the Carstairs mansion. Mrs. Vance had visited the house on the left early in the morning to trade coupons, a weekly ritual. A man on the right had been outside beating a rug. He'd seen the maid return shortly after lunch with a dress over her arm. "What about Evans? When did he leave?"

No one had seen the Carstairs's butler.

A nanny who lived catty-corner from Marian had been taking her charge out for a walk and bumped into Private Lake. "He walked right into me," she said. "I don't think he even saw us. He apologized profusely. Little Thomas was quite taken with him, a real soldier. The young man showed him how to carry a rifle and said to watch out for Germans."

I wrote this down. "Then he was happy?"

"No, I wouldn't say that." The young woman frowned. "More...distracted. He was definitely upset about something. I could tell he had to force himself to be kind to the child."

"Did he have blood on him?"

"Oh heavens no. I would've mentioned that to someone."

"Did you see him carryin' a pistol?"

She thought a moment. "I didn't see a gun. I suppose he could've had it in his pocket, but the weather was fairly warm. He wasn't wearing an overcoat.

CHAPTER TWENTY-TWO

Surely, I would've noticed the bulge."

"But he was in uniform."

"Oh yes. All dressed up, as though he was going somewhere important."

He thought he'd been meeting his long-lost mother. Of course, he would've wanted to look sharp. If he'd taken the gun away from the murder scene, he'd have had to stash it somewhere until he had a chance to toss it, and a pocket would be the place. "Then he was wearing a jacket of some kind."

"I guess you're right." She tapped her chin. "No, he didn't have a gun. I'm sure of it."

He hadn't tossed it away, not in this neighborhood. Someone woulda picked it up. If he'd left with the murder weapon, where did it go? "Did you see any other strangers around yesterday? Especially between ten in the morning and one in the afternoon."

"Sorry. Thomas takes up a lot of my time." She blushed. "But if you want gossip, you ought to talk to Mrs. Babbage. She lives right over there." She pointed to a house directly across the street from the Carstairs family.

"I'm less interested in tittle-tattle and more in what happened yesterday."

"Of course." The nanny's blush deepened. "I only mean she's a widow. She spends most of her time looking out her front window and knows everything about everybody on the street. Or that's how it seems. If you want to know who was around yesterday, she'll know. If she'll talk to you."

I moved to put away my notebook and paused. "What do you mean?"

"She's very difficult to deal with. Crotchety, I think you'd call it. She lost her husband in the Great War, and her sons are overseas now." The nanny shook her head. "I think she might be the only person in America who doesn't have a good opinion of the President."

"I'll try her anyway. Thank you." I headed for the Babbage house. Sam always said I was good at getting people to flap their gums. Maybe Mrs. Babbage *was* a cross old lady. I'd find a way to get her to open up.

Chapter Twenty-Three

The Babbage house was smaller compared to others on the street. At first glance, it didn't seem to be much different than its neighbors, a white house with dark blue trim set back from the street. But when I took a second look, I saw deeper than first appearances. The grass needed a trim. The hedges lining the front shot leggy branches every which way. No flowers lent cheerful color to the walkway. The paint didn't gleam. The windows were dull in the sunlight, most of 'em covered by the drawn curtains. Except the one in front. I could see an old woman looking out.

She looked me straight in the eye and crooked her finger.

It looked like an invitation to me. I mounted the steps to the porch and took note of the stars in the window, one blue, one gold. The nanny had mentioned sons overseas, but not that one had died. Did she know? I wondered if Mrs. Babbage had given up on maintenance. It seemed even the house mourned its lost resident.

I used a dull brass knocker to announce my presence. I had to do it twice, but eventually, the door opened. An older woman with a gravy-spattered apron stared at me. "Yes?"

The abrupt greeting caught me off guard, but I recovered and handed her a card. "I'm lookin' into the murder of Marian Carstairs. The family across the street? I was told Mrs. Babbage might be able to help me."

The woman, prob'ly a cook, took the card. "She won't see you. She never admits visitors. And she didn't like Miss Carstairs. Don't look for help in that matter."

"I think she might. She beckoned to me through the front window." *Why didn't she like Marian?*

"You must have imagined it. No sense wasting your time, dearie. Or mine. She's a sad, bitter old woman." The cook pushed at the door.

I stopped it with my hand. "Please. Ask her?"

The cook paused, then shook her head. "I will, but don't be surprised if she sends you away with a flea in your ear." She stood back to let me in, then bustled off. She returned less than a minute later. "I don't know what you did, but she said to come in. And mind you, wipe your feet first."

I obeyed and followed the cook to the front room. A heavyset, elderly woman dressed completely in black occupied the chair near the front window. Three picture frames, two of which were wrapped with a black ribbon, were on a small table near her elbow.

She stared at me, expression unreadable. "Leave us."

The cook hesitated. "Are you sure, ma'am?"

Mrs. Babbage turned a withering glance on her. "I'm quite sure. Bring tea. And any cookies or cake we might have."

After the cook left, I faced my hostess. "You asked me in, didn't you?"

She folded her hands across her ample stomach. "I've seen you coming in and out of the Carstairs house." She sniffed.

I noticed she didn't ask me to sit. "I'm lookin' into the death of Marian Carstairs, among other things."

"Awful family. Rude, proud, no manners to speak of. The only one who was half-decent is the youngest son, and even he had the poor taste to get involved with one of the maids."

She *did* know everything. She never left the window, but somehow, she had her finger in all the pies. I didn't know whether to be impressed or jealous. Maybe a little of both.

The cook returned with a tray of tea things. She set it on the table. "Will there be anything else, ma'am?"

Mrs. Babbage waved her away. Then she pointed at the couch. "Sit. Looking up hurts my neck."

I took my seat, careful to keep my back straight and my legs crossed at the ankle. Bein' as ladylike as possible could only help.

My hostess held out a cup. "Help yourself to sugar if you want it. My cook is excellent with coupon trading."

"No, thank you. I drink it black." I took my cup. It was a delicate china thing, not the sturdy ceramic mug I preferred, but I heard my mother whispering in my ear to be polite.

Mrs. Babbage poured her tea and stirred in a tiny spoonful of sugar. "Who are you? You don't look like you belong in this neighborhood."

I ignored the insult. "My name is Betty Ahern." I handed her a card.

She arched an eyebrow. "A private detective? What is the world coming to?"

"Hey, if the men are gonna go off and fight, the women have to step up, right?"

"Indeed." She handed it back. "Do you know why I called you in?"

"No, ma'am. But I sure would like to know."

She gave a small smile as she sipped her tea. "I have very little to do these days. The comings and goings interest me."

"Even when they concern a family you don't much like?"

"Especially then." She studied me. "What are you doing at the Carstairs house?"

I thought about how much to say. "I'm investigating Marian Carstairs's death."

"Isn't that the police department's job? I saw them visiting the house earlier." She eyed me. "Do you think they suspect Theodore? I read they already arrested a man."

The way she said it, I got the idea she was lookin' for my confirmation. "Yes. To all your questions."

"You don't believe them."

"Not a bit."

She tilted her head. "Why not?"

"I just don't." I weighed my words and decided to take a gamble. "Tell you what. Do you think Theo Carstairs is a killer?"

"I haven't talked to him in years. People change." She held up a finger. "However, the boy I knew would not take someone's life. Not in cold blood."

"What if I said you could help me prove that?"

A gleam of satisfaction came into her eye. "I'm an old woman, Miss Ahern. I never leave my window."

"You're a busybody." I waited for her to protest. "Give me the dope, and maybe I'll return the favor."

She studied me for a good long while. Finally, she said, "Okay, Miss Ahern. I'll help you. What is it you want to know?"

I wanted to sigh in relief, but I held it in. "Yesterday morning. Did you see Private Lake?"

"I didn't know his name then, of course, but yes. He appeared to have words with Evans, but then went inside."

I took out my notebook. "That's pretty far away."

"I have good eyesight. Besides, men are very obvious when they argue. It didn't come to blows, but Evans was not happy. Of course, he never is, horrid man."

Was there anybody in the Carstairs house Mrs. Babbage did approve of? "Why do you say that?"

She sniffed. "He's a sneak and a liar. Last year, he claimed my driver had backed into a tree that used to stand near the apron of their driveway. Fiddlesticks. With all the rationing, the only time I take that car out is to go to church on Sunday, so he couldn't have hit a tree on Wednesday."

Given my experience with Evans, the story didn't surprise me. "Back to Private Lake. Did you see him leave?"

"Yes, it was maybe fifteen minutes later. No more than twenty. He appeared to be agitated and strode off in the opposite direction."

"I don't s'pose you saw his face or anything."

She smiled. "My eyesight isn't *that* good. If you're wondering if he had blood on his clothes or hands, I'm afraid I can't tell you."

Drat. "What time was this?"

"Late morning. Mrs. Mills had taken away my tray."

Then Private Lake had not gone directly to see Marian. It would've been better if he'd rushed off immediately after leaving Teddy's. By waiting, they'd say he knew exactly what he was gonna do. "I'm told all the staff was out.

Did you see 'em?"

"Yes. The housekeeper, Mrs. Vance, left early to do her shopping, as usual. The younger girl, I think she's the remaining maid, left around midmorning."

"And Evans, when did he leave?"

"Evans didn't go anywhere."

Oh really? "Are you sure?"

Mrs. Babbage drew herself up. "Quite. I keep a sharp eye out for that man." She set down her tea. "Evans opened the door to admit Private Lake. That much I saw. I didn't see him again until late afternoon when the police arrived."

So much for Evans's claim he'd been out of the house. "Did anybody else visit the Carstairs home?"

"A young woman came late morning. I say young, but really, she was perhaps in her forties. Not a society woman. Neatly dressed but out at the elbows, I'd wager. The dress was years out of fashion. I don't know who let her in, but she left about half an hour later."

I needed to write this down. I looked about for a place to put my teacup, set it back on the tray, and pulled out my notebook. "You've never seen her before?"

"No."

"Was that everyone?"

"Yes. Well, I saw the man who delivers the mail. But I don't think that's who you care about."

"No, ma'am." I scanned what I'd written. "You don't much care for Evans. Is it 'cause of what you said earlier?"

"He's no gentleman's servant, that's for sure." She gazed out the window. "Ten years he's worked for that family and never once had a kind word for anyone. He was horrid to my boys when they were younger."

I looked up. "I'd heard he's worked for the family for twice that."

"See? A liar through and through."

Why would Evans exaggerate? "Tell me about the Carstairs family."

"I didn't know the oldest boy well." She settled her bulk back in her chair. "He seemed polite enough, although a bit stiff. His father was arrogant and cruel. He was connected to the steel industry and thought that made him special. Marian took after her father. She had a young man once. He married someone else and was forever grateful for it."

It wasn't quite the story I'd gotten from Hazel. "Marian was jilted?"

"I don't know that I'd go that far." She selected a cookie from the tray. "After Anthony died, Mr. Carstairs took on a protegé, a young man named Robert. Why he didn't rely on poor Theodore, I'll never know. The boy was profligate, true, but had he been given some responsibility, he might have shaped up fine." She sighed.

I'd never heard the word *profligate*. Based on what everybody said about Theo, I guessed it had something to do with his playboy lifestyle.

Mrs. Babbage continued. "Anyway, Marian took a fancy to Robert. The rumor was he turned her down. The funny thing is he continued to work for Mr. Carstairs for many years. I did hear they eventually parted company. I was surprised the elder Carstairs didn't turn him out immediately, for rejecting Marian. She always was a shrew. I haven't talked to her often in the last few years, but even back then, she had a hard edge to her."

"Do you know anything about her going away?"

"Only what was generally known. Which was all poppycock, if you ask me. I think she went away to escape the embarrassment of not getting engaged after the event had been predicted. Too proud, I tell you." She sniffed. "As if no other girl had ever been passed over by a man."

For an old woman at a window, Mrs. Babbage sure knew a lot. 'Course, if this is all she had to do all day, look out a window and watch people, it wasn't surprising. "Did Theo really fall in love with Marian's maid, Noemi?"

Mrs. Babbage finished her cookie and brushed crumbs from her bosom. "He was the only decent one in the family, in my opinion. Always had a kind word when I saw him on the street. Yes, he was smitten with Noemi, and she with him. Theodore looked out for my boys after their father died, almost like an older brother. He was heartbroken when Noemi was sent away, her pregnant and everything."

I gave her a sharp look. "You know that for a fact?"

Her answering look was indignant. "I certainly do. Noemi was friends with a young girl I employ. She worked full-time back then. Now she only does for me in the afternoon. She came to visit, Noemi, I mean. I heard them in the kitchen." Mrs. Babbage folded her arms. "I almost said something, but I didn't think it was my place. Considering what happened to her and the child, them dying, I regret that. Carstairs should have let his son be happy. Who cares if the girl wasn't from a so-called good family? Life is too short." She touched her dead son's picture.

Ha, she doesn't know everything. Private Lake's appearance told me Noemi could also be alive. "I imagine Theo was crushed."

"Something in him died when she left." She looked at me. "Arrogant and cruel, Miss Ahern. Remember that. Both of them, the elder Carstairs and his daughter. You will reap what you sow. That's what the Bible tells us. You mark my words. That's exactly what happened to Marian Carstairs."

We sat in silence for a couple minutes while I reviewed my notes.

Mrs. Babbage broke the silence. "Well, Miss Ahern? I held up my end of the bargain. Do you have anything to tell me?"

Should I? Why not? "You liked Theo. What about Noemi?"

"She was a sweet girl."

I leaned forward. "What if I told you their son was alive?"

Judging from her answering grin, I'd given her pure gossip gold. "And his mother?"

"I don't know, but I'm gonna find out."

She nodded in satisfaction. "You do that, Miss Ahern. And if you need to ask me any more questions, my door will be open."

Chapter Twenty-Four

Mrs. Babbage wouldn't let me leave until I promised to tell her how everything turned out with my "poor young man." Even though it was five o'clock, my first stop was a drugstore with a payphone to call Sam. I knew he'd be workin' late considering the fact he had a murder to solve. "Sam, I don't have enough nickels to tell you the whole story, but I got a lead for you." I told him what I'd learned.

"A middle-aged woman in plain dress, huh?" The crinkle of paper came over the line. "This the Babbage address?" He read it off.

"Yes."

"Looks like there wasn't anyone home when we visited. Thanks for the tip." He mumbled under his breath. "The old lady didn't give you a better description?"

"No, she woulda been too far away. But if Evans wasn't there, like he claims, who let her in?"

"Spoken like a true detective." A note of approval sounded in Sam's voice.

"I have another lead for you." I told him about Evans and his fibs. "Marian woulda been thirty or thereabouts when he came to work for her. Why'd he say he's known her since girlhood?"

"Good point. I'll look into him." Sam paused. "Will you be at Teddy's tomorrow morning?"

"I dunno. I've got a few things to check out."

"One of these days, you're going to tell me about your private and what's up with him."

"I will. As soon as I think it's safe." I ended the call with Sam and used another nickel to call home and let them know I'd be late.

What else did I need to do? I had to talk to Evans. He'd lied to me. Why? And who exactly was he, anyway? I remembered what Lee had said about the engraving. Maybe Mr. Dumonde could tell me something about that, even if he hadn't done the work himself. If his store was open at this hour.

I wondered if I should visit Private Lake again now that I knew who his parents were. Between what Theo and Mrs. Babbage had told me, it was as good as a birth certificate. No, I'd put that off until I knew what had happened to Noemi. That way, I could tell the whole story.

Sam was gonna dive into Evans's background. I would, too, but I couldn't do anything until tomorrow. I glanced at my watch. It was a little after five. Dumonde's store might be closed. But since it was kinda on my way back to the First Ward, I decided to stop.

The jeweler was locking his door when I arrived. "I'm glad I caught you. I wanted to ask you another question about the St. Christopher medal."

He pocketed his keys. "I've already told you everything I know. I am on my way home. Come back on Monday."

I plucked at his sleeve as he stepped away. "Monday might be too late. Please. All I need is five minutes."

He pulled away.

"There's a soldier sittin' in jail charged with murder. I gotta get his name cleared so he can go back to his duty. I swear, this won't take long."

"I'm sorry, no."

"Here's the deal." I spilled everything about Private Lake and Noemi, and Theo Carstairs, including the thwarted love affair. "My client has grown up without parents. Noemi, she's almost your countrywoman, right? Same language? Aren't most French romantics at heart? You gotta help me."

Mr. Dumonde sighed. "Paris is the city of love, this is true. But we Frenchmen also like to keep our wives happy. And that means being home on time."

I put on my best pleading look. "If you're late, I'll call your wife and tell her it was my fault."

He shook his head, but he took his keys out of his pocket. "Come in. I can spare five more minutes, no more." He flipped on the lights. "What is it you want to know?"

I handed him the St. Christopher. "When I was here before, you said this was old. What about the engraving on the back? Is there any way to tell when that was done?"

"You ask the impossible." But he took the chain and fetched his jeweler's loupe. He ran his thumb over the engraving, all the while making *hmm* noises and murmuring in French.

"Well?" I didn't want him to use up all my precious time examining the thing and walk out without giving me an answer.

"I am thinking, yes, maybe, possibly, the engraving was done well after the medal was cast." He handed it back. "But I cannot be sure. I do not do this kind of work, you understand."

It was one of the most unhelpful responses I'd ever gotten from a source. I took the jewelry back. "Do you know anyone who does?"

He took a notepad and scribbled a few names. "Here. These are men I know who do jewelry engraving. At least they did. You may have luck with them." He put away his loupe. "You are still looking for your missing woman, yes?"

"I am." I slipped the names in my purse. "I'm pretty sure I know who she is, and I know who her lover was. That's not enough. I want to know what happened to her. This may be one way to do that."

"I wish you success." Mr. Dumonde led me out of the store, and he once again locked his door. "You are quite right, Miss Ahern. Not all Frenchmen are romantics. But I am. I wish you success in finding the mademoiselle. *Bonne chance.*"

* * *

I made it to Teddy's with five minutes to spare. I took a seat in my usual booth and ordered two cups of coffee. I was starved, but I didn't know if Mrs. Vance would want to eat. Chowing down in front of her didn't feel very professional. I told my stomach to sit tight and waited.

And waited some more.

When it got to be ten to seven, I decided Mrs. Vance wasn't coming. I'd drunk both cups of coffee. The woman wouldn't want stone-cold java. I gathered my things to leave when I heard the chimes above the door tinkle. I looked over.

Mrs. Vance, her cheeks pink, hurried toward me. "I'm sorry I'm late. I almost didn't come."

I resumed my seat. "Why not?"

"I thought it would be disrespectful. Disloyal, even. I've worked for the Carstairs family for a long time. I thought telling their secrets would be a betrayal of their trust." She set her pocketbook down beside her and ran her fingers over the table.

The evening waitress came over. "Coffee? Do you want a menu?"

"A cup of tea, if you please." Mrs. Vance straightened the salt and pepper shakers. "A slice of lemon and a little milk."

"You got it." The waitress looked at me, but at my slight head shake, she bounced off.

I got out my notebook and pencil. "What changed your mind?"

Mrs. Vance traced patterns on the tabletop with her finger and didn't meet my gaze. "Noemi. That poor girl. She deserved better. From the Carstairs family and from me. I didn't stand up for her then. I owe it to her to do so now."

I flipped to a clean page. "How can you owe somethin' to someone after she's dead?"

Mrs. Vance's head jerked up. "Oh, no, I mean…I heard the story from Mr. Carstairs. I only meant, well, I don't know exactly *what* I meant, except this is my chance to do the right thing."

"Why don't you start at the beginning?" I set down my pencil and prepared myself for a long, wandering story.

However, Mrs. Vance proved to be direct once she got started. "Noemi was quite young when she was hired. Barely seventeen, if I recall. Everybody in the family loved her."

"Some more than others."

She blushed. "Well, yes. Mr. Theodore and Noemi. They tried to keep it quiet. But anybody with two eyes could tell they were deeply in love."

"How did Marian feel about that?"

Mrs. Vance shifted in her seat. "Much like her father did. That is to say, she was not happy. As nice as Noemi was, she was a servant."

I knew the tune. "And even though Theo was a second son, there'd be expectations for him. I get the impression old Mr. Carstairs had definite opinions on who were worthy matches."

"Exactly."

I had heard this before. I wanted her to skip to the part where Noemi was sent away. But I also didn't want to be rude. "You overheard me with Mr. Theodore. I think I have a pretty good handle on what happened. Did he leave anything important out?"

She smoothed the tabletop. "No. Not from what I overheard."

"Did she tell you about the baby?"

"She didn't, not at first." Mrs. Vance's voice held a note of sadness. "She didn't trust me, not then. I believe she confided in a fellow maid, one employed by Mrs. Babbage, who lives across the street. Of course, once it was out, I learned of it. I helped her as best I could. She tried to hide her condition, but that was not possible for long. As soon as Mr. Carstairs found out, she was dismissed. Especially once it was known who the father was."

I leaned forward. "Then he knew. About Theo."

"Oh yes."

"Noemi didn't go away with Marian?"

"Mr. Carstairs forbade it. He told her the whole story after she returned. I was a little surprised he didn't come up with some fabrication, but she has long been his favorite. Even before Anthony died." She stopped and pressed her lips together.

Mrs. Babbage was right. Marian had gone for a cure over a broken heart. "Was that the last time you saw Noemi?"

Mrs. Vance lifted her head. "Oh no. I continued to visit her frequently. We became close. She was the daughter I never had. In fact, I was in attendance when her son was born. Such a beautiful child. Babies are rather like wrinkled dolls when they first come into the world, but the boy was lovely from the start."

"Yet she gave him away. Why?" And how did she afford to live?

Mrs. Vance squirmed. "I…I don't like to say."

But you know. "Ma'am, you've been a good employee for a lot of years and kept this secret. I appreciate that. But think of your friend, the girl you called almost a daughter. Think of Mr. Theodore. If you love them, tell me what you know."

She closed her eyes, and her lips moved in silent speech. A prayer of some kind? Finally, she opened her peepers. "You must understand. Noemi was desperate. She tried to get another job, but she was a single, pregnant girl. The most she could obtain were odd jobs, and as her pregnancy progressed, she was able to do less and less hard work. The money was a godsend. Even if it did come with a price."

I had a suspicion I knew what that had been, but I wanted to hear it. "Go on."

She seemed to make a decision. "Mr. Carstairs offered her a generous sum as payment. But she had to go away, cut all ties with Theo, and give the baby up for adoption. A few days after the birth, he came and paid her off. He took the child. He wouldn't say where. Noemi wasn't allowed to know."

"But she gave him her St. Christopher medal."

Mrs. Vance nodded. "To protect him on his journey."

"Did you know it was engraved?"

Her expression was blank. "I know nothing about that. She said it had been handed down through her family."

If Theo had loved her as much as Mrs. Vance claimed, it could be he had it engraved for his lover as a gift. "When was the last time you saw Noemi?"

"That night." She wiped her cheeks, tears leaking from her eyes. "I went back on my next day off. The room was empty. The landlord didn't know where she'd gone. Mr. Carstairs had paid for it, you see."

"But she didn't die."

She refused to meet my gaze. "Not in childbirth and not before she left the tenement. I haven't heard hide nor hair of her."

Her words rang false. I believed she hadn't seen Noemi, but she knew more than she was lettin' on. I pushed my notebook to her. "Write down the address, please."

She did and handed it back. "Is that all?"

"Two more things. Miss Marian. Why did she go away?" I wasn't quite sure why I wanted to know, 'cept that it was more background on Marian and might relate to her murder, even twenty years later.

Mrs. Vance drew a line, though. "No, I won't tell you that. It's private information. I'll help you find Noemi, if possible, for Mr. Theo's sake, but I won't besmirch the Carstairs family."

It wasn't an unexpected response, but it was frustrating. "Last question. How long has Evans worked for the Carstairses?"

She blinked at the sudden change in topic. "Evans? Oh, ten years, maybe? No more than that. The stock market had crashed a few years previously. Our old butler left to go back to his family in Pennsylvania, and there was some discussion about the advisability of hiring another one."

"I see. Well, thanks for the help. If you change your mind about talkin' about Marian, or if you remember anything else about Noemi, please call me."

She stood. "I wish I could help you more."

She could, but I didn't think it was worth sayin' that. Instead, I thanked her again, and she left.

I ordered another cup of coffee and thought about what I'd learned. I'd visit the last place Noemi had been seen tomorrow. It was a holiday, but no matter. Someone would be there.

Chapter Twenty-Five

When I got back to the First Ward, the sun was lower in the sky, but there was at least an hour of light left. Mary Kate ran up to greet me, trailed by Cat. "I've been waitin' for you, Betty. We saved you some supper. You got this." She held out a red-and-blue striped V-mail envelope.

Finally, mail from Tom! I checked the postmark. It had been sent in early May. I wondered if the censors had marked it up a lot, 'cause it felt like it had taken longer than usual to arrive. I ruffled my sister's hair. "That's swell. I'm gonna go see Dot first."

My sister fell into step beside me. "Is it about your case? You can talk to me, you know. What does Tom have to say?"

"I haven't opened the letter yet." So many questions. My sister was sixteen, but as curious as when she was much younger. She wasn't old enough to discuss murder, though. "I need to ask Dot something. I promise I'll tell you all about the letter when I get home."

"Okay." She skipped off. I smiled. In front of a boy, Mary Kate would act quite different. At home, she was still a kid.

I ripped open the letter and read.

Dear Betty,

I finally have a quiet moment to write. I hope everything is good with you and you're staying out of trouble. I mean with your detecting. I got a letter from Lee, and I think you've been holding out on me a little. You're not "solving puzzles". You're hunting killers. And it's put you in danger. More than once.

I gotta be honest. I don't know how I feel about that. When..."

A big chunk of what he'd written was blacked out. His writing continued at the end of the paragraph.

...I could think of you safe at home. But were you? And when I return, and we get married, will I be sitting at home, wondering where you are and if you're okay?

I can't stop you while I'm here, and I know you better than to expect you will. But please, Betty. Think of us and our future, will you?

Stay my girl,

Tom

I looked at the second paragraph and the thick black lines where the censor had struck out the words. Tom must've really been upset. He was usually a lot more careful. His response didn't shock me. Deep down, I'd known he'd worry about me. I re-read the letter. This time, my eyes caught on Lee's name. What had he said?

Cat decided to follow me. I knocked on the door of the Kilbride house. "Wanna take a walk?" I asked when Dot answered.

"Goin' out with Betty," she called over her shoulder. Before her folks answered, she closed the door.

"What happened to askin' permission?" At this hour, I was used to Dot looking for approval before she went out.

She tossed her curls. "I'm nineteen. I'm not goin' to a dance. I'm takin' a stroll with my best friend." She looped her arm through mine.

Gettin' together with Lee had changed her. "I was gonna stop by the Tillotson house, too. Lee's got some explainin' to do." I thrust out the letter.

She read it, lip caught between her teeth. "Now, Betty, don't flip your wig. I'm sure this is a misunderstanding. Lee wouldn't snitch on you."

"What else could it mean? He told Tom everything, even though he knew I didn't want to worry Tom with all the gritty details."

"Well, I don't know. But stay calm and let Lee explain."

I grabbed the letter back. "He's my best friend. How could he do this to me?"

"Because he's Tom's best friend, too."

She had a point. But I'd helped Lee, doggone it. I saved his bacon from a lifetime in the pokey or worse. His thanks was to run behind my back and tell tales, which I'm sure were exaggerated, to my fiancé?

Cat gave his most pitiful *meow*.

She scooped him up. "You don't like it when we argue, do you kitty?"

He nuzzled her chin, then gave me a feline glare.

"Traitor," I muttered.

We found Lee in his backyard, finishing up some chores. He told his mother he was goin' out with us. We made our way to Conway Park. Dot dropped Cat for her boyfriend's embrace. *As it should be*, I thought, watching them out of the corner of my eye. They could be sappy sweet together, but mostly, they kept it in check in front of me. I didn't forget my anger at Lee, but seein' my two friends happy did soften it a tiny bit. But only a smidge.

Cat was less impressed and stalked over to me.

"What's shakin', Betty?" Lee asked when we got to the park. He lit a cigarette and held out his lighter for me to do the same.

"I have a bone to pick with you. What do you think you're doin', ratting me out to Tom?"

"I don't know what you mean."

"Maybe this'll jog your memory." I handed him Tom's letter.

As he read, he had the grace to blush. "I told him the truth. About my dad. Face it, you've gotten yourself in some tight spots."

"I've wiggled outta them. You make it sound like I'm regularly held at gunpoint or worse."

"I figured you'd brag to Tom every chance you got. About how clever you'd been and stuff." He folded the paper and handed it back. "I told you ages ago. I promised Tom I'd look after you. I had to make sure he knew that I always have your back when you were off bein' Sam Spade, and I'd at least tried to keep my word."

I stepped closer. "I'm no damsel in distress, Lee. I don't need savin'. I'm half-tempted to cut you out of the loop."

"I never said you needed saving." Lee also took a step. We were almost nose to nose. His voice rose. "But I ain't gonna stand by and let you get into scrapes, and I ain't gonna lie to Tom about it."

CHAPTER TWENTY-FIVE

"You know, Frank thinks I can do this. He said—"

"Frank Hicks?" Lee was so close, I could smell the smoke on his breath. "Don't tell me you're still seein' that smooth-talkin', yellow-bellied conchie. I got a limp, but don't think I can't turn you over the knee on this bum leg and give you a whoopin'. You got a ring on that finger, and don't you forget it."

Dot squeezed between us. "Stop it, you two." She pushed us apart. "Lee, you are not going to spank Betty like she's a child. Betty, you're not going to keep Lee in the dark. You both know it. Quit being childish. And there's no reason to bring Frank Hicks into this." She shot me a warning look.

Lee looked at the grass and scuffed his foot. I hoped I didn't look as embarrassed. What I'd told Dot about Frank and my feelings was between us girls, and I'd nearly blown it.

"Are we square?" Dot waited. "Now, apologize."

While I was tryin' to find words, Lee beat me to it. "Betty, I really did think you told Tom everything."

"I did mostly, but I didn't want him to worry. I never said anything about all the scrapes." The sight of my oldest friend looking like a humbled schoolboy stabbed me. "Sorry. I shouldn't have yelled at you. You're no tattle-tale."

He raised his eyes. "Why are you runnin' around with Frank Hicks?"

I snuck a quick look at Dot, who held up her hands. "He's the one who sent Private Lake to me. I had to interview him." The memory twisted my gut. Frank's smile, his dimple. Deep brown eyes that I got lost in every time. More important, his belief in me. *He'd never write a letter like Tom's.* I pushed that aside. "I haven't seen him since. I swear. It was all business."

Lee took a deep breath and held out his hand. *"Pax?"*

I pulled him in for a hug.

Dot gave a satisfied nod, like she'd won a major victory. Which she had, if I was honest. "Now, tell us what you did today."

"I found Christopher Lake's mother. For certain, this time." I told them about Theo and Noemi and what I'd learned from Mrs. Babbage and Mrs. Vance as Cat wound himself around my ankles.

Dot spoke first. "How sad. Like that play by Shakespeare."

Of course, Lee knew right off what she meant. *"Romeo and Juliet?"*

"Yes." She plopped down on the grass. "Two lovers, kept apart by their families. At least Theo might get to know his son. You know, if Betty can clear Private Lake for his aunt's murder."

I tapped ash from my smoke. "Not only that, I'm not sure Noemi is dead." She cocked her head. "You're not?"

"Think about it. She got paid a lot of dough by the old Mr. Carstairs to vamoose. Part of me is mad she abandoned her son, but part of me understands. In the twenties, it woulda been tough for her to get hired with a baby in tow. If she'd kicked the bucket, you'd think one of her friends would have heard." Or if she'd gotten married, if she'd given up on Theo.

Lee clamped his gasper between his lips. "Can I see that St. Christopher again?"

I handed it to him.

"The jeweler figures the engraving is newer?"

"He said maybe it was." I told Lee about my visit with Mr. Dumonde. "He gave me some names of people who might know, but I'm wonderin' if it's even important. That's a lover's inscription, not a parent's. My money is on Theo getting the medal engraved for Noemi."

"Why not give her something else?" Dot pulled up tufts of grass. "A religious medal isn't exactly romantic."

"Maybe he couldn't." I flicked away my cigarette and flung myself down next to her. Cat curled up in my lap, and I stroked his back. "I think it was hers. If they were tryin' to hide their relationship from his family, he wouldn't give her somethin' flash or a Carstairs heirloom. But he could engrave a piece she already had. Then she passed it on to Private Lake before he went to the orphanage."

Dot nodded slowly, following my words. "Why did Mr. Carstairs take the baby?"

Lee pitched away his spent cigarette. "To make sure it happened. Noemi coulda taken the cabbage and run with the baby. Old Man Carstairs woulda wanted to make sure she kept the deal. The rat."

"He doesn't sound like a nice man, that's for sure." Dot sounded like a prim miss as she gave her opinion.

I pulled up a dandelion. "There's more." I told them what I'd learned about the woman visitor, Robert Newcombe, and Evans. The butler interested them the most.

"It's such a dumb lie." Lee leaned against a tree and rubbed his bum leg. "As soon as anyone asked they'd know he hadn't worked for the Carstairses that long."

"Thing is, I'm not sure it *is* a lie." I tickled Cat's nose with the fluffy yellow petals of the weed. He sneezed and batted it away.

"What do you mean?"

"I've been thinkin' about his behavior, and something's wrong. He's too..." I searched for the word. "Cocky. As though he think's he's the one in charge."

Lee eased himself down to the ground. "Isn't that his job as a butler? To run the household?"

"It's more than that. I don't know. It's hard to explain. But that's the impression I got when he talked to Marian. Like he was puttin' one over on her." Of that, I was sure. Thinking back over my first visit with the pair, I realized I'd felt a thinly veiled hostility from Evans where Marian was concerned. There was a story there. "I need to find out more about him."

"How are you gonna do that?"

"I don't know. I'll ask Sam." I popped the head off the dandelion. Cat leapt after it. "I hate waiting, though. Not only is it a weekend, it's a holiday. Nothing will be open." Sunday was the Fourth of July. I didn't feel much like celebrating, not with Tom and Sean in a war, and God knew where. I didn't want to go to a parade, with all the flag waving, or to a movie where I'd have to see tributes before the picture. Pop would be workin', so I knew my family wasn't planning much. The younger kids would have sparklers for the night, but rationing made a picnic almost impossible. No, I'd rather spend my time workin' my case than mopin' around, worrying about my loved ones.

Dot musta sensed my thoughts 'cause she reached over and squeezed my hand. "You're stuck until Monday?"

"Nope." I tossed away the headless dandelion stem, got to my feet, and brushed grass from my backside. "I'm gonna keep lookin' for Noemi. I've got her last address, and apartment managers aren't off 'cause of a weekend, holiday or not." I grinned at my friends. "If you don't have to work, how'd you like to tag along?"

They both clambered to their feet, Lee a little awkwardly. He slung an arm around each of us. "Sure. Someone's gotta keep you out of trouble."

Chapter Twenty-Six

Saturday dawned with a perfect blue sky and a day that promised to be warm, but not too hot. I dressed in a pair of blue jeans left over from my days of working at Bell and a simple white short-sleeve blouse. I expected I'd be doing a lot of walking, so I pulled out my scuffed but comfortable Mary Janes. I thought about wearing a light sweater but ditched the idea. I might be cool now, but it'd warm up, and I didn't want to lug it all over Buffalo.

I met Dot and Lee at the bus stop. She was dressed a lot like me, 'cept she'd added a bandanna to hold back her curls. Lee looked like he did on a workday, squashy newsboy cap and all. Both had also skipped jackets. "You ready for a long day?" I asked.

Dot's eyes shone with enthusiasm. "Just like old times."

Lee consulted the posted schedule. "Where are we goin'?"

I gave him the address on Normal Avenue. "Mrs. Vance said that's where Noemi gave birth. I hope we'll get a lead from there."

Once we were on the bus, Lee swung himself sideways to look at me. "I was thinkin' last night about Robert Newcombe. You said he was the golden boy after Mr. Carstair's eldest son died, right?"

"That's what I've been told."

"Here's my question. His wife made it sound like he'd been cut off somehow, and the reason was 'cause he married Hazel. That line about 'his due.' But he worked for the company for a long time, you said. So whatever it is, or was, it can't be about jilting the boss's daughter. Old Man Carstairs woulda kicked him to the curb back in the early twenties. What else coulda happened?"

"I don't know a lot about it, to be honest. Guess I should find out."

"And if Marian was really involved with him *and* who woulda cared about it. How'd he die?"

He was right. "He committed suicide. But I don't see how it would matter now."

Lee crossed his arms and gave me a lopsided grin. "Bitterness doesn't blow over quickly, Betty. It coulda festered. If Hazel Newcombe thinks Marian owes her something 'cause of whatever happened in the past, maybe she lost her temper."

It didn't feel strong enough to me. But it was the seed of an idea. "We'll look into it."

Dot, who sat next to me, pulled her gaze away from the window. "I only got today off, Betty. I gotta go to work on Monday."

"I was talkin' about Emmeline."

"Oh. Right." She shot a sideways glance at Lee, who gave a tiny shake of his head. "What's the plan when we get to the apartment?"

"First, we cross our fingers and hope the manager hasn't died and the current one knows how to find him. It's been so long I don't think the same man is workin' there. Then we hope even harder that he, or someone who lives there, has a clue about where Noemi went after she left."

Lee took off his cap, brushed back his hair, and tugged it back on. "That's a lot of hoping. It sounds to me like you're winging it."

I spread my hands. "What can I say? I kinda am."

He shifted to lean back against his seat and closed his eyes. "I wish you the best, Betty. But I'll keep my job at GM, thanks. At least there, I know exactly what I'm doin.'"

Dot clambered over me to sit with her beau. She whispered in his ear. He murmured something in return.

What were they tryin' to hide? "All right, you two. Spill."

Dot heaved a sigh and faced me. "It's like this. After you left last night, Lee and I got to talkin' and, well, we aren't sure there's a place for us in this whole detection thing."

My jaw dropped. "What? How can you say that? I was gonna include you in the firm."

Dot's lip trembled.

Lee moved her outta his line of sight. "Betty, be reasonable. It's not that we don't like you. Or that we don't enjoy when you ask us for help. But be logical."

He would be that.

"First, Dot and I have jobs. We aren't available all the time."

"You'd be part of the gig, I told you."

He waved his hand. "When will that be? You can't even afford to pay Emmeline or rent an office. It's bad business, addin' employees when you can't pay 'em."

"Lee, I—"

"Second." He held up a finger, warning me not to speak. "Yes, we came today. But this isn't our idea of fun, Betty. We were gonna go to the beach and then catch the new picture with Claire Trevor and Edgar Buchanan."

"*Good Luck, Mr. Yates,*" Dot said.

My cheeks warmed. "Then why'd you come?"

"'Cause you asked." Lee's voice stayed patient. "But this isn't what we wanna do full time. We're happy to help, but detecting is your game."

Dot grabbed Lee's hand. "Plus, we wanna get married and start a family. I can't be a mother and run around Buffalo digging up clues."

The statement didn't surprise me. I'd known deep in my gut my friends were gonna get hitched. They were both right, not that I wanted to admit it. I'd always seen us all together. "I hear you. I understand. But you gotta promise me one thing."

"What?" they said together.

I leaned over the aisle to hug them. "Don't have the wedding until after this case is over."

* * *

We got to the neighborhood on Normal Street early. Kids were in the streets, waving sparklers, even though the holiday wasn't until tomorrow. Many of the boys ran around pretendin' to be soldiers fighting Germans or airplane pilots shooting down Japanese planes. A couple youngsters, maybe six or seven years old, buzzed by me, making rat-a-tat noises.

Dot watched them go. "Do they really think war is fun?"

My mind flashed to Sean and Tom. "Prob'ly. They're too young to know any better."

"Someone oughta tell them." She took a step.

Lee gently tugged on her arm. "Leave 'em be. They got plenty of time to grow up and learn life isn't all fun and games." He would know. He was only nineteen, but Mr. Tillotson had been murdered last spring, which forced my friend into the "man of the house" role before he even had a girlfriend.

We walked halfway down the street, checking house numbers as we went. I stopped in front of a plain building with a small porch and grimy redbrick walls. "This is it."

Dot wrinkled her nose. "Not very fancy. You think Mr. Carstairs coulda done better."

Lee mounted the steps. "His son carried on with the hired help, and she got pregnant. It was a scandal. He wasn't gonna put her up at the Ritz."

Dot followed him. "Maybe not, but this place is downright depressing. What a place to have a baby."

I brought up the rear. I agreed with Dot. It wasn't a happy-looking spot. I wasn't clear if old Mr. Carstairs had merely paid the rent or if he'd picked this run-down neighborhood. It coulda been all that Noemi could afford. 'Course, it mighta looked better twenty years ago, but somehow I doubted it.

Inside, I scanned the dingy hallway for a door marked "manager" or a similar word. "Look down there." I pointed. The last door on the right had the remnants of some letters on the scuffed paint, but enough remained that I could tell it said "supervisor." I knocked.

Dot sidled next to Lee. "Is anyone even home?"

I knocked again. "I s'pose he could be with family, but being a building manager isn't a nine-to-five job."

CHAPTER TWENTY-SIX

"Here, let me." Lee came over and fairly pounded on the wood.

A voice came through the door. "All right, keep your shirt on." It flew open. "What on God's green earth can you want on a Saturday and the day before the Fourth of July at that? Don't tell me the pipes in Mrs. Slattery's kitchen have burst again."

The manager looked younger than I expected, maybe only a year or two past the maximum draft age. His rail-thin body was stringy, but undoubtedly had what Pop would call a wiry strength. His dark, bushy hair flopped over his eyes. He wore a faded undershirt and blue pants held up by black suspenders. As he held the door partially open, I noticed his cuticles, black with dirt. The sound of a radio program filtered from the room behind him. He inhaled on a Chesterfield and blew the smoke at us. "You don't live here. Who are you, and what the heck do you want?"

Dot coughed, and Lee muttered under his breath.

"Are you the building manager?" I asked, fighting the urge to wave my hand in front of my face.

"That's me. We don't got any vacancies. You're interrupting my Saturday morning. You ain't residents, so you ain't bringing me a complaint. Scram." He exhaled another cloud, clearly thinkin' I'd turn tail and run.

I wasn't gonna give him the satisfaction. I handed him a business card. "I'm looking for a woman named Noemi Gerard. At least information about her. This building is the last address I have for her. She'd be memorable. An unmarried girl, Belgian. She gave birth here twenty years ago."

He took the card but didn't look at it. "That was before my time." He tried to close the door.

I stopped him. "Do you know where I can find the manager from back then? This is important."

He sighed. "Yeah, he's sittin' in my living room. My father had the job before I did. But he don't wanna talk to you."

Lee pushed his way forward. "How would you know? You haven't asked."

The stringy manager eyed my friend. "'Cause he's listening to his Saturday radio show, that's how. Besides, the old man is deaf as a post. You ain't gonna get nothing out of him." He stared down Lee.

Lee didn't flinch. "We sure would like to try."

The two men didn't break eye contact. Finally, the manager said, "You oughta be overseas, boy. Why aren't you?"

Again, Lee's expression didn't change. "That's my business. Now, are you gonna call your dad, or do we have to bust in here? Because Betty needs to talk to him, and I'm here to make sure she gets to do what she wants."

For a moment, I thought the manager was gonna slam the door in Lee's face. But he clamped his Chesterfield between his lips. "Suit yourself." He waved us in. "But I'm telling you. He ain't gonna hear but half of what you say unless you have a bullhorn. His hearing is shot." He led us to the front room and clapped the shoulder of an old man sitting in a faded armchair. "Pops! Visitors! Turn that thing down." He walked over to the radio and turned the volume knob to a normal level.

The man in the chair had a face like a walnut. White hair floated around his head like dandelion fuzz. His body was twisted with arthritis, but his dark eyes sparked like hot coals. "Lizards, you say? Why on earth would we have lizards?"

"Not lizards, you old coot. Visitors, guests." The son pointed our way.

But the old man didn't turn his head. "Gusts of what? I didn't think it was that windy."

His son threw up his hands in disgust. "I told you, deaf as a post. Good luck." He stomped off, and a moment later, we heard the door slam.

The old man chuckled.

"Sir, my name is Betty Ahern." I held out my hand and spoke in the same voice I'd used on the floor at Bell, makin' sure to say each word clearly. "These are my friends—"

"Don't shout at me, young lady," he snapped. "I can hear you fine."

Dot appeared flustered. "But your son said..." She appealed to me for assistance.

He cackled. "Serves the young buck right. I do it to annoy him. He's been giving me lip since he was knee-high to a grasshopper. I put up with him for years. It's my turn to have a bit of fun." He sat back. "Have a seat. The furniture is old, but it won't fall apart on you."

Lee and Dot sat on a couch that had definitely seen better days while I perched on a chair next to the old man. "I didn't get your name, sir."

"Don't you call me 'sir.' I worked for a living. Henry Jennings. Folks call me Hank." He gave me a beady-eyed stare. "Betty, huh? Nice plain name. What are you doin' here?"

I introduced my friends and explained our purpose. "I hoped you remembered a little about what happened."

"More than a little." Hank's skinny chest puffed up. "Darn rheumatism's ruined my body, but I've got a mind like a steel trap. I remember the girl. And her whelp."

Dot leaned forward. "What happened to her?"

Hank fixed her with a lewd stare, and she shrank back. "She had her brat, don't know much else. Sweet young thing she was. Looked fit to burst when she showed up on the door. She didn't have much money, but my missus, God rest her soul, took pity on her and rented out our smallest unit on the cheap. She always was a soft touch, no business sense at all. Another woman used to come see the girl, looked like a servant of some kind."

It must have been Mrs. Vance. I took out my notebook. "You said Noemi had the baby here. When?"

"Oh, lemme see." Hank leaned back. "Not long after she came, a month maybe? No more. The other woman, she was here when it happened. Lusty set of lungs that kid had. Woke me up from a sound sleep, and that's sayin' something."

"Do you remember a man? He would have been older, obviously wealthy."

Hank studied the ceiling. "Come to think of it, I do. He showed up a day or so later. Funny, I didn't hear the baby at all after that."

Lee, Dot, and I exchanged looks. "You didn't see him leave with the child?" I asked.

"I don't think so, but I wasn't payin' close attention. None of my business. Why, was it his? Some by-blow of the master's born on the wrong side of the sheets?" Hank's laughter this time was derisive.

"Not exactly." I wasn't sure I liked this man. "What happened to Noemi, the girl?"

"Dunno. She left, oh, 'bout a week after the birth. Soon as she was able to. Packed up her few belongings, left a note and a fiver for the missus, and disappeared." Hank's beady black eyes burned with a light, but not mirth.

Lee broke in. "She didn't die?"

Hank snorted. "Not in this place. Least no one smuggled out a dead body, and they'd have had a hard time doin' that. No, siree. She took that cash and hopped the first train out of Buffalo. That's my guess. She knew how to play the game." He licked his lips. "Too bad, 'cause she was a pretty slip of a thing, even when she was knocked up."

Lee raised his eyebrows. "How do you know he paid her? Do you listen at doors?"

Hank leered. "I told you, she was a cutie. I had a peephole. I saw the swell come in and figured somethin' was goin' on. I watched 'em."

Dot wrinkled her nose. "You thought you'd take advantage of the situation, didn't you?"

"Man's gotta make a living. But I didn't get squat." Hank's voice was nonchalant, like he spied on people all the time. He prob'ly did.

I steered the talk back to the point I'd noticed, letting the suggestive ones slide by me. "But you don't know for sure what she did?"

"Don't know, don't care." Hank returned his gaze to me. "Question is, missy, why do you? She a relative of yours? She owe you money?" He sneered. "Maybe you got another reason for wanting to find her huh? She your mama, too?"

No, I definitely didn't like Hank. I stood. "That's my affair. Thanks for your time. We'll show ourselves out."

Hank threw us a dirty look. "If you pass my son, tell him to get in here and make me some breakfast."

Lee tipped his cap. "We won't."

We left, Hank's howls chasing after us.

Dot drew in a lungful of fresh air once we were outside. "What an awful old man. That was one of the worst-smelling places I've ever been in, including the paint bays at Bell."

"With his wife gone, I don't think he or his son clean very well." Lee

158

scrubbed his hand through his hair and settled his cap. "Noemi didn't die in childbirth. Where would she go? And how are you gonna find out, Betty?"

They were good questions. "I'm gonna take out a few classified ads."

Chapter Twenty-Seven

I had Sam's telephone number from a previous case. Before we left the old apartment building on Normal, I dropped a nickel and called his house to give him notice we were on our way. When we arrived, he was in the backyard, standing over a small grill cooking hotdogs. "I can't believe you called me at home on a weekend." He turned a hotdog and took a drink from a bottle of beer. "What am I saying? Of course, you would. How'd you know I was home? I could have been out working the Carstairs case."

I shrugged. "It was a gamble. If you're comin' up as empty as I am, I figured you'd take the day off."

He pointed to the house. "Beer is in the fridge if you want it."

Lee disappeared into the house.

I sat on the metal lawn chair near the grill. "Sahlen's wieners, right?"

Sam's face took on an offended expression. "Would a Buffalo boy cook anything else?"

Lee reappeared holding three bottles of Iroquois ale. He'd already removed the caps. Dot waved him off, but I accepted one. "I should hope not. You got relish?"

Sam once again turned the hot dogs. "All the fixings are also inside."

Lee looked for a place to set down the other two bottles, but Dot put a hand on his shoulder. "Sit and drink your beer." She looked over at me. "I s'pose you wanna talk to the detective. I'll bring out the spread."

"Thanks." I turned to Sam. "I'm surprised you're cooking all this for yourself."

"I put it on after you called. I won't have much for tomorrow, but that's okay. I'm not hosting a party." He moved the dogs, now the perfect shade of dark brown, off the heat. "I was going to spend a quiet evening in. Maybe listen to the Dodgers game on the radio."

"Sorry about ruining your plans."

Lee eased down to the step. "You know Betty. There's no stopping her once she gets goin'." He clinked his bottle against Sam's.

"Don't I know it." Sam took a long pull from his beer. "What's the emergency this time?"

"It's not so much an emergency as you prob'ly have better sources." I tipped back my drink. "I figured I'd give you some names now and, you could maybe dig into them? After all, they prob'ly affect your investigation too." I rolled the bottle in my hands. "You find any other fingerprints or anything at the murder scene? Beyond what you already told me."

"Oh no. You aren't sharing with me. I'm done sharing with you. I warned you last time." He took the wieners off the grill and put them on a plate.

"I don't want you usin' anything I tell you against my client."

Dot came out of the house carrying paper plates and all the fixin's for our meal. "Betty, c'mon. You know the detective better than that. You want information from him, you gotta play nice."

I nearly dropped my beer. "Whose side are you on?"

"Yours." She deposited the goods on the table. "But be fair. Detective MacKinnon isn't gonna string up Private Lake unless there's proof he did the crime. Are you, Detective?" She turned her sunny face to Sam.

He held up two fingers. "Scout's honor."

I scowled. "Were you even a Boy Scout?"

"Sure was." Sam brought the food to the table. "Made it all the way to Eagle Scout. Do you want to see the award?"

"I'll take your word for it."

Lee limped over to the table and slathered relish on his hotdog. "Dot's right. You can't be all take and no give."

I didn't much like it, but my friends had a good point. My thoughts flashed back to my talk with Mrs. Babbage. *Sometimes, you gotta give a little to get a little.* "Okay, here's the skinny." I ran down the story on Private Lake, including everything we'd learned about Noemi and Theo, and our visit to Noemi's old apartment earlier.

Sam listened without interruption. Then he spoke. "You shouldn't have told him anything, until you were sure. Private Lake, I mean."

"Rub my nose in it, why don't you." I deserved the reproach. "I shoulda kept my yap shut, true. But you don't understand. He was so intense. I was afraid if I didn't give him a scrap, he'd do somethin' stupid."

Lee stopped in the process of bringing his hotdog to his mouth. "Didn't he do exactly that anyway?"

I pointed a finger at him. "He didn't shoot Marian. He dressed up 'cause he was goin' to see the woman he thought was his long-lost mother. He wanted to make a good impression."

"But when it didn't go as planned, he did argue with her loudly enough to be heard and was seen in the neighborhood." He bit the wiener, and relish oozed out.

Sam hadn't touched the food, but he aimed his beer at Lee. "That's what got him arrested. The prosecution will argue that he confronted the woman he thought was his mother, she spurned him, and he shot her out of rage. They'll argue he used the piece that Marian owned. It'll only bolster the whole 'crime of passion' angle."

I couldn't believe what I heard. "He shot her with a pistol that hasn't been fired and doesn't have his prints on it? How does that wash?"

"Easy. He could have left a dummy on the floor and thrown away the gun anywhere after he left the house." Sam held up his hand. "I didn't say that's what I believe. But you can be certain that's the argument the district attorney will make." He paused. "Tell me. What's your opinion of Christopher Lake? His personality, I mean."

"Does it matter?"

"Of course it does. I respect your instincts." He brought the bottle to his lips.

I thought about what I'd learned and how Private Lake acted around me. "He's a kid, really. I mean, sure, he's a grown man, a soldier. But in some ways, he's still a boy. If you're gonna ask me if I think he's capable of murder, sure I do. I've learned anybody is. I think he'd get in a dumb argument, lose his temper, and could kill someone. But shoot them, use a *different* gun, leave a clean decoy, and skedaddle? No, I can't believe it. He doesn't think ahead enough. Every decision he makes, it's like that." I snapped my fingers. "He wouldn't think of the consequences. And I spoke to a woman, a nanny, who saw him after the crime. He played with her boy, calm as anything, although she did say he looked upset. He wouldn't be able to hold it together at all if he'd shot a woman minutes earlier. 'Specially under the circumstances you describe."

Dot piped up. "But the nanny said he was out of sorts."

"He'd been turned away by who he believed was his mother." I studied my wiener. "There's a difference between bein' off-kilter 'cause you had an argument and havin' committed cold-blooded murder less than five minutes earlier."

Sam listened, then nodded. "I agree. I interrogated him before and after he was arrested. Of course, as soon as the JAG lawyer showed up, the private stayed mum. I didn't get the impression he was a world-class criminal." He sighed. "But he argued with the victim, he was there, and based on what you told me, he has a heck of a motive. Spurned by your mother after years of hoping to meet her?"

I rolled Sam's words around in my head. "Your turn. Did you find anything else at the scene?"

"Not much." He went to the table and made up a plate. "I already told you about the gun. They also turned up two sets of unknown fingerprints." He licked mustard off his finger. "

"You should check out Robert and Hazel Newcombe." I explained their connection to Marian. "Robert is dead, suicide. Could be an avenging relative. I also have my suspicions about the butler." I told Sam about Evans and his claims, which had to be false.

Sam fetched a notepad and pencil. He had me repeat the names. "I'll do what I can."

Dot clapped. "I love bein' around you two. It's like living in an Agatha

Christie novel."

Sam and I exchanged a glance. "Better than Dashiell Hammett," I said, biting into my hotdog.

Lee raised an eyebrow. "Why's that?"

I wiped ketchup from my chin. "There are fewer shoot-outs in Mrs. Christie's books."

Chapter Twenty-Eight

I went to early Mass with my family on the Fourth of July. After we got home, the younger kids went out to play with their sparklers. Pop departed for work. Mom retired to the living room for a little quiet time.

I sat on the front porch and thought about my case.

I was still there, smoking, when Dot appeared. "Whatcha doin?" She sat next to me. Cat appeared from outta nowhere and curled up on her lap, where she automatically gave him the attention he demanded.

"I'm planning my next move." I ashed my gasper in the garden.

"It's Sunday. And a holiday. What can you possibly do today?"

"I don't know. But I gotta do somethin'. Private Lake is s'posed to ship out this Friday. He can't do that if he's bein' held in a Buffalo jail cell." I hadn't seen him in three days. The poor guy had to be goin' out of his mind.

Dot ran Cat's tail through her fingers. "Have you told him about his mother and father?"

"Not yet. It feels cruel."

"He needs to know."

"Now?"

She tickled Cat under his chin. "'Specially now. You should try and convince Theo to go see his son, too. I think it would do both of 'em a lot of good. I'll come with you, if you'd like. Lee got called into GM, and my parents don't like the noise on the Fourth. We aren't doin' anything special."

I stood. "Are you sure?"

She set Cat aside. He gave an indignant *meow*, but when she ignored him,

165

he stalked off, tail swishing. "Positive. What else am I gonna do? Sit at home and sew all day? No way."

I let Mom know I was headed out with Dot. We took the bus down to the jail. Lots of women were there to see family members who were behind bars.

When Private Lake came out, I nearly cried. They'd swapped out his uniform for prison duds. There were purplish circles under his eyes. All the spark in him was snuffed out. "Hello, Betty." Even his voice was dull. "Surprised you came to see me."

"'Course I did. They treating you okay?"

He gave me a flat look.

"I mean, okay, considering it's jail and all."

"I guess. I can't decide which chow is worse. On the front or in here." He glanced at Dot. "Who is she?"

I introduced my friend. "She helps me out on occasion."

"Pleased to meet you." Dot held out her hand but withdrew it almost immediately at Private Lake's expression.

"Why are you even here?" he asked in a harsh tone.

"I have an update on your case." I told him about Noemi and Theo.

The emotions flickered across his puss as I talked. "Then the man I saw that day, the murdered woman's brother, he's my dad?"

"Seems that way, yes."

Finally, life came into his eyes, an angry light. "Why didn't he say anything? Why didn't he acknowledge me?"

I laid my hand on his. "Don't get sore at him. He didn't know who you were. He didn't get along with his sister very well." I did not say anything about Theo possibly bein' drunk that early in the morning.

"He thought you were dead." Dot's hands twitched, but she kept them in her lap. "You and your mother. His father and his sister lied to him."

I thought of something. "You saw him?"

Private Lake looked at his hands. "Only for a moment. He was on the stairs. Heading up, I think."

A thought tickled my brain, but it flitted away before I could catch it.

He looked from Dot to me. "Did he find out? I mean, after I left. Did he ask her who I was and why I'd come?"

I bit my lip. "I'm not sure, but he might have."

Understanding dawned behind his peepers. "Then he coulda killed his sister. Right? If he loved my mother, he'd be angry. I would be. But he must not care about me, or why'd he let me get arrested?" His voice rose as he spoke.

The guard looked over at us, hand on his nightstick. "Is there a problem over there?"

"No, sir, we're fine." I laid my finger on my lips. "Quiet down before they throw you back in your cell. I can't answer your questions, at least not right this minute." I paused and shot a look at Dot, who gave me an encouraging nod. "I plan to see him after I leave here. I...would you like him to come and visit? He can tell you about your mom. The two of you can get to know each other a little bit."

Private Lake gave me a flat stare. He looked like he wanted to slug me. Instead, he took a deep breath and stood, hands clenched in white-knuckled fists. "I don't want to see him, not a man who shot his sister and abandoned my mother and me. As far as I'm concerned, he can go to Hell." He returned to the guard, who took him through the door and to the cells.

I stared after him.

"Well." Dot sounded as taken aback as I felt. "That didn't go as planned, did it?"

* * *

From the jail, we traveled to Delaware Park. Festivities there were a bit quieter than the First Ward. No children roamed the streets, but squeals of laughter and the scent of charcoal told me the swells were celebrating in their neatly landscaped backyards. I looked over to the Babbage house. Mrs. Babbage was clearly visible in her front window. Prob'ly keeping an eye out for troublemakers. I waved, and she nodded in return.

I knocked on the door to the Carstairs mansion. After a few minutes,

Theo opened it. There were new lines on his face. Why? The stress of managing things now that his sister was gone? Or something else? "Miss Ahern. I don't mean to be rude, but why are you here?" He looked at Dot. "Who is this?"

I introduced my friend. "Where is Evans?"

"Damned if I know. He said he had an errand to run and left Friday afternoon. No one has seen him since." He pulled at his beard. "Mrs. Vance is trying to hold things together, but the whole household is topsy-turvy. No one is quite sure if he'll be back or when, and I'm answering my own door. All in addition to trying to plan Marian's funeral." In that moment, he looked very much like his son. Completely lost.

My first thought was that Evans's disappearance, especially under the circumstances, was fishy. He lied about how long he'd known his mistress, and now he'd vanished without a trace? But that was a matter for another time. "I came to see you. I, uh, have some news."

He twitched. "About Marian?"

"Not exactly. May we come in? This might be better to talk about somewhere private. Or at least where there are chairs."

He waved us in and directed us to his study. Once there, he went to the bar in the corner and held up a glass bottle. "Would either of you like a bourbon?"

I remembered the burn from my drink in Gladys's office. "No, thank you." I nodded toward a couch across the room, and we sat.

Dot murmured what I assumed was a decline.

He splashed some in a glass and took a seat across from us. "If this isn't about my sister, what can it be? Whatever it is, it's serious. I can tell from your faces."

I wasn't exactly sure how to start, so I jumped right in. "I have some news about Noemi. And her baby."

Theo's hand shook, and some bourbon spilled out of the glass, which had been halfway to his mouth, and into his lap. He ignored it. "What about them? They're dead."

I glanced at Dot, who merely gave a slight twitch of her shoulders. "I'm pretty sure they're alive. Well, your son is, that's definite."

"How do you know?"

"Because he was the young soldier who came to see Marian the day she died." I waited for the words to sink in. "That's who I got the medal from."

It took less time than expected. Theo placed the tumbler on the table next to him with a great deal of care. Then he leaned his forearms on his knees. "Miss Ahern. I'm not in a joking mood. If this is your idea of a prank, you can get out of my house and not come back."

Dot spoke up. "It's not a prank." Theo fixed her with a murderous look, and she squeaked.

"Let me explain." I once again told the story of Private Lake finding and hiring me. I went through everything I'd learned from Mrs. Vance, right up to my visit with Hank, the unsavory building manager.

Theo's body quivered. "Mrs. Vance knew about him? And that Noemi was alive?"

I held out a hand. "Sort of. Now, don't snap your cap. She knew your son had been born. That's it. She said she hasn't seen Noemi since."

His voice dropped further, now holding an unmistakable note of rage. "But she knew where Noemi had gone. About my father and what he did? Where he'd taken my son?"

Oh boy. I hoped Mrs. Vance wasn't gonna pay for her mistake. 'Course, she had withheld the knowledge from Theo for years. She coulda told him the truth on the sly. "I don't think she had the first clue about what happened to Noemi after the baby was born or where your father had taken him. There were a couple of orphanages in Buffalo back then. Still are. Noemi chose to disappear."

He clenched his hands in white-knuckled fists. "I can't believe it. I don't for one second think she'd take the money and run. We loved each other. She would find a way to let me know what happened."

Dot braved speech, even though Theo clearly terrified her. "Maybe she didn't think she had a choice. Maybe your dad threatened her. She was a girl, wasn't she? What did she know? She couldn't raise a baby by herself. Maybe she thought she was doin' what was best for you and your son."

Theo glared at her from beetled eyebrows. "I would have taken care of her."

I'd already seen his anger. I knew I was takin' my safety into my hands, mine and Dot's. But I had to speak. "Why would she have believed that? Had you stood up to your father? Had you said the heck with him, you'd marry Noemi anyway? From what I've learned, you decided to stick with your soft life and knuckle under. Like you always did." I could see my words hit close to home. I continued. "It doesn't matter what happened back then. Your son is sittin' in the Buffalo jail, accused of murder. You should go and see him."

Theo croaked out his words. "Why? What good will it do? I wouldn't be surprised if he hates me. He has every right to."

"You could bail him out and bring him here. Me, I think he's innocent. There are other people involved who have doubts, too." I didn't mention the fact that Theo was a good suspect. His anger could be an act. He might have found out about Private Lake, argued with Marian, and killed her.

But wouldn't he have stepped in to save his son?

Not if he only knew the boy was alive, and Marian hadn't told him Private Lake was that long-lost baby.

Theo didn't say anything. I kept talkin'. "I intend to solve this case, Mr. Carstairs. Theo."

The silence stretched between us. Finally, he stood up. "You do that, Miss Ahern. You find Marian's killer, locate Noemi, or at least learn what happened to her, and I'll make it worth your time." He rushed out of the room.

* * *

Dot and I let ourselves out. I thought I saw Mrs. Vance, but she disappeared like quicksilver. Outside, I stood on the sidewalk and surveyed the neighborhood. All these homes, all stately and reserved. How many more of 'em hid secrets?

Lots, I'd imagine.

Dot tugged on my elbow. "Betty? Not that I doubt you or anything, but how on earth are you gonna do what you said? Solve this murder and find Noemi?"

"I don't know."

She paused. "You think Theo is gonna go see his son?"

I replayed our interview. "Not yet. He's gonna be mad for a while, I think. Then he'll feel guilty. He might wait to see what I learn. But I think he'll go eventually. Although I'm not sure what he's gonna say."

"Do you think Theo killed his sister?"

"I think it's a lot more likely he did than Private Lake." Theo'd been in the house that day. It wasn't that hard to pretend to be drunk. Detective MacKinnon hadn't mentioned him as a suspect, though. From what people had told me, and what Theo had said himself, he had always been soft, weak. But I knew he could lash out. He might very well have shot Marian in a fit of rage. But unlike Private Lake, I thought Theo was more capable of covering up what he'd done. Still, I couldn't believe he'd let his boy, the child he'd had with the woman he loved, take the fall.

As long as he knew who that child was.

I spoke while I thought. "I think whoever killed Marian had a motive rooted in the past. She had a secret, or they did. It stayed quiet for a lot of years. What happened to set it off? That's the question." I ran down my list of suspects. "Private Lake. I don't think he's the killer, but I can't deny he had a motive."

Dot bit her lip. "No one likes being rejected, and it would have been especially painful for him."

"Exactly. Then there's Theo. We've already talked about him." I took out my notepad. "Robert Newcombe. I don't know enough about him. Or Hazel or what happened. But there's gotta be a more recent motive there. Otherwise, it's a stretch." I flipped the notepad shut.

Dot tilted her head. "Why?"

"Timing. And the fact Robert worked for Old Man Carstairs for years. If he doted on his daughter, why hire the man who rejected her?" I stared at Mrs. Babbage in her window. She stared back. I felt like she was daring me to come talk to her again.

I made up my mind and crossed the street.

Dot trotted after me. "Where are you goin'?"

"Noemi was friends with Mrs. Babbage's maid. She still works there a couple afternoons a week." I knocked on the door. "Let's see what she has to say."

Chapter Twenty-Nine

T his time, the door was opened by a plain-faced woman who mighta been in her forties. Judging by her black dress, it was Mrs. Babbage's maid. "May I help you?"

"I sure hope so." I held out a business card.

She took it but didn't even look at the script. "Mrs. Babbage isn't seeing visitors right now."

"That's okay because I'm lookin' for you. At least, I think I am."

She gulped. "Me? Whatever for?"

I pointed at the card. "I'm searching for Noemi Gerard."

The woman studied the card, a line appearing between her eyes. "I still don't understand."

Dot, still behind me, gave a *hmph* of impatience.

A thought occurred to me. "Can you read?"

The woman's head came up. "Of course, I can read." She thrust the card back at me. "You must be the girl who came yesterday or the day before, or whenever it was. Cook told me. I have nothing to say to you. Goodbye." She pushed the door shut.

Dot put her hands on her hips. "That was rude."

I wasn't gonna be put off easily. "C'mon." I walked around the back of the house to the back door. I could see the older woman who'd greeted me the first time through the window. She must be Cook, which meant that room must be the kitchen. A dented trashcan occupied the space next to the door. Handy for throwing out garbage. I peeked in the can. A soggy paper bag was at the bottom, perhaps holding scraps.

"Are you gonna knock?" Dot craned her neck to see around me.

"No, I'm gonna wait. Let them think we left. When someone opens the door, we'll pounce."

It didn't take long, maybe fifteen minutes, for the door to open. The maid stepped out. "I'll drag the can to the garage and be right back to help with those potatoes." She dropped another bag into the can and grabbed the handle.

I stepped out from around the corner of the house. "Hello again."

The woman fairly jumped and laid a hand on her chest. "Goodness gracious. I thought you left."

"Not yet." I stepped closer but kept some space between us. I didn't want her to feel crowded. "You knew Noemi, didn't you? It's okay. Mrs. Babbage already told me you did."

She flushed. "Yes, we were friends, of a sort. She would come for tea when Miss Carstairs didn't need her, that sort of thing."

Dot came forward. "You had to know about the baby. She must have told you. About her and Theo Carstairs."

The red in the woman's cheeks deepened. "I don't see where that's any of your business. I have chores to do." She tried to escape, but Dot blocked her.

"Please. I need your help." I held up my hands. "What's your name?"

She licked her lips. "Nancy."

"Nancy, I already know some. A lot, actually. You don't have to worry about gossiping or telling tales. Nobody is gonna get into trouble." I stepped closer. "Noemi's son, Christopher, hired me to find her. Anything you can tell me would be swell."

Nancy threw a panicked look at the closed kitchen door. Then she stared at the ground. "I was told she died in childbirth. With the baby."

"That's a lie, and you know it." I waited. She didn't look up at me. "Did you know Christopher has been arrested for killing Miss Carstairs?"

Again, the desperate look to the door. Then she glanced at Dot before gripping the handles of the can. "I read it in the paper. I can't help you. Noemi is gone."

Gone, she said. Not "dead." It clicked into place. She had known all along where Noemi had moved to. What else did she know? "Have you heard from her?"

She tried to muscle the can past Dot, who refused to budge. Nancy swung to face me. "Please let me be. She won't be happy with me."

I wondered who *she* was. Certainly not Mrs. Babbage. I couldn't see where the old lady would much care. The cook? She wouldn't care, either. "You mean Marian? Nancy, she's dead. So's her dad. No one's left to hassle you. Mr. Carstairs, Theo, he practically asked me to find Noemi. If you know somethin', now's the time. Her son could be executed for murder and die without knowing his mother. You want that on your conscience?"

"Not Miss Carstairs." Tears ran down Nancy's face. Her words came in a whisper. "I promised her."

Dot took away the trashcan. "I'd say things have changed."

Nancy wrung her hands and took a deep breath. "She wrote to me, Noemi did. Not regular like, but I'd get a note or a postcard every couple of months. She never said much, only that she was doing okay, and she...she hoped Theo was well. Once or twice, she mentioned the baby, how maybe she'd made a mistake, but hopefully he'd forgive her, wherever he was."

I guided Nancy to a stone bench under a tree near a birdbath. I gave her my handkerchief. "Did you write back?"

She sniffled. "A couple of times, at the return address. But my very last letter came back to me stamped return to sender."

"Was it in Buffalo? The address?"

"Yes."

Buffalo wasn't a big city, not on the scale of New York, but big enough. "Do you still have them?" I crossed my fingers.

She nodded. "Do you really know her baby? And did Mr. Theodore truly hire you?"

Dot sat on the other side of her. "Yes on both counts. We wanna find her, Nancy."

She wiped her eyes. "Wait here."

She went inside and returned a few minutes later, holding a packet of letters. "Here." She held them out. "I always felt bad for Noemi. Miss Carstairs, she wasn't a pleasant woman to work for, even when she was young. I always hoped Theo would stand up to her and his father, but he couldn't live without the money, I guess. He did love Noemi, but she said he had no skills, no talent. No way of supporting her. She knew their love was doomed."

I skimmed through the letters and cards. The latest was postmarked two years ago. It showed the Hotel Statler from down on Niagara Square, but could prob'ly be bought anywhere in the city. The elegant script on the back only said, "Homer died. Thinking of you. And Theo. Still hoping for brighter days. N." Could Homer be a man she married after she left Delaware Park? I asked Nancy.

She sniffled. "Yes. I don't think it was a love match, though. She needed a husband, and Homer was there."

Dot reached over and took Nancy's hand. "Thank you."

Nancy ignored her. "Find her, Miss Ahern. She was a good girl."

"I'm gonna try. May I keep these? You'll get 'em back, I promise." I stood. Nancy nodded.

I dropped the packet of letters in my purse. "You said Theo Carstairs was weak, but he loved Noemi. Tell me. If he found out his sister had lied to him, that his father had bribed Noemi to leave, and Marian had helped sell the lie, what would he do?"

Nancy wiped her eyes with the back of her hand. "He's not a strong man, but he has an awful temper. Mr. Theodore. I don't know if you know that."

I thought of the shattered whiskey tumbler. "I've seen it."

"I think he'd be furious." Nancy steadied herself. "Yes, Miss Ahern. I know what you're asking. He'd be angry enough to commit murder."

Doggone it. It wasn't quite what I wanted to hear.

* * *

We left Nancy in the back yard after Dot lugged the trash to the garage. It was the least we could do for her, considerin' she'd helped us out. Dot checked her watch. "It's two o'clock. I'm starved. We missed lunch."

"Unless you can find a joint that's open on the Fourth, we're outta luck." I read letters as I walked, occasionally glancing up to make sure I wasn't gonna run into anything. They were always short. No more than a quick hello, a brief update, thoughts about Theo and the baby, and well wishes. I'd been right. It seemed Homer and Noemi had only been married for a few years before he died from injuries he'd suffered at his job at the docks. She never mentioned children. I assumed they didn't have any. The return address was always the same, though. Even before her marriage. It struck me as odd. Why hadn't she moved in with her husband? "This address. I'm not sure it's even in a residential area of the city." Could it be an apartment building?

"I haven't even seen a corner store open where I can get a box of Cracker Jack. Don't you carry food with you?" Dot grumbled beside me.

"Sorry, fresh out." I looked at the postmark of the most recent postcard, the one of the Statler. "Do you know of any way to identify the post office that processed a piece of mail?"

"I can't believe you're asking me that. What would it matter, anyway?" Dot rummaged in her purse. "Why is that important?"

"I'm not exactly sure where this address is. If I can find the post office, it might be a clue to where Noemi was living. Or working, depending on the neighborhood." I glanced at my friend. "Oh, come on. You can't be that hungry."

"I'm famished." Her bottom lip quivered.

"Oh, for heaven's sake." I stopped and looked through my handbag. "I have a squashed Hershey bar. Take it."

She grabbed it from my hand and unwrapped it. From her expression after the first bite, you'd have thought she hadn't eaten in days. "Maybe Detective MacKinnon would know about the post office."

"Prob'ly, but I've hassled him enough this weekend." It seemed I'd hit a snag in my search for Noemi.

Dot spoke around a mouthful of chocolate. "What'd you think of Nancy's opinion of Theo?"

"I half expected it. I don't *want* the killer to be Theo. In my book, the best solution is that Marian's murder is related to some other grudge. I find Noemi and reunite her, Theo, and Private Lake."

"A happy ending."

'Cept I knew those kinds of things were a lot rarer than Hollywood wanted us to think. "Now that you've filled your belly, are you up for a little more sleuthing?"

She licked her fingers and crumpled the candy bar wrapper. "What's the plan?"

"We're gonna visit Hazel Newcombe." I flipped to the page in my notebook with Hazel's address. It was over on Saybrook Avenue, a relatively short bus ride from our current spot.

Sam said there'd been two sets of unknown fingerprints in the Carstairs house. Mrs. Babbage had seen a woman visit the Carstairses on the day of Marian's death. I wasn't getting too lucky with Noemi. Hopefully, a trip to see Hazel would give me better results.

Chapter Thirty

Dot and I didn't talk much on the trip to Hazel's. I was lost in my thoughts. Noemi was alive. At least, she had been two years ago. Had she ever tried to find her son? I didn't think she'd held out much hope for Theo. Or had she? I couldn't get the rage in Theo's eyes outta my head either.

"Them," I said, jolting Dot back to attention.

"What did you say?"

I looked at her. "When Sam told me about the German pistol, he said the maid told him Old Man Carstairs brought 'them' back from the Great War as souvenirs."

Dot's expression was baffled. "So?"

"Don't you see? The guns have to be the same, or close. Whoever killed Marian *knew* about the second gun. That wouldn't be Private Lake."

"But it could be Theo."

Talk about an inconvenient fact. It almost guaranteed Marian's killer was a member of the Carstairs household. I wanted to get off the bus and find a payphone. Did Sam know? He had to. He was a smart cookie. But maybe he didn't. "If Mr. Carstairs brought back two pistols of the same make, that would explain why the bullets are similar to what woulda been used by the gun found by Marian's body, but not an exact match." Maybe I could pull the emergency handle. It would make the other passengers madder than wet hens, but I'd be on the street.

It didn't come to that. The bus rumbled to a stop, and I bolted out the door. "Look for a phone." I scanned the street.

Dot waved. "Over there."

I ran over while I searched my coin purse. "Got a nickel?"

She handed me one.

"I'll pay you back." I dialed Sam's number, praying he was home.

He answered on the fourth ring.

"Sam, there's two of the same gun."

"Slow down, Betty." His voice was indistinct, like he had a mouth full of something. "What's got you in such a dither?"

I explained my reasoning about the guns. "Search the house. But I don't know if you'll find it." A smart killer woulda thrown it away.

Sam musta thought the same. "You realize this doesn't exonerate your private. He could have taken the gun Marian threatened him with, found the second, dropped it, and disposed of the first. It would explain the lack of fingerprints."

"I find it as unlikely that Private Lake woulda thought to search that room, find a second gun, and pick it up with a hankie as I did that he'd think to wipe off the one he used to shoot Marian. That's too planned out. If he's the killer, he acted on impulse, and what happened later requires too much thinking."

I knew Sam was stumped, because he was quiet for a bit. "God help me. I'll find a judge, get a warrant signed, and get over there. I will be the least popular detective on the force for a while, but I'll do it." He hung up.

Mollified, I faced Dot. "He's gonna go look."

She looked up and down the street. "Are we goin' back?"

"I can't help Sam. But I can interview Hazel Newcombe."

We'd gotten off the bus a good three blocks from Hazel's house. I set a brisk pace. Dot didn't complain, but she did have to trot to keep up. The saving grace was that the day wasn't too hot. Still, I could feel the sweat between my shoulder blades by the time we arrived. Dot's face shone, and she had to pause to catch her breath. I checked the address against my notes. "This is it."

"What do you think you'll learn?"

"I'm not sure, but hopefully, something that makes her a good suspect for

Marian's murder. Or at least takes Private Lake outta the frame."

The Newcombe house looked sad. There was no other way to describe it. The grass was overgrown. The paint peeled. The windows were slightly opaque in the light, showing a need for a bucket of soapy water and a rag. Hazel was a widow. She wouldn't be able to do all this work by herself. Obviously, she couldn't pay a neighborhood boy to do it. The houses on either side were much cleaner. I wondered if the neighbors complained or if they left her alone on account of her situation.

There wasn't a knocker. I rapped on the door, rehearsing what I'd say in my head.

The woman who answered appeared as sad as her house. She couldn't have been that old, maybe in her early forties, but her once-brown hair showed a liberal amount of gray. Her face was lined, her eyes tired. She wore a shapeless housedress and carpet slippers. "I don't know you." She started to close the door.

"Wait, Mrs. Newcombe. We spoke on the telephone. My name is Betty Ahern."

She paused. "Yes, you called looking for my husband. I told you, he's dead." Again, the door moved to shut.

"Yes, you did. I need a few minutes of your time, that's all."

Her stare was blank. "Whatever for? Why would you be interested in a dead man?"

I sensed I needed to convince her quickly. "I think I told you, I'm a private detective. I'm investigating the death of Marian Carstairs."

Marian's name brought a flicker of light to Hazel's dull eyes. "Why bother?"

From her tone of voice, I didn't think she was talkin' about me being involved in a police matter. "You didn't like Marian."

"I didn't care about her one way or the other. After what that family did to my Robert…" She gripped the door.

Dot stepped forward. "Maybe we could come in, and you can tell us about it?"

"I have no interest in the Carstairs family. Not any longer." Hazel's voice sounded flat and uncaring.

Sympathy for Marian, or her family, was not gonna win the day. I played my card. "Do you care about justice? 'Cause there's a young man sittin' in a jail cell for a crime he didn't commit. If you don't care about catchin' the real killer, would you at least help free him?" I crossed my fingers.

"No."

The answer caught me off guard. I studied her. "Suit yourself. But you won't be able to put off the cops. Have a nice day." I turned to leave.

"Wait."

Gotcha. I looked back at her. "Yes?"

"If I talk to you, will the police leave me alone?"

I spread my hands. "I can't guarantee it. I'm sure they'll want to talk to you. But I *am* friendly with the detective in charge. I could put in a good word for you." Not that it would do much, but she didn't have to know that part.

Hazel didn't move. Then she turned around. "Come in."

I glanced at Dot, who shrugged. We went inside.

The interior of the house matched the exterior. The furniture had seen better days. The carpet needed to be taken out and beaten. The dust in the corners would've made Mom faint dead away.

Hazel pointed to a sagging couch. "You can sit there. I hope this won't take long."

I got straight to the point. "Did you always hate Marian Carstairs?"

Hazel worried the edge of her housedress. "Hate is a strong word. I don't particularly like her. That much is true. Robert worked for her father. After Marian's elder brother died, Robert's role in the company expanded. Her younger brother was a wastrel. Everyone knew that." She dismissed Theo with a wave. "That would've been fine, except the unthinkable happened."

"What was that?" Dot asked.

A triumphant look came into Hazel's eyes. "Marian tried to cozy up to the man she thought would be her father's successor. But Robert chose *me*. Even back then, Marian thought she was better than everybody. Unsurprising. Her father encouraged her thinkin. That didn't sit well with Robert. He wanted a partner, not to be a prop on someone's arm. Marian was absolutely green when he announced our engagement."

I s'posed if *Hazel* had been the one attacked, I mighta bought Marian as the guilty party. But why would Hazel shoot her rival twenty years later? Besides, Hazel'd won. No, that wasn't the motive. "What did Robert do at the company?"

"He was Mr. Carstairs's right-hand man. Everything Anthony, Marian's elder brother, had done, Robert stepped into. He ran the meetings, handled daily operations, negotiated contracts, all of it."

Those were all things Marian had done for the past fifteen years. "He didn't last. Why?"

Hazel twisted her lips in a grimace. "Robert was not well. He always had little tics, things he did in a certain way. I never thought anything of it. They were endearing. But over time, he became erratic, unstable."

"How do you mean?"

"He came home with the most unbelievable stories. Things Mr. Carstairs had done, both professionally and in his personal life, that were simply too outrageous to be true."

"What kind of accusations?"

Hazel lowered her gaze. "I'm afraid I didn't listen to him. I wish I had. I might have been able to help him."

Mr. Carstairs prob'ly couldn't put up with it. "Robert was fired. Then what?"

Hazel dabbed at her eyes. "Robert couldn't find a job after Mr. Carstairs let him go. In his delusions, Robert believed he'd been blackballed because he'd dared to accuse one of Buffalo's biggest shipping magnates of improper behavior. It took a toll on him. He'd fall into fits of depression, raving. After the stock market collapsed, he went back to the company, tried to patch it up. By then, Mr. Carstairs had died, and Marian was in charge. She refused to even see him. She called him a raving lunatic and had the police haul him off the property. Then she threatened to sue him for defamation of her father's character." She choked back a sob.

Dot passed her a handkerchief.

Hazel patted her eyes. "Robert hung himself three days after he received the letter about the possible lawsuit. Marian used his death to paint a picture of a man who'd clearly been out to cover something up, that his suicide showed he was unstable, and her father had been right to fire him."

"Why?" Dot asked.

"It was spite, pure and simple." Hazel twisted the fabric so hard it should have ripped. "She still hated him for choosing another woman. She paid him back by taking what little he had left away from him."

The story explained why Hazel thought so little of Marian, but not why she'd gone to visit. "You went to see Marian on the day she was murdered. Why?"

Hazel's head snapped up. She ran her tongue over her lips, maybe tryin' to come up with a lie. Either she couldn't, or she decided to be honest. "I found a box of Robert's papers. I know it doesn't seem like it, but I do try to clean." She attempted a smile and failed. "There was a letter marked 'return to sender' in the box. It was addressed to Anthony Carstairs, Junior, but had never been opened. The postmark was two weeks after Robert was fired. He apologized for his words and admitted everything he'd said was untrue." Her gaze dropped to her lap. "I thought if I showed it to Marian, she might feel a little pity and forgive a troubled man. You must understand, I couldn't even afford a decent headstone for my husband's grave, Miss Ahern. He had no insurance. Nothing to leave me. I only wanted enough money to buy a stone, maybe a little recompense for sullying his name." She sniffed. "I should have known better."

From what I'd learned of Marian, I guessed at her response. "She threw you out."

"Laughed in my face." Hazel's bitter tone returned. "She said I had a lot of nerve, trying to wheedle money out of her over things that had happened years ago. Now that she knew the truth, I wouldn't get a penny."

I held my breath and waited.

"I could have killed her on the spot. It was my last hope." Hazel seemed to come to her senses. "I didn't kill her. I wanted to, but I didn't."

The tale Hazel Newcombe told painted a picture of her as a sad, forlorn woman who'd gone to Marian looking for compassion. But I wasn't convinced. 'Course, I'd been around the block a few times now. Sam might say I'd gotten jaded. Would Hazel have known about the guns? Prob'ly not. Unless she'd learned of them from her husband. But maybe she was leavin' out part of the story. "She didn't threaten you with a pistol or anything like that?"

The response was too quick. "No."

I stood. "Thank you for your time, Mrs. Newcombe. I know it's years late, but I'm sorry for your loss." I moved toward the door.

Her voice stopped me. "You believe me, don't you?"

I opened my mouth to answer, but my attention snagged on a framed picture on the front table. "Who is this? Here, in this picture." I picked it up and held it out.

Hazel's expression flashed in panic, but she recovered. "That's my brother, Paul."

"Paul Evans?" The man was undoubtedly the Carstairs's butler. He was much younger, as many as thirty years, but there was no mistaking his nose. Had Hazel's maiden name been Evans?

Her expression showed confusion. "I have no idea who you're talking about. My brother's name is Paul Fasenmyr."

* * *

As soon as we left Hazel's house, I rushed to find a payphone. "Got another nickel? I have to call Sam."

Dot handed me a coin. "Ten years is a long time to wait to kill someone if you ask me. Even if old Mr. Carstairs and his daughter did wrong her husband."

"True. But we don't know what went on. It could be something happened recently to fan the old flames." There was no answer at Sam's house. He was prob'ly still out getting his warrant. Maybe he was even at the Carstairs house. I retrieved my nickel from the return slot and dialed.

Mrs. Vance answered the phone. "Carstairs residence, how may I help you?"

"Mrs. Vance, it's Betty Ahern. Is Detective MacKinnon there?"

"I don't want to talk about it right now." There was a click and dial tone, indicating she'd hung up.

Dot folded her arms. "I'm all outta nickels."

"He's not there. He's not home. Which means he's at the courthouse or the jail or somewhere else I can't reach him." There was no point running all over Buffalo. "Let's go back to the First Ward."

Independence Day celebrations, even scaled down because of the war, were in full swing on Mackinaw. All the neighborhood kids were out with sparklers or small fireworks. Flags snapped from almost every house. The scent of charcoal floated down the street. The United States might be at war, but that wasn't gonna stop the people from celebrating our independence from England.

Dot nudged me with her elbow. "Whatcha thinkin'?"

"Detective MacKinnon had to have been at the Carstairs house. Maybe been there and gone."

"What makes you say that?"

I sidestepped two boys chasing each other down the street. "Mrs. Vance. She said she didn't want to talk about it when I asked if he was there. If he hadn't been there, she'd have said that. Instead, she got mad. Which means he showed up and made trouble." Ahead of me, I saw Sam leave my house and lift his fedora to someone inside. "There he is. Let's go ask him."

He noticed us coming and waited on the front sidewalk. "Fancy meeting you here," he said when we got close.

I brushed aside the small talk. "What did you find at the Carstairs place? Anything?"

"Another German pistol, exactly the same as the one left by Marian Carstairs's body."

"Where?"

He held my gaze. "In Theo Carstairs's sock drawer."

Dot gasped and clapped her hands over her mouth.

I kept my attention on Sam. "Did he confess? Are his fingerprints on the gun?"

"Most of the prints were smudged, likely from being jammed under the wool." Sam spread his hands. "He says he didn't do it. No other explanation, no intricate reasoning. A simple declaration. I arrested him. He has means, motive, and opportunity."

"Then you'll be releasing Private Lake."

Sam didn't budge. "Not yet."

I narrowed my peepers. "'Cause it's Sunday and a holiday. But tomorrow morning, he's free as a bird."

"I called my captain at home when we brought Carstairs in. The captain is unwilling to release Private Lake at this time. He thinks there's a possibility the two men were accomplices. Especially given their relationship as father and son."

Outta the corner of my eye, I saw the flabbergasted expression on Dot's face. Me, I went for stoic calm. "That's a load of malarkey, and you know it. They didn't even know each other before, well, ever. I don't think they've met. Theo was truly amazed when I told him Noemi and his child were alive."

Sam spread his hands. "You know as well as I do, Betty. Good criminals can be good actors. How do you know the two have never met? Isn't it possible Theo Carstairs led you down the garden path? He has met his son and is trying to cover for him?"

"Private Lake woulda told me. Your captain is an idiot."

"If you ever meet him, you can tell him yourself." Sam tugged his fedora. "Look at it this way. If you're right, and the two men are strangers to each other, Carstairs and Lake will finally meet."

Yeah. In a jail cell. Not the place I had in mind. "Remember Evans? The butler?"

"You mean Paul Fasenmyr?" Sam grinned. "His name came up when we matched one of the two sets of unknown fingerprints from the murder scene. He has a record. Petty larceny, mostly. Seems he reinvented himself back in 1932 as Paul Evans. That was the year he started working for the Carstairs family."

"He's Hazel Newcombe's brother."

Sam's forehead wrinkled. "Who is that?"

I told him about the Robert-Marian-Hazel love triangle. "That explains why he said he knew Marian as a girl. Have you asked him why he changed his name?"

"We intend to. As soon as we find him. Have a nice evening, ladies." Sam gave us a faux salute and drove off.

I watched him go. Sam knew me well enough that he included me in that "we." The cops might stumble over Paul eventually. I intended to beat them to it.

Chapter Thirty-One

Monday morning, I was on my own again as both Dot and Lee had to work. It promised to be another sunny day, but the ever-present breeze off Lake Erie kept the air from being stifling. I warned Mom I would be out all day.

She hugged me. "You be careful."

"Tell Mary Kate not to overfeed Cat. He's lookin' a little plump."

Mom sighed. "Frankly, I don't know where that girl gets the scraps for a cat. Lord knows we don't have them in this house."

"I wouldn't be surprised if she was givin' him food from her plate. She's convinced he wouldn't survive otherwise."

"He's a cat, Betty. He'd get along fine."

I kissed her cheek. "You're talkin' to the wrong daughter."

I stopped at Teddy's for a cup of joe and a quick breakfast. While I ate, I scribbled notes. I could buy Theo as a murderer a lot better than Private Lake. But there was no way the two men were in cahoots. Yes, I knew criminals were liars. I'd run across more than one in my short career. But Private Lake hadn't been fibbing when he hired me, and the shock on Theo's face when I told him about Noemi had been real, I was sure of it.

Not that I wanted Theo to be the killer.

I was sure Hazel knew somethin'. Maybe about her brother and why he'd worked for the Carstairses under a false name for ten years. I also wanted to know why she'd really gone to see Marian. I didn't buy the "have pity on my poor, dead husband" tale for a minute. One person might be able to put me on the right track for all of it.

I arrived at the Carstairs mansion and strode to the front door. My brisk knock was answered by the person I wanted to see.

Mrs. Vance's mouth thinned. "I don't have anything to say to you."

I stopped the door with my hand. "That's not true."

She puffed up. "I tried to help. In return, the police came swarming over the house and dragged Mr. Theodore away in handcuffs."

"I don't think you helped me as much as you could have. If Theo means as much to you as you say, you wanna let me inside."

She hesitated but motioned me inside. "Very well." Once she closed the door, she folded her hands at her waist. "What more do you think I can tell you?"

"Where is Noemi? And why did you never tell anyone that Evans's real name was Paul Fasenmyr?"

She sputtered and looked at the ceiling. "Really, what an absurd question. I told you, the last time I saw Noemi was twenty years ago, right after she gave birth. As far as Evans, I have no idea what you're talking about."

"Noemi wrote postcards and letters to Mrs. Babbage's maid." I watched her face. "She was a lot closer to you. I can't believe she never let you know she was okay. Remember Hazel Fasenmyr? She married Robert Newcombe. He was reportedly Mr. Carstairs's protege, and Marian was in love with him. Evans is Hazel Newcombe's brother. Given your history with the Carstairs family, I can't believe you don't know about that."

Mrs. Vance was havin' trouble focusing on anything. Her gaze darted around the hallway. "Miss Ahern, you are mistaken. I haven't had any contact with Noemi, and I have no idea what you're talking about regarding Evans."

"You're a poor liar, ma'am." I stepped forward. "I'm not gonna beat around the bush. Frankly, I don't have time. This is your last chance to be straight with me."

She squeezed her peepers shut. "I don't know anything."

I wanted to shout at her, but that wouldn't help. "Mrs. Vance, the son of the woman you claim to have cared for is in jail. In four days, he's s'posed to ship out and go back to the front. Unless I clear his name, he's not gonna do that. Murder is a capital offense in New York. He could get the chair."

Tears leaked out of her closed eyelids.

"In addition, the man she loved, the father of that child and the employer you claim to be loyal to, is also in jail. I bet he's gonna be home soon. But the cops think he and his son coulda been in cahoots. Do you think Noemi would want him to go to prison if he's innocent? You've worked for this family for twenty years. I can't believe you are as ignorant as you claim." I felt a twinge of guilt as I twisted the screw tighter. But she wasn't leavin' me much choice. "I've told Theo about Christopher and how Noemi might be alive. He hired me to find her." Not in so many words, but I didn't say that.

Her head swayed from side to side.

"I think I can help. To do that, I need the truth, and I need it now."

She melted in front of me and buried her face in her hands. "No one was supposed to know about Noemi." She broke down in sobs.

"C'mon, let's go sit down." I started toward the kitchen, then changed my mind and went into Theo's study. I guided her to a chair. I went to the bar and poured a healthy amount of bourbon into a glass. "Here. Drink this."

She lifted her head. "We can't be in Mr. Theo's room."

"He's not here to use it, and I'll be gone before he gets home." At least, I thought I would.

"Are you sure he's coming back?"

"I bet he's already got a top-notch lawyer workin' for him. He's rich. He'll get out of jail, as long as the cops can't tie him to the murder of his sister. Unlike his son." I took out my notepad. "Have a drink."

She took a generous swallow of the whiskey. Unlike me, she didn't cough.

"Let's start with Noemi. When was the last time you saw her?"

Mrs. Vance swirled the contents of the glass. "I haven't seen her for at least six months. In fact, I didn't see her often. Maybe once or twice a year. Most of our contact was by mail. But every once in a while, she'd propose meeting for coffee."

"Where'd you go to see her?"

"Different places around the city, mostly on the East side. I got the feeling she picked locations that were not close to where she lived because she'd make a comment about needing to catch a bus or trolley." She took another drink.

"What did you talk about?"

"This and that. She told me about her life after here, the difficulty in getting a job. I asked what happened to the money from Mr. Carstairs. She told me she'd put it in bonds. She hoped someday to find her son and give them to him." Mrs. Vance hiccuped. "Early on, she asked about Theo and if he ever married. I never understood that. He didn't stand up for her, but she never stopped loving him. Maybe if they'd been allowed to be together, he would have turned out a different man."

Mom had always said the right woman could do wonders for a man. I didn't doubt it would've been true for the only surviving Carstairs son. "Did he know about her? Theo?"

"Oh heavens no." Her eyes grew to the size of saucers. "Noemi was very firm about that. She'd made a promise to Mr. Carstairs to stay away, and she would keep it, even though it broke her heart. She knew Marian would hold her to it as well, after the old man died. Noemi got married, eventually. I don't think it was out of love. It only lasted a couple of years. Widowhood gave her a little respectability, and she was able to work after that."

"Did you keep her letters? More importantly, do you have the envelopes?" She nodded. "Shall I get them?"

"In a minute." I thought about my next question. "You said you saw her six months ago. Was that the last time you heard from her?"

"No. Her last letter is from three months ago. She always wrote to me around her son's birthday. But if you're wondering if it contained any hints as to where she was, you'll be disappointed. All she talked about was the child. She called him Christophe. She'd left a medal with him of St. Christopher. She longed to see him but despaired of ever being able to do it. I think she tried to look for him once or twice, maybe recently, but she didn't have any luck."

"I know about the medal. That's why the nuns gave him that name." I twiddled my pencil. "Tell me about Evans." I had trouble thinkin' of him by any other name.

A light came into her eyes. "He just showed up here one day. He knew all the right names for references and said all the right things. Mr. Carstairs had been on the fence about getting a new butler, but I guess Evans offered to work for a lower-than-average wage. I overheard him talking to Marian about it. He said something about being able to afford the expense. I found that confusing. The family never seemed to be pinching pennies." She raised watery eyes to hold mine. "I'll be honest, I never liked him. His manner was too attentive. It was like he watched Mr. Carstairs's every step. Later, it was the same with Marian."

"But isn't that the butler's job?"

"This was different." She sniffled. "It always struck me that he was watching *for* something. What, I didn't know. But it went beyond being attentive to the family's needs. I didn't know he was related to Hazel Fasenmyr."

Mrs. Babbage had seen the same signs. "Did he live here?"

"No." She wiped her nose. "He has an apartment on East Ferry, up by Humboldt Parkway."

That was odd. Most butlers lived where they worked. "Did he tell you?"

"He didn't have to. He always complained about the trolley service between Humboldt and Delaware Park. If he's taking the trolley from there, he has to live within a block or two."

I made a note of the trolley stop. "Next question. Hazel told me a story about Robert Newcombe and his relationship with the family up until he was let go." I summarized the tale for her. "Was it true?"

"Marian was definitely in love with him. It seemed to be going well, and suddenly, he married Miss Fasenmyr. I wasn't privy to the details, but the split must have been traumatic for Marian. She went into a deep depression when he broke it off. That's why she went away." The chime of the grandfather clock sounded nine. Mrs. Vance took another slug of bourbon. "What you must think of me, drinking this early in the day."

"Don't worry, I'm the one who gave it to you. Medicinal purposes, as my grandpa would say." Why had Evans gotten a job with this family if they'd wronged his sister? It wasn't logical, and I'd become suspicious of things that didn't make sense. "One last question. How many people knew about the pair of German pistols?"

She thought. "Everybody in the house. Mr. Theodore, of course. It was common knowledge that Miss Marian kept at least one of them in the drawer of her desk. For safety, it was said. She was quite a good shot. Her father taught her not long after she returned from the sanatorium. I knew, which means Evans had to have known as well."

"Then if she'd felt threatened, she'd have no problem usin' one?"

Mrs. Vance pursed her lips. "Not at all. In fact, she had the personality that would enjoy waving a loaded gun to make a point. Oh, I don't think she'd use it. I think having her heart broken made her hard, though. She was determined never to be vulnerable again. Having the gun made her feel powerful, especially in an argument."

"Thank you." I stood, intending to leave, but a thought stopped me. "Sorry, one more question. If Evans were to go somewhere, someplace to hide, do you know where?"

"I wish I could help you, Miss Ahern." Mrs. Vance's gaze was mournful. "If for no other reason than to save Mr. Theodore and Christopher for Noemi. But I honestly have no idea. Shall I get you those envelopes?"

I'd almost forgotten. "Yes, please. Wait."

"Yes?"

"Where did Marian keep the pistols?" *Don't ever say, "One more question."*

"The top right drawer of her desk. She wanted them close. I'll be back in a moment." She left and returned minutes later. "I don't know what good it will do, but here. I would like the letter back."

I scanned the note, but Mrs. Vance had been truthful. There was nothin' in there that gave a hint as to where Noemi was. I turned over the envelope and looked at the return address. It was the same as the postcard of the Hotel Statler. "Before I go, can I use your telephone?" The telephone book would not help me connect an address with the name of a person. But I knew someone who almost certainly could.

* * *

Mrs. Vance showed me to a room off the main hall that looked like a library. Bookshelves lined the walls and a lamp with a fringed shade hung over a heavy leather chair in the corner. The telephone was on a small table inside the door. "When you're done, you can call for me, and I'll show you out."

"That's okay. I think I can find my way. Thank you for everything."

She murmured and closed the door.

I telephoned the offices of the *Courier* and asked for Melvin. After waitin' a few minutes, he came on the line. "This is Schlingmann."

"Melvin, it's me."

"Hey, Toots. What can I do for you?" The sound of typewriters in the background came through clearly.

"Question. How do you know what post office processed a piece of mail?"

"Easy. You don't."

My spirits sank. "There's no way at all?"

"Nope. A postmark from North Buffalo looks much like one from the First Ward."

Shoot.

His voice turned sharp. "Why do you want to know? Does it have to do with your missing person?"

"Yes. And maybe with the death of Marian Carstairs. The two could be connected."

He whistled. "Hot diggity dog. You do stumble on the juiciest stories. Where's the return address?"

I looked. "It's on the East Side. 4738 Bailey Avenue."

"That sounds familiar. Hang on."

I waited and listened to the background noises of the newsroom until he came back.

"What have you gotten yourself into, Toots?"

What had he found? "Just a regular case. Why? What's at the address?"

"Before I tell you, what do I get for helping you out?"

I could imagine the smirk on his face. "There's no story here, Melvin."

"Like heck, there isn't. You said it could be related to the Carstairs murder. That's news in my book. Especially if you nail the killer."

"Who said I'm investigatin' that?"

"I do. Because I know you." His voice became wheedling. "C'mon. I can tell you right now what's there, or you can eat up a few hours traveling to the East Side. Your call."

I knew what was comin'. "I promise you a scoop, and you'll tell me, is that it?"

"You're a smart cookie. What do you say?"

I closed my eyes. "Sure."

He whooped. "That is the address of Mother of Angels Home for Troubled Girls. They do charity stuff, like helping unwed mothers, girls who have been turned out of their homes, things like that."

I could understand why Noemi would have lived there twenty years ago. But now? She wasn't a girl. These letters were too recent. Or did she work there? "Thanks, Melvin. I owe you."

"Don't worry, I won't let you forget it." He hung up.

Chapter Thirty-Two

Mother of Angels Home for Troubled Girls was a demure gray building on Bailey. Only one story, the front was close to the sidewalk. I could see a fenced area in the back, tall enough to provide privacy, but the maple trees towering above the building led me to imagine a grassed area with benches for sitting and prob'ly a few religious statues providing spots for prayer and reflection.

The front doors led immediately to a lobby-like space, where a woman with gray hair confined to the tight bun so favored by her generation manned the desk. She wasn't dressed like a nun, but her severe blue dress and thick-soled shoes made me wonder if she'd worked with a religious community all her life. She looked up as I walked in. "May I help you?"

I remembered my reception at Father Baker's. I started with an intro-duction. "I'm lookin' for a woman. She may have worked here years ago, or maybe she lived here. I'm not sure. At the time, her name woulda been Noemi Gerard."

The woman's mouth thinned. "We do not provide personal information on our girls."

I took the packet of mail from my purse. "She's been usin' this as her return address. Can you at least tell me if you know her?"

"No, I cannot. I doubt anyone would use our address for personal reasons."

I held up the envelopes. "I have the canceled mail right here. You can see for yourself."

A slightly younger woman working in the back raised her head and frowned at me.

The older lady waved me off. "You're mistaken. Unless you are looking for services for yourself or someone you know, I'm very busy. Good day."

I caught the younger woman's eye. Her attention never wavered, but she also didn't budge.

I knew it was no use arguing with the older woman. She might very well know Noemi, but I knew the type. She wasn't gonna give up any personal information. I shot a quizzical glance at the younger woman.

She gave me a tiny nod and held up two fingers.

"Thank you anyway." I left under the matron's watchful gaze.

Once on the sidewalk, I lit a Lucky and strolled a little ways away from the front door. I examined the letters in my hand. This was definitely the return address. Noemi had been here. Or had at least known about the place.

A few minutes later, the younger woman appeared. She looked around, and once she saw me, she came over. "Let's go down to the corner. Mrs. Crump will not like it if she sees me talking to you."

I followed her. She was perhaps in her late thirties or early forties, around Noemi's age. Her soft blonde hair was clipped back in a ponytail. She didn't wear any makeup, and her clothes were not unlike what any woman would wear to an office.

She reached the corner and turned. "You've heard from Noemi?"

"That's what I wanted to ask you." I held out the letters. "I got these from a friend of hers. As you can see, she's been usin' the Mother of Angels return address. What's your name, and how do you know her?"

"Amelia Cartright. Noemi came to Mother Angels when I did, decades ago." Amelia didn't take the mail. "We became friends because our situations were similar. Both in love with men who couldn't, or wouldn't, marry us. My baby girl died in infancy. Noemi didn't tell me her whole story, but enough for me to know what had happened."

I put the mail back into my purse and took out my notes. "Then you were residents."

"Yes, for a time. Mother of Angels provides a home and education for girls in our situation. Some of us end up working here." She shrugged. "Often, it's because no one else will have a 'fallen' girl around."

"What did Noemi do? Did she work in the office like you?"

Amelia brushed back her hair. "At first, but her talents were working with the girls, especially those who came to us in the family way, as they used to call it."

I paused. "That's not everyone?"

"Oh, no." She checked the front of the building. "Girls come for all sorts of reasons. Some are pregnant out of wedlock, yes. Others have been turned out of their homes because of uncaring parents or step-parents. Sometimes, they are into drugs or alcohol. Some never finished school. We do our best to provide education and a temporary home and teach them skills that will at least allow them to get a job. The war effort has helped with that. Factories rarely care about social standing. They want reliable workers. Our girls can do that."

I couldn't imagine bein' kicked outta my home. "If I understand you, Noemi worked mostly with the unwed mothers."

"Correct. She went from resident to working here." Amelia's eyes took on a faraway look. "I asked her once why she didn't go home. But she said there was nothing for her there. No family would take her in."

"Then you knew she was from Belgium."

Amelia came back to the present. "She taught French to some of the girls. I think she enjoyed it, the opportunity to speak her native language. I can't remember now if she said she ever lived in Belgium. But her parents were from there, and she grew up speaking French. I think she might have gone back to Europe, but as I said, she didn't have any family left. At least none that would take her back."

No wonder she'd stayed at Mother of Angels. "How long did she work here?"

"Until she married Homer Glassman. He was much older than her but offered her stability and respectability." Amelia's brown eyes held a gaze that made her look older than her age. "Before the war, that was very important."

That had happened years ago. "I don't understand why she continued to put this address on her mail. Why not use her home address?"

Amelia's expression became guarded. "Before I answer you, tell me something. Why do you want to know?"

"I'm a private detective." I handed her my card. "I work for her son. He very much wants to find her."

"I see." Amelia turned my card over in her hands. She seemed to be pondering something. "Noemi told me it was very important that the family of the man she loved never find her. After she married Homer, we made a deal. She would continue to have her mail sent here. My job is to sort it every day, it was easy for me to put it aside. Mrs. Crump would not approve. We, Noemi and me, would meet every other week for coffee and I'd give her any mail that had arrived. In return, she paid me a dollar."

Eureka! It was the best lead I'd had in my hunt. "When was the last time you saw her?"

"Three months ago."

My bubble of excitement deflated a little. "Why'd she stop?"

"I don't know." Amelia twisted her fingers. "I'm afraid for her, Miss Ahern. I can't put my finger on it, but the last time I saw her, she said she'd be out of touch for a while, and she didn't expect to get any mail. But if anything did arrive, to put it aside, and maybe she'd come for it."

"Did she say why?"

"No, and she didn't seem scared or anything. That might be what frightened me the most." Amelia looked over my shoulder. "I've been gone too long. If I don't get back, Mrs. Crump will come out and see me. I hope you find Noemi. If you do, please tell her I pray for her every day." She hurried back to Mother of Angels.

The last letter Mrs. Vance had received was from three months ago. In it, Noemi had not mentioned anything about leaving Buffalo. Had something come up after she wrote? What would make her give up the arrangement with Amelia?

She'd been careful not to give an address, but mentioning her husband's name, Homer Glassman, that was a slip. I was surprised neither Mrs. Vance nor Amelia had never thought of lookin' it up. No matter. I had to find a phone book right after I put another search in action.

200

* * *

My next stop was the library, where I headed straight for the stacks. Emmeline was there, reshelving some magazines. "Good morning. Did you have a nice Fourth?"

"I worked all day. And it's almost noon." I leaned on the counter.

She set down her armful of magazines. "No rest for the wicked, huh?"

"Nope." I brought her up to speed on what I'd learned yesterday.

She tapped her chin. "Do you want me to find an address for Homer Glassman?"

"No, I'll get to that later. I've got a bigger project." I pulled out my notes. "I need you to find everything you can on two people. One is Robert Newcombe. Hazel claims he spurned Marian Carstairs for her, but I don't think I believe her." I told her why Hazel claimed to have visited Marian on the day of her death.

Emmeline took notes. "What do you think happened?"

"I don't know, which is why you're gonna see what you can find out. Then I want to know everything about his death."

She looked up. "You said he committed suicide."

"Yes, but I wanna know any official statements or stories. Did he leave a note, things like that."

"Why not ask his widow?"

"Because I don't trust her." I skimmed my notes.

Emmeline nodded slowly. "You're thinking maybe Robert didn't commit suicide?"

"That's why I wanna see the official story." I held out my notes. "Next assignment. I want anything you can find on this man. Paul Fasenmyr." I told her about Paul reinventing himself as Evans.

"Oh, please. The butler did it? Isn't that awfully cliche?"

It was, but I plowed on. "I can't figure why he got a job with the Carstairs family. I got a feeling that's important. Knowing more about him is key."

She read through her task list. "This will take hours. It could take days."

"We don't have that much time. This has gotta be cleared up by Friday."

She drummed her fingers on the counter. "I'll give it my best shot. You know, Private Lake could very well be guilty. I know you think he's an innocent child, but what about this? What if *Theo* found him in Marian's sitting room, holding the gun? Maybe Theo overheard the argument, realized Christopher was his son and tried to cover things up?"

I didn't want to consider it, but I realized the same thing that morning. The police already had, which is why they weren't gonna release Private Lake. "I don't like it. But yeah, it's possible." Theo hadn't stood up for Noemi all those years ago. Had he finally found some courage? 'Cept Private Lake was still in jail. If Theo really intended to be a patsy, why hadn't he arranged for his son to go free?

Chapter Thirty-Three

I knew what I'd asked Emmeline for wouldn't be easy. I coulda done it myself, but my Friday deadline loomed large. Pop preached dividing tasks according to talent. Emmeline was the researcher. I would be better off pounding the pavement looking for Evans and Noemi. If I thought about it, I only had until the end of the day on Thursday. I had to get Private Lake sprung in time to catch the train to New York.

Unless I was completely wrong and he *had* shot Marian. If she'd kept the guns in her desk drawer, he coulda seen them when she pulled out the one she used to threaten him. He'd have had to figure out a way to get at it, but it was a possibility.

A chill ran down my back despite the warm sunshine. Could I be wrong about my client? 'Course I could. What would that say about my judgment? Nothing good.

I shrugged off my doubts as unprofitable. Right now, I needed to find the man I still thought of as Evans.

The neighborhood off the trolley stop at Humboldt and East Ferry was as Mrs. Vance described. There were a lot of mom-and-pop stores and diners, including a small grocery and a corner drug store. I asked every one of 'em if they'd seen a man who looked like Evans. The result was a couple of maybes and a lot of nopes. I finally hit a possible lead in a small gin joint a block away from the trolley stop.

The bartender dried a glass. "I don't know about no Evans, but the guy you're describing sounds a lot like Paulie."

"Paul Fasenmyr?" I leaned on the bar rail.

"I don't know his last name. He said he works for one of the swells up in Delaware Park. Likes to end his day here, with the real people of Buffalo, as he calls us." He put the glass on a rack and reached for another.

I tamped down my excitement. "Does he live around here?"

"I think so. He drinks in here, don't he? Stays real late some nights. I can't imagine he'd do that if his place wasn't nearby."

"But he never said where?"

He paused in wiping his glass. "Why are you lookin' for him? I don't wanna get him in no trouble."

"I'm a private detective. He might have information about a case. No trouble intended." Which was true. I wasn't gonna get Evans in hot water on purpose. If it turned out he did it himself, I couldn't be held responsible.

The bartender paused, then lifted his massive shoulders. "I don't recall. But if you're lookin' for him, there are a few places that cater to single guys around here." He gave me some addresses to check.

I thanked him and left. Out in the sunshine, I blinked to let my eyes adjust to the brightness after the dim inside of the bar. As I did, I noticed a familiar shape come down the sidewalk.

It was Evans.

I sneaked up on him, keepin' people between us so he wouldn't see me until the last minute. I reached out and tapped his shoulder. "Hey, Paul Fasenmyr. I've been lookin' for you."

He didn't hesitate. He grabbed an old lady and shoved her into me. Then he bolted.

I made sure the woman was okay before I took off after him. He moved pretty fast for a middle-aged guy with a paunch, but I was in much better shape. Plus, I'd come dressed for a chase in sensible shoes and pants. I was hindered, however, by all the people on the sidewalk. I issued a steady stream of apologies as I slipped between older folks, women with baby carriages, and darted around sidewalk displays.

Ahead of me, Evans was not as polite. He shoved people out of his way willy-nilly, not caring if they hit the dirt or not. Reaching an intersection, he darted into the street.

Right in front of an oncoming truck.

Around the scene, people screamed as his body went flying. It hit the pavement so hard it bounced. He flopped over a couple of times and lay still.

The truck driver got out of the cab, cursing about pedestrians who didn't pay attention to traffic or the right-of-way. I ignored him and ran to the body in the middle of East Ferry. "You." I pointed at a grocer who stood, mouth open, a few feet away. "You got a telephone? Call for an ambulance."

The man nodded and went inside.

I approached Evans carefully. I could see blood from scraped palms and knees and a gash on his forehead. He didn't move. I steeled myself and touched his neck, but I didn't feel a pulse.

Evans, aka Paul Fasenmyr, was dead as a doornail.

* * *

I stood on the sidewalk, staring at the body draped with a sheet. The ambulance crew had come and gone. There was nothin' for them to do. I gave my statement to a uniformed beat cop. The meat wagon from the morgue showed up, and a couple of white-coated men got out to do whatever it was they had to do. As I watched them work, I became aware of a tug on my sleeve.

It was Sam. "Why am I not surprised to see you?"

"What are you doin' at an accident scene?"

"The patrol officer phoned in as soon as they had an ID on the body from your statement. There's an APB out across the city for Fasenmyr." His puss looked glum. "What happened?"

I pointed at the cop. "I already told him."

"Tell me."

I described my search for Evans, Fasenmyr, whatever you wanted to call him, including talking to the bartender, then seeing my quarry and chasing him down the street. "Dummy didn't even look both ways, just stepped off the curb." I glanced over at the truck. "How's the driver?"

"Pretty shook up. He won't get in any trouble, if that's what you're wondering."

"That's good." I watched as the morgue guys bundled the body onto a gurney and into the back of the wagon. "There goes a solid lead. Now we'll never know why he went to work for the Carstairses. And under a fake name, no less."

"Maybe, maybe not." Sam lit a cigarette. "You say his sister didn't know?"

"Well, that's what Hazel said. But you know how it goes." I ripped my attention away from the accident scene and felt my knees wobble.

Sam caught me by the elbow. "Steady there. Let's go sit."

He guided me into another neighborhood pub and deposited me in a booth. He went to the bar and came back with a glass of whiskey, which he set in front of me. "Drink up."

"No, thanks. Gladys gave me some of this stuff, and it's awful." I pushed the glass away.

"Who's Gladys?"

"Oh, a friend of Melvin's at the *Courier*. You remember him, right? The reporter?"

"I do. She probably had rot gut that was bottled last week. You need a bracer." He nudged it back towards me. "I'm pretty sure this is better quality. Small sips, that's the key."

Sam wouldn't leave me alone until I tried. Doubtful, I raised the glass to my lips and followed his instructions. This time, the alcohol slid down my throat with a slight warmth and only the hint of a burn.

"Better?" Sam arched an eyebrow.

I gave a grudging nod. "I've never seen anything like that before."

"I didn't think you had." He tipped back his fedora. "That's what I want to see. A little color in those cheeks."

I took another drink. It went down even smoother than the first.

"How much do you know about Fasenmyr?"

I set the whiskey aside. I felt a lot calmer. "Only what you told me before."

"I assume you'd like to know what else I've found."

I nodded.

Sam flipped open his notes. "Apparently, Fasenmyr went to work for the Carstairs family right after his brother-in-law's death. He presented himself with a new name and phony references."

"I can't believe no one recognized him. At least Marian should have."

"From what I can gather, if she did, she didn't say anything. He was several years older than his sister. He knew Marian from the society pages and Hazel's descriptions, but the two had not met, at least not more than once or twice. By the time he sought employment, he was older, heavier, and his nose had been broken in a street fight at least once."

It might have been enough to hide his identity. Maybe Marian thought he looked like a man she once met, but that would be it. "I've talked to Hazel. She plays it cool, but there's no love lost between her and Marian, even after all these years. I'm still not sure why he did it. Went to work for the Carstairses, I mean." I thought back to my meeting with Hazel.

"I'm not sure, but there would be a reason. You mentioned Robert Newcombe. His death was ruled a suicide. But there was some question at the time."

I wouldn't need to wait on Emmeline after all. "Like what?"

"His wife claimed she came home from shopping and found him seated in a chair, pistol on the floor beside him. He'd been shot through the right temple. However, police were unable to lift clear fingerprints from the gun. They were too smudged, and it was possible there were several sets on the grip. Also, the coroner waffled on whether the body was moved post-mortem." Sam switched his gaze to me.

Moved? "Was he right-handed?"

"Ambidextrous, according to people who knew him. He most often wrote with his right hand. At school, writing with his left would have been discouraged. But co-workers and friends said he did many other tasks with his left."

"Would he have used his right or his left to shoot?"

Sam reached for my whiskey. "Unknown. To make it more difficult, no one tested him for nitrite, which would have indicated if he'd fired a gun."

I chewed my thumbnail. "He left a note."

"Yes, allegedly. His wife said the handwriting wasn't his. Police experts weren't sure. There were differences, but they could have been caused by a distraught mind." Sam lifted the glass in an unspoken question.

I waved it off. I didn't need alcohol clouding my thoughts. "In other words, it mighta been murder."

"Or it could have been what it seemed. In the absence of a clear motive from anyone in his immediate circle, the death was ruled a suicide. But I've looked at the notes from the detective who was called to the scene. He had doubts, but no evidence." He downed the whiskey.

Interesting. Hazel claimed she hadn't been left any money when her husband died. If she had, that definitely woulda been motive for murder, which she'd tried to cover to look like suicide. But she hadn't. "Hazel also told me Robert believed Old Man Carstairs blackballed him over what she called 'outrageous stories.'" Stories. Why hadn't I seen it? "Do you think Robert coulda known about Noemi? If he ran his yap, that's how Hazel and her brother woulda learned about it."

Sam set down the glass. "That makes sense. Anthony Carstairs would have been desperate to keep the story from coming to light. But if Robert Newcombe had gone to him, maybe threatened to tell the truth, Carstairs would have fired him in a New York minute?"

I tried to imagine what I'd have done. "If Old Man Carstairs simply fired him, Robert still coulda gone public with what he knew, and the result would be the same. Instead, Mr. Carstairs painted his former employee as unstable and depressed and then showed him the door. This way, even if he did blab, anything he said would be discredited." How cruel could two people be? "Robert got a small pension. Hazel said it was for past service, but what if it was a payoff?" If Robert had killed himself, it was another reason Hazel might hold a grudge against Marian.

"It's certainly one possibility." Sam flipped his notebook shut and put it away. "Here's another one. Perhaps Hazel realized her husband's stories were true. She tells her brother. Both siblings needed money. What could they do with information about a scandal like that?"

I stared at my glass. "Blackmail."

"Bingo. If it had come to light that Anthony Carstairs had forced a woman to give up her child, even if he paid her, it would have ruined his reputation. Come to think of it, the money made it worse." Sam checked his notebook. "This isn't the 1800s, and it's not the British aristocracy. Snobbery, and keeping your son away from an undesirable marriage, is one thing. Forcibly separating a mother and child is completely different."

"But why the job? Why not take the dough and run?" I asked.

"That I don't know."

I didn't know if the whiskey had cleared my head, but I didn't feel woozy any longer. "I don't s'pose any of the people you talked to, or Robert's death report, said anything about a love triangle between him, Hazel, and Marian. I'd still like to know the truth about how that story played out."

"No. I can only assume it wasn't considered relevant at the time."

It might not have been important back then. But I sure would like to know the truth. There was one person left who might know. "Is Theo Carstairs still in jail?"

He played with his glass. "Before I answer that, there's one more question you haven't asked. A very important one."

What did he mean? I'd covered everything except…it hit me. "If Evans or his sister was blackmailing the Carstairs family, where's the money?"

"Precisely." He pushed away the glass. "That's what you need to find out."

"Why me? Wouldn't you have better resources?"

"Officially, my investigation is closed." He folded his hands. "As far as my superiors are concerned, Marian's homicide is solved. We got our man and now it's up to the lawyers."

My mouth hung open for a second. "But what about Evans and the blackmail? If Marian learned about it and threatened to go public, isn't that motive?"

"Yes, but where's the proof?" He held up his fingers. "We're guessing. There's no evidence Evans knew about Noemi or her baby. Neither Evans nor Hazel are living lavishly, raising a question of where they're getting the money. Neither of them have fat bank accounts that we know of. We found nothing in Marian Carstairs's personal effects to indicate she was being blackmailed. I'm stuck." He waited a beat. "But you aren't."

It took me a moment to work out what he meant. "I don't need reasonable doubt or warrants to keep nosing around. Is that what you mean?" What he said was true. But it also meant I had to get my hands on a lot more dope on the scene than I had. "I'll need a little help."

"Meet me at the soda shop that's kitty-corner from the Broadway Market tomorrow at lunch. I'll bring what I can." Sam stood. "As far as Theo Carstairs goes, rich men can afford good lawyers. He was released this morning. He should be at home." He took a few steps, then faced me. "If you're thinking of talking to him, though, his attorney almost certainly instructed him to clam up."

"I know." I picked up my purse. "But you always said I had a knack for getting people to talk."

Chapter Thirty-Four

The sun still shone in Delaware Park. The homes looked stately, and the breeze through the leaves gave it a peaceful air, but the mood came off as somber. Maybe it was me. Knowing what went on behind those dignified walls stripped away a lot of the glamor.

Theo opened the door. "You again."

I tried for a joke. "Still answerin' your own bell?"

"Mrs. Vance is busy, and my butler is in the wind. Somebody has to."

"I found him. Evans."

"Is he coming back to work?"

"Not exactly." I craned to look over his shoulder. "You're prob'ly not eager to talk, and I'm sure your lawyer told you to keep your yap shut."

"I'm not, and he did." His grip on the door didn't budge. "What do you mean by not exactly?"

I told him about the accident, and he barely reacted. "I'm still on Noemi's trail."

No response.

"Theo. I'm gonna be straight. I know you've had nothing but trouble since I showed up." I waited for him to slam the door in my puss. When he didn't, I continued. "I'm gonna do my best to find Noemi and who shot your sister. But I need your help. If you tell me to scram, I will. I hope you won't."

He stared at me, eyes almost dead. Then he walked away.

I interpreted that as an invitation. It might not be, but he could always call the cops. I pushed the door shut behind me.

He was busy at the bar in his study when I went in.

He didn't turn around. "Drink?"

"No, thank you." I was sure Theo's whiskey was as good, if not better, than what Sam had given me. But I didn't want to get used to the taste and it was early afternoon. I sat. I noticed he'd lined up three glasses and filled two of them with ice and alcohol. Who was he expectin'? "Did you see Private Lake while you were in the joint?"

"I deliberately avoided him. I didn't want the first meeting with my son to be while we were in jail." He stayed near the bar, tumbler in hand.

The doorbell rang. Theo didn't move this time. Mrs. Vance answered, and I heard muted voices. She entered. "There's someone to see you, Mr. Carstairs."

I barely recognized Private Lake as the spit and polished soldier I'd first met. His uniform was rumpled, and the shadow of stubble showed on his jaw. But it wasn't enough to mask the similarities with Theo. They were almost the same height. Theo was a little heavier and broader in the shoulder, but not much. The facial features that were sharp in him were a little softened in Private Lake, but not so much I couldn't tell these two were definitely related. Even their ears were shaped the same. Private Lake's hair was a little lighter, as were his eyes. *His mother's influence.* I watched them.

They stared at each other for a long moment. Private Lake held his cap in his hands. "Father?"

Theo didn't move. "You look like your mother."

The tension was thick, and I could cut it with a knife. "You know what? You two need to talk. Without me hangin' around. I'll go." I took a step.

Private Lake caught me by the sleeve. "Stay, please. I want you to."

"I don't know."

"I do." He faced his father. Emotions flashed across his face too quickly to identify. "Why'd you leave Mom? You never looked for her. Or me."

Theo grasped his glass. "They told me you were dead."

"You didn't try to find out for sure, did you?"

"What did you think I could do?" Theo put the whiskey on the bar in an over-careful movement. "You have to understand. You didn't know your grandfather. He was an…intimidating man. No, I didn't stand up to him. I'm ashamed of that. I won't deny it. But when Miss Ahern told me about you, I didn't rest. I was on the phone with my lawyer when the police showed up."

"Did you think getting me out of jail would make up for what you did?"

"I hoped it would be a start." Theo half-laughed. "Turns out I needed a lawyer myself."

I watched the men in front of me. I'd never been so uncomfortable in my life. "I really don't think I should be here."

"I told you to stay. You work for me, right?" Private Lake's voice was harsh, but his gaze was fixed on Theo. "Did Aunt Marian know about me?" He stumbled over the word "aunt." All these new relatives to deal with musta been difficult for him to work through. "When I came to see her."

His father gave a sad laugh. "Before that day? I don't know. But she rubbed it in my face after you left. She wanted me to know I'd lost you all over again."

"Did you kill her?"

"No!" A muscle near Theo's eye twitched. "That awful woman... Christopher, all I want is a chance. I've much to make up for. I've only begun. Please."

The private turned to me. "What do you think, Betty?"

Who was I to give advice? I thought of my own personal troubles, my conflicted feelings about Tom and Frank, and how jumbled everything was. I weighed my words carefully. "I'm no expert. But in my experience, cuttin' off someone who loves you is never a good thing. He is your father, Private. Sure, you might think he shoulda done more twenty years ago. That doesn't mean you shouldn't give him a chance to do the right thing now."

Private Lake was quiet for a long moment. Then he nodded. "I won't stick around if you're a murderer."

Again, a flicker of movement near Theo's eye. "I wouldn't expect you to." He looked like he wanted to embrace his son, but held himself back.

"Well, now that's out of the way, we can all have a chat." I glanced at Theo. "I hope you two intend to sit 'cause otherwise, I'm gonna have to stand, and that'll be awkward."

They both took seats. "Betty, why are you here anyway?" Private Lake asked.

"I wanted to talk to your dad. I didn't know you were comin'." I sent a quizzical look toward Theo.

He didn't move. "I said I didn't want to meet my son in jail, not that I didn't want to see him at all."

Private Lake looked from me to his father. "What do you want to talk about?"

I sat. "Here's the thing. I got a feeling these two events, Noemi goin' missing and Marian's death, are connected."

Private Lake blurted out the question. "How?"

"Not sure." I focused on Theo. "You said you didn't recognize Evans as Paul Fasenmyr. I've learned some stuff that makes me think he and his sister coulda been blackmailing your dad, the older Mr. Carstairs." I took out my notebook. "That's what I'd like to ask you about. That and the day of your sister's death."

Theo coulda been sculpted outta rock except for the movement of his hand as he drank.

"Let's start with Marian. You were the only one home that day. You had to see or hear something, maybe even the gunshot."

Theo's face didn't move. "I'm sorry to disappoint you."

I wanted to snap at him but sensed that wouldn't help. He was either lyin' or hidin' something. I looked at the glass in his hand. "Why do I get the feelin' you aren't telling me the truth?"

His eyes bored into mine. "I may have heard Christopher arrive. But not much after that."

"Were you sloshed?"

He lifted his glass.

I looked around the study. I'd been here a couple of days ago. How much whiskey had been in the decanter? It had been almost full, and it still was. I'd yet to see Theo without a drink in his hands, and he often poured himself two or more in front of me. How much did he drink? "Your father and sister didn't make life easy on you. Shut out of the business, scorned, not allowed free rein with your dough. It's enough to drive a man to drink." I paused. "I get that you don't wanna look bad in front of your son. But right now, he's on the hook for murder. What would you rather? Lose him again, for good this time? Or admit you hit the bottle more than you should?"

Private Lake faced his dad, drink forgotten. "Father, please. I don't want to go back to jail. I've spent almost twenty years thinking about who my family was. I don't know that I'm ready to forgive you, but if you know something that'll help me, now's the time to say it." He swallowed hard. "It doesn't matter if you were drunk. Heck, I don't care if you've been that way for years. Betty is a good egg. I know it. Be honest with her, and she'll get to the bottom of what happened."

I was touched by Private Lake's faith. With any luck, his appeal would get through where I'd failed.

Theo hung his head and swirled his whiskey. "That's what I'm afraid of. It's the story of my life. I'd rather it all went away. Whatever you imagined your father to be, I bet it wasn't a coward. I heard you arrive, the ensuing argument, and the front door slam. Afterward, Marian came in to see me. She taunted me, said I'd never guess who had been to see her. Then she told me it didn't matter because I'd never see you again. She'd make sure of that. In that moment, yes, I could have killed her. I wanted to, in fact. What kept me from doing it was the possibility I could find you again."

I glanced at Private Lake, then swung to face Theo. "After that, you did what you always did. Got drunk."

He pressed his hands to his eyes. "I seem to spend a lot of time that way. It's what happens when you don't have anything useful to do. I passed out cold. The next thing I remember is the maid screaming. I went into Marian's sitting room, and there she was."

I took out my notebook and reviewed what I'd written earlier. "What about the second visitor, Hazel?"

Theo's expression turned wary. "What about her?"

"You didn't hear her arrive?" I watched him.

"Perhaps you missed the part where I was unconscious." He got up and went to the bar.

I had to find out how soon Hazel had arrived after Private Lake left. I already knew from Mrs. Babbage that Evans woulda been here. Did he and his sister confront Marian together? "When was the last time you saw your father's pistols?"

"I can't tell you." He didn't look at me. "But you could have knocked me over with a feather when the police found one in my drawer."

"What time was this?" I asked.

He clenched his fists and snarled. "I wasn't paying attention to the clock. If I had known...I would have acted differently, but it's too late now."

If he'd known what? *He must mean that if he knew about Noemi and Private Lake back then, he wouldn't have knuckled under.* I paged back in my notes. "Was Marian in love with Robert Newcombe?"

Theo faced me. "They were engaged. Oh, it hadn't been announced yet, but Marian was over the moon."

"They were?" Hazel had led me to believe Robert had switched his affection before things got serious with Marian.

"Dad gloated about how my time as a layabout was coming to an end, and I'd better figure out what to do with myself." Theo picked up his tumbler and set it back down. "He was thrilled he'd be adding Robert to the family. Then, one day, the engagement was off. Dad didn't say anything about it. Marian lost her mind. Eventually, Dad sent her away to get her to 'snap out of it,' as he put it. I wasn't paying too much attention to Marian, to be honest. I had my own heartbreak."

I thought about my timeline. "That woulda been right around the time Noemi left."

A spasm of pain crossed Theo's face. "Yes. I knew she was pregnant. I was all set to tell my father I was leaving to marry her, but it was too late. She left behind a note saying she was very sorry, she loved me, but this was for the best." He shot a guilty look at Private Lake. "I regret that I didn't look for her. Instead..."

"You got drunk." Private Lake's voice was harsh, unforgiving.

Theo hung his head for a moment. "Noemi was sure it was not a simple case of a man changing his affections. Robert, I mean. She never liked Hazel, and she was quite sorry for Marian and her broken heart. Noemi was always a romantic."

I let the silence stretch, unwilling to break it. But I had to. "Last question. Did you ever think your dad, or Marian, was being blackmailed?"

Theo thought for a moment. "No clue. Then again, neither of them would have talked to me about it, and they deliberately shut me out of anything financial, both family and business." He gazed at his son. "I wish I'd stayed sober that day. None of this would have happened. It seems my life is marred with one bad decision after another. But now that Evans is dead, perhaps..." He switched his focus to me. "You're quite sure about that, Miss Ahern? No mistaken identity?"

"None at all."

Theo swirled the whiskey in his glass but didn't drink. "Then there's still time."

Chapter Thirty-Five

I left Private Lake and Theo alone. They had a lot to talk about and I didn't need to be listening in. My progress report about Noemi could wait. I'd learned my lesson about giving information too early. Theo clearly wanted to make up for all the years he'd lost out on. I wanted to reassure him, tell him of course he had plenty of time to get to know his son, and that Private Lake would forgive him eventually.

But a niggling doubt at the back of my mind kept me from sayin' any of it.

As I headed for the door, I saw Mrs. Vance. "Can I borrow your phone book?" I'd been so busy I hadn't looked up Homer Glassman to get an address. I wanted to go to Evans's apartment next, but I might as well see if I could knock off two tasks in a day.

Mrs. Vance brought me a thick book. "What are you looking up?"

"Homer Glassman."

"Noemi said her husband is dead. I don't see why you want to find him."

I thumbed to the G's. "'Cause if he still has a listing, she might live there. Or at least someone might know where to look next." I didn't think it was all that special, but Mrs. Vance sure looked impressed at my logic.

Unfortunately, there were four listings for a Homer, or H, Glassman. "May I borrow your telephone?"

She led me back to the library. "I'll give you some privacy." She closed the door.

The first listing was no longer in service. The other three denied knowing Noemi or a Belgian woman. I stared at the first address on Winslow Avenue. On a hunch, I scribbled it down. It wasn't far from East Ferry. I'd be able to make a visit after I finished up pokin' around at Evans's place.

I'd seen a couple of boarding houses and apartment buildings for single men. Evans's was definitely on the seedier side. It was a plain brick building, no frills, no balconies. The front was pushed right up next to the sidewalk, and the brickwork desperately needed a cleaning. Inside, a row of mailboxes lined the wall. I ran my finger down the names. Evans was written on a slip of paper for 1D. He'd played his role well.

I found the door to the building manager and knocked, but no one answered. After the third try, I wandered down the hallway. The door to 1D was scuffed along the bottom, and the numbers were in a dark metal of some kind. I had expected there to be crime scene tape, but there was none. Maybe the cops didn't have to seal off the apartment. Or they hadn't come. After all, he'd been killed in a truck accident. But after what I'd told Sam, I couldn't believe they'd ignore where he lived. I didn't expect an answer, but I tapped on the door, loud enough for anyone inside to hear, but quietly enough that I wouldn't disturb the neighbors.

Nothing.

I tried the handle, but the door was locked. I snuck a look up and down the deserted hallway. The man was dead, and odds were good I wouldn't be interruptin' the police. I needed to get inside. *What the heck?* I took my lock picks out of my purse. It wasn't like the last time I'd broken into a man's house. Right? That guy had still been alive.

In a jiffy, I had the door open, and I stepped inside. One word came to mind. Barren. There was a plain wooden table with one chair in the dining room. The living room had another chair, the brown fabric worn at the corners. A scattered pile of mail was on the table. I looked through it, but all was addressed to P. Evans. There were no pictures. Was I wrong about Evans bein' Hazel's brother? Or did I have the wrong Evans?

The medicine cabinet in the tiny bathroom held only a man's shaving kit and a bottle of aspirin. The cheap shower curtain around the claw-foot tub was stained at the bottom. A bar of plain, white soap was stuck to the enamel. Thin towels hung on the rack.

The bedroom wasn't much better. One twin bed, the sheets old enough you could see through 'em. The clothes in the closet showed a mix of butler's duds and a selection of shirts and pants any working man would wear. I must be in the right place, 'cause two butlers in Buffalo named Evans would be too much of a coincidence. One pair of shiny black shoes and one pair of scuffed loafers. Nothing on the top shelf. The chest of drawers held only underwear, socks, and a few plain cotton hankies. Whatever he'd done with the dough, assuming I was right about the blackmail, he wasn't spendin' it on clothes or his living space.

"What a bust." I knelt down to look under the bed. Nothing but dust. I ran my hand under the box spring and then the mattress but came up empty. A search of the small desk in the corner yielded only a few stamps and sheets of cheap stationery. "Either I'm wrong about this guy, or he's a better actor than Bogie." I thought about Hazel's reaction when I saw the picture of her brother. Fear, that's what had shown on her face. I couldn't be wrong. What would she be afraid of?

Where would a blackmailer stash his loot? And his proof?

I wandered back to the kitchen. In the movies, the crooks hid stuff in toilets, flour containers, or under loose floorboards. I dismissed the bathroom. Whatever Evans had would be too delicate for water. He wouldn't want it damaged, even if he wrapped it in oiled cloth. I looked at the floor. It was linoleum, a solid sheet that went from wall to wall. No loose floorboards there. Aside from a few chipped cups and some plates, I didn't see a container in Evans's cupboards big enough to hide anything more than a stamp.

I knelt and looked at the cabinet under the sink. He had a few bottles of cleaner. One of the pipes dripped into a bucket. The floor was covered by more linoleum. I was about to close the door when the glint of the light caught my eye. Was that a bump in the floor? I ran my hand over it. I hadn't imagined it. The area was small, but there was definitely something underneath the flooring.

I looked around for a tool and had to settle for a butter knife. I eased up the corner of the rubbery covering as I didn't want to rip whatever was underneath. It felt like it took forever, and I half-expected the building super to bust in on me at any moment, but eventually, my patience was rewarded.

It was an envelope of photographs. I sat cross-legged on the floor. Some of 'em were of a group of boys at play. I recognized the dome of Our Lady of Victory and the buildings of Father Baker's Home for Boys in the background. One boy was circled in black marker. Private Lake? I flipped them over. Each photo was dated. The most recent was ten years old.

The other pictures showed a woman. She was slim with medium-dark hair. None of the photos were close-ups. It was hard to make out her features, but they seemed soft and delicate. The snaps caught her in a number of places. I recognized the Broadway Market, the park up by the Albright Knox Art Gallery, and what might have been City Hall. I doubted she knew she was being photographed. Her clothes were plain, but still showed a girlish figure, even though the backgrounds betrayed the passage of time through seasons and small details, such as the prices at the Market. I looked at the back. These were also dated. The earliest ones had "N.G.?" written on 'em. The most recent was dated two months ago. I peered at it. That was Roesch's butcher shop at the Broadway Market. I was sure of it. The photographer had captured Noemi placing an order at the counter.

I had no doubt I was lookin' at the proof Evans had used to blackmail Old Man Carstairs and Marian. But it still didn't answer the question of why he'd stuck around so long.

A thump in the hallway startled me. I looked at the cheap wall clock. I'd been in the apartment for nearly an hour. Time to skedaddle. I slipped the envelope of pictures in my purse and smoothed down the linoleum, before sneaking out and making sure the door was locked behind me.

* * *

Luck stayed with me. I made it out of the building without being seen. Once on the sidewalk, I stopped and lit a cigarette. When I put the photographs together with what Mrs. Vance told me, it was clear that Evans had been followin' Noemi and her son, at least while he was a little kid. It had to be blackmail. Why else would he do it?

I blew smoke as I thought. Hazel wouldn't tell me if her brother had been up to no good. Especially if she was gettin' any of the dough. I'd have to find proof of my idea somewhere else.

I hurried across the street to a drugstore. I found the payphone and called the Carstairs house. Mrs. Vance answered. "I'm not letting you talk to Mr. Theodore. He's in his study with his son, and they need to be left in peace." Her voice was firm, but soft.

It seemed I'd gotten back in her good graces, at least a little bit, by reuniting the two men. "I don't need to talk to him. You said Evans was hired ten years ago."

"Give or take."

"Was Mr. Carstairs alive? I'm talkin' about Marian and Theo's dad."

"Yes."

I pulled my notebook out and licked my pencil stub. "Do you remember who hired him?"

"Oh, Mr. Carstairs personally approved all the household staff right up until the day before he died." Mrs. Vance paused. "Why does it matter?"

I thought about the pictures. "I found proof that Evans knew about Noemi and Christopher, which would mean he knew the official story was a lie. Could he have blackmailed Mr. Carstairs?"

"Oh, I don't think that would be true." She sounded very sure. "Mr. Carstairs was not a man to be trifled with."

"Not even if someone threatened to say he'd paid a young woman to leave his house and give up her baby? Would he really want that story spread around the city?" I waited a beat. "Mr. Carstairs, or Marian, never said or did anything to make you think that was happenin'?"

"Well, when you put it that way..." She paused. "No, I don't believe it. "You're causing trouble again. Mr. Carstairs would have had good reasons to hire Evans, and they would have had nothing to do with blackmail. I have work to do, Miss Ahern. Good-bye." She hung up.

Mrs. Vance didn't buy the story. I had no problem with it. The elder Carstairs wouldn't have wanted to look bad, and Marian would've done anything to keep her father's reputation intact. And there was only one way

Evans woulda known about Noemi and her baby.

His sister.

Hazel had seduced Robert, thinkin' he was set to inherit the Carstairs business. When that went off the rails, and he died, she'd have been left high and dry. She and her brother cooked up a scheme to squeeze Old Man Carstairs. If Robert's stories had been crazy, the old man wouldn't have paid. But he did. Perhaps they'd asked for a small amount the first time, just to test the water. "Then they kept goin' back to the well." That could be a reason Evans got the butler's job. To make sure Carstairs didn't go to the cops. Or to judge when the time was right to ask for another payment.

Private Lake's appearance would've given Marian an out. The prodigal son returns. All she had to do was reveal Christopher's existence, and her blackmailer's hold would be gone. She'd be able to reveal years of blackmail to the cops. Evans must have realized that when the private came to the house. To stay outta jail, he had to get rid of Marian.

Hazel had been there because her brother called her. To help stage another scene? Maybe Marian's death was s'posed to look like suicide, like Robert. Distraught over the secret of her father's actions all those years ago coming out, she'd taken her own life. Or so people were s'posed to think.

I liked that idea better than if Theo or Private Lake was guilty. But, at the moment, it was simply an idea. I couldn't ignore the possibility one of 'em really had pulled the trigger. Theo had plenty of motive, 'specially if Marian had taunted him with his son's existence.

Private Lake had admitted she'd threatened him with the pistol. But how would he know where to stash it? Easy. He coulda looked through the rooms and found one that seemed likely.

What I needed was the truth about Theo's relationship with his family. Had he really been meek? I made a call to the library. "Emmeline, I need you to do something."

"Now what? I'm not done researching Robert Newcombe."

Doggone it. In my haste to search Evans's apartment, I'd forgotten to call her after I left Sam. "I'm sorry. But I don't need that anymore." I told her about talkin' to Sam.

Her annoyance came through loud and clear. "Then I wasted my morning."

"That's my fault. I shoulda called you, but I got flustered. I'll try not to let it happen again."

She grumbled, and the sound of paper being crumpled came over the line. "All right. Shoot."

"Go back to at least one of those society mentions of the Carstairs family. Find me someone else who was there. A person who woulda been in the same social circle and might have been a friend of the family." I thought again about the missing money. "Also, think of how someone would hide dough they didn't want found." I explained my blackmail theory.

"Friend of family, how to hide illegal money, got it." She mumbled to herself. "What should I do when I'm done?"

"Call me at this number." I rattled off the digits. I'd have to stay nearby until she called back, but I'd use the time to put my thoughts in order.

"I'll get right on it."

I hung up. I had no doubt Emmeline would come up aces. I only hoped that when I tracked the person down, I'd get the story I wanted to hear.

Chapter Thirty-Six

I t took nearly an hour for Emmeline to call me back. "There were a lot of acquaintances in the stories, but this name keeps popping up. George Braxton. As close as I can tell, he was a friend of Anthony Carstairs, the father."

I wrote down the name. "You're tellin' me he's old."

"Mid to late seventies. But still alive. I have his address and phone number as well."

"Now we're cooking with gas. What are they?"

She read 'em off. "Anything else I can do for you?"

"I think that's it for now. Thanks." I hung up. The address she'd given me was on Windsor Avenue. It wasn't quite as swanky a neighborhood as where the Carstairses lived, but still pretty nice. That told me while Mr. Braxton might not have as much dough as the Carstairs family, he was still fairly well off. Since I wanted him to talk to me, I decided to call first, 'specially as it was gettin' on toward supper.

A man answered the phone. "Braxton here."

I'd expected to have to battle my way through servants. "Um, is this Mr. George Braxton?"

"That's me. Who are you?"

I identified myself.

"A woman private detective? That's a new one on me. What can I help you with?"

Mr. Braxton sure was talkative. Or he was about to pull the rug out from under me. "I'm told you were friendly with the Carstairs family back in the day."

He wheezed what might have been a laugh. "Carstairs? That old goat didn't have friends. I suppose I came as close as anyone. He didn't hate me or see me as a competitor. Say." The sound of his voice betrayed his curiosity. "You wouldn't be looking into the death of his daughter, would you? I read young Theo is in a spot of hot water over that. Boy always was impulsive."

I seized on the opening. "I am. You've prob'ly read about the arrest of another man as well. Some people, includin' me, have a lot of questions about the official story. I'm lookin' for someone who knew the family back in their heyday."

"And you think that's me?"

"You were at a lot of the same parties."

He gave another wheezy laugh. "That I was. I don't know how much I can help you. But I'm an old man with a lot of time on my hands. The Carstairs family has been considered uppercrust society in Buffalo for a long time, Anthony and his kids." There was a moment of silence. "Have you ever heard the saying 'old sins cast long shadows' Miss Ahern?"

"I have. My grandparents have said that many a time." I paused. "Are you sayin' there are a lot of old sins in that family?"

"I am." Mr. Braxton sounded solemn. "And it's high time some of their secrets came out before any more innocent people are hurt. Are you free this evening?"

My heart skipped a beat. "Yes."

"Then tell me when you think you'll be here. I'll have the coffee ready."

* * *

The late afternoon sun shone in my eyes when I got off the bus. Mr. Braxton had given me directions. I turned left down Windsor. His house was four down from the corner, a tall, narrow place painted dark blue with white trim. The neighborhood wasn't swanky, but all the homes were well cared for. It reminded me of the neighborhood around Buffalo State Hospital, where Frank lived. Moneyed, but not quite as much as the Buffalo elite. I wondered if Mr. Braxton had always lived here or if he'd started in Delaware Park and was forced to move after the stock market crashed.

I used the shiny brass knocker to bang on the door. Mr. Braxton had answered his own phone. Would he open the door, too?

My question was answered a minute later when an elderly man with a head of silver hair opened it. He would have been tall once, but age had bent him over. He was not stocky or especially thin. His hands were gnarled, the knuckles swollen. He wore a nice shirt and slacks, and loafers. "Mr. Braxton?"

"In the flesh. You must be Miss Ahern."

"Yes, sir. Sorry, I'm a little later than I said."

"No worries. I always add at least five minutes to a bus schedule. Please, come in." He stepped back.

I hesitated. Mr. Braxton seemed like a nice man. But now that I was there, I wondered at the wisdom of goin' into a strange man's house. Even if that man looked twisted up with age and arthritis. I figured I could beat him in a fight. But youth and agility wouldn't help if he decided to shoot me.

He chuckled, and his dark brown eyes twinkled. "Right now, you're thinking perhaps this isn't such a good idea, aren't you? Very wise, miss. Not many girls would stop to wonder. A jolly old man may not be as harmless as he seems."

Part of me felt ashamed. I should respect my elders, right? But I'd seen too much in my short detective career. "No offense, but that's exactly it."

"None taken. As I said, it's a smart decision." He patted his pockets, obviously looking for something. He pulled a ring of keys from one. Then he looked at the grandfather clock in the hall. "Are you hungry?"

My stomach rumbled, and the denial that had been on my lips died away. "Yeah, I don't remember what I had for lunch."

"There is a very nice Italian restaurant around the corner." He came outside and pulled the door shut. "My treat."

"That's not necessary. Besides, you brewed coffee."

"Nonsense." He offered me his arm. "I don't get out much these days. Any

227

excuse to avoid cooking is welcome. And the coffee is only chicory. No great loss there."

We chatted about this and that as we walked. The war, the weather, my detective career, and baseball. I didn't have to say much. Mr. Braxton dominated the conversation. I got the impression he liked to talk, and no one came around often enough to satisfy him. Once at the restaurant, I scanned the menu, looking for the cheapest meal. My eyes popped at the prices. Five bucks for plain old spaghetti? Sure, it came with bread and a salad, but still. *Maybe I should get the soup.*

An elderly waiter in a black suit came over to the table. "Are you ready?"

Mr. Braxton seemed to read my mind. "You order what you want and don't mind the cost."

I wondered why he was bein' generous. Did he expect I'd come home with him after dinner? "Spaghetti, thanks."

The waiter wrote my order. "With a meatball or sausage?"

"She'll have sausage," Mr. Braxton said. "I'll have the chicken parmigiana with a glass of chianti, please." He handed back his menu. "Anything for you Miss Ahern? If you'd rather have meatballs, that's fine. I took you for more of a sausage enthusiast."

I cleared my throat. "Water. Sausage is fine."

The waiter glided away as much as an old guy could.

I faced my host. "Mr. Braxton, I'm very grateful, don't get me wrong. But—"

He held up his hand. "Miss Ahern, I told you. I have very few visitors and none of the ones in recent memory were as charming as you. Besides, if I'm right, you're going to give me an opportunity to get some things off my chest that I've wanted to talk about for many years."

"Why haven't you? Talked to someone, I mean."

"You don't quite understand the power the Carstairs family wielded in society. First Anthony, then his daughter. No one wanted to cross them. Sadly, that included me." He rearranged his silverware. "Now they are both dead, and there are things that should be told. There is another reason, too."

"What's that?"

He held my gaze. "You are the first person who ever asked."

I spread my napkin, real linen that felt smooth as silk, on my lap. Taking notes would be out of the question. Not only was it outta place, I'd prob'ly get sauce all over the page. "How well did you know the Carstairs family?"

"Very." The waiter returned with a glass of wine, which Mr. Braxton accepted and sipped from.

"You weren't in the same business?"

"No. I owned a textile mill many years ago. I sold it in 1935. The market was too depressed, and I was too old. Anthony thought I was insane, of course, because if I'd held out, I could have gotten a much better price. But I'd made enough money. My wife had died. I spent time with my grandchildren until my son was transferred across the country by his company. I suppose working would have kept the loneliness of the last few years at bay, but my heart wasn't in it."

The waiter came with our bread and a dish of real butter. *Heaven.* I cut off a chunk of the creamy yellow goodness, not caring what Mr. Braxton thought. I'd had enough margarine to last a lifetime. "How'd you meet Mr. Carstairs?"

"Some party or other." Mr. Braxton spread a thick layer of butter on his own slice. Maybe he was tired of margarine, too. "Our sons were roughly the same age, Theodore and my David. I believe our first conversation was Anthony comparing the boys. I regret to say Theodore did not come out on top."

I took a moment to savor the creaminess of the butter. "I've been told old Mr. Carstairs and Marian didn't care much for Theo."

"The feeling was mutual."

"But Theo never did anything about it."

Mr. Braxton furrowed his bushy eyebrows. "Who told you that?" He took a bite of bread.

"He did. And their housekeeper, Mrs. Vance." I caught his knowing gaze. "You're about to tell me otherwise, aren't you?"

"Indeed." He wiped the corner of his mouth. "I'm not surprised about the housekeeper. She is very fond of Theo. She would want him to look sympathetic, the downtrodden younger son."

"You know about the maid, Noemi, and what happened?"

"Oh yes. That is, I know enough." He sipped his wine. "Theodore loved the Belgian girl, that was clear. There was a serious falling out, and she was let go. I heard rumors of a baby."

"It was more than a rumor." I popped the last bit of bread in my mouth.

He set down his wine. "That makes things much more logical. Theodore, while a very easygoing young man in most regards, has a terrible temper. Did you know that?"

I reached for the basket and nodded.

"I saw him nearly come to blows with his father on a couple of occasions. Not in public, of course. Or not at events, shall we say. Right after Noemi disappeared, I went to Anthony's house. When the butler let me in, I could hear a blazing fight between the two men and Marian. Theodore said, 'If I find out anything has happened to her, I'll kill you both.' He stormed out of Anthony's study after that. His father brushed it off, and I didn't pursue the matter."

"Did you believe him? Theo?"

"Without a doubt." Mr. Braxton sat back as the waiter placed a plate before him. "I've seen Theodore break things and throw objects. Expensive china and furniture. Marian stood up to him, but I could tell she felt at least a little fear. Fortunately for her, Theodore's temper flashes hot, then fades quickly. Otherwise, I'm quite sure one of them would have died years ago. He didn't have the opportunity to act immediately. I heard he did eventually try to hire an investigator, but his father put an end to that effort. Yes, in many ways, Theodore was a beaten man. Of course, such men are often the most dangerous."

Based on that description, it was a lot easier to see Theo shooting his sister. But why hide the gun in his own sock drawer? "What about Robert Newcombe? Did you know much about that?" The waiter put a plate heaped with pasta in front of me.

Mr. Braxton cut his chicken. "I was one of the few. That certainly stuck in Marian's craw."

"I'm surprised her father continued to employ a man who rejected her." He speared a piece of meat on his fork and ran it through the red sauce. "Truth be told, that affair bothered Marian much more than Anthony. He said any man whose mind could be changed that easily by a low-class trollop wasn't fit for his daughter. A good employee, yes. But not a suitor. Marian went to pieces. I believe it was the first time the girl had ever heard the word no. Anthony sent her away more to remove the embarrassment of her behavior than any real concern."

I thought about how much differently Pop would have acted. *Glad Anthony Carstairs wasn't my dad.*

"Business first, you see. Anthony was excellent at keeping the two areas separate. Robert had a sharp mind, at least at first. He made the company a lot of money, which is why Anthony kept him on. Pity what happened to him. Poor fellow had a nervous breakdown. Anthony eventually had to dismiss him, no matter what Robert's wife said after he died." He chewed.

My ears perked up. "That was Hazel, right? How does she come in?"

"She visited Marian and Anthony after Robert died. Anthony gave the widow a small pension. Robert had been a good worker before his illness. I heard Marian later cut it off. A woman scorned, and all that."

Interesting. Being snubbed as a girl might not be a good enough motive for blackmail. But if Marian had cut off Hazel's income, that might have pushed Hazel, and by extension Evans, over the line. I twirled up some spaghetti. "Did you know Evans, their butler, was Hazel's brother? His real name is Paul Fasenmyr. I found some evidence that he knew about Noemi. I think he mighta been using it to blackmail Mr. Carstairs."

Mr. Braxton looked up. "Was he now? You use the past tense. Did he quit?"

"He was hit by a truck."

"Well, well. That's interesting. It explains...I wonder." Mr. Braxton stopped chewing.

I waited, but he didn't speak. "You wonder what?"

He swallowed. "Anthony never said anything specific, but I got the impression he was unhappy about something. More than that, he was angry.

He'd had a little too much to drink at the club and said words that made me think there was a situation in his life he wanted to get rid of. He referred to it as 'death by a thousand cuts.'" He took a sip of wine. "When I pressed, Anthony waved it off as an unfortunate, but trivial, business arrangement. Now, I think he may have been talking about this Fasenmyr fellow."

My mind ran through what Mr. Braxton told me. I shook my head. "That doesn't make sense. Why would Mr. Carstairs employ a man who was blackmailing him?"

Mr. Braxton set down his glass. "Simple. Anthony didn't know Fasenmyr, or Evans, was the perpetrator."

He was right. And if Anthony Carstairs hadn't known about his butler, he sure wouldn't have suspected his butler's sister.

Chapter Thirty-Seven

I was full from dinner, so I got off the bus two blocks farther away from home to walk off the feeling. That and I needed to think. I strolled down Louisiana Street toward the First Ward, a lit cigarette in my hand, and studyin' the notes I'd scribbled while on the bus back from the restaurant.

Based on the photographs I'd found at Evans's apartment, I was sure they'd been blackmailing Old Man Carstairs and, later, Marian. That "pension" hadn't been for years of service. It had been to keep Robert quiet. Maybe Hazel and her brother had seen an opportunity for more dough once Hazel's husband had died. But why so many payments? A thought occurred to me. The brother and sister mighta wanted to keep it going, see how long the golden goose could keep laying that magical egg. Had one sibling come up with the idea, and the other went along for the ride?

A familiar voice jolted me out of my thoughts. "I hoped I would see you here. Before you reached home." It was Frank. He sauntered up the sidewalk, dressed casually in slacks and a button-down shirt open at the collar. The setting sun lit his dark hair, and his easy posture, hands in his pockets, once again reminded me of a young Jimmy Stewart, all boy next door. And a darned attractive one.

What was he doin' here? Technically, I had not reached the First Ward. There was still a couple of blocks before the border of my neighborhood. But it was too close for comfort. I pitched away my Lucky. "Why are you here?" The words came out harsher than I intended.

He didn't react. "I've looked at a map. There are two more intersections before the boundaries of the First Ward." He halted and put his hands out, palms up. "I found your family's phone number in the book. I called, but once I found out you weren't there, I decided to come over. I needed to see you." He took a step toward me. "I wanted to, is more like it. I've been tracing the bus stops, hoping to run across you. It's my lucky night."

I crossed my arms over my chest. "You phoned my house? Great. Now I gotta explain to my mother why strange men are calling me after business hours."

"I told them I was Private Lake." He was only an inch out of reach but seemed hesitant to get any closer. "He came to see me, by the way. I understand you found his father."

My head told me to move away. My heart wanted to get closer. I didn't give in to either of 'em. "How's it goin' with them? Did he say?"

"It's a work in progress." Frank seemed to sense my discomfort, because he stayed where he was. "Christopher has many years of resentment to overcome. But he's trying. He believes you may still find out what happened to his mother. But being in his father's house is strange."

"I bet." It was prob'ly difficult for Theo as well. Imagine bein' faced with the grown child you believed dead for nearly two decades. I wondered again about Theo. What I'd learned from Mr. Braxton made it even more possible Theo'd lashed out at his sister. How would that affect his relationship with Private Lake? "Why'd you come, Frank? If you've talked to Christopher, you know everything."

"I wanted to congratulate you."

"I haven't finished the job yet. I still don't know what happened to Noemi, and I don't know if Christopher shot his aunt."

"You don't believe that."

"It's not about belief. It's about proof." Sam would be proud of my response. "That doesn't really explain why you're here. I don't see you for days, and all of a sudden, you show up near my home? That doesn't make any kind of sense."

He lowered his head. After a moment, he looked up. "I've thought about you a lot, Betty. Perhaps more than I should, but I can't help it." He reached out but lowered his arm. "I know you're engaged. But my heart doesn't care. I needed to see you, tell you how I feel."

Run away. But I was rooted to the sidewalk. "You already have. My answer is the same. You can hop the next bus or trolley and scram." I hoped he didn't see me trembling as I fought to remain calm.

"Fair enough." He didn't move, though. "I respect your honesty and loyalty. Have you really not thought of me at all?"

I didn't trust myself to speak. Dot was wrong. It wasn't that I felt lonely. The man in front of me was more interesting than a new case. And more frightening than a killer.

His gaze searched my face. "I don't know if what I feel is love. Perhaps it's only the desire to want to find out. "

"Frank—"

He held up a finger. "I'm not finished. The country has been in the midst of uncertain times for quite a while. One could argue it started with the stock market crash fifteen years ago. I wrestled with my decision to see you and share my feelings. Ultimately, I didn't want to lose the opportunity. Now, I'll leave you alone. I'll be here when you are ready."

Had the night become warmer? I could feel him, smell the clean scent of his soap. I should answer, push him away, tell him I never wanted to see him again. But that wasn't true. The light brought out warm glints in his hair. My eyes drifted shut.

I felt the warmth of his lips on mine, as soft as dandelion down.

Then he was gone.

* * *

To my surprise, I managed to make it home. My legs were wobbly. They shouldn't have been able to hold me up. All thoughts of Private Lake, the death of Marian Carstairs, and what needed to happen were driven from my mind.

I should not have let Frank kiss me. I should have run the other way as soon as I saw him.

But you didn't.

He didn't know if he loved me? Then why did he come?

For the same reason you didn't skedaddle. He needs to figure out how he feels.

I know how this story ends. I marry Tom and am happy.

Do you?

The same thoughts ran around and around as I walked the last couple of blocks to the intersection of Mackinaw and Louisiana, like the spinning propeller on a brand-new P39.

Mary Kate ran toward me, interrupting the cycle. "Betty! You got a phone call."

I pulled up, a defensive argument on my lips. There was a perfectly good reason for Frank calling. But before I could respond, she rushed on.

"She said her name was Mrs. Vance, and you know who she is. She said it's real important to talk to you. Here's the message." My sister held out a slip of paper.

You goose. Not everything is about Frank Hicks. I read the note, which said Mrs. Vance would be at Teddy's at seven thirty. "What time is it?"

"Heck, I don't wear a watch."

I tilted mine so I could read the time. Almost quarter to eight. I crumpled the note. "Tell Mom and Pop I'll be home as soon as I can, but don't wait up for me."

She nodded. "By the way, that private called, too. He didn't leave a message."

I waved her off. "Don't worry about it. You better get home before Mom flips her wig."

My sister skipped away.

When I arrived at Teddy's, I easily spotted Mrs. Vance waiting in my usual booth. "Sorry I'm late. I got your note." I looked up at the night waitress. "Coffee, black, please."

Mrs. Vance had an untouched cup of java in front of her. She pushed a thick bundle of envelopes toward me. "Mr. Theodore told us what happened to Evans."

"Yeah, I saw it happen."

236

"I think I told you Evans did not live in the house. But he did keep some personal items there. An extra shirt and slacks, in case he needed to change, that sort of thing. Mr. Theodore asked me to bundle it up, although I don't know who will come claim it."

It was an interesting question. Would Hazel admit she was related to the man now that he was dead? Somehow, I doubted it. "Did Theo tell you what to do? Perhaps he wants you to give the stuff away."

"He said he'd take care of it."

That struck me as odd. Why not instruct Mrs. Vance to take it to a church or Goodwill, where they could give it to someone in need? "What's with the letters?"

She wrapped her hands around the mug, even though the liquid in it didn't give off steam. "I think you should see them. At first, I thought Evans had a sweetheart. I'm ashamed to admit my curiosity led me to read a couple. He was never a pleasant man. I wanted to know what kind of woman would find him attractive. When I saw what they were, I knew you had to have them."

The waitress delivered my joe. I took a sip, set it aside, and examined the pile.

The name and return address on the envelopes were the same. H. Fasenmyr, 634 Saybrook Place., Buffalo, NY. Slick. Hazel'd used her maiden name. Nobody knew Evans's real identity. But they'd been sent to Evans at his apartment, not to the Carstairs mansion. "Where'd you find them?"

"In the butler's closet, under a pile of spare clothes."

The dates of the letters went back almost ten years, to right after when Evans had been hired. *Thank you for the money. How clever, getting a position with Carstairs. We'll know everything he says and does now. I'm not surprised he doesn't want the secret to come out.* I flipped to another dated right after Robert Newcombe's death. *I'm almost out of dough. Do you think you can get Carstairs to make another payment?* A third was dated after Old Man Carstairs had died. *We need to tell Marian she has to keep it up unless she wants the story about what her father did to be splashed all over the society pages. She deserves it, especially after how they treated Robert. Can you do that without blowing your cover?* The others were similar, and they were all signed *H* in handwriting that definitely looked feminine.

Why had Evans hidden these in the Carstairs house? Surely they woulda been safer at his home. I thought about the gaps in the dates. "Are you sure there aren't any more letters?"

"Positive. Why? Who is H?"

"I think it's his sister." I explained about Hazel Newcombe and Evans's real identity.

Mrs. Vance paled. "I didn't know. Do you think they knew about Mr. Theodore and Noemi?"

"That wasn't the real money-maker." I told her about what I'd learned from Mrs. Babbage. "The secret is what happened afterward. To Noemi and the baby."

She clapped her hands over her mouth.

"Robert's ravings musta put them on the trail. Unfortunately, I can't ask Evans, and I doubt Hazel will tell me. Over the years, they'd ask for cabbage when they needed it." Evans had to have had a way of letting Mr. Carstairs and his daughter know the secret wasn't safe without lettin' it slip he was one of the blackmailers.

I gathered up the envelopes. "Can I have these?"

Mrs. Vance nodded. "I have no use for them. Will they help find Noemi or clear Private Lake?"

I guzzled my coffee. The clock read eight thirty. Way too late to do anything more tonight. "Find Noemi? Prob'ly not. Unless Hazel knows where she is." The letters helped explain why Evans had wanted to work for the Carstairs family. He needed to be on the spot in case the scheme went south. But how that figured into Marian's death, I still didn't know.

Chapter Thirty-Eight

I continued to puzzle over the letters from Hazel the next morning as I ate breakfast at Teddy's. Not the purpose of 'em. That was clear. Why hadn't the cops found more in Evans's apartment? Unless they did. Were there others?

It was Tuesday. Four more days, counting today, until Private Lake was due to ship out. Which meant I had to wrap this up in the next seventy-two hours.

Judy stopped at my table. "You've been holding that piece of toast for ten minutes, and you haven't taken a bite. What's wrong with it?"

"Nothing." I nibbled at a corner, but the bread was cold and hard. I set it down.

She leaned over to read the letters. "What are those?"

I told her. "The Carstairs's housekeeper found 'em when she was cleaning out the butler's stuff. He died yesterday in an accident."

Judy topped off the coffee in my mug. "You sure it was an accident? I'm no detective, but those letters don't look like a simple note to see how he was."

I rolled the words around. "I'm pretty sure he didn't plan on getting hit by a truck. There's no connection between the driver and anyone related to this case. No, that was dumb luck."

"Then what's botherin' you?"

I spread out the paper. "See these gaps in the dates? Either Hazel, that's the sister, wasn't writin' to him regular-like or these are only a sample."

"Makes sense."

"What doesn't square up is why they didn't take the money and run. Why drag it out?"

Judy set down the coffee pot and wiped up a spill. "But why kill the golden goose? If this man, and then his daughter, we're willing to keep paying, why not take advantage of it? That's the only reason I can think of."

Judy was right. "They were in this for the long haul, not a quick score. For all I know, they spent a little of each payment and socked away the rest for a rainy day. Heck, even if they refused to pay any more dough, the letters might be leverage to buy some time before Old Man Carstairs or Marian called the cops, and that would give Evans and Hazel the opportunity to get outta town."

"Sounds like a good idea to me." Judy tucked her towel back in her apron pocket. "One catch. You can't prove it if the man's dead."

I guzzled my coffee. "Oh yes, I can." I checked my watch. I needed to call Sam.

* * *

Sam wasn't at his office, and I didn't want to leave a message at police headquarters. *I'll call him later.* I took the bus and got off at the corner of Chapin Parkway and West Delavan, the closest I could to Saybrook. Hazel would not want to 'fess up, I knew that. I could only hope that confronting her with the facts would back her into a corner, and she'd spill what she knew about her brother's arrangement with the Carstairs family.

Hazel answered my knock. "I was wondering—" She pulled back. "What are you doin' here?" She wore a plain housedress and ratty bedroom slippers. Her hair hung limply over her shoulders and didn't look like it had been washed or set in a day or two.

She was expectin' someone, but not me. "I need to talk to you about your brother, Paul."

"What about him?"

"First, I wanted to tell you I'm sorry he died. He ought to have looked both ways before runnin' out into the street."

240

"What on earth are you talking about?" Her laugh sounded brittle, and the skin around her eyes tightened. "Paul isn't dead. I talked to him this morning."

Did she not know? Or was she tryin' to put me off? "What did you talk about?"

Her gaze drifted over my shoulder. "A little of this, a little of that. We talk often."

I coulda let her spin her tale to see where she'd go, but I didn't have time. "Mrs. Newcombe, don't lie to me. Paul was hit by a truck yesterday. I saw it happen. He left the Carstairs house. I don't know where he was goin', or if he finished the thing he intended to do, but that truck put an end to whatever it was."

Her knuckles turned white as she gripped the door. "You are insane." She tried to slam the door.

I stopped it with my hand and ignored the jolt of pain through my shoulder from the impact. I didn't say anything, though. Just stood there, bracing the door so she couldn't close it. "You tell me."

"I don't have to listen to this." She shoved the door again.

I threw all my weight against it to keep it open.

She stared at me for a good long time. "Yes, Paul was employed by that family. He went under another name, so they wouldn't know he was related to me. I told you before. Marian resented me after Robert broke off their engagement to marry me."

"That doesn't explain why your brother took a job there. He couldn't work anywhere else?"

"Times were hard, Miss Ahern. Paul did what he had to do to survive. Companies weren't hiring, and he decided to try his hand at a service job. Even after the crash, the Carstairs family had money. I was destitute after Robert died, and Paul was my only source of income. I didn't question his motives."

"About that." It wasn't my preference, but clearly, this whole conversation was gonna happen on her front steps. "I've talked to several people. Robert didn't fall in love with you, not at first. According to a lot of people who would know, you stole him away."

She lifted her chin. "What if I did?"

"Why'd you do it? And why pretend he decided to marry you because he liked you better?"

She bit her lip. "It was petty, I admit it. I went to school with Marian Carstairs. Did you know that? She thought she was better than all the other girls, including me. All because her family was wealthy."

How had these two women, from completely different social classes, gone to school together? "Where?"

"At Saint Augustine's. A Catholic school isn't the same as an exclusive private school. We were in the same classes for years. For her, everything was a competition. She had more money, she got better grades, the nuns liked her better."

"You hated her."

"I didn't say that. But no, we were never friends. She stole my boyfriend in high school. I thought I'd found the man I would marry. She used him and threw him away, like she always did. Instead of coming back to me, he left the city and went to Cleveland, where he wouldn't have to live with the embarrassment she'd caused. I'm quite sure she stole an essay I'd written and turned it in under her name, too. But I could never prove it." Hazel's gaze was locked on the ground. "As I said, she'd charmed the nuns quite well. They wouldn't hear a word against her. Looking back, it was all so childish. But we were very young."

"You got back at her with Robert Newcombe."

"I'm not proud of it, but yes." The words were barely audible. "I wanted her to see how it felt to lose for a change. As I said, petty and childish. She truly loved him. Eye for an eye, Miss Ahern. I didn't really love Robert, but he wasn't a bad sort, really." She blew out a breath. "But the joke was on me. He had a nervous breakdown and was never the same. He lost his job, then committed suicide. Once again, I got the short end of the stick. As Marian gleefully pointed out. After he died, Marian stopped the pension. Isn't there a saying about winning a battle but losing a war? That was me." She refused to meet my eye.

And that's why Evans decided to try his hand at blackmail. Without the pension, Hazel would be destitute. "Why'd you go see Marian the day she died?"

"You shouldn't listen to drunks. Marian Carstairs is part of my past, Miss Ahern. I admit I didn't always take the high ground, even after we left school, and I'm rather ashamed of that. But I'm a grown woman. I guess maybe I got the better hand in the end, seeing as I'm still alive, and she isn't. Now, it's time for me to move on. Good-bye." She overcame my resistance and shut the door.

Chapter Thirty-Nine

The address I had for Homer Glassman was on Winslow, an easy bus ride from Hazel's house. The neighborhood was neither rich nor poor. The houses were simple boxes, all of the same design, most of 'em painted white, gray, or light blue. The only thing keepin' them from being completely identical was the front decorations. Some had flower boxes, some windows were adorned with stars, and others had tiny Victory gardens. Here and there, bikes and children's toys lay scattered, as if their owners dropped them as soon as something else came along.

I knocked on the door to the Glassman house several times, but no one answered. I tried to peep in the windows, but the white curtains prevented me from seein' anything more than a slit of the front room. I wandered around to the side of the building. The door to the small garage was shut. I didn't spot a car when I looked through the window.

A woman called to me from the sidewalk, her voice carryin' a suspicious note. "Hey. What are you doing? I'll call the police, I will. This is a respectable neighborhood, but no one has anything worth stealing."

I went over to her. "I'm not a thief." I held out a business card. "I'm lookin' for Mrs. Homer Glassman."

The woman didn't take it. She was stout and looked to be a bit past middle age. A little older than Mom, not as old as my grandma. She carried several parcels wrapped in brown paper. "The Glassmans haven't lived here for years. You can clear off."

I reached for a package. "Those look heavy. Would you like some help?"

She yanked them out of my reach. "Give my groceries to a total stranger?

I think not. You'll not steal food from my family's mouths, missy."

"I told you, I'm no thief. I'm a detective." I smothered a sigh. "I'm told Mr. Glassman died several years ago. Is that right?"

She squinted at me. "Maybe."

"I'm lookin' for his wife. Did you know her?" I pulled the picture of Noemi from my purse. "This is her. Well, it's her as a young woman. But I don't s'pose she'd look much different after ten years. She wouldn't have changed so much you couldn't recognize her."

The woman ignored me. "You have five seconds to leave, or I'm going straight home to call the police."

This was goin' nowhere. "Never mind. You have a nice day, ma'am."

She sniffed and strode off, occasionally casting a furtive glance over her shoulder, as if to make sure I wasn't followin' her.

"Hey, lady."

I checked around for the owner of the voice, which was high and clear, one that belonged to a child. A boy, maybe ten years old, watched me from a yard across the street. "Did you say somethin'?" I asked.

"Yeah. Mrs. Mallory isn't very nice. There's no use talkin' to her."

I crossed the pavement. "I can tell. I don't s'pose you knew the people in that house, huh?"

"I might have." He wore a dirty shirt and pants. A beat-up baseball mitt lay at his feet, a well-worn ball nestled in it.

"Can you tell me about 'em?"

A cunning gleam came into his brown eyes. "Why d'you want to know?"

"I'm a private detective." I showed him my card. "I'm lookin' for a woman who used to live there."

"A real detective, like the movies?"

I nodded.

"Holy mackerel."

I waited. "Are you gonna tell me?"

He gave a gap-toothed grin. "In the pictures, detectives pay for dope about people."

I took out my change purse. "I'll give you a quarter."

"Heck, that ain't nothin'. I guess you don't want to know." He bent and picked up his mitt and ball.

"What's your name?"

"Billy."

"Okay, Billy, fifty cents." I held out the coins. "That's enough to buy yourself a new baseball."

He reached out a grubby hand.

I pulled the money away. "But only if what you tell me is true."

He licked his lips. "Deal. What do you wanna know?"

I hoisted my thumb over my shoulder at the Glassman house. "'Did you know the people who lived there?"

He bobbed his head. "Yep. Mr. and Mrs. Glassman. I didn't know him, though. He died, least that's what my ma told me. She sent me over to do chores for Miz Glassman before she moved. Ma didn't pay me nothing. She said it was our Christian duty to take care of a widow or somethin' like that, but Miz Glassman baked real yummy cookies, and she'd always let me have as many as I wanted. Once, she made waffles, all thick with sugar on 'em. But that was before the war."

"I don't s'pose you know how long she lived there."

The kid's shoulders went up and down.

"Anything else about her? What was she like?"

Billy's eyes sparkled. "She was the bee's knees. Me and Eddie, that's my best friend, we was playing ball in the street last summer and Eddie, he hit one right through her front window. Ma made us go and 'pologize. I thought we'd get in awful trouble, but Miz Glassman, she didn't even yell. 'S'matter of fact, she gave us cookies and milk! Can you believe it?"

Billy reminded me of my own brothers. "Did she say why?"

"Why what?"

"Why she wasn't angry."

He thought, his tongue poking out a little. "I dunno. I guess she liked boys. I mean, she liked all the kids on the street. But Eddie and me, and some other chaps, we always got more goodies than the girls."

That made sense, seein' as she'd had a son of her own, however briefly.

Perhaps she'd seen a little of what she missed in each of these children. "You prob'ly don't know when she moved."

"Sure do. Right after Thanksgiving. I told you, Miz Glassman baked the best cookies. They looked like the sugar cookies Ma bakes or used to before the war. 'Cept these don't have no frosting. But they was all cinnaminny." He licked his lips. "We always got some early in December, 'cause she said that's when Father Christmas brought presents back in her country."

He had to mean the feast of St. Nicholas. "Go on."

"Me and Eddie went to her house, but it was all locked up and no one was there. I told Ma, and she said Miz Glassman had moved." He stuffed his hands in his pockets. "She didn't even leave us cookies before she went."

Billy was too young to understand rationing. She may not have had enough sugar. "One more thing. Did Mrs. Glassman talk with an accent?"

"What d'ya mean?"

"Did she sound like your mom or like she came from somewhere else?"

"Oh." He tossed his ball into his mitt. "I guess she sounded a little funny when you first met her." He held out his hand. "I told you plenty. Gimme my two quarters."

It was doubtful a child could tell me anything more. I dropped the coins in his dirty palm. "Is your mother home?"

"Yeah, she's doin' the wash." Billy dashed down the street.

I walked up to Billy's house and knocked. A woman with a red face, strands of hair stuck to her forehead, answered the door. "May I help you?"

I handed her a card. "I was speaking with your son a moment ago."

She sighed. "What's he done now? Surely a private detective wouldn't be concerned with a child's actions."

From her voice, I guessed she was used to people showin' up to report on her son's misdeeds. "Nothing. He told me a little about Mrs. Glassman. She lived across the street. That's who I'm lookin' for." I pointed. "I hoped you could tell me a little more. He was mostly concerned with the quality of her baked goods." I grinned.

"I'm not sure there's more to tell, to be honest. Mrs. Glassman kept to herself, mostly. She spent more time with the neighborhood children than the adults."

"She didn't happen to look like this woman, did she?" I held out Noemi's picture.

Billy's mom took a long look and nodded. "That's her. Younger, of course, but I recognize her."

I put the picture back in my purse and took out my notebook. "Billy mentioned how she gave the kids cookies around St. Nicholas's feast day."

"Oh yes. She said it was a tradition in Belgium. That's where she came from."

"Did she tell you anything else about herself?"

The woman shook her head. "As I said, she was very private. I didn't even know her first name. The only reason she told me that much is because the first time Billy came home with a dozen cookies, I marched him straight back. I was sure he'd stolen them from somewhere."

"Billy said she left last year, after Thanksgiving. Did you see her before she moved?"

"No. One day she was there, the next the house was empty and there was a for sale sign in the yard." The woman spread her hands. "I have to go wring out my clothes." She glanced at the house. "Mrs. Glassman isn't in trouble, is she? Why are you looking for her?"

"If you mean trouble with the law, no, not that I know of. She had a baby, years ago, and was forced to give him up. He wants to find her."

Her hands flew to her mouth. "Oh, that's sad. It explains so much."

I waited.

"That day I took Billy over to return the cookies. She insisted they were a gift. She said something about not having a son to spoil. I thought she was simply childless, that she and Homer had never been blessed. I wish I could have done something for her."

"You did, ma'am." I put my notes away. "You gave her time with your son."

* * *

Noemi's old house wasn't that far from the Broadway Market, so I skipped the bus and hoofed it over. I wasn't sure the workers at Roesch's would remember her. Then again, with her foreign accent, different than the Poles or Germans, she coulda stood out. It was worth a shot.

War rationing or not, the Market was hoppin'. People bustled along, lookin' over the wares and stockin' up on groceries, coupons in hand. I loved the energy of the place. I also enjoyed seeing all the different nationalities of Buffalo. There were old Polish grandmas in their babushkas pressed right up against Italians from the East Side. I heard a sampling of every language in the city and English spoken in a variety of accents. I even saw a few colored people here and there.

I stopped at a Polish bakery and bought myself a bag of *bajaderki*, a type of soft ball-shaped treat. These were chocolate with nuts, and I swore I could taste a faint hint of rum. It was almost lunchtime, but I figured as long as I was at the Market, I had to buy something. I might as well satisfy my sweet tooth.

I licked the last crumbs of *bajaderki* from my fingers as I approached Roesch's, a popular butcher in the Market. An older man with a paunch, older than Pop, came to the counter. "May I help you, miss?"

I tucked the bag of treats in my purse and pulled out Noemi's picture. "I'm lookin' for this woman."

He barely looked at the photo. "You don't want to buy something?"

"I wasn't plannin' on it."

He shrugged and moved as if to go to the next customer.

Man's gotta make a living, I guess. Fortunately, I had my ration book on me. "Wait." I flipped through my coupons. "I'll take two pounds of beef." I held out the slip of paper.

He took it and went to the back. He returned with a hunk of roast, which he proceeded to weigh and trim to meet the allotted weight. "That's Mrs. Glassman." He wrapped my purchase in heavy white paper. "She comes in every other week."

I took my package. "When was the last time she was in?"

"Why should I tell you?"

"Her long-lost son hired me to find her." With my hands full, I couldn't get a business card. "I'm a private detective."

The suspicion from the butcher's face cleared. "Is that a fact?"

"Sure is. His name is Christopher Lake, and he's a private in the Army. He's home for a while and decided to try and locate her." I hadn't intended on shopping, so I hadn't brought a bag. "He leaves again on Friday. Any help you can give would be swell." No need to tell the man about the murder charge.

He leaned on the glass counter. "Come to think of it, she did mention a son last Mother's Day. We were watching all the women here with little boys. Mrs. Glassman said she'd lost him years ago. I thought he died, the way she was talking."

"He was taken from her and raised at Father Baker's."

The butcher slapped the glass. "That's outrageous. Who would do such a thing?"

"It's a long story, and you got other customers." The women next to me had decidedly impatient expressions, and one tapped her foot, clearly wantin' me to get outta the way. "When was the last time you saw her? Mrs. Glassman?"

He thought. "Must have been two weeks ago, at least. She wasn't here last week. In fact, I should see her today."

"She ever mention where she was from?"

He frowned. "France? No, Belgium. We were chatting about the war news as I wrapped up her order. I could tell she had an accent, thought she might be French. I mentioned the Huns romping through France, and she said it was an old story. The Germans did much the same to Belgium in the Great War."

I set the white-wrapped parcel on the counter. "I can see you got other people to wait on. Would you do me a favor?" I handed him a business card. "Next time you see her, would you call me at this number, please?"

He slipped the card into a pocket of his bloodstained apron. "It won't be until I can get to a telephone, and that might be hours later."

"It doesn't matter. Anything you can do will be jake." I thanked him and apologized to the waiting woman, who didn't look mollified. Then I took my purchase and left.

It was too bad I couldn't hang around and wait to see if Noemi turned up. But there were other leads to pursue, and I couldn't spend all afternoon at the Market. I'd have to hope the man at Roesch's could call me quickly.

The crowd had increased while I'd been there, and I dodged people constantly on my way out. Ahead of me, a slender, dark-haired woman handed some money to a vendor and put her purchase into her bag. She faced me.

"Noemi!" I almost dropped my package. "Noemi Gerard! I need to talk to you."

Chapter Forty

Noemi froze like a deer caught in the glare of a predator. Then, she fled in the opposite direction.

I uttered a constant stream of apologies as I threaded my way through the crowd, tryin' to keep her head of dark hair in sight. A knot of babbling Polish grandmas forced me to a halt. I hurried around them and almost slipped on a spill of liquid.

Noemi ducked around a stall. I tried to follow, but the crowd jostled me into an elderly lady. I grabbed her arm to keep her from falling. Once I was sure she was okay, I stood on my toes and searched the mass of people in front of me.

Noemi wasn't in sight.

I left the Market, cussing under my breath. I'd been so close. If only Noemi had let me talk to her. But at least I knew for certain she was alive. There had to be a way to find where she was livin'.

The sound of a man's voice made me stop. "Betty. Wait!"

It was Sam. He jogged up the sidewalk toward me.

"How'd you find me?"

"I've been tracing your movements all morning. I always seem to just miss you." He took off his fedora and wiped his forehead.

"Do you have the goods?"

He cast his gaze around the neighborhood. "Let's go in here." He nodded toward a drug store. "I'll buy you a malt."

"What am I gonna do with this beef?"

He grinned. "We'll get you a bag."

Inside the shop, he went to the counter and took out his wallet. "Vanilla or chocolate? And the lady needs a bag."

"Chocolate," I said to the waiting soda jerk, who nodded and busied himself with makin' my drink. I faced Sam. "You're bein' generous. Which means you're gonna help me, but it still won't be easy to get to the bottom of this mess."

"You're right, but get your malt first."

The soda jerk returned in no time, a frothy drink in one hand, a bag in the other. I took the icy glass and paper sack, and Sam paid him. Then we went to sit in a booth. "Okay, what do you have?" I sucked on the straw.

He pushed a folder across the counter to me. "It's not complete. I hadn't gotten to the real reason why Paul Fasenmyr, the man we know as Evans, was involved in all this."

"Oh, I know that. Least I'm pretty sure I do." I brought him up to speed on the blackmail scheme, the pictures I'd found in the apartment, and showed him the letters I'd gotten from Mrs. Vance. "Thing is, they have to be stashing the cabbage. They're not spendin' it, and that makes sense to me. If a butler and a poor widow are suddenly swimming in dough, people would get suspicious. I'm thinking they were saving as much as possible against the day they had to run for it."

Sam's forehead creased. "You think his sister, Hazel, was involved, not merely a beneficiary?"

"She mighta been. It might even have been her idea." I stirred the melting ice cream with my straw.

"Why not do it all by post? Send an anonymous letter, get the cash, and be done with it."

"I'm thinkin' they were greedy." I pointed at him. "After Robert's pension was pulled out from under her, Hazel decided to get revenge. It's not just pride. She needs the cabbage. She knew about what happened with Noemi from her husband's ramblings. She tells her brother. He does enough to learn Noemi is alive and track Private Lake down. Sister Francis, the nun I spoke to, mentioned a man hanging around Father Baker's years ago."

"Do you think Old Man Carstairs or Marian knew who he was?"

"No. It was all anonymous. Evans got the job so he could keep an eye on them, make sure they toed the line."

"Keep your friends close and your enemies closer, huh?" Sam tapped the table.

I sucked the last of my malt. "Every time Hazel and Evans needed a little dough, he was perfectly placed to drop another anonymous note and make sure they paid up."

Sam rubbed his chin. "Possible. Then you think Evans killed Marian?"

"It's likely. I think he definitely knew who did. But remember, Hazel was at the house that day. She denies it, but I have a witness who is pretty reliable. And Evans lied about bein' there at the time of the shooting."

Sam tapped his fingers on the table. "Yes, I know all that. The problem is, I can't draw a line between Hazel and her brother and the victim. Not well enough to get an arrest warrant or even a search warrant for Hazel's house."

"I gave you the letters!"

"Any defense attorney worth his fee would have a field day with your search. I can't use them." He held up a hand. "I have no proof. Speculation, yes, but on the surface, Evans was a perfectly respectable servant, and his sister merely came calling to ask for charity. The fact he changed his name doesn't mean anything. The captain is right. We arrested our suspect. Case closed."

I read the frustration on Sam's puss. I'd always thought of him as the guy with the answers, but now I knew what he meant when he talked about the difference between what he believed and what he could prove. "What do you think I can do better than you?" My words came slowly.

"You don't have to follow all the rules I do. Here." He withdrew a pack of paper from his coat. "These are copies of all the witness statements from the day of Marian's death. I always thought there was a funny stink about Evans's story, and what you told me about the blackmail confirms it. Keep digging." He stood. "When you figure out who killed Marian, call me." He left.

Talk about raising the stakes. I unfolded the sheets and read. Much of it I'd already heard. Mrs. Vance had been out, that was for certain. The maid had run an errand for Marian. But according to her, when she returned, Evans had told her not to disturb her mistress until tea time. "Well, how do you like them apples?" It wasn't only Mrs. Babbage who contradicted Evans's story. The maid had come back around two. She'd taken the tray in around four, which was when she found the body.

I shuffled the papers until I found Evans's statement. He said he'd been out "all day." Why didn't the cops jump on that difference? Unless they figured "all day" and "all morning" were somehow the same. The statements had all been signed by an Officer Carlton, but Sam wouldn't have been so sloppy as to not notice. Unless he hadn't been on the scene. I ran my finger down the reports. Sure enough, a different detective had been there. One not as precise as my friend.

I took out my notebook and flipped to a clean sheet. I needed a clear timeline.

8:00am - Private Lake learns about Marian; Mrs. Vance and maid leave for errands

10:00am - PL visits MC; argument; PL seen on street about thirty minutes later by nanny

11:00am - visit from Hazel (no one admits seeing Hazel leave)

2:00pm - maid returns, talks to Evans

4:00pm - MC found dead by maid and Theo (claims he was drunk in study)

Based on those times, Mrs. Vance and the maid were in the clear for Marian's death. Even if Evans had been somewhere else that day, he could easily have shot Marian before he left, assuming that had been after Hazel came. Or he coulda done it after he returned.

I studied the timeline again. If Hazel had talked to Marian, that cleared Private Lake, too, which meant he shouldn't have been arrested. Either the cops had proof he'd returned, and Sam didn't know it, or one of 'em was dirty and figured he could pin the murder on a helpless soldier.

A thought occurred to me. Hazel hadn't come lookin' for charity at all. Private Lake's appearance meant Marian didn't have to pay her blackmailer any longer. The secret would be out. After many years of hidin' it, it made sense Marian would no longer care. Her father'd been dead for a long time. Maybe she'd made a comment to that effect. Evans heard her and called his sister. They needed to get Marian back under their thumbs.

I looked for Theo's statement. He'd told the police he'd seen his sister at breakfast and "heard raised voices late in the morning" but couldn't make out the words. He'd heard the maid around four and "went to her." From what he'd told me, he'd been drinking and passed out shortly after Private Lake left, presumably in his study.

Wait a minute. I went back to the maid's statement. She claimed to have checked in on Theo when she returned, but his study had been empty. When he appeared after she screamed, he came from *upstairs*. He'd allowed people to assume he'd been downstairs. I only had his word he'd been passed out.

Then I remembered what Hazel said. I'd asked about her visit to Marian, and she replied, "You shouldn't listen to drunks." The only person who fit that description was Theo. Hazel thought he'd been the one who told me about her visit.

Which meant they'd seen each other, even if they hadn't spoken.

I scooped up the paper and checked the time. If I hurried, I could call Emmeline and still catch the next bus to Delaware Park.

* * *

I got off the bus at the corner of Delaware and Nottingham Terrace and saw Emmeline waitin' for me. "How long have you been sittin' on that bench?"

"About twenty minutes. I left as soon as I hung up with you." She looked around. "Are you going to the Carstairs mansion?"

"That was my plan." I tilted my head. "I get the feelin' you want to talk to me first."

"I do." She gave a sigh of exasperation. "Aren't there any places to be private around here?"

"It's not a neighborhood for corner stores." I checked around. "There's no one out. Tell me what you found."

"All right. Did you talk to Mr. Braxton?" She sat back down.

I took the spot next to her. "I did. He was very helpful." I went over my discussion. "What he said doesn't help me clear Theo, though. It's very possible he finally snapped."

"You're right, it doesn't, but this might." She handed over a notebook. "I know you pulled me off Robert Newcombe, but I'd already done a little work before you called. Reading between the lines, I think his death was definitely suicide."

I flipped through the notes. "I thought there were questions?"

"There were." She crossed her legs at the ankle. "Naturally, that would make you think a murder was being staged as a suicide. But I think it was the other way around."

I lifted my head. "Suicide made to look like murder? Why?"

She pointed at the notebook. "Robert had a life insurance policy, a small one. But it had a clause that said the policy wouldn't pay if the insured committed suicide. There were irregularities about the death scene, but I think it's because Hazel, after finding her husband had killed himself, tried to make it look like murder."

"She needed the cash."

Emmeline nodded. "But she wasn't good enough. The coroner ruled Robert's death a suicide anyway."

"Hazel got nothing." Which would make blackmailing the Carstairs family even more attractive. 'Specially if Marian killed the so-called pension after Robert's death. "What about how to hide some cabbage you don't want other people to know about?"

She gestured back at the notebook. "I called my friend who works at a bank and asked her about the easiest way to hide money. She told me the best way she knew would be to use a safe deposit box at a bank."

"For ten years' worth of cash, that's a big box."

Emmeline leaned forward. "Not if you use bearer bonds."

I read the notes, written in her crisp, clear handwriting. I tapped my chin. I liked the idea, but there was still a problem. "I searched Evans's apartment. I didn't find any bonds." I looked at Emmeline. "How big are these things?"

"You mean denomination or the physical size of the paper?"

"The size of the paper. I mean, how hard would they be to stash?"

She thought. "I'm pretty sure they'd be easy to hide, no bigger than a regular bond. You can buy them in small amounts, say a thousand dollars."

I laughed. "That isn't a small amount."

"It isn't for you. But not in terms of bond sales. Imagine having a slip of paper worth ten hundred-dollar bills, or fifty twenty-dollar ones." She raised her eyebrows.

"I see what you mean. You need a lot less space. Try this idea. Hazel and Evans blackmail Old Man Carstairs, and then Marian. They gotta spend some of the cash, but they tuck the rest away in bonds."

"Makes sense. They'd have a stream of income and some money for the future."

"But Evans can't hide 'em. He works for the family. And maybe he doesn't trust his sister not to run and leave him high and dry. So he doesn't give the bonds to her for safekeeping, either." A safe deposit box suddenly looked better. I looked at Emmeline. "Say, who can get into a safe deposit box?"

"Only the person with the key." Understanding dawned in her eyes. "And you're left alone when you access your box. My father had one, and no one could see what was in it, not even the bank manager. Do you think Evans or Hazel had a box?"

I stood. "It's possible. I've thought all along Theo Carstairs had somethin' more to say about Marian's death. I think it's time we found out."

Chapter Forty-One

This time, I strode up to the front door of the Carstairs mansion, Emmeline trotting behind me and pounded on the door. I didn't stop until someone opened it. "Mrs. Vance, hello. I need to talk to Theo."

She blocked the entry. "He's in the backyard. He's spending some time with his son. They have years of catching up to do, and Mr. Theodore has a lot to make up for."

If I was right, he had more to smooth over than she thought. "I understand, but this isn't a social call. I'm working for Theo." She opened her mouth, and I cut her off. "No, it won't wait."

She craned her neck to see behind me. "Who is with you?"

"Emmeline Schechter, my research associate."

Emmeline waved. "Pleased to meet you."

I cut off any further pleasantries. "Are you gonna show me to them? 'Cause if not, I'm gonna walk around the house and scale a fence if I have to."

Emmeline mumbled something about not bein' dressed for that kind of activity.

I didn't care. I was on a mission.

Mrs. Vance didn't move. "I don't know. Mr. Theodore was very adamant that he didn't want to be disturbed. No exceptions."

I could see she wanted to help me, but her loyalty to her boss was holding her back. "Let me put it to you this way. If you don't take me back there, it's very likely the next person to pound on your door will be the cops when

259

they come to take both Private Lake and Theo back to jail. Now, maybe Theo's lawyer is good enough to get them off. But if he isn't, both of 'em are at least going to prison for life, if not the chair. And Marian's real killers will go free."

Mrs. Vance wavered. "You think you know who shot her?"

"I do."

She seemed to make up her mind, 'cause she opened the door wide. "Follow me." She led us through the house to a backyard I mighta taken a moment to admire more if I hadn't been in such a hurry. The two men were seated at a wrought iron table, glasses of lemonade in front of 'em. Private Lake's was untouched. He was dressed in clothes he musta gotten from his father, a button-down shirt with the collar open and tan slacks that were made of good fabric, stuff that was outta reach on a soldier's salary.

Theo was similarly dressed and leaned on the table as though he'd been appealing to his son. He drew his eyebrows together as he looked at his housekeeper. "I thought I told you we weren't to be disturbed."

Mrs. Vance opened her mouth, but I stepped forward. "Don't blame her. I insisted. That's what you're payin' me for. You and Private Lake."

He faced me with a thundercloud expression that woulda scared someone else. "It's okay, Mrs. Vance. This time."

Maybe I'd have been intimidated a few days ago, but not now. "You've been holdin' out on me."

Private Lake's gaze flicked between his father and me, but he said nothing.

Theo threw a glance at him, then focused on me. "I told you everything."

"No, you haven't." I took the pile of statements I'd gotten from Sam out of my purse. "According to your statement, you did hear your sister's argument with Private Lake. But you never came outta your study and was awoken from a drunken stupor by the maid's scream when she found Marian's body."

Theo's body tensed. "That's correct."

I held up a finger. "Except the maid told the police that you came from *upstairs* after she called out. And she said nothing about you bein' drunk."

He clenched his fists.

"I also talked to Hazel." I watched him closely, but outta the corner of my eye, I could see Private Lake as well. His face had turned pale, two spots of color high on his cheeks. I couldn't imagine what he was thinkin'. "I know she visited the day Marian died, 'cause Mrs. Babbage saw her. You know Mrs. Babbage. She's the widow who lives across the street. Hazel admitted that and said she'd come to ask your sister for money outta pity."

Theo spoke behind clenched teeth. "The Babbage woman is a nosy old gossip. And Marian never felt pity for anybody."

"That's what I told Hazel." I took a breath. "When I confronted her again and suggested she'd come for another reason, she said an interesting thing. 'You shouldn't listen to drunks.' You're the only person in this house who that could be, Theo." I waited a beat, but he said nothing. "Admit it, you saw Hazel that day."

Private Lake shifted on his chair. "Father, what is she talking about?"

Theo didn't look at his son. "Nothing. She's mistaken."

I put my hands on my hips. "No, I'm not. Mrs. Vance tells me you're tryin' to patch things up with your son. That's admirable. But if you don't stop lyin' about the present, it's not gonna matter what you do about the past. You may have a swell lawyer. But twelve men are gonna sit in judgment of your son, and chances are good he's goin' to be convicted."

Private Lake didn't move. "I didn't shoot her, Father. I swear."

Theo slammed his hands on the table. "I know that! Oh God, trust me, I know." He buried his face in his hands.

Emmeline twitched, as though she was going over to him. I reached over and stopped her. Theo had admitted he would gladly have killed his sister. He knew about the guns. But I didn't think he had done it, either. I remembered something he'd said earlier about his habit of making bad decisions. *He wasn't talkin' about the past.* "Theo," I said, forcing myself to be calm. "This is your opportunity to come clean. If you don't tell the truth now, it isn't gonna matter what did or didn't happen twenty years ago. If you know something that could keep your boy outta jail, spill."

He rubbed his face, then looked at Private Lake. "What I said about hearing the argument between Christopher and Marian is true, as was my confrontation with her later. When she told me about him, that he was my son, and I realized Noemi might be alive, I truly did contemplate strangling her. But I didn't. I went to my study and slammed the door. But I didn't get drunk. All I could think of was finding them. I wasn't sure how I would do that. I didn't know any private investigators, not before I met you, Miss Ahern. Marian would never give me the money I needed, either." He glanced at me and rubbed his hands on his thighs.

"What happened next?" I asked.

Theo stood and paced, stopping next to a huge rhododendron bush with glossy green leaves. "I don't know how much later it was, but the bell rang. Before I could do anything, Evans answered the door. I heard a woman's voice. She and Evans sounded like they were arguing. Then I heard Marian. The women's voices got softer, but I went to my door to try and listen. It sounded as though all of them, including Evans, were fighting. I could tell it was escalating because the volume went up, and they talked faster. Evans sounded frantic, he said something like, 'Put it away, that's not necessary.'" He glanced at Private Lake. "Then I heard a gunshot."

Emmeline and Mrs. Vance gasped.

I stepped forward. "You didn't mention that before."

Theo swallowed. "I rushed into Marian's sitting room. The woman, Hazel, did you call her? She was holding the gun, which was still smoking. Marian was on the floor. Evans had grabbed his sister's hand, the one that held the gun. He was trying to get it away and was chastising her." He half-laughed. "That sounds so polished. He was swearing like a sailor. She looked frightened, but triumphant at the same time."

Private Lake leaned forward. "Why didn't you tell the police this?"

"I intended to. I even had my hand on the telephone. Evans told me to stop. He said he knew Noemi was alive, that he could find her. But if I called the cops, I'd never see her or you. I couldn't lose you both again." He plucked a leaf from the bush and crushed it in his hand. He stuffed his hands in his pockets and hung his head. "I helped them stage the scene under Hazel's direction. Evans and I moved Marian's body. I knew about the second gun. I picked it up with my handkerchief and dropped it on the floor. I said I would hide the one Hazel had used and dispose of it later."

I thought back. "Why'd you hire me? Evans was gonna bring you Noemi for nothing."

Theo swallowed hard. "He didn't know where she was, only that she was alive. If you found her first, I intended to call the police and tell them what really happened."

I hadn't been prepared for this. It didn't surprise me Hazel had been involved. After her husband's death, she had experience in manipulating the scene of a crime. "After Private Lake was arrested, why didn't you come forward?"

"I was afraid." He faced his son. "I knew what I'd done was illegal, and I'd go to jail. I thought maybe they'd charge me as an accessory. And there was the threat from Evans. I planned to get you the best lawyer money could buy. Then I was arrested. I felt confident I could evade jail time. If you were acquitted, or better yet, if the lawyer could get the charges dropped, I'd never need to tell you about my role in Marian's death."

"And after Evans died?" I pressed.

"There was still Hazel. I didn't know what she would do. If there was any chance I could see Noemi and my son again, I had to take it." He took a deep breath. "I'm sorry, Christopher."

Private Lake turned away from him.

I looked at Emmeline. "Do you still think a safe deposit box is the best candidate for a hidin' place?"

Her face was pale as new milk. Theo's confession had shocked her. But she pulled herself together. "I do. Especially if this house and his apartment have been searched."

I looked at Mrs. Vance. "Evans must have had a set of keys as a butler. Do you have them?"

Her wide-eyed stare was fixed on Theo, and she didn't respond.

I snapped my fingers in front of her. "Hey, did you hear me? I have work to do."

She pulled a bunch of keys outta her pocket. "Yes, he did. But I don't have them. I have spares, but he had his own set."

I thought. "I need to use your telephone."

263

She led me to the library, to the phone I'd used before. I called Sam's office and hoped he was there. "Sam," I said when he answered. "When you brought in Evans's body, did he have a ring of keys on him?"

"Let me see." Sam set down the handset of the phone. A minute later, he picked it up. "Yes, I have them. We haven't released his personal effects yet."

I crossed my fingers. "Is there one on there that looks like it could fit a safe deposit box?"

The keys jangled as Sam sorted through them. "Right here. Why?"

"Do you know if Evans had a bank account?"

"We found deposit slips for Manufacturer's & Trust in his apartment."

Perfect. "Meet me at the branch nearest his apartment in fifteen minutes. Bring those keys. And a warrant."

Sam sounded puzzled. "Why?"

I looked at Emmeline. "I think I found the blackmail stash. And Marian Carstairs's killer."

Chapter Forty-Two

Becuase Emmeline and I had to take the bus, Sam was waitin' in front when we hustled up to the door of the bank. He tossed aside his cigarette. "What took you so long?"

"Very funny, buster." Emmeline puffed like a steam engine and even I had to catch my breath. "You bring the keys?"

He held them out. "Right here. What's this about solving the Carstairs murder?"

I told him about Hazel and her brother as I searched the keyring. It didn't take long to find the odd-shaped one that prob'ly belonged to the safe deposit box.

He whistled. "I'm still surprised they didn't hit Carstairs up for a lump sum and skip town."

"You can ask Hazel about it when you arrest her." I glanced at him. "What about a warrant?"

He spread his hands in a helpless gesture. "The judge turned me down."

That complicated things, but I'd figure it out. "Let's go."

Inside, I asked the woman at the desk to see the manager. "It's a matter of some importance."

She folded her hands on her desk. "Mr. Southerland is in a meeting and cannot be disturbed."

Sam shouldered me aside and showed his badge. "I think he'll come out to see me."

Flustered, the secretary buzzed her boss.

A minute or two later, a portly man in a brown suit appeared, followed by a much younger man, also dressed in brown. "Yes, officer? What can I do for you?"

"Detective." Sam displayed his badge again. "This young lady has some questions for you, and I would appreciate your cooperation."

I stepped forward. "Do either Hazel Newcombe or Paul Evans have a safe deposit box here? It might be under the names Hazel or Paul Fasenmyr."

Mr. Southerland puffed up. "I don't know every person who rents a box with us. And it doesn't matter. I wouldn't tell you without a warrant."

Oh, brother. "I don't think you heard the detective. This is important."

"I don't care." Mr. Southerland smiled as though he knew how annoying he was. "No warrant, no information."

The other man piped up. "Getting a warrant would be futile, anyway. Mrs. Newcombe already emptied the box." He tried for a smug look but cringed as his boss wheeled around.

"Walker, can't you keep your mouth shut?" Mr. Southerland snapped.

Mr. Walker looked like he wanted to melt into the floor. "Sorry, sir."

I wanted to grin in satisfaction, but the truth was I had nothin' to be happy about. If Hazel had split with the goods, we needed to hurry. "Well, since the cat's outta the bag, when did she leave?"

Mr. Southerland scowled. "She came to see me about noon. Her brother paid for the box, but she was authorized to access it, and she had her own key. She told me her brother was indisposed, and she needed to get inside."

"Indisposed? That's one way of putting it," Emmeline said. "He's dead. She probably didn't mention that, did she?"

Mr. Southerland gaped at us.

I rolled on. "You don't happen to know what was in the box, do you?"

He shook himself, sorta like a bear after waking up from a nap. "No. The contents of a safe deposit box are known only to the owner. When someone comes in, we take them to the vault and leave them alone for as long as they need."

Darn it. I fixed both the manager and Mr. Walker with a glare. "Did either of you see her leave?"

"I...I did." Mr. Walker raised a trembling hand. "I don't know any more than Mr. Southerland about the contents. But whatever it was couldn't be very big. She had a case with her, no bigger than a man's briefcase. Whatever she took had to have fit in there."

I checked with Emmeline, who nodded. The bearer bonds woulda fit inside. I faced the bank men again. "Did she say where she was goin'?"

Mr. Walker shook his head. "She said something about Toronto weather being wonderful this time of year, but that's all."

Sam and I spoke at the same time. "Train station."

* * *

Thanks to Sam and his car, it didn't take us long to get to Buffalo's Central Terminal. I patted the stuffed buffalo that soldiers often touched for good luck when they left town, as we hurried inside. The first thing I did was check the day's departures. "There's a train leaving for Toronto, Ontario, in forty minutes from platform five."

"Good. The Mounties are good to work with, but I'd rather catch her before she crosses the border." Sam checked his gun. "Let's go."

We arrived at the platform with thirty minutes to spare. I could see some of the passengers had boarded. Others bought a paper to read from a nearby vendor. Conductors and red caps roamed outside, leading people to their seats and loadin' baggage. Sam corralled a conductor. While he explained the situation, I gave Emmeline a description of our quarry. Then we got on board and searched through the cars.

Fortunately, the train wasn't a sleeper. Hazel wouldn't be holed up in a private compartment.

Emmeline tapped my shoulder. "She's up there."

I looked in the direction she was pointin'. Hazel's head was bent, maybe to keep her face averted from anyone until the train was safely away. I couldn't call out to her. She had a clear path to the far door. I didn't fancy a footrace through the cars. She might jump off at any point and be lost in the crowd. I laid my finger across my lips and tipped my head toward Hazel, hoping Emmeline got the message.

She must have, 'cause she gave a quick nod.

We walked slowly toward our suspect. But before we got close enough, Hazel looked up. The second she saw us, she left her seat, a brown leather case in hand, and hurried to the door at the far end of the carriage.

At that moment, Sam appeared in the doorway, blocking her. "Hazel Newcombe, you're under arrest for the murder of Marian Carstairs."

Hazel froze, but only for a second. She grabbed a young woman who had been stowing something in the upper rack and pulled a pistol out of her jacket pocket. "Back off, or I'll shoot her."

The woman screamed. Sam pulled his own gun and aimed at Hazel.

I reached out. "It's okay, ma'am. She's not gonna hurt you."

Hazel's laugh was harsh. "Who says? After all, I shot Marian."

She didn't even bother to deny it. "Hazel, don't be a sap," I said as I tried to catch Sam's eye. "Look around. You're gonna shoot some poor innocent bystander in here? All that'll happen is you'll go down for two murders instead of one. You can't get off the train without runnin' into me, Detective MacKinnon, or someone from the railway. You might get life without parole for killing one person. But two? You'll definitely get the chair."

Hazel jammed the gun into her hostage's side. "Try me."

The woman whimpered. "Please. I have children."

"Can it." Hazel looked around the compartment. "You, missy. Back up. Detective, I'd put down your gun. You don't want this nice woman to get hurt, do you?"

I felt Emmeline touch my back. "Keep her talking," she whispered.

I had no idea what Emmeline intended to do, but I couldn't worry about that. "Hazel, don't be foolish. Let her go." I checked on Sam, who hadn't budged an inch. "We know about the blackmail and why you did it. We know about Private Lake turning up, and Marian threatening to shut it down." I slid toward her. "When you confronted her, she didn't call it off quietly, did she? She prob'ly threatened you with jail, a lawsuit, heck, with anything she could think of."

Hazel's eyes moved side to side, like she was afraid to take her focus off either Sam or me. "You have no idea."

"Why'd you stick around?" Sam asked. "Why not take the money and run?"

"Paul wanted to. But I thought we could milk it. Paul was on the spot as the butler, so he could slip Carstairs the notes. He could tip me off if old Carstairs or Marian got wise, and we'd scram. After that private showed up, Paul called me. He said Marian was going to go to the cops, tell them everything about the blackmail, and let them hunt down the culprits. I went over to persuade her otherwise." Hazel licked her lips. "She told me she was going to turn me in, but she still didn't have a clue about Paul or who he was. There she was, waving that stupid pistol. I had to stop her."

I moved to make sure Hazel was hemmed in. "And after Marian died? You didn't vamoose."

"We were going to. I didn't want to leave Buffalo too quickly and raise suspicion. Someone might have seen me that day."

Sam inched closer.

Hazel squeezed her hostage. "I told you, Detective. Don't move. Now." She focused on me. "Let *me* tell *you* what's going to happen, Miss Ahern. You're going to get out of my way. I'm going to leave with this nice lady. You and the detective will count to two hundred. Let's see if you can catch me. I'm—"

The window behind Hazel shattered.

She flinched at the flying glass, and the woman threw herself into an empty seat.

Sam darted forward and brought down the butt of his gun on Hazel's wrist. Her pistol clattered to the floor.

I launched myself forward and tackled her, We tussled in the tight space, but growin' up with brothers had taught me a thing or two. It took a minute, but I managed to get on top of her, clamping her hands between mine. "Sam, I sure hope you got handcuffs."

Emmeline stuck her head through the door. "Did you get her? Did anyone else get hurt?"

Sam took charge of the prisoner, and I heaved myself to my feet. "We did." I brushed hair outta my eyes. "Fortunately, no one was sittin' with her, so the glass didn't hit anyone." I looked behind me. A large rock, the kind they used to weigh down stacks of newspapers to keep 'em from blowin' away, was on the floor between the seats. "Did you throw that through a train window?"

Emmeline blushed. "I wanted to distract her, and it was the first thing I saw. I didn't want to break the window, honest. Do you think they'll make me pay for it?"

I checked on the hostage, who was unnerved, but unhurt. Then I got off the train. "We'll talk to Sam and get it smoothed over. Quick thinkin'. But next time, maybe look for something a little smaller."

Emmeline's cheeks got redder. "There will be a next time?"

I thought of Lee and Dot. They were my pals, but they were right. They had lives, and plans, of their own. Ones that didn't include bein' junior gumshoes. I hooked my arm through Emmeline's. "It's a done deal. There's an associate spot with your name on it at Ahern's Detective Agency. Between this fee and what I've saved from my last one, we might be ready to take the next step."

She spun to give me a bear hug. "Thank you! Oh, thank you! Wait until I tell my parents."

We headed for the main entrance to the terminal, following Sam and his prisoner. "I told you," I said. "You might want to wait until I got a real office before you do that."

Chapter Forty-Three

S am called for a uniformed officer to transport Hazel to the city jail. "I'll be in touch," he said, one foot in his car. "I'll need statements from you and Miss Schechter on this one, since it was your work that nabbed Marian's killer. And uncovered ten years' worth of blackmail."

I saw the case on his front seat. "Have you looked inside yet?"

He followed my gaze. "No. But don't worry. I'll tell you how much is there when we process the evidence. Thousands, I'm sure. Had Hazel made it over the border, she would have had a nice little nest egg to start her life over somewhere, most likely with a new name."

"What about Private Lake?" I asked.

"I'll start the paperwork to get the charges dropped as soon as I get back to the office." He sobered. "Theo Carstairs won't evade jail time in this. I doubt the DA will want to try him as a co-conspirator, but he did help cover up the crime."

"He knows. But he's rich. I bet his lawyer will make sure he serves the least amount of time necessary." I thought. "If the attorney is really good, he might even get Theo off with time served."

"Quite honestly, I wouldn't be completely surprised if the charges end up being dropped completely. Especially if he turns state's evidence. That's the way it works with the upper class. Fortunately, that's not my mess to deal with. Ladies." He tipped his fedora to us and opened the door to his car.

"Wait a minute." I aimed a finger at him. "I take down a murderer, and this is the thanks I get? You strand us? Least you could do is give us money for the bus."

He pulled out his wallet and took out a couple of bills. "Take a cab. My treat." He got in his car and left.

I grumbled, but I took the dough and headed for the taxi stands.

Emmeline walked backward so she could talk to me face-to-face. "Is that it? Do we go somewhere to celebrate?"

"Nope." I took out a Lucky and lit it. Then I exhaled. "We have one more thing to do. The original job."

Emmeline's expression showed her confusion.

"Findin' Noemi." I clamped my cigarette between my lips and took out my notebook. "It looks like Private Lake is gonna make that boat on Friday, the one that'll take him back to Europe. Which means I have two days to find his mother." I reviewed my notes.

"Do you think you can?"

I put the notebook back and ashed my smoke. "I think I'll have it done by the end of today." I took off toward the nearest taxi stop.

"Where are we going?" Emmeline hustled behind me.

"The Broadway Market."

Once there, I bought a bag of roasted peanuts and headed for Roesch's. "Hey there." I greeted the same butcher I'd spoken to yesterday.

"You're back," he said. He handed some change to a customer and faced me. "What do you want now?"

"Has Noemi Glassman been here today? You know, the woman I was lookin' for yesterday?" I held out the bag to Emmeline.

"Not yet. She didn't come by yesterday, either." The butcher eyed me. "Did you have anything to do with that?"

"Maybe, well, prob'ly. I spotted her, but she ran away before I could talk to her." I surveyed the crowd, but it was mostly old women. "What time do you close?"

"We're done at six."

"Is there someplace we can sit and watch for her?"

The man waved toward a small grouping of tables. "Over there. I assume you mean a place where she wouldn't see you immediately and be scared off. If she looks straight at you, you'll be out of luck. But I don't think that's likely. She missed her shopping yesterday. I think she'll be more interested in me."

I thanked him. Emmeline and I took our seats so we could keep an eye on Roesch's storefront.

She took a handful of peanuts. "Do you think she'll come back?"

"Fingers crossed." If she didn't, I'd come back the next day and stake out the butcher again. It was the last place I'd seen her, and she had to buy her meat ration eventually, didn't she?

We waited an hour. Emmeline gathered her purse to leave, but I stopped her. "There she is." I nodded toward the crowd.

Noemi walked up to the counter. She cast a look around her, but then caught the butcher's attention and gave her order.

Thankfully, he didn't give Emmeline and I away by lookin' at us. We got up and approached cautiously.

"Excuse me." I cleared my throat. "Noemi Glassman? I've been lookin' for you."

She startled and whipped around, but there were too many people in front of her to run off immediately.

I had to stop her. "Wait! Christopher says hello. Your son. He'd like to meet you."

She froze and turned. "You know my boy?"

Now that she was closer, it was clear Noemi hadn't changed much. She was dressed more like a matron. But her face was still smooth, her hair as dark as it was in the picture I'd gotten from Mrs. Vance. "I do. He hired me to find you." I held out my card.

She didn't take it. "His name is Christopher, you said?" Her voice was mellow, with the faintest trace of an accent.

"The nuns at the orphanage gave him that name. Because of the St. Christopher medal you left with him." I took it out of my pocket, where I'd been carryin' it all this time. "This one." I held it out.

Next to me, I heard Emmeline sniffle.

Noemi's fingers trembled as she accepted the medal. "He kept it. All these years, he kept it."

"Of course he did. They told him at Father Baker's he'd had it when he arrived."

She ran a finger over the silver disc. "Did they tell him why I let him go? But of course, they couldn't. That horrible man, he probably did not say a word."

"Mr. Carstairs? No, he didn't." I watched her. "But one of the nuns, she suspected somethin' wasn't quite right. She'd seen him when he brought your baby. In fact, she set me on the path to findin' you. Nancy and Mrs. Vance, they helped." I smiled at her surprise. "Don't be mad at 'em for spillin' your secret. I can be terribly stubborn when I want things. At least, that's what I've been told."

Next to me, Emmeline mumbled what sounded like agreement. I elbowed her.

Noemi turned the medal over. "My dearest Theo. I hated lying to him."

I pointed at the necklace. "He had that engraved for you, he said. He was gonna stand up to his father. He told me so. But Mr. Carstairs told him you were dead, you and the baby. Theo never got married, did you know that?"

Her eyes widened. "You've seen him, too?"

"We've talked. He's very anxious to find you." I left out the bit about Marian taunting him after Private Lake's visit and her murder. I wondered if Sam had arrested Theo yet. I hoped not. *Take your time on this one, Sam.* I sent a quick prayer to the Virgin Mary, too. After all, she was a mother. Surely, she'd lend a hand. "I can take you to them, both of 'em, if you want. Christopher is in the Army. He leaves on Friday. If we go now, you can spend between now and then gettin' to know him."

Noemi curled her hand around the St. Christopher. She wiped her eyes. "I think, Miss Ahern, I would like that very much."

Chapter Forty-Four

I arrived at the Carstairs mansion for the second time that day. But this time, I didn't pound on the door. Instead, I knocked politely and stood in front of Noemi, shielding her from view.

Mrs. Vance answered. "Miss Ahern. Did they get her? Mrs. Newcombe?" *Thank you, Sam. And Mother Mary.* "Yes. I'm surprised Detective MacKinnon hasn't been to see you or called."

"No, we haven't heard anything." She sagged with relief. "It isn't a good time, Miss Ahern. The men are in the garden, trying to…work things out, I think you might call it. They need to be alone."

"I brought someone who might help with that."

She shook her head at Emmeline. "I don't think your associate, as nice a girl as she is, will be able to smooth this over."

"I didn't mean her." I stepped aside.

The expression on Mrs. Vance's face transformed from sadness to surprise to joy in less than a second. "Oh, my dear. You've come home!" She opened her arms and rushed to embrace Noemi.

Noemi murmured in response, her face buried in Mrs. Vance's shoulder. She pulled away. "You told her about me?"

Mrs. Vance brushed at her eyes. "I'm sorry. I had to. She's very stubborn." She shook a finger at me.

I spread my hands. "It's part of my job."

Noemi patted her friend's face. "I forgive you. He is here? Both of them?"

"Yes." Mrs. Vance beckoned. "Mr. Theodore is in the garden with your boy. Come." She led us through the house again.

I heard the men's voices long before we reached the back. *Oh boy.*

Private Lake was visible through the glass of the French doors, his back ramrod straight. "I'm not going back to jail, Father."

Theo paced the edge of the patio. "For the thousandth time, of course, you're not. I'll make sure of that. Even if they don't catch that woman, I'll see to it your name is cleared in plenty of time for you to make your deployment date."

"And what about you?"

Theo waved his hand. "In a way, I think I deserve what I get. After all I've done to you, why do you care?"

Private Lake looked like he was carryin' on a battle in his head. "It's true, you've not been a model father. But I don't think I want to lose you, not the only parent I have."

I brushed past Mrs. Vance and stepped outside. "Evening, gentlemen."

Neither of them moved. "This isn't the time for a visit, Miss Ahern," Theo said.

"With all due respect, Mr. Carstairs, I didn't come to see you." I hoped my use of a formal name would set the tone. I pointed at Private Lake. "I've got something for my client."

He tore his gaze away from his father. "Did you catch her? That woman who killed Ma...Aunt Marian?"

"Hazel Newcombe? Oh yeah. She's going away for a long time, I suspect. But that's not why I'm here." I enjoyed the confusion on his face, but only for a moment. No sense in torturing the guy. "You hired me for a job. I finished it." I stepped aside. "I found your mother."

Noemi stood there, hands clasped together. "Hello, Theo, Christopher."

Before Private Lake could budge, Theo rushed over. "My darling, you're alive!" He held Noemi tightly and kissed her.

She stiffened at first but melted into his arms quick enough.

I heard Emmeline sniff again. Wordlessly, I held out a handkerchief. Would that be Tom and me when he got home? Once, I'd have said yes without question. These days, I wasn't sure. One thing I did know was that the two people in front of me were madly in love, even twenty years later.

276

It didn't matter to Theo that Noemi had gotten married to someone else, or that she worked, or she wasn't a fine society girl. That's what I wanted. A man who accepted me for who I was, no questions asked.

Was that Tom? Not based on his last letter, although maybe he'd change his mind after the war. *After the war.* Who knew how long that would be or even if Tom would come home at all.

Frank's face appeared in my mind. He didn't look at me with quite the same tenderness as Theo, but I remembered that kiss, soft as the fluttery wings of a butterfly. What had he said? He didn't know if he loved me, but he wanted to find out. Could I take that kind of gamble?

Noemi pulled away and cupped her lover's face. "What does Christopher mean, Theo? Why are you going to jail? And why have you grown that ridiculous beard?"

His face reddened. "I'll shave it off. As for jail, we'll talk later."

Her voice hardened. "No, Theo. Now." It was pretty clear who would wear the pants in this house should Noemi stay.

He looked from me to Private Lake. "I've done something rather stupid." He told her about his role in Marian's death. "But my lawyer called not long ago. He thinks if I testify against Hazel, he can get me a minimal sentence. Maybe even get the charges dropped."

Sam was right. Rich guys always knew how to work the system.

I stared at the lovers. My heart ached for them and for me. Theo had never been a strong man, but I saw a new light in his eyes. Perhaps Noemi's reappearance was what he needed.

What did I need?

Noemi sighed. "Oh, Theo. Have you not grown up? Still the little boy. We will talk about this later." She took a step toward Private Lake. "Miss Ahern tells me the nuns named you Christopher. That you came looking for me."

He nodded, mute, but the look in his eyes left no doubt about his feelings.

"I am sorry, my son. I did not want to give you up. But I was young and alone. I had no money. No one would hire a pregnant girl." She half-reached toward him but lowered her arm. "You have grown up strong, I see that. It is what I wanted for you. Now, I can only hope that the nuns taught you to forgive me. And your father."

Private Lake said nothing.

Theo cleared his throat. "I was going to search for you, Noemi. My father be damned, I was going to marry you. But he told me you died. I never looked at another woman, no matter how many debutantes Dad paraded in front of me." He checked with Mrs. Vance, who gave him an encouraging nod. "I know I was a spoiled child back then. I don't deserve forgiveness from either you or Christopher. But please, give me a second chance, and I'll do better. I promise."

To my surprise, Private Lake fixed his attention on me. "What do you think, Betty?"

Shoot, why was he askin' me? I chose my words carefully. "I think you hired me to do a job, Private, and I've finished it. I found not only your mother, but your father. What you decide to do now is up to you. Sure, you can hold their choices against 'em, mistakes they made when they were not much older than you are now. Heck, your mom was younger." I studied the family before me. "Or you can give 'em a chance. And yourself. Who knows, you all might even be happy. It's up to you."

He thought a moment, then his face screwed up, and he nodded. He held out his arms. "Mother?"

Noemi held him gently. After a moment, Theo went over and wrapped his arms around both the woman he loved and the son he'd thought he lost. Tears coated both Noemi's and Private Lake's faces.

Emmeline blew her nose. Even I had to hold myself back from cryin'. I nudged her. "It's time for us to go. We've got no place here."

Theo pulled away from his family. "Wait."

I faced him. "Yes, Mr. Carstairs?"

"I told you, call me Theo." He sounded annoyed. He really didn't like bein' reminded of his dad, but he *was* Mr. Carstairs now. He'd get used to it. "I told you if you found Noemi, as well as Marian's killer, I'd make it worth your time. Mrs. Vance, get my checkbook."

She bobbed a curtsy and went inside.

I raised my eyebrows. "Since when do you have a checkbook? I wouldn't think Marian would let you have such a thing."

"She didn't. I got an allowance in cash every week." A ghost of a grin flitted across his face. "But I *am* head of the family now. I went to the bank the day after she died and signed all the paperwork." His face softened as he looked at Noemi. "Now I'll have to go back and put my wife on the account."

Noemi sighed. "There is no rush, Theo. It will take months to plan the wedding."

"If you think I'm waiting another day to marry you, think again. I never got rid of the ring. Tomorrow, we'll go downtown and take care of it. And don't talk to me about a license." He winked. "I'm sure if we ask nicely, Christopher will be a witness."

"It would be my pleasure," Private Lake said.

Mrs. Vance returned with the checkbook and a pen. "Sir."

Theo took it and hastily scribbled on the top check. He tore it off and handed it to me. "Thank you, Miss Ahern. I'd double that, but something tells me I'll have to argue with you to accept this much."

The check was for five hundred dollars. "Oh, Mr. Carstairs—"

"For the last time. Theo."

"Theo." I held it out. "I'm flattered and all, but I don't know what I'd do with that much cabbage."

He refused to take it. "Christopher tells me you conduct business out of a diner."

"Yes. Teddy's, down in the First Ward. You prob'ly don't know it, bein' all swanky like you are."

Theo checked on his family, then put his hands in his pockets. "Perhaps you should look for a place of your own. If all your investigations are as successful as this one, you'll need it."

Chapter Forty-Five

Theo and Noemi invited Emmeline and me to dinner, but we said no. They, plus their son, didn't need outsiders at their first meal as a family. Besides, I expected Sam to show his puss any moment, unless he was deliberately delaying his arrival to give the reunited family some time together. I wouldn't put it past him.

Mrs. Vance showed us to the door. "You'll be at the wedding, right? After all, Noemi did say she needs a bridesmaid."

"Uh, sure," I said. "Theo said tomorrow?" Heck, if he could get outta criminal charges, he prob'ly could wangle his way out of needing a marriage license.

"That might be a little overly optimistic on his part. I'll call you with the details. Good night." She closed the door.

Emmeline and I walked down the driveway. From across the street, I saw Mrs. Babbage at her window and waved. She returned the gesture. She was sure to have seen Private Lake's arrival. After the ceremony, I'd have to stop and give her the story. After all, she'd helped me crack the case. But not tonight. I was bushed. And I had to call Melvin at the *Courier*. I owed him a scoop. I sighed.

"Why are you glum?" Emmeline asked as we walked to the bus stop. "I thought you'd be over the moon. You solved the murder and found Private Lake's family. And made a bucketload of money! Are you gonna take Theo's advice and find an office?"

"Guess I should. I need to get a business account at the bank, too. Pop will help me with that." I still had most of the fee from my last case in a cigar box in my desk. Now, there was this check. I didn't think all my cases would bring in hundreds of dollars, but at the same time, I couldn't keep it all in a box. "I'm not sad. A little overwhelmed, is all. Workin' for the swells is fine, but I'm more at ease with my own people." Plus, there was the scene of Theo, Noemi, and Christopher, grouped together on the patio. Not a perfect family, but one that was tryin' their best. Was that my future?

Somehow, I didn't think so.

Emmeline bade me farewell at the bus stop. "Call me when you hear from Mrs. Vance tomorrow. I want to be at the wedding."

I promised her I would, and she got on the newly arrived bus. I checked the schedule. The next ride I could take back to the First Ward didn't arrive for half an hour. But I didn't want to go home. Normally, I'd write to Tom and tell him all about my latest triumph. That was before his latest letter, the one where he made it pretty clear he didn't like the idea of me bein' a detective and puttin' myself in danger. I thought of Hazel and her gun, Emmeline tossin' a brick through the train window as a distraction, me tacklin' Hazel, gun and all. What if it had gone off? What if she'd shot that woman and then me? Sure, Sam had been right there and the odds of that happenin' were low, but there was no doubt I coulda been hurt. It hadn't occurred to me at the time, I'd been focused on Hazel. But there was no gettin' around the fact it was a possibility. After all, Sam wouldn't always be there to back me up.

No, Tom wouldn't want to hear about that.

I left the bus stop and wandered the streets through the soft July night. I could hear cicadas buzzin' in the trees and the call of night birds. Delaware Park was a lot quieter than the First Ward. I'd go home to tell Lee and Dot the full story, of course. They'd want to know. But that could wait.

Right now, I wanted to talk to someone who was interested in *me*. What I'd done, not who I was in relation to them. Not a parent, but a friend. Someone who'd hear about my accomplishments and be proud of me, not tell me how irresponsible I'd been by not thinkin' of the effect on other people.

I didn't do it consciously, but I wasn't terribly surprised when my wanderings had me hop a bus and get off in the neighborhood near Buffalo State Hospital. Did I dare? I guess I did, because I found myself knockin' on the door to Frank's apartment.

He answered, lookin' as good as ever in slacks and a short-sleeve cotton shirt, no shoes on his feet. "Betty, this is a surprise. It's rather late, isn't it? I would have expected you'd be either pounding the pavement or at home for dinner."

I rocked on my heels. "Evening. I, uh, wanted to let you know I found Private Lake's mom."

"I had no doubt you would." He flashed a smile. "You came all this way to tell me that?"

"Yeah, uh, since you sent him to me, I figured you'd want to know."

"You could have telephoned to tell me that."

Was he bein' deliberately ignorant, or was he playin' with me? Did women always show up on his doorstep? His eyes twinkled, and there was enough of a smile on his face to show the hint of the dimple. I thought about our last meeting, his whisper-soft kiss. "The last time we talked, you said some things."

"I did."

"Did you mean them?"

He studied my face. "Yes."

I felt the ring on my finger. I needed to talk to Tom, but who knew when that would happen? Meantime, I also had to sort out my emotions where Frank was concerned. "You said you'd be there when I was ready. Well, here I am. Want to go grab a cup of coffee? Maybe something to eat? I can tell you all about Private Lake's case and we can, how did you put it? Find out how we feel."

The silence went on forever. I was about to call it off when he spoke. "Let me get a shirt and shoes. I know a place around the corner."

A Note from the Author

Once again, I've mined Buffalo history for this book. Father Baker's Home for Boys was a real orphanage. Father Nelson Baker originally founded OLV Infant Home by a dredged section of the Erie Canal. The home provided sanctuary for unwed mothers and their infants, without questions asked. Mothers who did not want to keep their babies could leave the child to be raised there, an operation that was thoroughly disapproved of by locals who believed unwed mothers had to "pay" for their sins by raising their children in poverty. Father Baker added a maternity hospital in 1919, which was later converted into a general hospital.

In 1921, Father Baker began his "project of love," construction of a shrine to Our Lady of Victory. Completed in 1926, it was then elevated to the dignity of "basilica," becoming one of only two minor basilicas in the United States.

Father Baker died in 1936. He was beatified by as "Venerable" Father Baker in 1987. The cause for his canonization continues to this day.

Acknowledgements

As always, a million thanks to all of the following people:

- My superb critique group – Annette Dashofy, Jeff Boarts, and Peter WJ Hayes – for keeping me on point and historically accurate.
- The women at Level Best Books – Verena Rose, Shawn Reilly Simmons, and editor emeritus Harriette Sackler – for embracing Betty and the gang and helping bring them to the page.
- My father, Gary Lederman, for always being willing to respond to my myriad of questions about Buffalo history minutiae.
- My tribe, Sisters in Crime and Pennwriters, for support, celebration, encouragement, and the resources to make me a better writer.
- Mark Baker at Carstairs Considers for championing The Homefront Mysteries through his reviews.
- My family, for not thinking I'm (too) crazy spending my free time plotting fictional murder and mayhem.

Love you all!

About the Author

A recovering technical writer, Liz Milliron is the author of The Laurel Highlands Mysteries and The Homefront Mysteries. Her most recent release, *Thicker Than Water*, is the sixth in the Laurel Highlands Mysteries series. Short fiction has appeared in multiple anthologies, including the Anthony Award-winning *Blood on the Bayou*; *Mystery Most Historical*; *Fish Out of Water*, A Guppy anthology, and the upcoming *Mystery Most International*. She is a member of Pennwriters, Sisters in Crime, International Thriller Writers, and The Historical Novel Society. Liz lives in Pittsburgh with her son and a very spoiled retired racer greyhound.

SOCIAL MEDIA HANDLES:
  Facebook: www.facebook.com/LizMilliron
  Instagram: @LizMilliron
  Threads: @LizMilliron

AUTHOR WEBSITE:
  http://lizmilliron.com

Also by Liz Milliron

The Homefront Mysteries

The Truth We Hide

The Lessons We Learn

The Stories We Tell

The Enemy We Don't Know

The Laurel Highlands Mysteries

Thicker Than Water

Lie Down with Dogs

Harm Not the Earth

Broken Trust

Heaven Has No Rage

Root of All Evil